12/00   6 00

5 00

"THE SPECIAL PATHOS, THE AMBIGUOUS HOPELESSNESS, THE SURREALIST COURAGE AND WIT THAT EMANATE FROM THESE PAGES ARE UNIQUE TO THE GAY MALE AUTHOR TODAY . . . He is a writer beleaguered and thus must be heeded. The humor and sorrow of his words stem from the mystery of the AIDS plague as surely as Boccaccio's *Decameron* stemmed from the Bubonic Plague, and every one of us can learn from him."
—Ned Rorem

"SOME OF THE BEST GAY FICTION, PAST, PRESENT AND FUTURE. . . . It's a treat to have it conveniently collected. And it's a treat to read. Hopefully the word will now spread about the riches of gay writing."
—Martin Bauml Duberman,
Distinguished Professor of History
Lehman College of the City University
of New York

"A DAZZLING COLLECTION OF SOME OF THE BEST NEW FICTION I'VE READ IN YEARS . . . should be of interest to all readers who are interested in the contemporary world and in contemporary literature."—Julia Markus

"MEMORABLE . . . NOTHING IN THIS COLLECTION SHOULD BE OVERLOOKED . . . DESERVES WIDE READERSHIP."—James Purdy

GEORGE STAMBOLIAN teaches at Wellesley College. The author of *Marcel Proust and the Creative Encounter* and *M-l-* *P-* *-* *Realities* and editor of *Twentieth C* *-* *Homosexualities and French Literature,* *The Advocate* and *The New York Na*

D0954605

TO RICHARD UMANS

MEN·ON·MEN

·BEST·NEW·GAY·FICTION·

EDITED AND WITH AN INTRODUCTION BY

GEORGE STAMBOLIAN

A PLUME BOOK

PLUME
Published by the Penguin Group
Penguin Books USA Inc., 375 Hudson Street, New York, New York 10014, U.S.A.
Penguin Books Ltd, 27 Wrights Lane, London W8 5TZ, England
Penguin Books Australia Ltd, Ringwood, Victoria, Australia
Penguin Books Canada Ltd, 2801 John Street, Markham, Ontario, Canada L3R 1B4
Penguin Books (N.Z.) Ltd, 182-190 Wairau Road, Auckland 10, New Zealand

Penguin Books Ltd, Registered Offices: Harmondsworth, Middlesex, England

Published by Plume, an imprint of New American Library, a division of Penguin
Books USA Inc.

PUBLISHER'S NOTE

These stories are works of fiction. Names, characters, places, and incidents
are either the products of the author's imagination or are used fictitiously,
and any resemblance to actual persons, living or dead, events, or locales is
entirely coincidental.

BOOKS ARE AVAILABLE AT QUANTITY DISCOUNTS WHEN USED TO PROMOTE
PRODUCTS OR SERVICES. FOR INFORMATION PLEASE WRITE TO PREMIUM
MARKETING DIVISION, PENGUIN BOOKS USA INC., 375 HUDSON STREET,
NEW YORK, NEW YORK 10014.

Introduction copyright © 1986 by George Stambolian

"David's Charm" by Bruce Boone. Copyright © 1986 by Bruce Boone.
Published by permission of the author.
"A Queer Red Spirit" by C. F. Borgman. Copyright © 1986 by C. F. Borgman.
Published by permission of the author.
"The Outsiders" by Dennis Cooper. Copyright © 1986 by Dennis Cooper.
Published by permission of the author.
"Nothing Ever Just Disappears" by Sam D'Allesandro. First published in *No
Apologies*. Copyright © 1984 by Sam D'Allesandro. Reprinted by permission of the
author.
"Second Son" by Robert Ferro. Copyright © 1986 by Robert Ferro. Published
by permission of the author.
"Choice" by John Fox. Copyright © 1986 by John Fox. Published by
permission of the author.
"Sex Story" by Robert Glück. Published in *Elements of a Coffee Service*.
Copyright © 1982 by Robert Glück. Reprinted by permission of Four Seasons
Foundation.
"Maine" by Brad Gooch. Published in *Jailbait and Other Stories*. Copyright ©
1984 by Brad Gooch. Reprinted by permission of the SeaHorse Press.
"Life Drawing" by Michael Grumley. Copyright © 1986 by Michael Grumley.
Published by permission of the author.
"Backwards" by Richard Hall. Published in *Letter From a Great-Uncle and Other
Stories*. Copyright © 1985 by Richard Hall. Reprinted by permission of the Grey
Fox Press.
"Bad Pictures" by Patrick Hoctel. First published in *Mirage*. Copyright © 1985
by Patrick Hoctel. Reprinted by permission of the author.

The following page constitutes an extension of this copyright page.

"Friends at Evening" by Andrew Holleran. Copyright © 1986 by Andrew Holleran. Published by permission of the author.

"September" by Kevin Killian. Copyright © 1986 by Kevin Killian. Published by permission of the author.

"Hardhats" by Ethan Mordden. First published in *Christopher Street*. Copyright © 1985 by Ethan Mordden. Reprinted by permission of the author.

"Street Star" by Wallace Parr. Copyright © 1986 by Wallace Parr. Published by permission of the author.

"The Most Golden Bulgari" by Felice Picano. Copyright © 1986 by Felice Picano. Published by permission of the author.

"Speech" by Richard Umans. First published by *The James White Review*. Copyright © 1984 by Richard Umans. Reprinted by permission of Michael Brennen.

"An Oracle" by Edmund White. First published in *Christopher Street*. Copyright © 1986 by Edmund White. Reprinted by permission of the author.

All rights reserved

Lyrics from the song MELE KALIKIMAKA, written by R. Alex Anderson, appear in the story *Choice*, by John Fox. Copyright © 1949, 1950. Copyright Renewed and Assigned to Bibo Music Publishers (c/o The Welk Music Group, Santa Monica, California 90401). International Copyright Secured. All Rights Reserved. Used by Permission.

Library of Congress Cataloging in Publication Data

Men on men.

1. Homosexuality, Male—Fiction. 2. American
fiction—20th century. 3. American fiction—Men
authors. 4. Men—Fiction. I. Stambolian, George.
PS648.H57M46 1986   813'.01'08353   86-12856
ISBN 0-452-25882-0

 REGISTERED TRADEMARK—MARCA REGISTRADA

First Printing, November, 1986

9 10 11 12 13 14 15

PRINTED IN THE UNITED STATES OF AMERICA

CONTENTS

CONTENTS

INTRODUCTION

I AGREED TO EDIT this anthology because its publisher, New American Library, expressed a lively interest in giving it a large printing and wide distribution. In matters of gay writing I confess to having the zeal of a missionary for whom nothing is more tempting than a chance to reach new audiences. This book celebrates those readers, new and old, whose numbers have grown steadily over the past ten years, just as it celebrates the richness and variety of the works that are offered here for their pleasure.

From the beginning, I decided to limit the collection to works of fiction by contemporary writers most directly concerned with issues confronting gay men in America. This meant that poetry and plays, fiction by foreign and older American writers, as well as works by women would not be included. I also decided to exclude genres like science fiction and murder mysteries even though they represent a significant portion of recent gay fiction and have attracted many gifted writers. My purpose throughout was to maintain a focus for the collection that would at the same time reveal a range of expression within the limits I had established.

I invited writers to submit, whenever possible, new and preferably unpublished stories or autonomous sections of novels in progress. By abandoning the usual procedure of making a selection from published works only, I knew I would introduce an element of risk and would be obliged to involve myself more deeply in the editorial process. My intention was not simply to entice readers with fresh works, especially by more established authors, but to make certain that the collection would reflect the rapid changes taking place in the gay world—particularly those changes produced by the devastation of AIDS. This was essential because the collection is dedicated to a close friend who recently died of an AIDS-related illness, and who symbolizes for all of us the loss of so many talented men.

The first writers I contacted were Robert Ferro, Michael Grumley, Andrew Holleran, Felice Picano, and Edmund White. These men, together with Christopher Cox and George Whitmore, had all been members of the legendary Violet Quill Club, the most productive workshop for gay writers in the post-Stonewall period. Building on the unprecedented success of novels by Holleran, White, and Picano—*Dancer From the Dance, Nocturnes for the King of Naples, The Lure*—the VQ met informally between the summer of 1979 and the winter of 1981 to explore the problems of autobiographical fiction which represented a second and more delicate stage of a literary coming-out process. The works that grew from these meetings have now been widely read: Whitmore's *The Confessions of Danny Slocum*, White's *A Boy's Own Story*, Holleran's *Nights in Aruba*, Ferro's *The Family of Max Desir*, Picano's *Ambidextrous*.

With other writers of the same period, such as Richard Hall, Larry Kramer, Armistead Maupin, Rita Mae Brown, Bertha Harris, and Jane DeLynn, these men were also among the first to produce works that testified to the emergence of a self-aware gay community in America. Their novels and stories effectively moved the focus of gay literature away from the lonely homosexual figure doomed to unhappiness toward the elaboration of a world in which homosexuality was no longer an exclusively psychological issue shrouded in secrecy and guilt but a social reality. Above all, the new literary forms and subjects they developed, and are still exploring, encouraged a whole generation of writers by forever dispelling the notion so often repeated by hostile critics that gay fiction must inevitably be second-rate because homosexuality itself is somehow incomplete.

Once I had received commitments from this first group of writers, I decided to devote as much of the remaining space in the collection as possible to stories by younger or less established authors. I contacted John Fox, whose novel *Boys on the Rock* had made a powerful debut, and Brad Gooch, whose *Jailbait and Other Stories* had received much praise. I also wrote to four present or former Californians who, like Gooch, had impressed me by their interest in literary experimentation: Dennis Cooper, Robert Glück, Bruce Boone, and Kevin Killian. In works such as Cooper's *Safe* and Glück's *Jack the Modernist* these men, like many other contemporary American writers, had moved away from traditional narrative forms by freely using elements drawn from poetry, drama, pornography, and the philosophical essay. Admired by a small but devoted following, they seemed ready to attract a larger audience.

I discovered the remaining writers in the collection through extensive reading and a few fortuitous introductions. My investigation of the California literary scene led me to Sam D'Allesandro's story in *No Apologies* and Patrick Hoctel's in *Mirage*. Robert Glück sent me copies of stories that Wallace Parr had presented to his San Francisco Writers' Workshop. After reading several unpublished pieces by Richard Umans, I chose one that had appeared in *The James White Review*, a journal that has provided an important forum for writers in the Midwest. Thanks to Stan Leventhal, I read C. F. Borgman's work, which satisfied for me the dream every editor has of presenting a new author's first published story. Finally, I selected a new piece from Ethan Mordden's popular series in *Christopher Street*.

There were disappointments: One writer was unable to finish his story because of illness. Another could not withdraw from contractual obligations to his publisher. Two sent novel-length manuscripts from which it was impossible to extract shorter sections. In my search for stories by gay black men I discovered that a number of authors had already committed new works to a forthcoming anthology of black writing. And most regrettably, unavoidable restrictions in space forced me to abandon excellent stories by Steve Abbott, Christopher Davis, and Harlan Greene.

Every collection reflects its editor's tastes, and this one is no exception. Although I tried to present works on a variety of topics, my final choices were determined, as they must be, by judgments of artistic quality. Nothing would delight me more than to speak about the pleasure I had in reading each of these pieces—to describe, for example, Holleran's masterful use of dialogue, the richness of White's or Ferro's prose, Picano's narrative exuberance, or the stylistic precision Cooper and Glück reveal in their writing. But the relative newness of gay fiction and the fact that it continues to exist in a politically charged climate require some discussion of its evolving historical and critical context in order to enhance the reader's own enjoyment of its artistic achievements.

Gay fiction often tells us "tales of the city," to borrow the title of Armistead Maupin's popular novel, because it was in cities like New York and San Francisco that gay communities first developed in the post-Stonewall period. "The city gives you the chance to make yourself up," Richard Sennett has remarked, and gay culture is to a large extent a made-up thing, an existential invention constantly proposing new values and codes of conduct. Even today much of the excitement of gay fiction comes from this sense of witnessing the creation of a new life.

The central importance of the modern city gives an added interest to variations on this setting. Felice Picano's description of Rome in "The Most Golden Bulgari" reminds us that European cities were gay meccas at a time when American cities were still repressive. Part of the fascination of Edmund White's story, "An Oracle," comes from placing a highly evolved gay New Yorker in the very different homosexual world of Crete, whereas the resolutely rural setting of Brad Gooch's "Maine" strikes us with its simplicity compared with the bustling intensity of San Francisco in the stories by Robert Glück and Bruce Boone.

A growing number of writers in recent years have remained outside the gay capitals and have written about their own regions of the country—Kevin Esser in Illinois, Harlan Greene in South Carolina, Roy F. Wood in rural Georgia. But even the stories and novels of Andrew Holleran, so closely associated with the fast-paced life of New York City, reveal a sensitivity to social and regional differences. When I asked Holleran recently if he had an ideal reader, he replied: "It would be an odd combination of a youth I've never seen in a library in Kansas and a queen from Fire Island who is very witty and critical. If you can please both, you've done it right."

Holleran's remark provides an interesting perspective on his own story in this collection, but it also reveals a desire to reach different segments of the gay community. In the 1970s writers such as Holleran, Picano, White, Maupin, and Brown criss-crossed the country in a conscious effort to develop new audiences for their work. Thanks to their readings, book signings, and lectures thousands learned for the first time that a whole new body of gay fiction was being created. The excitement their novels and stories generated was accompanied, however, by criticism from competing political groups within the gay community. Writers were attacked for supposedly favoring one life-style over another or for offering images of gay life that were not representative of the majority of gay men and women. There were even people who felt uncomfortable with the entire enter-prise of "making public" previously secret aspects of our lives.

The rapid expansion of the gay community and the broad-ening of its political base have somewhat diminished these fears. At the same time, the fact that books now exist on almost every aspect of gay life means that no one can view any single work as representing the entire gay world. This growing pluralism of gay literature and its readers explains why attempts to define an overall "gay sensibility" have all but ceased. Readers are more interested in particular genres and more conscious of the individ-ual sensibilities of their favorite authors. The proliferation of gay books and their increasing availability throughout the country have also served to familiarize readers with the new signs, codes, and narrative forms of gay writing. A significant number of readers now share with writers a "common language" that tran-scends social and political differences.

Fiction frequently includes its readers within its cast of char-acters. When writers in the 1970s began showing gay people in groups, as friends and as members of a community, that same emerging community was also the primary audience for their work. One way of defining contemporary gay fiction is to say that it now assumes the existence of a more or less sympathetic gay audience. Earlier writers usually addressed an audience assumed to be heterosexual and generally hostile. This often forced them to explain homosexuality to their readers and to justify it. For many writers Gay Liberation signaled the end of this obligation. Instead of explaining homosexuality they could now describe the diverse expressions of gay life.

The stories in this collection present a variety of gay subcultures. C. F. Borgman's "A Queer Red Spirit" reproduces the world of a fifties homosexual and juxtaposes it to the easier life of a very contemporary gay man. Wallace Parr's "Street Star" introduces us to the strange and eerily comic existence of a sixties street queen, whereas Ethan Mordden in "Hardhats" explores the uncharted brotherhood and sexuality of construction workers. Even those writers who make no reference to the gay world or its history know that many of their readers will have some understanding of the place of their work within this larger context.

Gay stories, like heterosexual stories, are often about love affairs that dramatize the passionate conflicts of human relations —but there is a difference. Homosexual relationships usually operate with fewer conventions governing sexual roles. There are also fewer literary conventions or patterns of inherited imagery for the writer to fall back on. A long tradition of writing on homosexual love certainly exists, but given the changes in those few conventions that used to surround same-sex relationships, its value to the contemporary writer is limited. Gay love today continues to be a testing of possibilities that is often quite varied, because the relative absence of conventions makes it easier for homosexuals to cross social, economic, racial, and cultural barriers.

The stories in this collection describe many such crossings made all the more intriguing by unexpected complications. In Richard Umans's "Speech" a young man's love for an older man is dramatized by the mutual need to overcome the obstacle of mutism. The menace of compulsive behavior adds a new dimension to the interracial adventure portrayed in Michael Grumley's "Life Drawing." Edmund White's account of an affair between a middle-aged American and a Cretan boy takes place under the shadow of death. And Felice Picano treats us to the surprising liaison between a young American social worker and an older European film director who happens to be a former Communist. These last three narratives are also interesting in the way they follow the movement of an affair through its different crises and resolutions. Sam D'Allesandro does a poetic variation on this form by concentrating on the essential moments of a relationship. By telling his story backward, Richard Hall gives us a startlingly new perspective on how one relationship fits into the broader pattern of a man's life.

Most love stories end unhappily, but in gay life failed love has had a controversial history. In the days when homosexuality meant doom, love was often an impossibility made all the more difficult by overwhelming social constraints. Later, in the post-Stonewall period, writers frequently employed the absence or failure of love as a powerful device for criticizing the impersonality of gay life, its sexual excesses, or its lack of social cohesion. Although this kind of vital criticism continues, reactions to it have begun to change. A story like Kevin Killian's "September," which describes how a retarded boy is brutalized by a sadistic and self-hating older man, would have been attacked in the past for not providing "positive role models" or "self-affirming images." But today most readers will see it as a strangely moving love story that ultimately explores the way language confers power on those who control it. Similarly, Patrick Hoctel's "Bad Pictures," which dramatizes repeated failures in love, cannot be judged solely as a criticism of gay life. Contemporary readers are more likely to appreciate all the dimensions of a work, from its politics to its art, and to understand that a story or novel is not a factual report but an imaginary construct, a work of fiction.

Sex is one issue that has remained controversial. For writers in the 1970s, liberation meant they could write more explicitly about sex and begin the crucial process of demystifying gay sexual practices that were still unmentionable. Here again their efforts met with criticism from the gay press. Some attacked these writers for giving too much attention to sex and other forms of "wasteful" pleasure instead of emphasizing the political and social problems of the time. Others denounced those who did not insist enough on the revolutionary aspects of gay sexuality. Today it is the menace of AIDS that has reawakened the controversy. Writers describing sexual practices know that their work will be subjected to close scrutiny, even if they as individuals are morally committed to fostering safer sex. This situation partly explains why many stories involving erotically unrestrained behavior are now habitually set in the years preceding the advent of AIDS.

I began this collection with Richard Umans's "Speech" because it describes in parable-like fashion an initiation into sex that is also an initiation into language and knowledge. Many other writers use that special knowledge to explore the literary possibilities of gay sexuality. Edmund White shows how effectively sexual acts reveal the psychological nuances of character. Michael Grumley develops a moral tale from the conflict between sex and love often found in gay fiction, where sex is seen alternately as a source of freedom and an imprisoning obsession. And C. F. Borgman uses different narrative points of view to re-create the eroticism of writing itself.

A new group of writers has brought equally new insights to the literary and social dimensions of pornography. In "Maine" Brad Gooch takes a situation typical of pornography and reverses its purpose: Instead of hot sex the characters speak of family ties, indulge in honesty, and develop friendship. Dennis Cooper in "The Outsiders" offers a detailed examination of the emotional distancing and perceptual misplacements produced by certain forms of the pornographic imagination. In "David's Charm" Bruce Boone employs fantasies of power and domination to study the psychological conflicts and erotic desires associated with class differences. And in "Sex Story" Robert Glück writes about sex without falling into the conventions—pornographic, romantic, demonic—that usually govern such writing. Glück deliberately plays with and against these conventions to describe what actually takes place in sex—not simply the acts, varied as they are, but also the emotions, thoughts, and events that surround them.

But it is death that has had the most troubled history in gay fiction. At one time homosexual characters seemed destined to die violently so that others' lives could go on. The "coming-out" story that emerged after Stonewall reversed this situation—the discovery of one's homosexuality became an affirmation of one's life and the revelation of a new future. But death persisted as a theme because gay men and women were now free to address the reality of the violence directed against them. Writers also turned to the sexual underground to study the violence gay men inflicted on each other. No one foresaw that the theme of death would be frighteningly transformed by AIDS.

Although works related to AIDS have begun to appear—Paul Reed's novel *Facing It* and plays like Larry Kramer's *The Normal Heart* and William Hoffman's *As Is*—it is certain that writers will be examining its effects on our lives for years to come. Without naming the disease, Sam D'Allesandro's story, "Nothing Ever Just Disappears," makes us feel the surprise and pain of loss. Andrew Holleran's "Friends at Evening" dramatizes the social repercussions of the epidemic in a long conversation whose bleakness is at once relieved and reinforced by an extraordinary play of humor. For Holleran AIDS represents a confrontation with the absurd and the decline of an entire generation and way of life. The same generation of gay men appears in Edmund White's story, but here the focus is on one man's efforts to reshape his life after his lover's death. By countering death with a rediscovery of the senses, "An Oracle" in effect renews the coming-out story with its life-affirming values. Once again these writers assume that the gay community exists, and will survive.

Two other narratives relate AIDS to problems gay men confront within another community—the family. In "Choice" John Fox captures the undeniable alienation and paranoia that AIDS has produced in many men and examines the elaborate rituals of denial by which one family attempts to save appearances in order to escape unpleasant truths. He reveals the comic aspects of these rituals but also their sad irony, because his hero himself succumbs to their demands. Unlike the other writers, Robert Ferro in "Second Son" tells his story from the point of view of a man afflicted by the disease, but he is less interested in the nature of the illness than in the way it connects the present to the past, one life to another. Faced by the possibility of death, Ferro's protagonist ponders the nature of his role within a family whose love at once sustains him and reminds him of his solitude and irreducible difference.

The conflicts between gay children and their parents have been the subject of several books, including Ferro's *The Family of Max Desir*, White's *A Boy's Own Story*, and Holleran's *Nights in Aruba*. These books have also been among the most successful in attracting heterosexual readers who often feel more comfortable with gay works in which their own lives are portrayed. Indeed, nongay readers have frequently criticized gay fiction for being too "self-absorbed," by which they usually mean that it excludes them. Some established critics have unfortunately used this same impression to support the notion that gay fiction lacks universality.

But to a disinterested observer, gay fiction would appear no more self-absorbed than heterosexual fiction where the absence of gay characters has hardly been noticed. Gay readers themselves long ago developed the habit of drawing meaning from works that ignored their existence. On the other hand, one continuing purpose of gay fiction is to prove, as Sartre said of Genet's work, that homosexuals do in fact exist, that we speak and judge for ourselves instead of being merely observed and judged by others, and that our lives are to be taken as seriously as anyone else's. This fundamental need to demonstrate the authenticity of the gay experience partly explains the strong autobiographical presence in many gay works, including several stories in this collection, in which the writer retains his individuality yet serves as an example to the community whose story he tells by telling his own.

Despite this sense of community, there is hardly an author of gay books who has not protested at some time against being called a "gay writer." Writers know this label can be dangerous when it suggests that their work has meaning only to a limited audience, making it easier for others to dismiss them as "minority writers." There is also the fact that many so-called gay writers have written on a variety of subjects in their fiction and nonfiction. The literary careers of Picano, White, Ferro, Grumley, and Mordden are exemplary in this respect.

But to the extent that the world views them as members of a minority, writers of gay fiction have a particular interest in reaching a larger audience. Some believe that for a work to succeed it must not be too gay, and that if sex must be described, it is better to omit the details. Others contend that a writer should emphasize precisely those desires, practices, places, and mores that are unique to gay life. The majority of writers insist, however, that whatever the requirements of success, they must not involve the sacrifice of artistic integrity or submission either to the "friendly" censorship of editors and publishers or to the far more insidious demands of self-censorship. Contemporary gay fiction like contemporary gay culture in general is the result of a massive lifting of self-censorship, and for most writers regression is unthinkable.

The importance of these issues may be diminishing as more gay books, such as this one, are published by mainstream presses. I have suggested that the growth over the past decade of a sizable gay audience has contributed greatly to this development. But just as there are many gay people who never read gay books, there are many heterosexuals who do. Some of these nongay readers were first attracted to gay fiction in the post-Stonewall period by the popularity of novels such as Patricia Nell Warren's *The Front Runner*, Gordon Merrick's *The Lord Won't Mind*, Mary Renault's *The Persian Boy*, Rita Mae Brown's *Rubyfruit Jungle*, and John Rechy's *Sexual Outlaw*. The growing awareness of gay life in all segments of the American population has also produced a renewed interest in the earlier works of Isherwood, Vidal, Baldwin, Burroughs, and Purdy. And today, there is every indication that increasing numbers of nongay readers have begun to read books from small gay presses, which continue to serve the vital function of nurturing new talent by publishing works that, for whatever reason, have a more limited commercial appeal. Despite the persistent reluctance of many mainstream critics to acknowledge the phenomenon, gay fiction is an exciting and undeniable reality.

It is not enough, however, to say that sooner or later artistic quality is always recognized. New subjects like new forms of art make new demands on readers by obliging them to modify their beliefs and habits of perception. The demands made by gay fiction—and many of its rewards—will be great as long as gay life itself remains morally and politically controversial. The heterosexual audience has been learning to read gay fiction just as the gay audience has learned in the years since Stonewall to overcome its own fears and prejudices. The exact composition of this nongay audience is unknown, but it is certain that it includes not only the parents and friends of gay people but also students, urban professionals, other writers, those who follow their favorite authors no matter what subjects they treat, and people who simply enjoy good writing.

—George Stambolian

SPEECH

• RICHARD UMANS •

DANNY MURRAY AND I were best friends for years, through elementary school all the way into junior high. We never had to ask if we'd be spending Saturday together, just what we'd be doing. Weather permitting, we'd usually ride bikes. Danny and I were great bikers.

Our Saturday afternoon expeditions took us not over country roads but into city streets, far from the calm predictability of our boring suburb. We explored much of the city on our bicycles, sailing freely through unfamiliar neighborhoods, walking our bikes past the exotic window displays downtown. We imagined ourselves tough city kids, looking for a gang to join. In fact, without knowing it, we were practicing for times to come, when this city or its like would provide the setting for our high school dating, our college adventures, our adult careers.

We were not without safe havens, even downtown. My uncle had a shoe store on Clarendon Street. He would sometimes take us for sandwiches or at least treat us to ice cream. But the real excitement lay all the way in the downtown shopping center, on Washington Street, where Danny's father's store stood. My uncle's little shoe shop paled by comparison.

I. J. Murray occupied its own six-story building. The first three floors were retail space, selling women's clothing, especially furs. Danny and I, unlike mere customers, were allowed to ride the service elevator to the top three floors, where the furs were stored, cut, and stitched into coats. We would visit Danny's father's grand fourth-floor office and be treated to lunch. And we had the run of the place.

The most absorbing area was the fifth-floor cutting rooms. Here the furs would be laid out, backed, and cut to shape by skilled craftsmen. The process remained forever magical to me, and two factors gave it special meaning. First, a single mistake could cost hundreds, even thousands, of dollars. Second, one of the cutters was Danny's Uncle Leo.

Leo Murray was dashingly handsome. Even in a long grey work apron, his fine slacks and pure white shirt set him worlds apart from the other cutters. His hair gleamed with sleek blackness, one curl sometimes tumbling Gene Vincent-like over the crest of his forehead. His large black eyes gazed with sensitive alertness, and his jaw stood square and firm, framing thick, straight lips. Altogether, he reminded me of Superman, barely disguised as Clark Kent.

When Danny and I entered the cutting room, Uncle Leo stopped whatever he was doing. He gave Danny a long, powerful hug, his face brilliant with delight, and they would talk. Uncle Leo's voice would soar and whoop, and Danny's mouth would silently form big, emphatic words. I never learned to understand more than a little of Uncle Leo's strange speech, and Danny told me that most people had the same problem. But Danny, his deaf uncle's favorite, had grown up hearing that speech and understood it with ease.

Danny's sharing of a secret language with this intriguing adult, who would drop everything to hurry over and chat, seemed to me the height of special friendship. In my school, some of the girls had trained themselves to speak a variation of Pig Latin, at lightning speed, in order to confound the boys and undermine the teachers. Since I'd long ago learned to decipher my parents' use of spelled words when they wished to disguise their meaning from me, nothing had so excluded me as the girls' annoying gobbledygook. Miffed, I'd taught myself through lonely practice to understand it, though speaking it in public was beneath masculine dignity.

Danny's conversations with Uncle Leo remained impenetrable to me, however. Far more than schoolgirls' nonsense talk, the excited exchanges of my best friend and his dazzling uncle thrilled me with a sense of witnessing a rare intimacy, a bond between man and boy that crossed social boundaries. It was the kind of buddyhood common on television, where heroes often had a young sidekick—the Range Rider and Dick West, The Rifleman and Mark, even Tarzan and Boy. But real life held few openings for sidekicks. My friends and I all had harried, overworked fathers, well-meaning but locked within their own worlds. Other male grownups—gym teachers, camp counselors —managed us where necessary, but always from the unbridgeable distance of their adulthood.

Only Danny Murray, of all the boys I knew, seemed able to enter the private world of an adult male—not only adult, but moviestar glamorous, and appealingly set off from the rest of the world by his mysterious speech. Danny had a rare and precious access, and I watched enviously as Danny communicated with his uncle with far greater ease than even Mr. Murray, Danny's father, who was Uncle Leo's brother and boss.

Only Ernie, Uncle Leo's elderly co-worker, seemed able to understand him as well as Danny did. Ernie, Danny said, had trained Leo Murray as a fur-cutter when the youth had come out of a prestigious school for the deaf with few skills in lipreading or speech and little academic training of any kind. Uncle Leo had always been a rebel, Danny confided. He'd been thrown out of school several times, and only his father's wealth and position had gotten him back in. Crusty old I. J. Murray had intended for young Leo to "overcome" his deafness and become an executive like his older brother. Instead, Leo had taken avidly to the craftsmanship of cutting fur, married a deaf woman from school, fathered three hearing children, and moved into a lesser neighborhood of the same suburb where Danny and I lived.

Sometimes Uncle Leo would pull Danny and me over to his work table to show us what he was working on or lead us to the storage vaults to show us a new shipment of gleaming pelts. His voice would swoop like a crazed sparrow, his hands and face signaling most of his intent. I would smile and nod along, imagining I understood. Then Danny and his uncle, and sometimes old Ernie as well, would explode into laughter at a remark of Leo's, a remark I could no more distinguish from the cascade of his vocalizing than a particular quart of water from a gushing torrent. Danny would translate for me, and I would laugh energetically, glad to be part of the interchange once more, even if emptily, and too late.

One summer afternoon, on a trip home in my late twenties, I chanced to visit a small country club in a suburb near the one in which I'd grown up. The country club had no golf course, only a pool and clubhouse, and it failed to hold its own against clubs that offered golf and tennis. Some gay entrepreneurs had bought it, and now it was prospering as a gay pool club.

The poolside atmosphere was pleasant and low-pressure, with people who had moved to the suburbs for many of the same reasons as my parents. The men lounged and chatted, and the women horsed around. A few show-offs practiced diving or swam self-conscious laps in the pool. Here and there sat pairs of recent lovers, with eyes for no one but each other.

A tall, handsome man in his early forties strode past. Shocked, I determined to listen for the voice, but the black, sympathetic eyes were the giveaway. At once I fell to smoothing my hair and sucking in my stomach. Then I realized that I had with any luck changed far too much in fifteen years for Leo Murray to recognize me now.

He still looked fine. His body was thicker, but not fat, and his hair was wavy and dark, greying slightly at the temples. I watched him cross to his lounge chair and sit beside a tall, skinny blond, with whom he began to talk comfortably. His eyes still flashed with lively humor.

Screwing up my courage, I approached Leo Murray and his companion and introduced myself as Danny Murray's boyhood chum. Leo's face enlivened instantly, just the way I remembered, though his friend's held some residual suspicion. As I asked for details of Danny's recent years, however, Carl had to repeat most of Leo's answers for me, and he began to warm to his role as go-between.

I quickly satisfied myself regarding Danny's progress and pressed on about Leo himself. He obliged me with the information that he was divorced, his kids grown, and he still worked for I. J. Murray, though the firm was much reduced by declines in the fur market. He lived, he said, with his sister. Carl, though obviously close, was apparently not Leo's lover.

I listened greedily. Leo Murray's voice still darted wildly up and down, detached from the meaning of his words. But reading the constant flicker of emotion across his face, I felt the remembered impression of comprehending his message without actually making out his words. It was as pleasing a sensation now as then, a kind of private, prelingual communication, full of intimacy even in blazing sunlight beside a crowded pool. I sat talking long after there was anything left to say.

Returning to my own friends at their lounges, I found myself making disparaging remarks—not about Leo, whom I simply described as an acquaintance from childhood, but about Carl. Cattily I described his skinny body, his pockmarked face, his lisping, pretentious speech. Slowly it dawned on me that I was jealous. Once again I had had to speak to Leo Murray through an intermediary. Once again he had chosen another to be his intimate. Why not me? Why was I again, unfairly, too late?

Several years later, on another pass through town, I was left with two hours to kill before my train left. It was an awkward space of time, not enough to call friends, too much to spend comfortably in a train station. I rented a locker for my suitcase and went for a walk.

The train station stood alongside the financial district, and at early evening the sidewalks were already nearly empty. There was only one movie theater in this end of town, and my timing would be unlikely to permit me a full feature. At this theater, however, it mattered little at what point you walked in. I paid the high admission fee and went in to watch the grainy, scratched film with its mismatched soundtrack.

When I entered, all eyes turned to survey the new arrival. The audience was all male, as I knew it would be. Men were seated at odd intervals throughout the small theater, occasionally in pairs. There was a cluster standing behind the back row of seats. A steady stream of individuals trooped back and forth from the lounges located at the very front of the theater, behind the screen.

I watched the film for a few minutes, and the crowd. Then I took a walk through the lounge area. It was dimly lit. There were men standing within and outside both bathrooms. Some of the stall doors stood ajar. No one spoke. The shadowy figures passed in and out in silence, sometimes lingering, blending into deeper shadows. Back in the theater, the flickering light of the movie made the spectators' closed faces superficially alive.

On my second pass through the lounge area, I spotted Leo Murray. He was cruising the same way I was, moving slowly through the hallway, which was lined with slouched figures. He looked me full in the face, but I couldn't tell whether he recognized me or not. His eyes were already wide, engorged with perception, before he caught sight of me.

I carefully passed him two or three more times, doing everything possible within the conventions of this place to alert him to my presence. Reluctantly I refrained from planting myself in front of him, tapping him on the shoulder, or signaling him directly. I slowed to a crawl each time he approached; I eyed him sullenly. He simply moved past like a figure in a dream, at ease in this silent world, his black eyes glinting, bottomless. We each glided along like the others, stopping sometimes to cling to a wall, otherwise floating past each other in the purgatory murk. Different stall doors stood ajar.

At length I drifted back out to the theater. I took a seat as far as possible from everyone else and applied myself to the unwatchable movie. Some minutes later a figure joined me in my row. It was Leo Murray, watching the screen with a gentle, beatific smile illuminating his face. I moved over two seats and sat beside him. Like a spotlight on a pivot, he turned and flooded me with his smile. His eyes glowed, black and wet.

I placed a daring hand on his knee. The fabric of the slacks was thick, luxurious, elegant. His own hand danced across my thigh, and he turned toward me further. Then he spoke to me, only to me, and I dropped my head back and listened.

CHOICE

• JOHN FOX •

JIMMY ARBOOZ WAS having dinner with his mother Flo Arbooz in a restaurant on Columbus Avenue, five blocks from his building, a cab ride from Flo's office. It was his neighborhood, a newly fashionable one. He was comfortable in this restaurant: the tables weren't crammed an inch apart from one another. They were talking about work, their jobs. He crossed his legs; he liked his socks.

They do this from time to time. The dinners are planned a couple of days ahead so that Flo can tell Jimmy's father Dan Arbooz and Dan will know he'll have to make his own supper in two days. He doesn't mind this but she feels he ought to be forewarned.

"Your sister isn't going to marry Ted," Flo said, bringing up the subject, rubbing her ear; she'd just removed a jade-and-onyx earring.

Jimmy watched the other one come off; then he was surprised his sister wasn't going to marry Ted.

"She isn't?" he said.

"He reconciled with the wife."

The two earrings were on the table; he wished she'd left them on.

"What wife?" he said. "I thought he was divorced."

"That was all a lie—they were just legally separated." She

was talking with extreme nonchalance, almost a monotone. Barbara was already once divorced, and now this. She took out a lipstick and pocket mirror; Jimmy was glad she was reapplying. Her casual manner was a front, but she was by this time so used to talking about her daughter in this way with Jimmy that it came nearly without effort.

"Do you like my socks?" he asked her, wagging his foot up and around, not changing the subject.

"Mm hm," Flo said. She didn't look at the socks—she'd already noticed them. They were a black-and-red checkerboard pattern. The other things on his feet were white patent-leather loafers he'd picked up in an antique shoe store on East 2nd Street. Flo didn't think that wearing loafers and having a flat-top in winter was such a good idea, but she keeps a tight rein on such opinions when they're out in public.

"Well, I hate to say I told you so," Jimmy said. "I've said all along he's a sack of shit."

"P.S.," Flo added, dropping the lipstick into her huge pock-etbook, "he's got two kids, not one."

Jimmy rolled his eyes. He lit Flo's cigarette. He felt badly for his sister.

"I don't know why she can't find the right man," Flo sighed, waving her own smoke away from her face. "But I'll tell you something: Barbara would still be married to Steve this very day if Ted hadn't come into the picture."

"Big deal. He was a jerk too." What Jimmy didn't say is that he doesn't think Barbara is such a prize herself. "She must be a total mess."

"Be a little charitable," Flo said. "You know what she's been through, James."

Jimmy flinched slightly around one side of his mouth, and his cheeks flushed. He hates it when his mother does that—shifts alliances on him or scolds him on neutral territory or, as in this case, both. One minute they'll be talking like a couple of sophisticates—friends—confidantes—and then suddenly he'll feel as if he was eight and just got spanked. He also hates being called James. When he was eighteen, seven years ago, he announced that that's what he wanted to be called from then on, not Jimmy, and not Jim. He thought James was elegant. His father and sister both ignored this request; now he wishes his mother had; he thinks it sounds silly, pretentious.

"Yes," he said, "I do know what she's been going through."

She sipped her brandy Alexander. "Mm, that's good." She flagged the waiter and asked him nicely to put some more nutmeg in it. This made Jimmy happy. It wasn't a gratuitous or boorish request; she just wanted more nutmeg. Jimmy watched the waiter to see if he'd give his mother an attitude. He didn't. There was no reason to; this was Columbus Avenue: waiters are actors, dancers and singers. Waiters are gay; they love fifty-year-old women with burgundy hair. His father would have gotten embarrassed and asked her what she needed more nutmeg for.

"Is she still going to have Christmas dinner?" Jimmy wanted to know. Christmas was ten days away.

"She said she was. Which I think is a good idea."

He agreed for stiff-upper-lip reasons, but he wished she'd decided to cancel it. He hates going to his sister's. "What do you want for Christmas, anyway?" he asked, this time deliberately changing the subject.

"Oh," Flo said. "Oh! You know what I would love to have?"

"What."

"But it's very expensive." She named a new, very expensive French perfume.

"Oh yeah, you mentioned that at Thanksgiving."

"And your sister won't get it."

"I know she won't." He also knew that Barbara does all of Dan Arbooz's Christmas shopping. On Thanksgiving when Flo dropped the hint about the perfume—which she first smelled on a promotional insert wrapped in cellophane and enclosed with her Macy's bill—Barbara pointed out that Flo had at least a dozen bottles of perfume on her dresser that were all full. Half-full, Flo had said. She likes perfume but tires of the scents and enjoys getting new ones.

They rehashed Barbara's divorce and her now-canceled second marriage plans. She told him about who on the block dropped dead and who got engaged and who's moving to Maryland and who had a second child but shouldn't have because they seem so unhappy. Jimmy inhaled cigarettes deeply and exhaled a lot of smoke expressively while he listened to some of what she said. His mother should know by now that he doesn't want his ear bent with this stuff when they go out, and he often suspects from her flat tone that she no longer cares about neighborhood gossip anyway, but the only aspect of his life either of them feels comfortable discussing with the other is his job, so she often has to hold up his end of the conversation once they've exhausted the details of Barbara's life. He smokes cigarettes in restaurants with her but never at his parents' house nor his sister's. He never addresses her (Mom, Ma, Mommy) when they're in public together. He sees no resemblance between them—he is hawk-faced like his father, she is all mouth and jaw —and he sometimes hopes people thinks he's a gigolo.

A minute later he had tuned her out completely and the following speech was batting against the backs of his teeth: *You expect me to have charitable feelings and get all involved in conversations about divorces and canceled marriages and babies but my life is a total blank to you and Daddy. I've been through worse than her but you don't want to hear about it—the thought of it is too disgusting. I broke up with a man I lived with for four years, twice as long as her marriage, but it's unmentionable, the breakup, the whole relationship. For all I know I could have AIDS. I could be dead in a year.*

"I'm not going to Barbara's on Christmas," he suddenly blurted, interrupting her in midsentence.

"Why?" Flo said once she'd caught her bearings.

"Because I don't feel like looking at her being all miserable and nervous."

"I don't think that's very nice of you, James." It wasn't a conscious attempt to instill guilt; she was just thinking of her daughter's feelings. "I think it's good for her that she didn't cancel it," she said, reaching for her pocketbook.

"Well, I'm not going," he said, infuriated, and Flo got up to go to the ladies' room. He undressed a few waiters and a few flirted with him. He particularly hoped they thought he was a gigolo. He tamped out Flo's cigarette and lit a fresh one for himself, recalling the one and only time he ever smoked in his parents' house—he was still living there—five years ago, in the basement, in the dark, when he told her he was gay—he'd gotten drunk first—and she asked him if he was sure. He said that was like asking him if he was sure he had arms and legs. She thought there were ways of changing, she said. He said he didn't want to change. She didn't understand this. He said it was part of him, like his heart. She asked him if there was anything she had done to cause it. No, he said; definitely not. No one "caused" it. He was born that way. He said this so she wouldn't feel guilty but now he believes it, most of the time. They talked for an hour, chain-smoking, his father asleep above them. He said it was up to her whether or not she told him; he said he didn't care. She said she didn't know he smoked cigarettes.

When he reached puberty, and for a couple years afterward, he kept dreading the moment when his father would bring up the subject of girls; it never came, and Jimmy's reaction went from relief to bewilderment to resentment. His sexuality—whatever its nature, the mere basic fact of it—remained unacknowledged until that night in the basement when he dropped his bombshell on Flo, and also disclosed, while he was at it, that he'd been smoking for years and that he would do so in the house from then on. Fine, Flo had said, blasted, nodding at the floor, like the mother of an abducted child quietly acquiescing to the ultimatums of kidnappers. Jimmy didn't realize that she would have cut off her right arm for none of it to be true, so a few times in the weeks following he attempted to talk to her about the way he was in real life, as he put it, in an indirect breezy manner, but it clearly made her uncomfortable and it quickly became an untopic, an unfact, verboten. To this day he doesn't know if she ever told his father or sister—although he assumes that even they must have figured it out by now—and he never smoked in the house again.

He had Flo to his apartment once, shortly after he moved into it after splitting up with Dean six months ago, and made a point of not removing a "Swimmers & Surfers" beefcake calendar from its prominent position on the refrigerator. She seemed unfazed by it, but Jimmy knew that she'd become an expert at veiling her feelings by then, so during cocktails he kept trying to think of a pretense for turning it over, and by the time he served coffee he wanted to tear it off the refrigerator and ram it in a drawer. Flo understands her son's need for love and companionship; she has even grown to accept his wanting it with another man. What she can't see is the sex part.

They've continued to meet for dinner, but always in restaurants like this one, where he was still stewing in his juices when she returned from the ladies' room, and he could plainly see that she'd removed her girdle.

Startled—amused—he quickly uncrossed his legs and sat up straight. He chuckled. He leaned forward, beaming, and clasped his hands on the table.

"What is it?" Flo asked, smiling right at him, having no idea what he'd reacted to. He flushed; he flexed the tendons in back of his knees—right, left, rapidly back and forth. Flo can be a charming and amusing person, but Jimmy tends to forget this because he's usually carrying her around in the back of his neck, part of a tight muscle that gets massaged every two weeks at a health club. "I'll call you later in the week about Christmas," he said sheepishly.

"Oh. Fine," she replied, cupping her mouth, yawning elaborately. It was her pleasant, "time-to-call-it-a-night" yawn. She got a cab to the Yonkers express bus and Jimmy wandered around the neighborhood.

He stopped along the avenue and joined a small crowd watch a street comedian do an imitation of a roach stuck and writhing in a Roach Motel. He laughed out loud. He bought a pear at a fruit market and ate it as he walked. This was to look casual and health-conscious. He passed the custom-frame shop he manages, dark and gated. He wished it were lit and open and that he was in it and that it was the next day, even though when he's there he wishes he were someplace else. He paused in front of a bar on the next block but didn't like the way he was dressed for this place so he kept going. He wasn't going to go home, change, and come back, either. He knew what it would be like: he'd lean against a wall and watch a porn video on a TV suspended above the heads of a small group of regulars who'd be carrying on a lively conversation at one end of the bar. About ten other men, alone, would be scattered around in various attitudes, watching the video, acting, like Jimmy, as though that's what they'd come in for, and only occasionally copping rapid fish-eyed peeks at one another. Jimmy's furtive bar attitude is exactly the same as it was before the health crisis, when it was due to his fear of rejection and his need to reject; but now in addition to that he has no way of knowing who has AIDS, plus he figures if he seems too cruisy he might appear promiscuous, and therefore that much more likely to have contracted it himself. He swears that if they were to find a cure tomorrow he'll suddenly be all gregarious and chummy.

In order to get into his building he had to climb over four Hispanic men—beer-bellied, sweaty even in the cold, drinking out of paper bags—whose enduring presence in his gentrifying neighborhood riles him. They're there day and night, yabbering away and laughing, and he always wonders what they could possibly have to talk about since they don't do anything and don't go anywhere. He calls them Hispanics, though. It's the correct thing to call them. Like "physically challenged," not handicapped. Like "gay," not homosexual. Like "person with AIDS," not AIDS victim.

He doesn't know a single person with AIDS and hopes he never does. He wouldn't want to have to cook up excuses not to visit the hospital. He wouldn't even want to get letters from such a person and have to worry that the licked portion of the envelope might be infected. That's the way he thinks. The previous summer he wore shorts almost every day to show off his lesion-free legs.

Upstairs he ran into his neighbor Tabitha in the hall. She always seems to be in the hall—throwing out garbage, getting the mail, coming or going with her half-wit kid Charles. "Hi," Jimmy said. "Fine," Tabitha said. He doesn't like her. She's pushy, yet has a somnolent air about her. And he'll never figure out why some black people answer the greeting "Hi" by telling you how they are. She asked him if he was giving the super anything for Christmas. He said he was. How much, she wanted to know. He said he wasn't sure yet. He knew how much but didn't think it was any of her business.

"Do you think five dollars is enough?" she pressed.

"Well, you know, whatever you can afford." He would have given nothing at all before five bucks. "See ya," and he went inside.

He stood there staring at his bed—six months old and no one but him had ever been in it. Long before he moved out of his ex-boyfriend's, who he'd met at a bar in the West Village, sex had become the only reason to stay together—they figured they were both relatively "safe." The days when they couldn't keep their hands off each other were gone however, and the apartment was thick with tension, which would have been only slightly relieved by occasional visits to back rooms or baths, but even these outlets were precluded by their fear of death. Now he masturbates a lot—twice a day, minimum—usually with porn magazines that he keeps piled under his bed, and sometimes with photos of Dean sprawled and propped up around him on pillows.

He opened his sock-and-underwear drawer and removed a pack of them—snapshots he took on the beach in Provincetown shortly after they'd met. *You know you're welcome to bring a friend.* That's the way he has always imagined his mother would put it, her hand on her throat, gagging on the word "friend," if she ever broke down and invited him to bring someone to the house. Dozens of times over the course of his four years with Dean he pictured what this would be like. Perusing the photos, he pictured it now and saw his parents and sister visualizing the two of them "sodomizing" each other, while they all bent over backwards trying to act normal and easygoing. He wouldn't have accepted such an invitation; he will when he knows he'll feel comfortable holding a man's hand on the couch, just as his sister used to do with her husband Steve; and he'll introduce the man as his boyfriend, not his friend.

What invitation. What man.

He stuffed the pictures back in the drawer and made a beeline for the phone. "I'm not going to Barbara's on Christmas," he told his mother. "I've made up my mind."

On Christmas afternoon, Jimmy and Flo were sitting next to each other on one half of Barbara's L-shaped sectional sofa. Flo had sat first, Jimmy after getting himself a scotch-and-soda. His feet were flat on the floor and he was slumped back into the sofa, watching his knees, as though afloat on an inner tube. A fist, shoved against his face, was forcing his mouth off to one side and his elbow was embedded in the foam-rubber arm of the sofa.

Flo dipped a potato chip into a bowl of onion dip but the chip cracked and three-quarters of it remained stuck in the dip so she left it there and while chewing on the undipped piece she said, very low but still using her vocal cords, "They're whispering in the kitchen."

Out from around his fist Jimmy muttered, "She should have the crinkly kind so they don't break."

Flo lit a cigarette and crossed a leg, then crisscrossed her wrists on her knee and held the cigarette between two fingers that pointed straight up. If not for her cigarette and his drink, they would have passed for a couple of unpopular relations at a wake.

"What do you think they're whispering about?" he asked.

"Who the hell knows," she answered quickly, looking away at the Christmas tree, exhaling smoke at it.

He looked sidelong at her leg. "You have a very small run in your panty hose."

All in a split second she looked at his eyes, he saw her do this out of his peripheral vision so he looked away, and she looked at her leg. "Where?"

"There."

"I can't even see it. Don't point things out, James, if you can hardly see them."

The blender was going in the kitchen now, competing with Barbara's voice—two shrill whines.

Jimmy took a ceramic figurine from the end table next to him. "This is the mouse I gave her last year."

Flo glanced at it. Her daughter collects mice. Mice hugging. Mice in bed—snugly, asleep. Mice kissing—hands behind backs, faces bent toward each other, eyes closed. Mostly from card shops, although last year Jimmy discovered some quality mouse collectibles and decided to try and improve his sister's taste by starting her on a particular Irish set he thought was the least corny.

"I'm sure she thinks it cost the same as the Hallmark crap," he said, gesturing at the other mice, but also taking in, while he was at it, the kitschy Christmas decorations that covered every flat surface and much of the wall space. "I don't know why I bother to spend money on good things when people don't appreciate it. Daddy would—"

"Oh, shoosh."

"He'd just as soon have a Milky Way than—"

"Use a coaster."

"—than the candy I get him from Li-lac."

"Be nice, will you, please?"

"I have all intentions of being nice," he said, replacing the mouse.

Flo sighed. She flicked an ash fleck off the gray wool pleated skirt Jimmy had given her that morning. She was also wearing his most recent Mother's Day and birthday gifts: an off-white silk blouse and dark burgundy pumps that matched her hair. They were all going to exchange presents there at Barbara's, but Jimmy had figured Flo might want to wear her present so he gave it to her at his parents' house, three blocks away. He'd done his shopping at a Fifth Avenue department store, and when he had the skirt wrapped he chose a box with the store logo rather than the generic Christmas one. The expensive French perfume, which came in its own box, was in a small shopping bag at his feet, with the Li-lac candy and a new mouse.

"James, use a coaster."

"All her furniture has a Formica coating. You don't need a coaster."

Fluttering her eyes closed, Flo looked away at the tree again, shaking the foot of the crossed leg. "She's got that blender on too long," she said just as it was shut off. In a minute, Barbara came in with a tray, followed by her father.

"Ooh, chi-chis!" Flo exclaimed, dinching the cigarette.

Barbara smiled stiffly and placed the tray on the coffee table. Three stemmed glasses were filled with a white frothy concoction. Barbara and Dan sat next to each other on the other half of the L-shaped sectional. She perched herself on the edge of it; he sat back comfortably, his bony knees in the air, like Jimmy's, only he wasn't deliberately slumped. The coffee table held the chips and dip, cheddar cheese and Ritz crackers, Hershey balls wrapped in festive foil, and mixed salted nuts. A roast was in the oven, almost well-done.

"Well," Dan Arbooz said, raising his glass, smiling self-consciously, "Merry Christmas, everybody." Not one with words, and gawky with displays of sentiment, he was Bob Cratchit-shy now. Jimmy would have found this endearing in a twelve-year-old boy.

"I think I left the blender on too long," Barbara said. "Are they too watery?" She was looking at her drink when she asked this.

"No, no," Flo answered, knowing the question had been directed at her. She tipped the glass away and dabbed her mouth with a paper Santa cocktail napkin. "Perfect."

"Christmas in Hawaii," Dan chuckled.

Jimmy began to sing. "Mele Kalikimaka is the thing to say—"

"On a bright Hawaiian Christmas daay-y," his mother joined in, laughing.

Barbara turned the sides of her mouth up; this was a smile.

Her father remembered the tune but couldn't place it. "What's that from?" he asked.

"The Arthur Godfrey Christmas album," said Jimmy. "You still have it, you know. I saw it this morning."

"Oh, we should have brought it," Flo said, lighting another cigarette.

"I have Christmas albums," Barbara said, waving the smoke away. She'd been a popular, pretty girl in high school, but now, at twenty-seven, her face is tight and pinched; she has large hips and shapeless legs, easily bruised, and a high-pressure job that she hates but says she likes. A Christmas album of hers was playing at that moment, one by a famous mellow-pop songstress whom Jimmy loathes. The A-side had been on when Jimmy, Flo and Dan got there. Jimmy had wanted to take the arm and press the needle screeching across the record—it's what Barbara did once when he was eleven and she was thirteen to a record of his when he refused to lower the volume. A slapping and hair-tugging fight ensued but Dan Arbooz interceded and separated the two while Flo screamed at the top of her lungs from the kitchen: "You goddamn ungrateful snots! Why did I ever have children!" Dan told Jimmy never to hit a girl in the stomach because it might prevent her from having babies. He hadn't been anywhere near her stomach but rather than pursue this point he said that he would feel sorry for any baby *she* ever had. It was said in anger but he meant it and he still thinks it. Long after brother and sister had barricaded themselves in separate rooms and Dan had gone outside to hose down the sidewalk, Flo continued to rant and rave in intermittent bursts until she'd finished making supper. In those days she flew off the handle whenever her children fought like cats and dogs—an almost daily occurrence—but after she went back to her secretarial job Barbara and Jimmy fought less and when they did Flo usually ignored them. Years later, by the time Barbara married that moron Steve, her fits were rare and always directed at Dan. They ceased completely once her only son and favorite child broke her heart.

"Where'd you hear about these again?" Dan asked his daughter, raising his glass.

"Hawaii!" Jimmy said. "Where else? That's why I thought of the song!" He might have been talking to an idiot. Flo tossed him a quick combination of knitted brows and pursed lips, instantly gone. Barbara was chewing a nut and fingering another one. "This dip is delicious, Barbara," Flo said. Jimmy got up to refill his scotch-and-soda. He hates drinking in the daytime.

Barbara and her ex-husband Steve discovered chi-chis on their honeymoon in Honolulu; they are the same thing as piña coladas, only with vodka, not rum. During their two years of marriage she made them whenever they had her parents over but she stopped after the divorce. Dan Arbooz liked Steve; they were both route salesmen—Steve for Miller beer and Dan for Drakes Cakes. They used to talk about "stale" and "returns." Dan misses him because no one else is interested in this topic.

The fact that Barbara was now miserable over her breakup with Ted enabled her to quit being miserable over her divorce from Steve. Jimmy and Flo both understood that the revival of the chi-chis was meant to signal this, but Dan didn't get it because he didn't remember that Barbara had stopped serving them in the first place.

"Let's open the presents," Flo cheerfully suggested. Her cheerfulness in the presence of her daughter, whose very sight depresses her, comes automatically, like the nonchalant manner in which she talks about her to Jimmy.

Barbara took a pile of presents from under the tree and Jimmy noticed, on top, a wrapped box the exact shape and size as the perfume he'd bought. Dan self-amusedly rubbed his hands together at the sight of the wrapped loot. Among other things, Flo and Dan gave Jimmy three books from a long list he'd given Flo. He was very appreciative; he admired the books, riffled and smelled their pages. Dan got what he always got— pajamas, shirts, socks and underwear—and was very happy. Jimmy was trying to decide what to do about the perfume.

Barbara opened one of her presents and removed a matching skirt and jacket; she said nothing.

"You don't like it," Flo said, watching her daughter scrutinize the cut. "I think it's beautiful."

Jimmy was about to agree but he kept his mouth shut.

"I don't know," Barbara said tonelessly. "I'll have to try it on."

"I have the receipt with me," Flo said.

Barbara suddenly looked right at her mother for the first time that day. "You always buy what *you* like—what you think I should like."

"Take it back. I have the receipt."

"You always do this. It would be nice to get something from you for a change that I don't have to return. You must know my taste by now."

No one moved.

"It's a beautiful suit," Flo said. "Vicky was with me. She even said, 'Oh Flo, Barbara will love this.' "

Barbara's eyes watered; she sprang up and rushed into the bedroom. Dan Arbooz hadn't said a word during the exchange but now he sat forward and clasped his hands.

"You better go in there," Flo said to him.

"Why?"

"Because. She's crying."

Dan got up and went down the hall and knocked on the door; it opened and he went in.

Flo stood; she went to the window and looked out at the snowless, sunny, almost balmy day. Jimmy watched her as she adjusted the blinds to admit more, then less, light, as though signaling an SOS to someone across the street. His insides surged with apology. He wanted to save her. *Let's leave*, he wanted to say.

"See if there's any more in that blender, will you?" she said.

He picked himself up and went into the kitchen. "It's empty."

"Fix me a vodka-and-tonic, honey."

He also made himself another scotch-and-soda. He sniffed the air. He opened the oven door a crack and looked in. "Looks like an extremely well-done roast beef in there."

"Shut that. And don't say a thing about it."

"*Oh,*" he said, bringing their drinks, "I just remembered."

"What," she said, turning from the window.

"*A Christmas Carol* is on—the good one. The one with Alastair Sim. We can just catch the end."

"Put it on," she said and sat back down. "And don't flick the stations so fast."

Finally Dan and Barbara emerged from the bedroom and went into the kitchen. Barbara opened the oven door. "Oh, great," she said to her father. "Well, there isn't going to be any gravy," Flo and Jimmy heard her say. "There's no juice in this pan. It's all dried up. Everything's going to be all dried up," she said, slamming the oven door. Jimmy wanted to slap her.

"It will be delicious!" Flo bellowed from the living room. "It smells delicious!"

Jimmy suddenly took the perfume from his shopping bag and thrust it at his mother. "Merry Christmas!"

"Oh, James! *Another* present?"

Barbara materialized in the archway between the dining room and living room with an oven mitt poised against her thigh. She looked as though she might pull a small pistol out of it.

"Oh, I don't believe it!" Flo exclaimed, delighted. "Oh, James I never expected . . ." She made a great fuss. She dabbed perfume behind her ears and on her wrists. She was very happy. She really hadn't expected it. Barbara's face was flushed and her jaw had clamped shut. She marched over to what was left of the pile of presents on the coffee table and grabbed the perfume she had bought. "Don't even bother opening this. It's the same thing." She tossed it back under the tree.

"Oh, no!" Flo laughed. "So, I'll have two!"

"Don't be ridiculous. You'll never finish *one*. You'll get tired of the smell and want a different kind within a year."

Flo placed the perfume on her pile and lit another cigarette.

"Do you have to chain-smoke?" Barbara said. "You're stinking up my apartment."

Flo turned to the TV and ran her tongue across her upper lip, shaking her head slightly, but Jimmy couldn't keep his mouth shut. "You knew she chain-smoked when you invited her here."

"Shush up," Flo said to the TV screen.

He turned back to the TV and stuck with it. He felt Barbara's eyes riveting him; he half-expected the sofa to flip over backwards. Dan Arbooz was in the kitchen all this while, carving meat, listening but not saying a word, as though he'd been hired for the day. Barbara stood there facing them, her feet spread wide, her hands—one of them still in the oven mitt—on her waist. She looked defiant, courageous, and somehow only a bit ridiculous.

She looked at the TV. It was her TV. Jimmy looked at Barbara. Barbara looked at him. He looked at her TV.

"We're just watching the end," Flo said. "It's 'Scrooge.' "

It was the part where Scrooge does the jig with his shocked housekeeper. "I'm as merry as a schoolboy; I'm as giddy as a drunken man."

Barbara turned on her heels and went back into the kitchen

where her father was still carving the roast. "Now we have to watch a *movie*," she said for the benefit of the two in the other room. "While my dinner gets cold."

"Jesus Christ Almighty," Flo murmured to herself and to Jimmy. Then, "Shut it off, James," and she got up.

Jimmy shut it off just as a reformed and contrite Uncle Ebenezer was being admitted to his nephew's home, a scene of merriment and familial bliss. The obvious irony—the kind that happens all the time in life but never in good fiction—was not lost on Jimmy or Flo.

The dinner was uneventful. They discussed what movies they'd seen lately. There was a big, very popular one they'd all loved except Jimmy who found it "sloppily sentimental." This did not cause an argument, just a few moments of silence, and then a change of subject. It went on like that and then Flo, Dan, and Jimmy left right after coffee. In the car, Jimmy swore aloud from the middle of the backseat that he would never go to his sister's again. He watched the backs of his parents' heads, looking from one to the other four or five times, waiting for a reaction, and when none came he slumped and felt like a jerk.

They drove him to the express bus. He thanked them for the presents and they thanked him. He leaned over and shook his father's hand. He kissed his mother's cheek and she held the side of his head while he did so.

"Get home safe," she said; then, suddenly, and with genuine enthusiasm, "Call me and we'll have dinner soon."

"I will!" he said, opening the door.

"I enjoy that," she added, almost to herself, while her husband sat with two hands on the steering wheel, facing front, as detached as a chauffeur.

From the curb Jimmy turned to wave but she was looking down, digging for something in her pocketbook. A handkerchief, he hoped; but no, a cigarette. The car swerved into a U-turn and he looked away before his father's side came into view.

He was unpacking his presents—he'd been home for ten minutes—when he heard a loud noise from the hall. WooooOO

—WOOO*OOOO*. The sound of a toy train. It kept repeating. It made his right ear throb. Then he heard a woman's voice—Tabitha's. He listened to the noise for about five minutes, hoping it would stop. It didn't. He put on something neutral and homey—worn jeans, sweatshirt, and slippers—and went for the door. The boy, Charles, had never played in the hall before and he was going to nip this in the bud. He stopped, and stuck a pencil behind his ear. He unbolted the door; he opened it and there was Tabitha handling a foot-long locomotive—one of those friction things. "Tabitha?" he said.

"Huh?" she answered.

He spotted Charles standing in the shadow of the stairwell, mutely staring at him, his face vacant. Unnerved by the motionless boy, Jimmy asked her in a nastier tone than he'd intended if she would please take the train into her apartment. She strolled over with it instead. "He lost the screws," she said. "I'm trying to get the bottom back on."

Jimmy feigned interest in the toy. Charles looked like he couldn't care less about it and just continued to stare at Jimmy who was still holding the door half-open with his foot, hadn't expected this to take so long.

"Do you have any screws?" Tabitha asked him.

"Uh, no, I don't—none that small." He suggested she put rubber bands around the thing. Awkwardly, he said, "Well, so long," and opened his door wider to go back in, but Charles bolted and darted over his foot into the apartment and expressionlessly, silently, ran around in small circles while Jimmy, appalled—after all, there was that damn calendar still in plain view on the refrigerator—pretended to be friendly and amused. "You want to move in here, Charles?" he said, fake-laughing, addressing the boy for the first time.

"Come on, Charles," Tabitha said, and he ran out and down the hall. Jimmy, all smiley: "See ya, Tabitha." She didn't say anything. He shut the door cozily, like he'd opened it for a nice chat. He glared at the smiling stud on the calendar as though it were a boxing opponent, taunting and belittling him. He glanced from it to the garbage can, clenching and unclenching his fists. He marched over to it, grabbed the pencil from behind his ear, and wrote "CALL MOM RE DINNER" in one of the boxes below Mr. December's gorgeous thighs.

He switched on his FM receiver and rolled the dial rapidly from one end of the band to the other, trying to find a song he liked, but he couldn't. He put on a record and lifted the arm to the last cut on the side, knowing he'd done this so often that it had to have caused an aural scratch. He regretted this even though he didn't like the next-to-last song and knew he'd probably never play it again. He turned up the volume and ground his teeth rhythmically to the music. He thought of going out but rejected this idea: he wouldn't have been caught dead in a bar on Christmas. He decided to start saving for a video-cassette player so he could watch porn videos in the privacy of his own home. Then, as though performing a routine chore, he hauled out the stack of magazines from under his bed and plopped them on top of it. He knew he wouldn't look at them all—only two or three. Whenever he goes on a trip, he also overpacks. He has always loved the luxury of choice.

A QUEER RED SPIRIT

• C. F. BORGMAN •

MY . . .

I have him by the loose leaf. I have him by the pen.

My name is . . .

He's exhausted and spent. He moves the pen. I write through him.

My name is Brian Malv . . .

He's bandaging his guilt for having forgotten to call Benjamin by writing a story about him. Clever of me, a spirit, to pick such a hunk for my medium. I've done it before. I get so physical, speaking metaphysically of course.

Brian wants to write about Benjamin Quinn and he knows very little. I, on the other hand, know Benjamin's spirit. We are old friends. I've known him since Sodom, possibly even before that, but Sodom was where we got close. He's a queer red. I'm a queer blue. I know only three purples.

My spirit colleagues scoff at my choice of Brian for a medium. They take communication between planes so seriously. "He's shallow," one spirit says. I answer, "He's cute. He's easy. He grows on me."

So here Brian sits writing frantically at his desk, spaced out of his

*gorgeous head. Let it spill, Brian. It will dry. It will cake and make
sense. You're the icing, honey. The content is mine. The veil is drawn
open, brushing the sweat from your hot brow. What were you saying?*

My name is Brian Malventano. I live out here in Rockaway
Beach, Queens. I feel so tight. All muscle. No fat. Hard. In me
there is a blue sea center. I am the sky. I thrive on high drive
sex. It's in the air. I breathe it. I taste it. Maybe there's something out of kilter in my gland secretions. Maybe it's in the
brain. All I know is I love men. I am constantly overcome with
lust. I've made all sex be my religion. Orgasm is the highest
sacrament. Vera, my psychic friend from Bay Ridge, once said,
"Brian, you're so physical that your mind is like free to roam all
the layers of life. Your senses rule you. Your antennae receive
and send out more than just sexual signals. You're like a lighthouse in like some crazy psychic sea." Vera has always had the
hots for me. She really wanted to fuck around.

I see a trail of hair descending toward the elastic waistband
of some runner's shorts, and inside I scream, "Give me that!
Strip for me!" I burn up. I feel the blood pumping through me.
I am alive! It's more than flesh. Sex is everything to me. Sex is
in the stars. In the spice rack. In the sand. I see the hands of two
lovers on the beach. I see their fingernails caked with sex. Sometimes at night, I dig a hole in the sand. It is wet and still warm
from the day's sun. I fuck the Earth. I come. Tears pour free. It
makes me spiritual.

Anyway, I remember Benjamin singing in his shaky British
accent, "The birds and the bees do it, let's do it, da da da dada
da." We sat on his porch out here in Rockaway. I got him talking
about sex. He could tell stories. He was old, an old queen from
all over the world. He spoke with exaggerated movements and
precise diction, and whenever he used a sexually explicit word,
he whispered it. He sat in his "queen's chair," a high fan-backed
rattan one. I sat on the rotting steps to his porch.

"Brian, dearie," he said, and it always sounded like he was
saying, "brandy," "you've have the stars on your side. And you
can thank your lucky stars for your big cock." He leaned forward and whispered "cock." "Just do what you do and enjoy it.

Call it a religion if you will. God knows there are a lot of bodies that should be worshipped. I've genuflected in front of quite a few golden calves in my day, dearie."

Benjamin lived next door to my uncle's house out here. When Uncle Sal was killed, it turned out he had left the house to me. I moved in two years ago, and that's when I met Benjamin. He screamed at me for cutting the climbing roses from my side of the fence. His house is covered with climbing roses. I was in my shorts, and as we spoke, I kept snapping my shears in the air. I knew he was queer right off the bat. I can tell right away. I made sure that my sexual equipment jutted out as far as possible. I snapped the shears nearer and nearer to my cock. Benjamin turned red. Finally he blurted out, "Cut what you will from your side of the fence, but be careful down there." His shaky arm extended toward my crotch. I laughed. I assured him, "Hey, man, I'm as gay as a goose. Don't be embarrassed. Believe me, I'd never cut it off." And from then on, we were friends. I know he wanted to suck me off at times, but that would have been like getting a blow job from my mother. Benjamin was like my mother. I'd done it with older men, maybe fifty tops, but that was way back when I was a teenager and making bucks from it. Now at twenty-four, I'd rather expend my sex free into the sand and into the asses of muscle I fall for. I'll save the royalty for my own old age, which gets me back to Benjamin's porch.

Benjamin said, "You think I'm all dried up and old, dearie, but just because there's snow on the roof, that doesn't mean the fire has gone out of the stove."

I thought, "Sure, I get it. You mean you can still get it up even though you've got white hair, but Benjamin, your highness baby, your hair is gone, and you wear a dark toupee." You see, he's always worn a brown rug taped to his skull. It looks fake. Sometimes I noticed the tape edges on his forehead. I should have said some sort of joke at the fence that first day we met, like, "Hey, that almost looks real," or, "That's a very realistic hairpiece," or something that would have made it clear to him that I knew it was fake. Then it never would have bothered me. Hell, what do I care what he puts on his head. I dyed my hair maroon last winter. But anyway, I was afraid that I might hurt his feelings. I figured that in his head, he thought it looked good, and who was I to say anything.

Once I accepted the lie of the rug on his head, though, I always felt off a bit when I looked at Benjamin. I worried for him when it was windy in the Shop-Rite parking lot and I was helping him to my car and his hands were full of bagged groceries and I could see the toupee about to fly off his head. I would grab the bags and look away, giving him time to straighten the hair back on. And I never just barged into his house, especially in the hot days of summer. I always made noise outside on the porch, knowing he would surely be inside watching television, bald, airing off his skull. I would give him a minute to slap the thing on before I walked in. God, I remember talking at the fence during August and the sweat would be pouring from his adhesive hairline, and I'd want to yell, "Just take the damn thing off!"

Believe it or not, I think I was on the same wavelength as Benjamin. There was something in him that intrigued me. I would watch him putter in his overgrown garden from my bedroom window. He seemed content to spend his days either in the garden or watching television. I really had nothing in common with him. He was old, I was young. He was bald, I was hirsute. Not apish, just hairy enough in all the right places. Did he have a hairy chest? No, I remember pink, and I think he had a few white hairs growing around his teats. I was "out," and he was still "whispering." I was openly gay and he was just openly swishy.

Whoa! I wonder about Vera the Psychic. I let her read the preceding page, and she said she felt, I mean FELT, that I had looked up the word "hirsute," which I didn't. Tony Santini, this guy I used to sleep with, used to say his dad, Angelo "Big Deal" Santini, was hirsute. "Hairsuit," we called him. I'm beginning to wonder about Vera reading any more of this story. Oh, and then she said that she thought "swishy" and "gay" were similar, not opposites! I said, "The day I sway around like Benjamin Quinn, is the day they castrate me. I am not a swish, Vera, and I'm as gay as a goose!"

Okay, so Benjamin and I had nothing in common except that we lived next door to each other, and we were both bent. *Bent Neighbors!* That's what I should call this story.

Anyway, my point is, there was something magnetic about Benjamin to me. I certainly wasn't sexually attracted to him, I mean fuck my own mother! But I loved him. He was a character. He was a gay one who had made it to old age next door to me. We were in the same tribe. Maybe it was meant to be, us being neighbors, so I could write this story. I psyched into him. I understood his vanity. Hell, I wouldn't want to be bald. I mean balled, yes, but not bald unless I chose to shave my head. But really the hair thing was no big deal now that I think of it. I was just trying to show what he looked like and that was the first thing that came to mind. He was so odd. I'm not odd. That's another difference.

One too many differences!! This has gone on too long, Brian. Make your point and move on. And while I'm at it, honey, let's keep Vera away from these papers. Can you hear me, Brian? That's it, let me in here on your lap.

The young man means well. It's true he is full of psychic energy. I love to play with him. I work him up, lapping his ideas with my tongue. Sex is the key to his spirit. I get him so hard that he moans for release. And that's where I slip in. I must get off in time to get through. That's the catch, trying to jump back into time. I am a spirit. Time is like a Broadway show, and getting into time is like getting cast in the show. You wait and wait for the callback. Well, this stud with the urge to write is my show. As long as he is here in this time of yours, I can slip onto the stage. You see, Brian is tuned to my wavelength, a queer blue wavelength. His confused but enthusiastic brain has all the letters, even a few ideas, waiting to be assembled. When I get him receptive, I can write through him, pushing his pen, revealing the truth. Truth is revealed in many ways. As I said before (Oh, I do love this time thing— before, after, then, way back, all those words), as I said before, some spirit communicators possess stuffy academic types. I go for the physical. Why be so serious? That's what I love about Red. He has a sense of humor too. Brian is a young Italian stud. I love it!

Hey! he is really into me! Wait till I tell Vera.

Brian, relax. Feel this? Feel that? Mmmmm. That's it.

I turn you on, man. The goddamned spirits are into me!

I read that Jack Kerouac wrote on a roll of shelf paper, non-stop, on speed, running the roll through the typewriter. This spirit might have a lot to say. If this works out, maybe I should get a typewriter to take with me when I move to Mark's apartment in Soho. I am, as Vera says, a lighthouse. Mmmmm, I feel so good. Like standing on a rock, getting drenched by warm waves, salty naked burning. So, this spirit thinks I'm hot. Hey, I can dig it. Vera said to surround myself with white light and no spirit can harm me, and I dig the attention. Beat. He fights me on my using "into" but I say, Hey, then go find a science freak. I am "into" writing the story of my dear neighbor, Benjamin Quinn. I wish I knew more about him. I am into erections and shooting stars!

Come, come. That's it. Now Brian is relaxed and receptive and I can tell the story of Benjamin Quinn who was born in Australia in 1917.

There is a ship in the North Atlantic. On the deck of the ship, which is headed for the Great War in France, stands a handsome drunken sailor named Teddy Purnhagen.

Hey! I am into Teddy Purnhagen! I am into Teddy's pants!

Brian, don't fight me. He focuses on the sailor's erection. I too focus on the erection.

Teddy Purnhagen rubs his crotch, unbuttons his pants, and pulls his penis in the moonlight. It is midnight. The deck is deserted. Teddy's legs flex and he moans and ejaculates. He finishes the last of the whiskey from the flask his father had given him at the train station in Ohio. Teddy slips from the deck into the ocean and is drowned beneath the hull and mangled by the ship. His twentieth-century life (He was born in 1900 and had always thought of his life as innovative. He was going to explore the world beyond Ohio. A new generation, a new century) came to an abrupt end in this drunken, drained slide into the Atlantic.

In that dark night there were millions of stars visible. The star pinpointed above the ship became Teddy Purnhagen's signature star on his short life. Just as the Big Dipper is connected by stars, everyone has his own constellation. If all the high points of Teddy's life were connected, the picture, the symbol that would appear would look very much like a man with an erection.

Teddy Purnhagen's signature star, which is the dickhead on the man with the erection, is Benjamin Quinn's first star. As Teddy's spirit, my friend, Red, surfaced from the Atlantic, it soared to the dingy flat above the bakery in New South Wales, Australia, where baby Benjamin was being born. Red, exhausted from the whole Purnhagen confusion and the flight, nestled deep into the new safe pure innocence of the baby. Benjamin cried. The midwife whacked him on the buttocks. He cried louder, but was soon coaxed to sleep by a very tired red spirit.

Catherine Quinn and her husband, the baker, were thrilled with their new son. He was to be their only child. Benjamin's father burned to death when the oven ignited his apron and the entire bakery, while two-month-old Benjamin was out for a ride in the new baby carriage his mother pushed. His father had worked overtime baking for three weddings and four wakes in order to save enough money to buy the best baby carriage for his son, and because of his exhaustion, he became careless, and as he fumbled with a tray of biscuits near the ovens, his apron caught fire. Catherine proudly pushed her son, letting herself dare to show off for once. She felt that people seeing the new pram and the handsome child were envious of her. She let herself feel lucky and well off, and then with her head held high, she noticed the smoke rising above the buildings and she returned to her street to find her husband charred and dead, pulled from the fire, and their home burned to ruins. At that moment,

Catherine felt she was being punished for her brief moment of pride. The guilt she accepted fertilized the seed of cancer that was in her uterus.

She took the baby and the buggy and moved to Sydney where she was hired as a cook for a wealthy banking family. Catherine and Benjamin were given two rooms off the kitchen in the banker's mansion. She wrote to her only living relative, her sister Evelyn, who lived in London: "Heartache upon heartache, the Lord works in strange ways. I accept that and pray for forgiveness for my wrongdoings. My little Benjamin is the only joy I know. He is a very quiet obedient child. The family has given us two extravagant rooms. One has a carpet covered in red roses. The lady of the house told me that the carpet came from Hong Kong. I admit that I have overheard her tell guests that all of their furniture is imported. That is how rich they are. Pray for your poor sister and nephew. Your sister, Catherine."

Red, Teddy Purnhagen's spirit, or I should say, Red, the spirit that had leased Teddy, was completely at home with Benjamin in the big house in Sydney. He's a pushover for comfort.

Benjamin learned to crawl and babble and delight his mother. Catherine shushed him whenever he cried or raised his voice, telling him, "We don't want the family to be disturbed." Benjamin would be quiet. He would always be quiet, never disturbing anyone if he could help it, for the rest of his life.

The rose carpet from Hong Kong was thick and warm. Benjamin's first word was "rose." Throughout his life, within his dreams, roses bloomed when the emotion his unconscious was translating signified comfort, warmth and innocence.

The carpet star above Hong Kong appears in Benjamin's constellation.

And Red, Benjamin's pulsing spirit, became sensual and warm as the knees crawled across the carpet and he remembered similar carpets from centuries gone. The sailor that Teddy Purnhagen had been in love with, the young man that Teddy had exposed himself to, blaming alcohol for his bold and sinful behavior, this man who slept below as Teddy ejaculated and drowned, never to know the confused love of queers in war, this young man had the same carpet as the banker in Sydney. It was made at the same mill in Hong Kong, the same week. Nothing is a coincidence.

Catherine Quinn died of cancer of the uterus in 1925. Her spirit was worn to thin gauzy shreds and faded in ecstatic relief having had its fill of human life. Evelyn, Catherine's sister, half-heartedly sent for Benjamin. Benjamin wanted to scream and cry, but he bit his lip and watched his mother's casket be lowered into the ground. He threw a rose in the hole and was led away by the wealthy banker to the ship that would take him to England, on his own, at the age of eight. As Benjamin stood on the freighter, waving good-bye to the banker and Australia, he felt defiant and strong and not as sad as he thought he should. A young sailor was directed to look over the boy. He went up to Benjamin and said, "There's nothing to be afraid of," and, "You're a brave lad so don't be scared." Benjamin shook his head in agreement. At eight, he knew, thanks to Red's strength, that he would get by. He was a polite and obedient and handsome child. He waved to the banker again, with the young sailor at his side waving also. Benjamin felt free and good. The banker, who for all of his money, had the gray spirit of an idiot, wiped a tear from his eye and felt the poor boy had a wretched life ahead of him, but also told himself that he had done more for the boy than most would for domestics. Benjamin stopped waving and wrapped his arms around himself. The young sailor talked to him about England.

On her deathbed, Catherine had glimpsed Benjamin's queer spirit for a moment. Benjamin was standing at the bed, shocked at the impending desertion. He could see every bone in his mother's skull. She took his fleshy hand in hers.

"Forgive me, Benjamin," she muttered.

Because she had asked for forgiveness, Benjamin felt she had a choice in the matter. She was choosing to die, to desert him, and therefore was asking for forgiveness.

He asked, "Why do you hate me?"

"I love you. God loves you. You're an angel," she whispered.

But Catherine saw Red as clear as she saw her son. She saw

strength and she saw sex. She remembered the fire and the pram and her pride. She closed her eyes and prayed that the devil would leave her son. "One final torture for my sins," she thought. She was paying for her pride. And, as I said, her spirit was spent, she was full of idols and Bible fears and thought Benjamin's spirit was Satan. (This was not the first time Red has been taken for a fictional character.) There was no doubt in Catherine's eye that Benjamin was possessed, so Red, in the clarity and purity of death, stepped forward and rocked her forlorn confused spirit to sleep, comforting her, as if she were an infant.

Benjamin let go of her lifeless hand. He was turning cold. Catherine saw, in that last light of life where the truth is simple and clear, that for him to survive, he would shed few tears. He had to withdraw from her. His spirit was showing hers that there was nothing to fear.

Before he lost sight of Australia, on the deck of the freighter, with the young sailor at his side, having said he would be Benjamin's big brother for the voyage, Benjamin said out loud to his mother fading at the horizon, "You and your Lord are selfish."

The sailor said, "I like shellfish."

The sailor was looking forward to bedding down with the boy. He wanted and hoped to fuck the boy's tight little butt.

Brian!

Hey! Give in to what you see in your mind's eye. Vera always says that. One night, I know this has nothing to do with Benjamin, but anyway, one night when I was twenty-two, or maybe even twenty-one, Vera and I were sitting by candlelight on the bare floor in her apartment in Brooklyn, and she told me, "Brian you are sooooooo empty. You are empty enough to be filled with the spirits." She said I was vacant enough to be rented. She told me that I could receive energy from other worlds that are all around us. It kind of freaked me out at first, but she told me about that white light thing, and then she said she wanted me to fuck her. She said it wasn't fair that I was gay. I said, hey, there have always been gays and that it had nothing to do with fairness, and she tried to talk me into going beyond the male-female costume trip, but I said, "Whoa, Vera, my cock is my antenna and I know what I can pick up and what I can't." She said she couldn't wait for cable to be installed and we both laughed and stayed friends, but I still think she is coming on to me sometimes.

Anyway, so about this story, let me just say this: Vera gave me a book to read on "automatic writing" a while ago, and the spirit, named William James, said it doesn't matter if you believe it. When it is necessary, you will remember that you read about it, and belief or disbelief will be irrelevant. The facts will be clear. Sometimes, if I'm stoned, I'll think, "Yeah, it all makes sense," then sometimes I think, "What the fuck is this all about?"

I stripped down because it's so hot at my desk. I wait for my spirit writer to manhandle me. From the window I see the ocean beyond Benjamin's yard. His yard is really overgrown now. Roses are even in the gutters and chimney. I wait for the spirit. Take me.

I must have dozed, but no new lines. The moon is full over the Atlantic. It is bright enough to still see color, bluish colors. The moon is a fluorescent jawbreaker that I suck and take out of my mouth to check for changes, then reinsert, running my tongue round and round its sweet surface. My lips are blue from sucking the moon. I relax, take deeps breaths, digging the ink drip after drip after drip.

The coquette boy on the freighter. Benjamin. He did bed down with the young sailor. At eight, he fell in love with the young man. He wanted to be fucked. His spirit knew what he wanted. "Bugger" was what the sailor called it.

Benjamin's bugger star rises over the Indian Ocean.

On the last night, before docking in England, the sailor held the boy close in their bunk. He ran his fingers through Benjamin's fine golden hair and patted his pink behind.

He whispered into the boy's ear, "This has been our secret. Do you understand?"

"Yes," he answered, "I'll never tell."

The warmth that Benjamin felt from that sailor on the freighter was enough heat to keep the boy alive during the first years at Aunt Evelyn's house on Gale Street in London. He had a secret. He daydreamed of the sailor holding him tight and protecting him from all the bullies. He knew that someday he would find that closeness again. The word "queer" excited him. With the sailor as guide, he had learned of the sensual touch that he would hunt for the rest of his life, no matter how secretive he had to be.

With Aunt Ev's came religion classes and he soon learned why his desires were to be kept secret. He told himself that since he was an orphan, God would consider his sinful thoughts less heinous than those of parented children.

Benjamin was not close to his aunt or uncle, and of his three cousins, only Duncan, who was two years older than him, treated him like a brother. The other two made it clear to Benjamin that he was an outcast, and never let him forget that he was "extra." Duncan told him one night, after the two younger children were asleep, that the reason they resented Benjamin was because he was "extra," and, Duncan said, "extra means extra special."

Benjamin was an obedient child. He did the chores required of him, and made good grades in school, and never made noises or disturbances that would make his presence felt. He always took less than the others at meals, and if there was ever a question of blame among the children, Benjamin would accept it.

At fourteen, he had grown into a handsome, lean, young man. He was shy, and had the reputation of being a "goody-goody." Only at night, in his bed, did the noise and screams and anger and tears come. He would bite into his pillow to stifle the sounds, and finally fall asleep. One night Duncan heard him crying and asked what was the matter.

"Nothing," Benjamin heaved, "I'm sorry."

Duncan held him close and patted his pink behind and ran

his fingers through Benjamin's darkening hair, and the two boys masturbated each other.

Duncan whispered, "This is our secret."

Benjamin said, "I know."

The noises Benjamin heard in his head were his own words, the yells he would have made to the boys at school for making fun of him for coming from the "land of convicts," or for being a "sissied orphan lad." The noise was every feeling he suppressed, and the tears were for the need to be touched and held. Since the day he dropped his mother's hand, he had only been held by the sailor on the freighter and Duncan. And with Duncan, he learned to fall asleep soundly, holding on to the older boy's arm, forgetting the rest of the world and all the meanness.

In 1933 Duncan left for the Navy. Benjamin never saw him again. He was killed in World War II. And Benjamin left Aunt Ev's to work for a man he had met on a park bench.

"Who is this man?" Aunt Ev asked as Benjamin packed his suitcase.

"He works in the theater," Benjamin said, "and he will give me a room and board and a small salary. I've written the address here."

He handed the woman the paper, knowing she would soon misplace it, knowing she was only upset because her obedient servant was departing.

"Well, Benjamin," she said at the door, "I see your mind is made up. Remember to let us know how you are, times are hard, and remember, our home is your home."

He thought that one day he would be honest with her and write her a letter and tell her that every time she said, "Our home is your home," she was really making it quite clear to him that he was a guest, an "extra." He never did write that letter. After one Christmas exchange, they were never in touch again.

A bench star over London. Benjamin becomes a houseboy for one of the queens of England.

The man on the park bench was an actor named John Wyatt. Benjamin was attracted to him and took a seat on the opposite bench. John Wyatt introduced himself as "John Q. Wyatt, actor extraordinaire, and"—he raised an eyebrow and lowered his voice to a throaty theatrical growl—"the Q in the middle stands for one of the swellest queens this side of the Channel."

Benjamin smiled, but did not quite understand the humor. He sensed that the actor was implying a queerness, and he could see there was a sexual arousal, but he felt it was so public. The man's bold gesture to Benjamin's thigh was no secret to the people walking past the bench.

John Wyatt introduced Benjamin to his friends, all of them had something to do with theater. For the first time in his life, Benjamin felt free to be fey. He loved John Wyatt and learned to mimic his humor till he too found the humor in it. He learned to touch freely within the theatrical circle and he learned the sexual exercises of the professional. Benjamin became the darling of the queens. They called him "princess," and when John Wyatt traveled to Cornwall to "serve penance" with his wife and child, "for appearance sake, I mean, my God, I am a public figure with a growing reputation to protect, can you imagine," Benjamin remained in their London flat and was besieged by proposals from the other queens. He lived with John Wyatt for four years.

"There is magic in the red," Benjamin said of the theater lights. He had gone onstage to retrieve John Wyatt's cigarette lighter, and in what was a very bold move for him, he lingered and turned and bowed to the empty house. The red stage lights warmed him and embraced him and he pretended for a moment that he was inside a character. He returned to John Wyatt's dressing room flush with the din of imagined applause and announced that he too wanted to become an actor.

"Dearie," John Wyatt sighed, flaunting his unlit cigarette in Benjamin's face, "I think you would make a better actress. Light me, damn it."

Benjamin lit his cigarette and looked hurt, so the actor added, "Dearie, there's only room for one actress in our little family."

The following weeks were full of bickering between the actor and Benjamin. Benjamin was feeling, for the first time, that he could be someone. He threw back to John Wyatt what the actor had said to him so often, "You can get by on looks for just so long, dearie."

During an all-night party of the *Royal Family of Picadilly*, Benjamin and another "princess" were inebriated to the point where they allowed themselves to be photographed wearing tinsel crowns and nothing else. They posed, to the cheers of the guests, with tongues lapping at each other's cocks. John Wyatt had planned the so-called impromptu "photographic entertainment" and he paid the photographer for the pictures and threatened Benjamin with exposure if he ever tried to "make a name" for himself.

Benjamin moved out and into a flat with another stagehand who worked at the Old Vic. John Wyatt pursued him, begging him to come home, but he would not relinquish the photographs to Benjamin, and so, Benjamin threw him out. John Wyatt was gone, but the term "dearie" remained with Benjamin for his life. He found himself on his own and forced to accept a job backstage at the Windmill Burlesque in order to survive. The seediness of his shared flat, and his exaggerated dignity, the latter coming from associating with "royalty," was rationalized in one newfound phrase that Benjamin repeated often: "The Theater is my life!"

In 1940, at the age of 23, Benjamin met Queen Mary at a party, and fell in love. Queen Mary was truly famous. He had film roles and stage roles and was about to go to Hollywood. He was married to a lesbian and their marriage was a perfect disguise.

I think Vera is a lesbian sometimes. We were at the beach before and she pointed out two women that she thought looked great in bikinis. Then this hot stud who works at O'Casey's on Beach Boulevard came over to our blanket and stood there talking to us, his equipment was bulging out of his trunks. It was hanging right by our faces, and I would look up to him, then down to his bulge, and then to Vera, and there she was, still staring at the two women in bikinis, and here's this huge thing hanging in front of her face. His name was Scotty. He told me that O'Casey's has a happy hour when all drinks are only fifty cents!

What has that to do with Benjamin?

Don't I have a say in this story? It's my paper. My idea. My desk. Benjamin was my friend. It was my fault he went to Rodeo looking for me. Weiner, my dachshund, still sits at the fence waiting for Benjamin. From my window I can see him sitting there, as if Benjamin will be coming out with a bone for him. He just waits there. Dogs don't know about time.

Neither does Brian.

Benjamin fell in love with the wealth and fame of Queen Mary's world. He lived among original paintings in gilded frames and red velvet couches and servants. Queen Mary gave him a fur-trimmed dressing robe. The famous actor's closet was the size of the room Benjamin had been living in.

"My home is your home, darling," the Queen said.

And this time, Benjamin took advantage of that line he had heard so often on Gale Street. In the plush safety of the man's house, he became a snob. He learned to find the best tweeds. He learned to order the servants about. And, he found the nightly blackouts during the war "such a bloody bother." The Queen had procured a military deferment for him.

The Queen was twenty years older than Benjamin. He treated the handsome young man tenderly, doting on his whims, surprising him with gifts, and only expected loyalty and sex in return. Benjamin felt contented and loved and surrounded himself with more and more objects. He felt the Queen was magical. The red of the theater world was in every room, every carpet, every goblet, and in every dramatic gesture either man made. When he was not worshipping the Queen, he was worshipping the Queen's world. The only time that Benjamin found himself pulled from the magic was when he read of Duncan's death in the war. Even then, he expressed his grief by reprimanding the maid who had delivered the paper with breakfast to his bedside table.

Benjamin traveled as Queen Mary's personal manager to Toronto in 1949 for the run of *Macbeth* in which the Queen starred. The years of rich red bliss holding each other under the silk sheets as the bombs dropped on London, declaring undying love, had yielded with time to routine accusations and suspicions of affairs whenever either was apart. Benjamin maintained the house in London and entertained tricks, while the Queen was in Hollywood filming and having every young available man up to his suite. To save the marriage, they decided it best to travel together.

Benjamin befriended the stage manager of the theater in Toronto, and confided in him, "I'm just the Queen's lady in waiting, his plaything, and meanwhile my own career in the theater has gone stale. I had aspirations once. And there's nothing I do right for him. And what about when I get old. He resents my being with him here, I can tell, because he's used to having all his young things, and he can't with me around."

The stage manager invited Benjamin to stay in Toronto, saying that a temporary separation might help. When Benjamin announced to the Queen that he would not continue with the tour of *Macbeth* and he wanted a separation, the actor feigned hurt and anger, but Benjamin could read through his act, and could see relief written on his face.

Six months later, Benjamin returned to London, having decided to settle down in Toronto. He packed his trunks. Queen Mary had returned triumphant from the tour, and did not have another young man living in the house as Benjamin had expected. The actor was unusually subtle, Benjamin thought, in his plea for reconciliation.

Benjamin said, "You've acquired a certain believability and sincerity since your film acting has developed. I almost believe you."

The Queen said, "You will realize, my darling, that you will never be as comfortable as you have been with me. Hasn't Toronto taught you anything? What can that fool in Canada offer you?"

"Nothing," Benjamin said. "We are only rooming together. I am not his lover, and before it's too late, I want to try to establish my own career, for myself. I've always been someone else's patsy."

"Patsy!" the Queen gasped, losing his film nuance and becoming theatrically demonstrative. "Your career is with me! You are something with me! You have earned a prominent place in my biography if fame is what you're looking for, and don't scoff! You'll be back. With your tail between your legs. All the Marys in Canada cannot compare to me and you know it!"

Then the actor's voice lowered and he climbed atop the coffee table and looked down and almost whispered, "And darling, how dare you think that I am not aware of my many many moods. Of course you don't understand, of course you get hurt. I am an artiste!" His voice enlarged and now echoed, "And you say I have boys everywhere! Well? Well? So bloody what! And you say that I never say I love you? Well look around, darling. I say I love you by letting you live here. By letting you into my inner sanctum!"

Benjamin closed the trunks. He closed his feelings for the actor and told himself that the histrionics were merely ridiculous and further confirmation of the end. He was no longer the giddy girl he'd been when he and the Queen of British theater had danced drunken about the house during those first years. He now had a life in Canada. He was studying acting. He had studied speech. He did not tell the Queen that he had auditioned and been hired at a new little television station in Toronto, and that he was to be the weatherman. He knew the Queen would ridicule that. Television was a fad. He kissed the Queen good-bye and had the servants help him with his trunks.

"How dare you steal from me!" Queen Mary screamed as the door closed.

What I know about Benjamin is that he never talked about wanting to be an actor, but I guess I believe it's true if I wrote it. I believe and then I think that this is all inspiration and I'm just gifted, then I feel so tired and I conk out like in a trance, and then I come to and I've ejaculated in my underwear and I read this stuff and it's just so weird, and it's even weirder that Vera told me that I went off with that guy Scotty at the beach and gave him a blow job under the boardwalk, and I came back to the blanket and told her about it. I don't remember that. This is the first time ever that I don't remember doing it, unless Vera's lying. Hell, I want to be into sex. Maybe I'm cracking up like in the movies. Maybe I'm a murderer too. Maybe I've fucked Vera. God. I need to turn on every white light in my house.

I have control over my young man. I might add that Scotty was not so hot. Once Brian came, I was bored and Brian finished Scotty off by hand. Sperm is nectar for us queer spirits, and I have Brian by his delectable Italian balls. I remember when Red, Benjamin's spirit, and I were in Rome. Caligula was possessed by a queer purple spirit and a powerful electrical green spirit, and it was bizarre, but that's another story.

The weather star over Toronto. The pinnacle of achievement for Benjamin.

Although he thought he was on the first rung of a ladder, he had reached his peak. Television was primitive. There were only a few thousand sets within the signal of Benjamin's station, but he was recognized on the street.

"Aren't you the weatherman?" people would ask.

He loved that. He did miss the opulence of his life with the Queen, but drinking seemed to take the edge off his regrets. In 1951, at the age of thirty-four, Benjamin rented his first apartment. He had a steady income, a degree of notoriety, and he was working in the warmth of the bright studio lights. He was distant from the other people at the station; most of them were also in radio. He didn't feel included in their world, and he didn't want them to know of his secret world. He knew he would be fired. He did keep three very secretive friendships with three queens he'd met through his old roommate. They called him Mary Weathergirl. When they would get together after a week of pent-up lust and sham, they would get drunk and silly and sashay about whoever's house they were in, and "let loose" purging their hidden lives in screeching camp, mimicking the people they mutually knew, but could never know.

Benjamin moved to New York after being fired from the weatherman's job in 1953. He was a drinker, a heavy drinker. He had, after all, Red, Teddy Purnhagen's spirit, and although he preferred highballs to whiskey from a flask on a slippery deck with leg muscles spent from orgasm, Benjamin had begun to mix screwdrivers in a thermos and drink at the station.

One day he received a warning from the management that he had been monitored slurring his words and swaying during the noon broadcast. He was told that it should not happen again. Benjamin wanted to explain how monotonous the wait between shows was, and why he was so careless, but there was no way he could be honest and blame it on Queen Mary. No one would believe him.

What happened was, Queen Mary was in town playing *Othello*, and he and Benjamin had had a few dates, drinking each other under the table. The actor ridiculed Benjamin's silly occupation and accused him of wasting his life.

"You were something when you were with me. You were there on stage with me in every performance, and now look at you. Didn't I warn you? Didn't I tell you? You didn't know how good you had it, did you, darling?"

Benjamin mixed more drinks in the Queen's suite, and tried to explain that his job was only the first step, that television was the theater of the future, but he was interrupted by the drunken voice that could "hush a thousand cries."

"To where? Where can you go? You don't know the first thing about weather. I can see your eyes reading on camera, darling. Why you don't know if the sun or the moon is out! You never knew if it was raining or foggy. Be serious. Really. Where do you plan to go? Newsman? How droll! And you're not getting any younger. Your hair is thinning. I could tell when you stood at that shaky weather map. They must have a light spot shining directly down on you. It's unflattering. There's a shine. Powder might help, darling, but why don't you give up and come tour with me."

Benjamin felt his hairline. He was drunk out of reason. He

admitted that he had noticed some hairs in his brush. He admitted that the excitement was limited and more and more people from radio were coming into the station taking new positions.

The next day, during the evening news broadcast, he knocked the map over and blurted out in disgust that the weather was once again going to be "bloody wet!" and he was fired. He went to the Queen's suite and accused him of deliberately getting him drunk in order to undermine his burgeoning career in television, and he told the actor that there was no way in hell that he would tour with *Othello*.

"I'm leaving Toronto and moving down to the States, to New York," he said.

In New York, Benjamin was hired to play Cooky the Clown on the local children's program, "Flying High with Captain Windy." He wore a rubber hat that made him look bald, and a yellow suit with a polka dot tie that hung to the floor. He was hit with pies, squirted with water, did pratfalls over his tie, and directed guest children down the slide. Essentially his job was to keep the children in front of the camera.

A dim clown star over Manhattan for Benjamin Quinn.

Benjamin was definitely balding. He claimed that wearing the rubber bald cap under the hot lights as Cooky the Clown was what was causing him to lose his hair. He no longer felt like the handsome youth or the dapper man, and the "somebody" he had set out to be was an unrecognizable sidekick to an egomaniac named Captain Windy. Benjamin read of a hair specialist in Rockaway, Queens, and he took the train there and bought his first toupee.

"You look like a twenty-year-old!" the specialist exclaimed.

And so Benjamin moved from his apartment in Gramercy Park, to a new place in Greenwich Village. The people in his old building would know he was wearing a hairpiece, but the neighbors in his new area would think he was young. And in 1957, beatniks and artists and queers were welcome in Greenwich Village. Benjamin took an apartment above the restaurant that would one day be the bar called Rodeo. He never really liked the apartment. He claimed that the smells from the restaurant below bothered him, and he found that keeping something baking in his oven disguised the greasy smells from downstairs. But the real reason he never felt comfortable in the apartment was that his spirit knew of the Rodeo Bar to be, and knew that Benjamin would die there, and Benjamin sensed a gray doom whenever he was at home for long. He took to bars. He was an alcoholic, and with his new habit of baking, he was also getting fat.

"Captain Windy" went off the air in 1958 and Benjamin quit television for good, telling a friend, "The Golden Age is over, it's all ratings now." And that same friend found Benjamin a job as a supernumerary with the Metropolitan Opera.

At the Met, he met a dresser named Robert Winters. Robert was 57, sixteen years older than Benjamin. Robert had white hair and worn pink skin. He was meticulous and very proper. Benjamin was flattered by Robert's attentions, and he knew that as his lover, he would always be younger. Benjamin believed that Robert was deceived by the toupee he wore. Robert, on the other hand, never mentioned the hairpiece because he knew how vain Benjamin was. And he liked it. Benjamin proposed they live together at Robert's apartment on the Upper East Side. Benjamin never wanted to return to that strange apartment on Christopher Street.

When one of his three queen friends from Toronto visited, Benjamin explained, "I was so tired of living alone. I need to be with someone. He's so much older than me, and so set in his ways, but we keep each other cheered up."

And during a visit from an old friend from London, he said, "Oh, it's not like it was with the Queen, you know how wild that time was, but Babs is kind and cultured." Babs was Benjamin's pet name for Robert, and Cooky was Robert's pet name for Benjamin. He continued, "Babs is sweet to me. I'm content for once in my life."

Both Babs and Cooky would wear silk dressing gowns around their apartment, and Babs convinced Cooky to attend a few drag balls. Benjamin never admitted to Robert just how much he loved wearing those full wigs. And Benjamin redecorated the apartment, wanting to make his mark, making it as red as possible. Sexually, they had very little together. Benjamin saw Robert buy a trick in a bar one night and was shocked. He swore he'd never stoop to such humiliation. But seeing the satisfaction on Babs's face soon convinced him to try it. He found that once he was the buyer, he could be selective, and, in turn, he found himself realizing just what his tastes in men were. And Benjamin prided himself on being an expert shopper. He found bargains at auctions, and attended closeout sales in order to get the most for his money. And so, he soon found out what kind of trick he wanted to hire for an evening. He found that he liked "Big colored bangers."

Babs made him promise to never bring a colored trick home to their apartment, fearing that they might be robbed or tied up or murdered, "If not by your trick, then by our neighbors, Cooky. This is uptown, Park Avenue, not Harlem or the Village."

Benjamin became a dresser like Robert in 1965. There were times when he would reflect on his life and feel that he had never applied himself toward success. But he still had hope. He played sweepstakes. He entered contests that came in the mail. He always had the feeling that one day he would be the big winner, something that would thrust him into the spotlight, like it had been in Toronto. He thought that if he could write down some of his clever and funny ideas, he could write a hilarious musical. Babs had been working on a "musical" for years. That was the other thing, aside from the toupee, that Babs never talked about with Benjamin. He never let Cooky read it.

"Please," Benjamin asked. "What are you afraid of? If it's so funny, let me in on the joke."

"No," Robert said. "It's not finished. It's my art. I will know when it's ready to be read."

Benjamin decided that collecting antiques and cooking were his arts. He planned elegant dinners that reminded him of his days at Queen Mary's house in London. He would have guests up to the apartment and they would rave about the decor and whether they meant it or not, they always told Benjamin and Robert that their apartment was "out of *House and Garden*."

Benjamin would modestly shrug and claim, "Oh, I just put it all together, with no rhyme or reason. It's just a talent I have for color and fabric, and everything was a bargain. That settee was only two hundred at Sotheby's auction." Thus, he was able to point out his shopping expertise along with his keen design eye.

As a dresser with the Met, Benjamin traveled to Los Angeles. Queen Mary was in Hollywood doing a film. He was not starring, but he talked as if he did have the pivotal role as he and Benjamin dined.

"I haven't had as many offers, but my new agent insists that I be seen. There's a new generation that, as hard as you may find this to believe, might not know my name. He's talking commercials for television, but I said, 'Never!' "

Benjamin started to say, "There just aren't as many roles for older—" but Queen Mary grasped his hand across the table and interrupted.

"Don't say it. Don't you dare. I am still an honored actor (he'd been knighted in 1964) and I can bring a touch of class to any dismal B movie, and by the way darling, that rug looks ridiculous."

Benjamin blushed, then hissed and felt his heart sharply stab in his chest. He hissed again, insinuating the Queen was just being catty, and he said as clear voiced as he could, "No one knows, not even my lover. They all think it's real."

"Yes, darling, believe what you must, but the truth is, no one has the nerve to tell you. Darling, it doesn't look natural."

Benjamin faked a laugh. "You wouldn't know 'natural' if it came up and wagged itself in front of your face. And you couldn't see anything anyway without your specs."

The actor patted Benjamin's hand and said in a motherly manner, "Darling, trust me on this."

That was the last time Benjamin spoke with the Queen. The Queen died later that year of heart failure. The director of the film was interviewed concerning completion of the picture without the celebrated actor, and he said, "He will be greatly missed, but he had completed his part in the film, it was not big, but it was pivotal."

But that final talk with the Queen in Los Angeles triggered Benjamin's vanity block and fixed his vanity star, and set in motion his eventual end. The year was 1967. Benjamin was about to turn fifty, which is somewhat late for a vanity star, but in this case that was when the block was finally assembled. Benjamin returned to his hotel room, leaving the Queen at the table with the check forever. He swore as he rode the elevator that he would never see the Queen again. He was furious over such catty remarks that had been made about his hair. Certainly Robert would have said something, he thought. He remembered the years at Aunt Ev's when he would take the blame for something he hadn't done. He remembered the pent-up noise that would ring in his ears as he screamed into his pillow. He fell into his bed at the hotel room. He felt the pressure in his skull, and he felt the pulse of his veins against the tape on his head. He wanted to rip the wig from his skin and throw it out the window. He knew that he had been trying to be something other than himself, a younger, happier, sexier, richer person than he was. He went to the mirror. He stood for a moment, looking. He lifted the hairpiece slightly, and then the noise in his head stopped. It was quiet. The block, a block of compressed tears and mucus, dried with fifty years of screams, absorbed the din, calmed his heart, and padded his mind. He straightened the toupee. He looked fine. He looked closer to thirty than fifty, he thought. He held his stomach in and moved a few feet back from the mirror. From there, he was quite the "turn on," he thought. He found his hand mirror to see the reflection of the back of his head in the dresser glass. Then he made a quick turn to catch his image in a complete look of surprise. He turned the lights on and off. He made lewd and lecherous looks, and he shook his hair in a free-spirited manner. It still looked real. The Queen was old and jealous. The mirror would never lie, he decided.

The vanity star over Los Angeles.

Most vanity stars appear when inner aches and outer lines and sags appear. When youth is noticed and envied, and you're not within it. In L.A., Benjamin had the opportunity to con-

front himself, to age with honesty, gracefully. The hairpiece was
merely the catalyst. The point is, he completely stopped hearing
his heart, he stopped hearing Red. All spirits come through the
heart. He stopped loving himself, if only a sliver, and chose to
be blind and deaf. The energy used to keep up the facade could
have been spent on health, but instead, his muscles soon degen-
erated, he needed glasses (which he never wore in public), and
his heart developed a murmur. The vanity block had not happened overnight. He'd been wearing the toupee for ten years.
But his confrontation with himself in the mirror was the last
straw. From then on, in his heart, he would feel superficial. He
would always know that what someone was seeing in him might
be the fake part. His smile, his eyes, his waistline, no part of
him would be genuine to his conscious mind, there would always be costumes and roles. Block after block would assemble
till it formed a tomb, and Benjamin's queer red spirit would
have to hack deathblows to escape.

On his return to New York with the Met, Benjamin was
shocked at how old Robert looked and acted. Robert felt the
distance from Benjamin but thought that it came from being
apart for months. Benjamin, determined to "live, live, live,"
wanted everything changed. He announced to Babs, "Red is
out. Psychedelic purple would be wild. I want to get all the
furniture reupholstered."

Hey, I wonder if Benjamin ever dropped acid. Man, that
might of cleared up whatever the hell was going with him about
his looks. It sounds like too big of a deal. He was still pretty cool
for an old gay man on his own. I bet if he'd dropped acid, he
would have melted away all that shit. I know that the first time
I dropped acid, I saw how fake everything was. I got to the
core. I felt in tune with the universe. And sexually, I felt like a
horse. I have this animal inside. Butts are horses, butts. Those
muscles! I see these guys in their tight trunks and they're stal-
lions. I want to ride them!

Benjamin was offered drugs by one of his tricks. He never
dared try them, afraid of losing control. Like I said, he was

expending an enormous amount of energy on his blocked head. Robert was in the hospital undergoing chemotherapy and offered pills to Benjamin, but he refused, saying the only pill he could tolerate was Valium.

In 1972, Robert died. Benjamin was with him at the hospital. He remembered watching his mother die. He held Babs's hand and tried not to care what anyone would think if they saw him. When he was going through Robert's papers, he found the "musical" Babs had been writing, tied with a ribbon and accompanied with a note, "For you to read, Cooky, it's finished."

The play was set on Wall Street and was called *Summer Stock*. A stockbroker falls in love with a struggling actress and so on. It was not original. It was not very funny. It did not "make mincemeat out of all the clichés we work on," as Babs had claimed to Benjamin. They both had become dressers for Broadway shows. Anyway, the play was not finished and had never been read. It never played anywhere but in Robert's head, but what a glorious run it had there. There were constant rewrites and sex changes and new songs. As Robert had aged, all the characters had aged, and the styles changed as his own wardrobe was updated. It closed when he died. It had a brief revival as Benjamin read it. There was a character in the play that wore a toupee, but Benjamin did not see himself in it. And now the play is on a shelf in Benjamin's house under his stack of *Playbills*, and Brian, who will inherit the house and its contents, will never read the entire draft. He'll be curious, after this, to read it, but he'll be easily bored.

I inherit Benjamin's house!

Benjamin bought the house with money Robert willed to him. He was out in Rockaway at his confessor's hair shop. This man was the only person Benjamin patronized. There, in the sanctuary of the shop, Benjamin could complain of the itch he felt, or the discomfort of the new adhesive he'd tried. He always felt cleansed after a visit to the specialist in Rockaway, and one day, on his way to the train, he passed a real estate office that displayed beach bungalow photographs in its window.

The landowner star rises off the coast of Long Island.

The bungalow Benjamin bought was built on a sandy soil. He loved the roses that climbed over trellises throughout the yard, and along the whitewashed clapboard siding. It seemed to him to be a lot like an English cottage. The real estate agent wisely left Benjamin alone in the house as he talked with the sellers on the front porch. Benjamin imagined all of his purple furniture and his paintings in the rooms. He imagined fresh cut roses on the tables. He asked about television reception after a plane crossed overhead, landing at JFK airport. And the decision was settled as he stood at the kitchen sink and thought, "I'll have to make a concentrated effort at collecting vases. I'll need so many."

Benjamin moved from Manhattan with Felicia, the Siamese cat he had given to Robert. His few friends had discouraged the move, telling him that he would be spending all of his time commuting. And, during a particularly deep sodomizing by Cal, one of Benjamin's regular tricks, he doubted whether Cal would be willing to take the train way out to Rockaway, and he thought he would have to pay extra, and possibly let the tricks sleep over, and he worried what the neighbors would think, and then he squealed as Cal shot his load and his mind went blank.

Cal always thought he was "nailing it to whitey" when he worked on Benjamin. He told Benjamin, "I don't know, man, that's way the ways out. I'd have to charge more."

Despite the long commute to Broadway and the late hour when he returned, Benjamin would usually wake at seven and put on the big teakettle he had received from Queen Mary's widow. She had remained in touch with Benjamin over the years, and she wrote a note that accompanied the kettle: "He would have wanted you to have this. I'm sure you remember how particular he was about his tea. Remember him fondly. He always referred to you as his young 'darling.' " Benjamin would watch the "Today" show, then "Phil Donahue," and then game shows and drink tea the entire morning. During the warmer months, the roses and the garden and the stray cats would win out over television, at least for part of the day.

He rarely went to the beach. When a friend could be persuaded to make the trek out to Rockaway, they would want to see the beach, and he would walk with them if coaxed, but he would wear a hat, claiming the sun hurt his skin, "I have the fair skin of British aristocracy." And he rarely went to the queen bars that he and Babs had always frequented. Only on matinee days, when he had time to kill between shows, did he go to a bar, or he would go to a porno book store. He had sex less because of the higher prices.

Brian's uncle, Salvatore Malventano, next door was not at all friendly to Benjamin. He sensed that "that Quinn character is a real oddball, real fairy acting." And his suspicions were confirmed when one morning he saw Benjamin kiss a black boy in the doorway, behind the screen. Salvatore spread the word about his queer neighbor, hoping to run him out of the neighborhood, but most of the people he talked with didn't believe homosexuals could own a house or would want to live outside of Greenwich Village. "You're a bigot, Sal," one neighbor said, and "Leave the old man alone, he's harmless," another said.

Salvatore Malventano also had a queer spirit. That was why Benjamin's existence was so disturbing to him. He had fought that spirit his whole life, and with the assistance of the Church he was able to suppress his desires to the death. His "toupee" was his entire being. He was completely unaware of the value of life. He had tried to have sexual relations with an "easy" girl back when he was seventeen, and he failed. He considered the seminary, but he was attracted to the young priests. His block was completely in place by the age of nineteen. He could have been a fag-basher or worse, if he hadn't found certain strange releases for his frustration. He never married. He became a transit worker. And he once baby-sat for his nephew Brian, when the boy was two. In a heady stupor, having had a fifth of gin, he set Brian in a chair and stripped down in front of the boy, and let the boy play with his genitals. The man shot cum into Brian's milk bottle and tried to force the boy to drink it.

The cum was too thick to come through the nipple. And suddenly Salvatore returned to his senses and grabbed the bottle from the boy, throwing it against the wall. His guilt made him leave Brian his house in his will. Salvatore was electrocuted on the third rail of the BMT subway line in 1982.

My uncle never did that to me. I mean, wouldn't I remember something that kinky, especially from old straitlaced Sal? And he was no fag-basher either. He never got pissed at me for being gay. I mean, I came right out and told him when I was sixteen and he kept asking me about what pussies I'd eaten and what girls I'd gone all the way with, and I said, "Hold on to yourself, Uncle Sal, but this guy here is gay, and proud of it." I had just been at a meeting in the Village with another guy from high school who turned me on to this support group in the city, and I went there and I was like, freed, seeing all these other guys who had the same feelings I did. Anyway, Uncle Sal never acted like he hated me. He didn't seem queer either. He seemed sexless. Hell, he left me his house, so he must have favored me above the other relatives. He was closer to me than my parents. They were, and still are, "full of shame." "Shame on you," they said to me. I said, "Adios."

In 1979, Benjamin became the dresser for the Che Guevara character in *Evita* on Broadway. It was his last regular show. He had developed the reputation among the stagehands and actors of being a cook. One matinee day, he brought in the makings for a stew, "the way the British do it," and a slow cooker. In the past, he had provided plum puddings, biscuits, and sometimes cakes for a cast member's birthday. At the Hadassah Thrift Store on Beach Boulevard, he had found a bargain: an electric Crockpot for one dollar. As it happened that day, Che needed a button sewn on, and another dresser was out sick, and Benjamin completely forgot to check on the stew. The frayed cord of the Crockpot began to smoke and then ignited a nearby towel and it set off the alarms and sprinkler system under the stage during the "Don't Cry for Me, Argentina" song. When Benjamin was confronted by the stage manager, he tried to blame the Hadassah for selling faulty merchandise, but the man was already filling out the forms for Benjamin to take to the union for his severance pay. "You're a danger to the theater," the stage manager said, knowing he would now have to answer to the higher-ups who would probably fire him for letting any cooking go on in the first place.

I remember him telling me about that Crockpot. He said he was not about to bring in an expensive new one because it might be stolen while he was busy with costume changes. I asked him who would want to steal a hot pan of stew during a Broadway show and so what if they did, and he said, "Well, dearie, you never know with all the weirdos out there. And when that witch at the Hadassah wouldn't give me my dollar back, I told them I'd never shop there again."

He was that way, though. Indignant. He told me that TV shows like "The Joker's Wild" and "Tic Tac Dough" were rigged and crooked and unfair.

"Brian, dearie," he explained, "they pick the people and tell them the answers. I know because when I was in L.A. once, I went to their open call for contestants, and they said I didn't pass the test! I told them that I knew every bloody answer to every question, but thinking about it later that night as I helped fit that fat bitch into her Carmen, I realized that they knew that I would win all the money. The test was to pick the idiots for their shows!"

I said something about television being all fake, and I remember he said, "Not in the Golden Age when I was working!" And then he told me about the early days in Toronto and all the funny mistakes that happened like . . .

We are coming to the end of this story. We have already covered Benjamin's Toronto days, Brian.

Okay. Okay. After *Evita*, Benjamin subbed for other dressers, but found himself more and more content to stay in Rockaway and watch television, and tend his garden, and when Brian moved in next door in 1983, he rarely made the trip into the city. He considered Brian his friend, and in a way, his son. He enjoyed embellishing stories of his past and telling Brian these stories on his porch on cool summer nights. For sex, he bought a video-cassette player and ordered porno tapes. He was not lonely. He was content. He spoke to the cat, Felicia, and he spoke to his friends on the phone about which new shows would fail or succeed. He was really only lonely when he was with a group of people. Then he saw how comfortable they seemed with each other, and he felt awkward and shy. He would see himself outside their circle (due to his block). If he was invited to a cast party, he would go, wearing his cleanest hairpiece and dousing himself with cologne, imagining the most magical of meetings that he believed possible (similar to winning a sweep-stakes), but when he arrived, he clammed up. He felt he was acting cordial or interested in what was being said, but all the time there, he was wondering what people were thinking about him, and if they thought he was handsome and polite, and he would drink, trying to loosen up, but the more he drank the more his block soaked up. Everyone seemed to be acting happy. He felt they were all phonies. He usually found himself in the corner at a party drunk and thinking about the long trip home and the TV movie he was missing. Everyone became an outsider to him but Brian by 1984. By then he refused the few invitations he received, and he was content to talk on the porch and watch television and video.

Sometimes Benjamin seemed to be senile to me. I would be up in my bedroom doing my special form of yoga. I would strip down and stretch and twist and concentrate on my third eye (the pisshole in my dickhead), and out the window I'd see Ben-jamin stumbling on his patio carrying a pie pan tin full of mushy brown stuff for the stray cats in the neighborhood, and he would be wearing these skimpy paisley bikini briefs, and his big gut was hanging over the paisleys like a balloon. He made a squeaky whistling sound and in baby talk he would call, "Pussy! Mommy! (Mommy was the mother of most of the strays on the street) Pussy! Mommy!" Then he seemed to wander about mak-ing his way to the fence where my dog, Weiner, was barking and whining for a treat, and Benjamin would set a bone down and yell, "Down, Weiner! Be patient! Down!" And beyond his little square of yard, I could see the other boxed-in squares, on down to the boardwalk, and beyond that, the Atlantic Ocean. Benjamin looked so small and feeble there in his square compared to all the rest of the world, and it looked like the ocean was about to lap him up. I pulled my bamboo blind down and went back to my dickhead meditation, or I should say I tried to, but outside I kept hearing "Pussy! Mommy!" and his whistling and cooing. I just couldn't get into it with him out there.

Brian has served me well. He has satisfied me with his receptive fingers. Now, at last, we have reached the scene at Rodeo.

Rodeo is the name of Brian's favorite bar on Christopher Street in the West Village. Benjamin once lived above the place when it was a restaurant. Brian went there at least three nights a week, and sometimes in the day. He met three different lovers there. He thought it was his lucky home away from home. Benjamin had asked him about the place, remembering when he had lived there.

"It's got a great jukebox," Brian said, "and it's a good place to just hang out. You know, check out who's there and have a beer and maybe check in the john if you just want to get off."

Benjamin fed Weiner daily, and when Brian had not been around in four days, Benjamin began to worry. Weiner whined at the fence till Benjamin finally brought him into the house, terrorizing the cat, Felicia. And finally, Benjamin decided to go into Manhattan to find Brian. He had to return his friend's *That's Entertainment Two* video-cassette anyway, and he figured that Rodeo would be a good place to find Brian. He would ask if he'd been in and if anyone knew his whereabouts. He took the tape to his friend's apartment. Then Benjamin walked through Chelsea and he spotted an all day breakfast special for 99 cents, so he had what was to be his last meal, and his last bargain. Two eggs over easy, home fries, toast, and tea. He walked from Chelsea to the Village, passing many young men that looked like Brian. He found the bar. He looked up to his old apartment window.

That was where he first wore a toupee. It seemed like a snap of the fingers had passed since then, and then he felt as if he had never lived there, that he was someone else in a different life. He thought, outside the door to Rodeo, "I used to get fucked by Sir Queen Mary," and he thought with added dignity, "And I was in television in the Golden Age."

All of these thoughts were used to bolster himself before he entered the bar where he knew he would be shunned. He too had been that way, when he was young. In his head, he still shunned the old. He remembered hating Robert's age. He knew that even though he was 68, minus ten or fifteen years for his hair, he was still about to enter a place where age is not only hidden but found repulsive. But it was the only place he knew to find Brian. As he pulled open the door, the few people at the bar turned to see who had arrived. They immediately turned away seeing the old man. "Just dust," one stud said. Benjamin said to himself, "I was the lover of Sir Queen Mary, who all of you now worship and whose film retrospectives you all now attend at the Museum of Modern Art." He remembered the Queen's words about being a part of his inner sanctum, as if that were enough to live for, and Benjamin thought that he should possibly write an exposé of Sir Queen Mary's "real" life. He stood in the dark corner by the wall. The bartender, Art, came over.

"Can I help you?" he asked.

Benjamin jumped, and wanted to thank the man for speaking kindly to him, but he blurted out, "Brian Malventano. I'm looking for him. His dog Weiner. He's my neighbor. Has he been here? His dog, you see, and he's not been home . . ."

"Sure, sure," Art said, misunderstanding and turning to the bar announcing, "Has anyone seen a lost dog around here?" then back to Benjamin, "What kind of dog was . . ."

Benjamin stopped him, "No, no, no. I have the dog. The dog is at my house! I'm looking for Brian. Brian Malventano."

Art understood. "Forget it," he said to the bar which had been unresponsive anyway. "Nah, pal, I don't know any . . . Brian, oh, Rockaway Brian you mean?" Art acted a little more familiar with Benjamin then. "Yeah, yeah, he should be in. No

guarantee, but he usually comes in later. He was here last night
with this hot number."

"I'll wait then," Benjamin said.

Art looked doubtful and said, "No telling when he'll show
you know."

"It's important I know he's all right," Benjamin said.

"Want a drink?" Art asked.

"Whiskey," Benjamin said, feeling that he should pay to stay
there.

*Red! Red! How are you, sweetie? I was hoping you'd pull yourself
out when you got word of my little tale.*

ENGLISH. ENGLISH. I'VE BEEN HEARING NOTH-
ING BUT RUSSIAN.

*This is one of the warmest and most fitting voices to tell of Benjamin's
last hours—his own spirit. Red, this is my little horse, Brian. He's a
doll, huh? And feel that, pretty nice, huh?*

MMMMMM, NICE BODY. NICE EVERYTHING. (I
MUST EXPLAIN, WORDS DON'T COME EASY. I'VE
BEEN IN A RUSSIAN WOMB FOR SEVEN MONTHS
NOW.) SO, WE WENT TO THE BAR NAMED RODEO.
I WANTED BENJAMIN TO BREAK DOWN. TO GET
ANGRY WITH HIMSELF. TO CRACK THE DEAD
BLOCK. THERE HE WOULD BE IGNORED. CLASPS
AND SNAPS WOULD POP IN HIS BRAIN. HE WOULD
BECOME UNHINGED, WHICH FOR ME WOULD BE A
RELIEF. I WANTED HIM TO BE ALONE, BE SAD, BE
OLD. BUT NO, HE WOULD NOT SEE HIS FOLLY. HE
SHOOK. HE WAS STRONG AS THE DAY WE SAILED
FROM AUSTRALIA. (MMMM I REMEMBER THAT
YOUNG SAILOR.) HE WAS FINISHED FOR ME IN
THAT BAR. LET ME OUT! I AM A FLAME. I AM A
DRIVE. I AM PERSECUTED, BECAUSE I BUCK AND I
AM ORIGINAL. I WILL FIND MY OWN HOLE TO FILL
IF I CHOOSE. IT HAS MADE ME STRONG AND IT

HAS MADE THE LIVES I'VE LED WILD AND EMO-
TIONAL. REMEMBER ROME AND CALIGULA, BLUE?
I LIVE TO THE HILT WHEN I CAN. I MADE TEDDY
PURNHAGEN'S BRIEF SPIN REAL. BEFORE WE
BOARDED THAT SHIP WE HAD ONE HELL OF A
TIME. AND WITH BENJAMIN, I KNEW IT WAS OVER.
I'D JUST ABOUT FALLEN ASLEEP. I WANTED OUT. I
WAS TIRED OF JANE PAULEY'S FACE AND WATCH-
ING PEOPLE WHO HAD ANSWERED QUESTIONS
CORRECTLY FOAM AT THE MOUTH OVER A WEEK-
END TRIP TO PALM SPRINGS. GIVE ME BEDSPRINGS
BABY! ANYWHERE! I KNEW I HAD TO GET BENJA-
MIN OUT. HE WOULD HAVE TO OPEN HIS HEART
AND FREE ME. BRIAN MET A SUCKY YOUNG MAN
AT RODEO AND FELL HEAD OVER HEELS FOR HIM
AND SPENT FOUR DAYS WITH HIM, FORGETTING
COMPLETELY ABOUT DOGS AND NEIGHBORS
BACK IN ROCKAWAY. AND ROCKAWAY, FOR THAT
MATTER, WAS BORING TOO. BENJAMIN HAD EN-
TOMBED HIMSELF WITH ME, PULLING THE
SHADES ON A CLEAR DAY SO HE COULD FLIP OFF
HIS WIG AND MASTURBATE TO PORN VIDEO. NOT
MUCH FUN AFTER A WHILE. I AM A SEXUAL SPIRIT.
I KNOW THE OTHER QUEER SPIRITS. WE LIVE IN
SACRED HEARTS. ALL HEARTS ARE, YOU KNOW.
SACRED. AND WE SHOOT ARROWS THROUGH THE
EYES OF YOUR MEN AND WOMEN. WE ARE GET-
TING STRONGER AND LIGHTER, NOT DARKER
WITH BLINDS PULLED. I FOUGHT MY WAY OUT OF
BENJAMIN WITH THE HELP OF ALL THE SPIRITS IN
RODEO, AND FINALLY WAS FREE AND DASHING
FROM DICK TO DICK TO DICK TO DICK. I MADE
THE ROOM HOT. BENJAMIN COLLAPSED, HOLD-
ING HIMSELF TO THE WALL. HE SWORE, "I WILL
LIVE." AND HIS HEART ATTACK STARTED. HE WAS
INVISIBLE. SOMEONE CALLED HIM AN OLD
DRUNK. SOMEONE ELSE SAID THE BAR HAD HAD
IT BECAUSE OF PEOPLE LIKE HIM, BUT BENJAMIN

STOOD THERE. HE JUST STOOD THERE AS HE HAD AT AUNT EV'S AND TOOK IT. HE WITHSTOOD THE PAIN OF LOSING ME, AND FINALLY GAVE UP THE GHOST, AS THEY SAY. AND AS HE SLID TO THE FLOOR, NOW GET THIS—HERE THIS MAN IS DYING, AND HE IS RECALLING THE ENTIRE SPLENDOR OF HIS LIFE, AND BELIEVE ME, IT IS ALL SPLENDOR AS YOU ARE BIDDING FAREWELL TO YOURSELF, AND GET THIS—HIS FINAL THOUGHT WAS, "FALL SO YOUR HAIR STAYS IN PLACE." THAT WAS HIS DAMN VANITY STAR, WHICH I HOPE IN THIS NEXT TEMPLE WILL BE A LITTLE MORE REALISTIC. YOU SEE, AS I LEFT RODEO AND BENJAMIN, THERE WAS THIS MAN PASSING SPERM INTO A WOMAN IN A SMALL FLAT IN A TOWN ON THE BLACK SEA, AND HER WOMB LOOKED VERY INVITING AND WARM, AND I SETTLED IN WITH THIS SWEET LITTLE SPUD OF A STUD, WHO IS DEFINITELY GOING TO BE RED IN ALL WAYS, AND I SEE QUEER VODKA DAYS AHEAD TILL WE DEFECT.

Hmmmmm, that's that then, another one down for the count.

ONLY ON HIS TERMS, DOWN ONLY ON HIS TERMS. WE KNOW BETTER.

Don't go yet, Red. Let me finish this. Brian is getting itchy, anyway. We can go out. Ride music. Separate from these grave souls for the night.

WE CAN TANGO AND SING SIOUX SONGS.

Oh, the Sioux. Don't remind me! The Sioux!

AND THE MONASTERY CHANTS. YOU LOVE THOSE.

You'll never let me forget it either, will you, Friar?

I'LL WAIT, COMRADE.

Good. And that was Benjamin's Red Spirit. Benjamin's body was taken to St. Vincent's Hospital where he was pronounced dead from a massive heart attack. An attack similar to that of Sir Queen's. He had made out a will, thanks to Phil Donahue's show, and left his house and his possessions to Brian with one stipulation—that Brian take care of Felicia.

The last star over the Rodeo Bar. Benjamin's constellation encircles the Earth, wrapping petals, forming a rose in bud. And now, Red and I are going out for a while to reminisce.

No good-byes? Nothing? I wait for my blue spirit. I sit at the desk. Naked. Hard and waiting. I read all of this. I should have given Benjamin a call. He really cared about me. Mark was just such a knockout. He's a dancer. He loves to show off. He can be a saint in the Church of Brian Malventano, and I'll make Benjamin an angel. My religion of sexual meditation will flourish. I'm going to take Weiner and Felicia, and I'll rent out both the houses out here in boring Rockaway, and I'll move into Mark's apartment in Soho. I hope pets are allowed. I wait. I stare at the paper. I'm waiting. Hard and waiting. I'm waiting.

MAINE

• BRAD GOOCH •

Russ, a not-*that*-young-anymore guy, is walking down a dirt road. He has on khaki shorts, a white T-shirt, tennis sneaks with no socks; a short sprouting haircut. Summertime. The T-shirt obviously washed recently.

Russ gets to a rocky area in the middle of which is a swimming hole. A few teens are jumping and dipping. He sits on a pile of cut-down wood. The sun is nearly in its eleven o'clock position. Big rock music sound is trying to make itself heard from a little transistor box set on a nearby boulder. The swimming kids' skins are shiny like wet seals.

Russ gets up, already stuffed with just hanging around. Makes his way farther down the road. Through a tunnel of dark green saturated leaves. Russ is from a small town in Pennsylvania. He is spending the summer up here in a rented cabin secluded away from all the other houses on Vinalhaven, Maine. Vinalhaven was a big supplier of marble at the turn of the century. For example, the marble pillars inside the Cathedral of St. John the Divine in New York City. Now most of its men are lobster fishers. Their sons all seem to drive Camaros. Russ is using the inheritance from his father's death to rent his cabin.

Gets to the end of the dirt road, which opens out now to scratchy pastures broken off at the landsend. Big cliffs drop dramatically down into the glittering Atlantic Ocean. Vinalhaven is far out into the water; the island reached only by ferry; and so the ocean seems more wildly itself than the tamer ocean which washes the vacation beaches of New Jersey. Asbury Park is the closest Russ ever was before. Water is slapping the rigid rocks.

Over there, beyond a brown weedy patch, he sees three local guys. With them are two chunky Labrador dogs, frisking away like mad. Russ heads over to the group, his heart warming up, like coffee seeping into the conical filter paper when boiling water is being poured gradually in.

The dogs continue animatedly, but the three locals just look up at Russ first with uncomprehending dull looks. Finally Jason, one of them, starts to speak. He is the one dressed in blue-jean overalls with no shirt underneath. His skinny handsome arms are covered with the same black hair as on his head.

JASON: You're one of the summer people.

RUSS: My name's Russ.

JASON: I'm Jason.

RUSS: Who are your friends?

JASON: Bill (a pudgy, mean one) and Teddy (short and blond and ready to go for it).

Russ bows at them. Bill smiles "Hello." Teddy puts his Nike-running-sneakered foot up on a mound, and stares out to sea.

JASON: You wanna talk to us about something?

RUSS: It's just I've been on this island for two weeks now. I've got a house on the other side, on an inlet sort of. And now, just last night, and today, I've started going batty from no one to talk to. (Forces a series of little laughs) I guess you don't get that way living here.

Things quiet down in the circle, as Bill and Teddy and the dogs rustle themselves and go for a walk into the even hotter horizon. Sounds of wood being chopped close by. Jason is scraping a mud blob off black penny loafers he is wearing with no socks. Shiny enough otherwise for the black wax to reflect a pale sun glare.

JASON: Where you from?

RUSS: Nanticoke, Pennsylvania.

JASON: What are you doing stuck there for Chrise' sake?

RUSS: How do you know what kind of place it is?

Jason stands up, impatiently, looks around to see if he can see his friends, obviously fed up somehow with Russ.

JASON: Most of the summer people come from New York City, or Europe. The kinds of places I want to get to.

RUSS: If you come by the house I've got Tequila. You know it? It's powerful stuff. From Mexico.

JASON: Not in the daytime. (He makes horizontal slats out of his black eyes.)

RUSS: Tonight? I'll explain how to get there. And you can drive up. . . . You can bring a friend if you want, too.

JASON: Yeah?

Russ gives directions. They split up. Jason makes tracks as he slides down the cliffs and off around a corner to look for the rest. Russ goes back the way he came, through the inky leaves, past the chilly empty swimming hole, over to a bush full of berries. He lifts up his bike which he had left leaning into the damaged bush, a black Schwinn with clunky cross-bar—not the kind with ten speeds—gets on, wheels off.

Russ's cabin is a new-style A frame with a wraparound terrace, all made from the same authentic, yet spruced up, wood planking. There are large glass sheets for windows. Inside, a fireplace in which he has built the beginnings of a fire. Right now Russ is relaxing with his legs up on the railing, looking out over the inlet waters as the sun finally spreads over the entire land, leaving the sky to the dark. Russ is sketching a drawing of a dragon eating a sun which looks, because of its many lively jagged rays, like an octopus.

Russ runs a one man advertising shop in Nanticoke. He is a rare bird who would stay in an immobile town like that, with no prospects, and would come on vacation himself to this kind of island, with not much tourism, most visitors coming regularly each summer to family houses, left over from richer days, and then the inbred lobster-fishing villagers. The air is getting cooler now. Is dark enough for Jason to use the headlights on the little metal truck he is driving up the driveway in. He is with a girl, Sharon.

Russ is happy to see them. These people have come all the way out here to meet him. They will all three try to beat time together. The regular Vinalhaven people usually turn in by ten. By now it is already nine. Russ goes out to shake hands with his guests, the first since he arrived.

RUSS: Jason. I'm glad you were adventurous enough to come.

JASON: There's no adventure in me going anywhere on this island. This is Sharon.

Sharon looks about eighteen or nineteen. She has light brown scraggly hair. Almond eyes. Is dressed in blue flannel shirt and cheap green cords with pink beat-up canvas shoes. She is rubbing her hands flat upon one another. If Sharon were a rock, rather than a girl, she would be limestone.

RUSS: I just put up some coffee to boil. But you're still welcome to have the Tequila, the Tequila I promised this afternoon.

JASON: (Caveman bluntness) Good. (Then, pronouncing out all the vowels) *Te*-kee-*la*.

They go inside. It is now definitely black outside. So their shapes are reflected in the large windows. Russ is drinking a mug of coffee. Jason and Sharon, short yellowy glasses of Tequila.

SHARON: I'm pregnant.

RUSS: (Jaw actually does drop) No. You're kidding. You're so young.

SHARON: It's true.

RUSS: By Jason? (to Jason) By you?

JASON: Seems that way. Born in a car near where we were today.

SHARON: (Rolling eyes) Not born. Conceived.

RUSS: How do you know?

JASON: By figuring out the months.

Russ stands up, feeling himself lighter now, having lost the pressure on his shoulders and in his back; not needing to entertain himself anymore; or to try to get anything rolling on the island; he has just been admitted into the center, or one of the centers, of its life. Vacation, tourism, reflection, are notions fast slipping out behind him in the exhaust.

RUSS: Why are you telling *me*?

SHARON: 'Cause we can't tell anyone yet on the island. So you seem the safest bet. And we couldn't stand not telling anyone. We talked about it in the truck on the way up.

Sharon pours the rest of her hot drink down her tired-out-from-telling-about-the-baby throat.

RUSS: (to Jason) Is there somewhere we can all walk to?

JASON: No. No use walking around at night. Bears. Snakes.

SHARON: (Solicitously, to Jason) Plus we have to be getting back soon. I think I heard the curfew horn already.

JASON: (Slapping hands together, standing up, as if applauding) Right. Right.

Russ feels like he is a parked car, unattended on the street, with an alarm that won't shut off, its metal parts vibrating out of control. He also knows that this panic is completely inappropriate and tries to stall for time, wondering what to do next.

RUSS: But you guys just walked through the door. And it's a long way.

SHARON: I'm no guy.

Jason sits down again. Russ relaxes a little.

JASON: We're used to it. All we do around here is drive around in our buggies, listening to music from Rockport. At night that road leading to the cliffs is a make-out strip. Except when there's a full moon. The cops are in on it. Paid off. By a slush fund.

Russ laughs and laughs. He points at Sharon's still regular-looking stomach, implying that that's how she got the life growing inside her. In addition he is relieved the ball is still rolling.

SHARON: (Correcting) He means the younger kids. Fifteen. Sixteen. Not us. The ones who don't work yet. They make a slush fund together. Then in the summer, on Fridays, they line up all day in their cars to be sure to get a place on a ferry to get to the mainland. Every time a ferry is leaving they gotta be there to move theirs forward, or else lose it.

Sharon loves being an expert on something. In classrooms she is the kind who is never an expert, just a mimicker, trying to say what she's heard. Jason too feels pleased at this new dimension (tourist guide) brought out in Sharon by Russ.

RUSS: (Happy) One thing we could do to save time would be for you two to be my guests tonight.

JASON: (Slightly suspicious) We're already your guests tonight, Mr. Bozo.

RUSS: I mean you could sleep here. There's a bed and a couch and . . .

JASON: (Looking over at Sharon with an "I told you so" look, referring back to an earlier talk they had had in the truck about Russ) No way. Don't rush me, man. It would look funny.

RUSS: (Unusually involved) So you just come in and tell me, the only person on the island, that you're having this big secret, and then walk out? You know what I'm saying? Who's rushing who?

Quiet in the room, as vibes die down stirred up by Russ's convincing emotional shout.

SHARON: (Touching Jason on front shoulder area) He is right about *that*. I think.

JASON: (to Sharon) And what do you tell your mother? I mean mine don't care anymore, so long as I'm on my boat at five. But there's no way you can stay out all night with two guys in some out of the way . . .

RUSS: Or we could take Sharon home, if there's no other way, and then you and me, Jason, we could come back here, if there's no problem for you. That would be second-best.

JASON: I flat don't get it.

This time Russ touches Jason on the front shoulder.

RUSS: Come on. For more Tequila.

JASON: (Feeling excruciated inside) I have to work tomorrow. You don't have to worry. You're only a tourist.

SHARON: (Upset) Jason! How can you go off like that? Maybe he's not just a tourist.

JASON: (His jaw made out of stone as he says the words) Are you some kind of wild card?

RUSS: (Looking Jason in the eyes, saying each word deliberately) *No I am not a wild card.*

Jason puts his hand to his forehead. The one time he got in a fight in his life he just wanted to swing and sway until he got his way. Usually he just teases around in a fight and backs off in a frontwards way. But now he feels that spooky wanting-to-win coming on.

JASON: Sharon I'm . . . I'm waiting for you to smooth me out babe . . . baby. . . .

Russ is leaning hard into a kitchen counter, the Formica's angle making a slit across his tummy. He is watching Jason and Sharon reflected in the window. But then too he is remembering the advice of his social worker therapist in Nanticoke (the only licensed psychotherapist in town) about how he watches his life as though in a window and how he must stop that behavior right away. Russ shimmies his whole body, like a Tiki dancer, and then turns.

Sharon is writing her phone number on a pad.

SHARON: (to Russ) Call me if you want. *I'm* not a fighter. *I'm* a lover.

JASON: (Shaking his one hand loosely) Whoooa! Get a load of that. You should be the first female to run for office. Whoooa! (to Russ) How old are you?

RUSS: Twenty-seven.

JASON: Why didn't you tell me? I could've trusted you sooner. I'm only twenty.

RUSS: (Wisely) We're just animals, Jason. Animals. We had to test each other first. Like on *The Wide World of Sports*.

JASON: Huh! It's far out when it happens.

RUSS: (Feeling a twinge scared of Jason now, and of Jason's effect on him) So it *is* pretty late. I'll call that number, Sharon. Someday soon.

JASON: No that's OK. Deep down I really *want* to spend the night here. I mean if you can manage to get me rolling at five, out that door, with coffee. I could dig a night in the country. This is wilderness over here, compared to where Sharon and me live, or I mean the neighborhood, built up, where both our parents' houses are.

Sharon just sort of looks at Jason for a long while, her face thick, almost like thick paints have congealed to form her textured skin, like in the paintings of Italian women in religious poses on thick old canvases on which layer after layer was applied for some purpose. Then the ickiness seems to undo, as unexpectedly as it was roused up.

SHARON: There's no predicting you. You're like a cat. When you're in you wanna be out, and when you're out you wanna be in.

JASON: Come on. How often do I get to sleep outside that hot house?

Jason and Sharon and Russ crowd into the truck. Down and around some different roads. A little night animal crosses in headlights. A larger night animal, maybe a bear, or moose, is up along one bend. Then they get nearer the built up section. Most house lights are out. Little motorboats parked in the harbor are making slapping sounds from water rocking. Jason and Sharon are singing a song:

> *Billy Billy Bunting*
> *Went out for to go hunting*
> *He shot a deer he shot a bear*
> *And then he went off grunting.*

These were obviously words they made up themselves. Russ could tell, or thought he could, by the way they laughed at all the parts. They might as well have been two woodsy critters for all he understood of the meaning of their twitter. And yet their song did remind him of one his grandmother used to sing to him in Nanticoke, rocking him in a chair. Maybe one of his earliest memories. A song about a baby falling out of a tree in which somehow, maybe by the wind, he was being rocked. And then there was a similar song about Puss N Boots in a boat sailing through the starry sky. All these lyrics, and the rhythm of that great old moving chair, interrupted flat by the smell of a rabbit his uncle had shot, steaming on his grandmother's dining room table, came back. Lots of ogling faces of relatives.

RUSS: (Stopping his memories, and their giggling) Not many stars out tonight. Not what I'm used to up here.

JASON: (Leaning over to smack him once on thigh) That's

because, because we're in the busy part of town, with street lights, street lamps.

RUSS: (Sarcastic) Coulda' fooled me.

Sharon gets his joke and laughs a little, then kisses Russ on his soft cheek.

SHARON: That's one for tonight. From me.

The truck stops. Jason and Sharon squeeze each other, though without any lingering or passion. Russ gets down to let Sharon out. She is into her black doorway rectangle very soon.

Jason and Russ head back out to Russ's cottage. Lots of flacks on the way of lit-up stones. Then there.

They go inside. Russ lights a kerosene lamp over an open-out couch. Jason steps out of his overalls which he lets fall on the floor. He shivers and gets between prickly flannel blankets. Leans up on a folded-over arm in Russ's direction.

JASON: I'm glad you walked up Russ. Even if you did get me mad before. Except I forget why now. Ha! D'you remember?

Russ is sitting in an armchair. He has a kerosene lamp by him, too.

RUSS: (Hollow) I don't know what to call it.

JASON: Will you get me up?

RUSS: Sure. I don't sleep much anyway. That's one of the funny things about me. I get by on two or three hours sleep. And *that* half the time I take in the morning. . . . You look a little to me now like the lead singer in Modern English.

JASON: (Flattered) Yeah? I like their music. But I don't know what they look like.

RUSS: I went to a concert of theirs in Philadelphia last month. In an auditorium.

For a bit, the two of them just let the various night noises get louder and louder in the contained room. Russ's heart is percussive again. A black cloud passes through Jason, though.

JASON: I think Sharon is real wife material. Don't you? I mean I didn't think about it before, I mean before the baby, but even without the baby, I could see her being steady. She seems smarter in some ways than me.

RUSS: (Almost wishing he had Jason's kind of problems, instead of his own) But you must have a doctor who you told?

JASON: Why?

RUSS: Jealous I guess. (Rubbing his own chest) I guess I like being the only other one.

JASON: You're one lonesome dude. You don't have a wife do you?

RUSS: No. But I'm close to this woman who's a social worker and a psychotherapist in my town. She's not . . .

JASON: (Sensing a no-fun problem subject, stretching his arm up to the ceiling) Could you help me with this light here?

RUSS: Don't move a muscle.

JASON: Hah.

Russ is already over there where he douses Jason's lamp and comes back to sit down again. Jason is rolling his tongue inside one side of his cheek.

JASON: You could be from Mars for all I know. Getting me here for some brain secretions. This could be a lab.

Jason draws his leg up to make a tent in his bed, scratches the underside of his leg. Russ doesn't move.

JASON: Maybe you'll end up coming back to be best man. . . . And, if we two became friendly, like me and Bill and Teddy—not that you'd be in that group—I mean you're a special case. . . .

RUSS: (Feeling young again) I'll answer your question, Jason.

JASON: You don't even know what it is yet Rufus. . . . My question is . . . what kind of friends would we be? (At which Jason lies back down flat on his back, letting his head sink easily into the pillow)

Russ is left face-to-face with his own head reflected on the wall over Jason's lumpy body. He stands up, agitated, as if about to address a speech to his shadow. It is his turn to be just another ingredient in the big swirling soup which has now involved him in the uncontrollable spills and whirls.

RUSS: (Almost shrill, and overcompensating) All right. This is nineteen-eighty-something. And to answer your question I *am* definitely a "wild card." OK? And so I guess if we're going to be friends, we're going to be the kind of friends who know what's up with the other, really up. And if I could make you I'd love it. And if you'd rather not I'd love that exactly as much. So there you are. (Spreading his arms and hands out in a wide, exotic gesture, like a fortune teller lady in a storefront spreading out her plastic tarot deck) The secrets of the universe.

JASON: (Sits right up in bed, his eyes lit with charges) Yeah. That's it man. I wondered when you were gonna talk to me. You think I had all summer? . . . I knew something was up.

RUSS: (In a tough snarl) How?

JASON: (Speed talking) There was this painter, Robert Nyack, who has this house here. And he used to bring a hustler up every year. And then he and the hustler—and this guy was dumb, with tattoos and, you know, curly blond hair—they had a big fight. A lot of big fights. And Nyack threw him out. So this guy, the hustler, started screwing all the girls on the island. And then he was threatening to kill Nyack. He broke in a couple times and bruised . . . and he took him back and . . . anyway, it got so hairy the island council voted to ban the hustler from the island, and the ferry operators got instructions not to let him back on. Now I can tell you're not planning that, you're too . . . shy . . . but I like people who are different. . . . I'm outgrowing my others . . . or . . .

RUSS: (Generously) This is too good to be true.

JASON: (Crooked smile) That doesn't mean I want to get into dry dog humping, fellas. (Catches Russ about to go shrill again) Or vice versa. (Russ subsides; Jason leans back against the wall.) You're gonna have to hold all that back. The rest of me, like a friend, you've got.

RUSS: I don't know if I can take the suspense.

JASON: (Stage laugh) I like that OK. You're honest. Now that you're honest we can hang out more together.

RUSS: I can't believe we're having this talk.

JASON: There you go again. (Jason exhales and crashes back down flat on mattress.)

Russ goes out on the wood terrace. All the insects are string instruments. There is a nebula of stars whooshing through the sky gathering littler lights in its sweep. Russ stumbles down the steps and out a bit toward a dark rumpled shirt of surrounding woodsy hills. He looks down at the bay, pricked by reflections of steaming high-up stars. Remembers that the season here for falling stars begins soon. And then the unusual excitement subsides. Russ heads back to wait for morning.

Jason is swallowing noisily, an indication of active sleep.

Russ hums to himself. He is reading a nature book, actually written for young children, about the living habits of rabbits. For a while the pace of this short-enough book is steady. Then, quickly, with every page, the lightness outside goes up a notch. Up, up, up.

Russ comes over with a cup of coffee and nudges Jason with it. Jason gets up noiselessly, but is obviously not even close to *compos mentis*.

JASON: (Sitting cross-legged; gravel-voiced) What did you put in it to sweeten it?

RUSS: Maple syrup. People do that in the South, I read, to sweeten, they use maple syrup in coffee. And the tenants left some here on a shelf. Last year's tenants. Did you know who they were?

Jason gets up to collect his last night's overalls off the motionless rocking chair. Russ had picked them off the floor and folded them over its back when he returned from his walk.

JASON: (Shaking his head) You read a lot. Do you read that much where you're from? Or is it because you don't have a TV here?

Goes over and slaps Russ twice on his shoulder.

JASON: The lobsters are waiting for me.

RUSS: (Playing girl) Lucky lobsters.

JASON: Cut the comedy. Listen. You can come for supper some night at my Mom's and watch it. There's all that news now on the Nuclear Reactor Plant to be built in Maine. I may not vote for it in the referendum.

RUSS: (Sadly) I forgot all about the news, practically. I mean I remind myself more of a grandmother, sitting all night in this chair, reading a book.

JASON: (A broad, black silhouette standing framed in the sunny doorway; his voice from beyond) That's one thing we have in common. So far. There's no denying. We both come from family life.

Russ scrunches his forehead. Then walks Jason out to the

truck. He sees now that the truck is painted aquamarine, not dark blue. As the motor starts up, Russ touches his hand down for good-bye on the hood over the vibrating motor, the front of the truck. Then he feels the truck moving out from under his palm. Stands drenched in the morning wet.

Jason's mind is already on the road. But he senses, in no words, as he takes the curve, that last night he had matured in a way which had made him more marriageable.

At eight in the morning, when most people in Nanticoke are starting to have warm scrambled eggs and last night's pie (often eaten for breakfast in that part of the world), Russ is fast asleep on an Indian rug, squarely in the center of his inverted V-shaped bungalow. It is a pyramid for the common man. His arms and hands tucked up under his chin.

FRIENDS AT EVENING

• ANDREW HOLLERAN •

I SAW MISTER Lark at the Stanford Hotel last night—which, at Seventh Avenue and Twenty-second Street, is not a place history has noticed any more than the people who walk by. One block north is the Chelsea Hotel, whose rooms have housed, and still do, writers and musicians, poets and designers. But the Stanford Hotel has none of the reflected glory of the arts, or even of its seemingly English, substantial, semiaristocratic name —whatever it once was, it is now, to be perfectly frank, a welfare hotel. And like those big old establishments in Atlantic City whose names conjured up the great country houses of England —the Marlborough-Blenheim, for instance—but whose windows looked down on a wooden boardwalk, brown beach and umber surf, the Stanford Hotel surveys a very un-English scene: black and Hispanic women on the stoop watching their children skip rope, play hopscotch, do back flips, as if in the dirt road of a small Southern town or a village in the mountains above San Juan. In summer the entire hotel seems to be on the sidewalk, but even in winter, no matter what the weather, there are always a few people out—certainly children, doing flips and skipping rope while waiting for their parents to come out of the bar on the corner called Soul Heaven. The music at Soul Heaven is on tape, and the tapes are so good that when I walk past the bar I stop—no matter what the weather;

and even in a blizzard you can hear the music—to listen to a few songs.

Last night on my way to meet Mister Lark for Louis' funeral, it happened that Gladys Knight was singing the theme from "Claudine" ("Make Yours a Happy Home") and I had to ask myself where else on earth but this bar would I have been able to hear this song; one of my favorites a decade ago, one Louis and I used to dance to. A very light snowfall was trying to begin, but it was so feeble it resembled chips of paint falling from an apartment ceiling, and the children were skipping rope as if it were an August night. The song has just that unpretentious mix of happiness and sadness that one listens for in vain in so much contemporary music, and I was feeling very sentimental when who should come up with a little grocery bag in hand, the kind they give you for one small item, but Mister Lark.

"Mother of God, you're on time," he said in a murmur which melded his words together in one continuous stream—a sound that baffled me for years till I realized it was the sound the priest makes giving you absolution on the other side of the grille. "How few people one can even count on for that fundamental courtesy!" he said. "So small, yet so enormous! A real index of character! I do not want to be late for the service. He Who Gets Slapped expects us to pick him up on Madison Avenue. He'll pay for the cab downtown." He grabbed my arm. "Do you remember this song?" I said.

"Remember it?" he said. "It is the story of my life!" And we stood there listening for a moment; until, just as Gladys Knight was starting the final chorus, the pay phone on the corner rang. Mister Lark reached right out and picked it up, as if it were his own. (Perhaps it *was*. I was so accustomed to Mister Lark's phoning me from subway stations and street corners, I assumed he had no phone of his own.) He listened for a moment and then said, "No I am *not* horny. I am, in fact, on my way to a funeral . . . I know *perfectly well* which window you're in, and I have no intention of looking up . . . I find penis size irrelevant, I do not talk dirty on the phone. I think that is for people who have never *quite* grown up!" he said, and put the receiver down with a clatter.

A small group of children gathered round and were staring up at Mister Lark. "Hello Charles, hello Antoinette, hello Delores, hello Paul," he said. "How are you this evening? Aren't you supposed to be doing your homework?" He set his paper bag on the metal platform beside the telephone, reached into the pocket of his coat, pulled out a little book whose cover had been ripped off, and began to leaf through it. "Louis's phone book," he murmured. "His brother and I ripped it in half, to divide the job of notifying people about the funeral tonight. I have a few more people to get a hold of," he murmured, and then, after putting a coin in, dialed a number he read in the book. He turned and smiled at the children, who continued to stare. It was just as well—"Make Yours a Happy Home" was succeeded by David Ruffin singing "Love Is What You Need," another song I hadn't heard in a long time. Mister Lark, however, began to frown, deeper and deeper, and finally he looked at me and said: "Do you suppose there is some equivalent of methadone for people who *can*not stay off the phone? Could we set up toy telephone clinics for people who cannot bring themselves to hang up? There is, after all, such a thing as consideration for others. The telephone does not exist to be abused," he said. (I waited to see what he would do: Mister Lark was the only person I knew who told the operator it was an emergency if someone's line was busy. Then, after the operator had broken in to say, "I'm sorry, I've an emergency," and the person interrupted felt his heart go into his throat at the imminence of bad news, he would hear the murmurous incantation of "My dear boy I'm so sorry, but I had to tell you *not* to meet me at eight o'clock *at the fountain*, but *inside* Alice Tully Hall. All right?") He sighed as he leafed through the little book, the phone cradled between his chin and shoulder, and finally stamped his foot. "That's it!" he said. "I've done my best!" And he threw the telephone down onto the metal prongs. I waited for him to dial the operator and declare an emergency, but instead he sighed, put the book back in his pocket, and picked up the paper bag. "*Avanti*," he said, and held out a hand with his pinky extended, a little hook I was to grasp, and be pulled along in the wake of his big black overcoat, past the children with wide eyes and pigtails and, around the corner, the middle-aged women in dresses the color of Kool-Aid and nylon bomber jackets, and their male companions in straw hats and old pea coats, who, with their bottles of beer in hand, gave the whole block a theatrical, artificial air; as if it were merely a theater set for *Porgy and Bess*. Mister Lark turned to me in the garish fluorescent light of the small tiled lobby and said: "Forgive me if I make you walk. But I would no more go in that elevator than I would go to a party given by Bobby Durwood." On the last few words his voice got louder, his enunciation sharper, in the tone of abused tenants everywhere, and the bare beginnings of the half-snicker, half-snort Mister Lark used in place of a laugh were aborted in the face of the immediate task: ascending the narrow stairs on which people sat rolling joints and listening to portable radios in little clouds of bright fluorescent light on each tiled landing, till we arrived at the top, dim floor and Mister Lark, panting, filmed with sweat, unlocked the gray metal door to his apartment. There was someone inside already: a man whose face was vaguely familiar. "Do you know Ned Stouffer?" said Mister Lark as the man smiled and held out his hand; he'd been standing at the window with his hands on the windowsill looking out when the door swung open.

"I think we have met," said Ned, "at Curtis's New Year's Eve party. How are you," he said, and shook my hand.

"Ned is just back in town for Louis's funeral," said Mister Lark. "I'm sorry he had to come back for such an awful reason," he said, his voice low, murmurous, gloomy. Then he grasped his friend's hands. "But I'm so glad to see him again!" He reached down and picked up a magazine on the table and held it out to us. It was called *Black Woman, White Stud*. "Have you seen this?" he said. "The 'portfolio' of the woman who lived here before me with her eight-year-old son. I can't bring myself to throw it away. Oh God. Look at him now," he said. We turned and saw across the amber radiance of the streetlight outside the window a naked white man standing in his window masturbating. "Can you imagine?" said Mister Lark. "And I'm over here, reading Montaigne! Of course," he said as the man turned around and put his buttocks to the glass, "it might make a difference if he were twenty-nine, good-looking, and Brazilian. But with *that* ass! Wouldn't you *hide it from everyone?* Tell me, what would you like to drink?" He held out an arm to the refrigerator. "I've got apple juice, tap water, and puree of beets. Unless you'd like tea," he said. Ned took apple juice and I took tea, and we sat down on the Styrofoam cushion which occupied what might be called a windowseat overlooking the skip-rope and games of the children on Twenty-second Street.

"*Mi casa es su casa,*" said Mister Lark, his voice swelling with the pride of a host whose friends are finally under his roof. "In the words of the Supremes—someday we'll be together! At the Stanford Hotel. I'd like to say Eugene O'Neill wrote *Mourning Becomes Electra* here, but I'd be lying if I did. In fact, though every street in Manhattan but this was *once* the playground of the Astors, nothing ever happened here. I'm in famous company —just round the corner from the Chelsea, which I'm told is so social these days poor Chris Potter takes a room at the Y," he snicker-snorted, "when he wants to get some writing done. Otherwise it's up and down the halls in a frenzy of gossip. Only the other day my friend Nicky Nolledo was in the lobby when one of the guests who'd just died was carried past on a stretcher, and the man at the desk looked up and said: 'Checking out?' "

He snicker-snorted and said: "I just thought I'd share that with you, since I have no cakes and cookies to serve, not even an Entenmann's!" (The paper bag he'd brought back from the store contained, I saw now, a product whose blue-and-white box promised the *safe home removal of ear wax.*) He raised his teacup and said to us: "I am reminded of a line from the perhaps over-rated, but occasionally divine, Walt Whitman, which I shall use to toast you. 'It is enough to be with friends at evening,' " he said. We smiled. "Although," he added, putting his cup down, "the occasion that brings us here tonight, that is, the one we are going to, is not one Whitman would have imagined. Poor Louis! Lying in what I'm sure will be a closed coffin, considering how he looked the last time I went to the hospital."

"How did he die?" said Ned, frowning. "I mean, what was the final thing that did it?"

"The final thing, indeed," said Mister Lark. "I'm not sure,

exactly. An intestinal infection, I believe. There was also blindness and herpes of the brain. Ron Pratt died of a tuberculosis formerly found in *birds*. Peter Ord of CMV running riot in his veins. As to what in Louis's case—the heart just stopped beating. What made the heart stop beating I can't say. I saw on television last night a gazelle brought down by lions on the Serengeti—the claws, the teeth, the *weight* of two lions, and still the gazelle almost escaped! That's what it's like to kill a man. The virus has to work itself into a perfect rage, a swarm, an irresistible tide that pours through the broken gates before anything so big, so vital, so complex as a *man* can be killed. And then," he laughed, "what does the virus do? Dies, because the thing it's been feeding on is dead. Foolish, isn't it? A parasite is more sensible—it knows when to stop. It even establishes a relationship. But I find it hard to find a place in God's plan for the virus."

"I still can't believe it," said Ned, looking down at the floor. "I feel so bad I didn't visit him more."

"But you had to leave town!" said Mister Lark. "How is your father? Hmmmm?"

"Well," he said, "a stroke takes a long time to recover from. And of course you never know if there won't be another stroke. But we send him to physical therapy and—just live from day to day, I guess. Were you with Louis at the end?"

"I was just going up to the hospital," said Mister Lark. "It was last Saturday morning. I had a few errands to run uptown —I planned to be there at ten. But I called first from the bookstore. A nurse answered the phone, said he'd died. And would I come up and please collect his things? They don't wait, you know, they get the room ready for the next patient! The private duty nurse on the night shift called Louis's brother at three in the morning to say Louis was dead, and she could not find her check! Can you imagine? *Moving right along!* The heartlessness of people is incredible! When I got there, everything he owned was in a plastic bag. His room was like the church door Luther nailed his theses to. Plastered with big crosses, skull and bones. *Poison. Stay out. Do not enter without gloves and mask.* You'd have thought someone was making plutonium inside. But no," he said, "it was just darling Louis, looking more and more each day like the world's oldest man."

"Was he *very* skinny?" said Ned.

"Yes. One day he asked me to hand him the towel at the foot of his bed. And he lay it across his forehead. And I thought: What is he doing that for? And he said: 'Don't you think I look like Mother Theresa?' "

"Making a joke about it!" said Ned.

"Yes," said Mister Lark.

"And did he?" said Ned.

"Look like Mother Theresa?" said Mister Lark. "Exactly." A cockroach scuttled out onto the rug between us. Ned reached out with his foot and stepped on it. "We are to the gods as flies to wanton boys," Mister Lark intoned. "God just reached out with His foot and stepped on Louis. Only he didn't die *right away*."

"Is his family here?"

"Yes," said Mister Lark. "They flew up from Georgia. His brother lived with him the last three months, you know. An angel. Odd, isn't it, how at the end, the family takes you back? How many men have gone back home when they got sick."

"And how many men have been cared for by their friends," said Ned. "Like you. I'm sure there'll be a terrific turnout to-night."

"Well, he knew so many people," said Mister Lark, "from so many milieus! He was always at the newest nightclub, in the newest pants, doing the newest dance! Sometimes I think he died just because he did everything *first*—"

"That's a funny way to look at it," said Ned.

"Funny ha-ha, or funny peculiar?" said Mister Lark, as he opened a jar, scooped some cream out, and began to apply it to his face in small, ever-widening circles.

"Somewhere in between," said Ned.

"I suppose it is. But when I am lying awake at night, I think of it that way, sometimes. I think of it so many ways. My mind *swarms* with metaphor." His hands made tiny circles till his face was entirely green. He plucked a tissue from a box of Kleenex and began to remove it all in short, deft strokes.

"Do you think it's going to stop?" said Ned.

"No," said Mister Lark. "I think we're all going to die."

There was a silence; we could hear the throb of the bass of whatever song was playing in the bar below beating against the night. A few snowflakes began to meander down past the street-light when I turned to look behind us; the man across the street was now lying before his window with his legs thrown up into the air, and an index finger circling his asshole.

"Do you really," said Ned in a soft voice.

"Yes," said Mister Lark. "Think of how many people we know who are already dead. Don't you make lists? Lists of people dead, lists of people living you worry about, lists of people you don't worry about, lists of people who would tell you if they got it, lists of people who wouldn't," he said as he wiped his face with a tissue. "Lists of people *you'd* tell if *you* got it, lists of people you wouldn't. Lists of people you'd care for if they got sick, lists of people you *think* would care for you, lists of places you'd like to be when you get it, lists of methods of suicide in case you do." He sighed. "Dreadful lists!"

"But what about this list," said Ned. "Of people whose lovers have died of it, but who are perfectly all right themselves!"

"That list we recite several times each day," said Mister Lark. "That list is our only hope. Five men in New York who are perfectly intact, even though their entire household has died. Who will always wonder, like the survivors of any catastrophe, why was I spared?"

"So you think nothing will ever, ever be the same?" said Ned.

"Nothing," said Mister Lark, screwing the cap on his jar of face cream. "We're all going, in sequence, at different times. And will the last person please turn out the lights?"

"I agree," said Ned.

"And that's why," said Mister Lark as he stood up, "each moment is so precious! Each friend who's still alive! Let us go then, you and I, when the evening is spread out against the sky, like a patient etherized upon the table."

He bent down and picked up the dead roach with a napkin.

"I feel bad killing that cockroach," Ned said. "It's the same thing."

"I know," said Mister Lark.

Louis's phone book fell out of his pocket with a thud; he picked it up in his other hand, and straightened up. "Did I tell you who's in Louis's phone book?" he said, tossing the napkin and the roach into a wastebasket. "His brother and I ripped it in half to call people about the funeral." He opened the book up and began to read: "Mary Tyler Moore."

"Mary Tyler Moore!"

"Walter Cronkite."

"Walter Cronkite!"

"Lena Horne."

Ned smiled.

"Halston," Mister Lark said. "Dan Rather. Lauren Bacall. Jeff Aquilon. Roy Cohn. Liz Smith." He looked up. "He used them when he was arranging the fashion show for muscular dystrophy. But he put them in his book. Do you see? *He wanted Mary Tyler Moore in his phone book.*"

"That's *so* Louis," said Ned as he shook his head. "And what are the rest?"

"A lot of Spanish names," said Mister Lark, "of no particular importance."

"Not in official circles," said Ned.

"Shall we go?" said Mister Lark. "It's almost six o'clock." He looked at us. "We must make a stop uptown first. You know, He Who Gets Slapped is waiting."

"I'm so excited," Ned smiled as he stood up.

"No more than He Who Gets Slapped," said Mister Lark. "When I told him you were back, be began to sing on the telephone." We took our cups to the heaped sink—miraculous flies, even in the dead of winter, droned over the sticky patina on the dishes—put on our coats, and went out into the hall.

Mister Lark wrapped a long scarf around his neck so that it hung down his overcoat on either side, like the stole a priest wears to hear confession. "You never really know in the Stanford Hotel," he said as he went down the narrow, vomit-colored hall whose fluttering fluorescent light gave the place a nervous aspect, "if anything will be left when you get back. Imagine a methadone addict operating a hot plate! I *al*ways expect to see the towering inferno when I come up out of the IRT. So I follow the advice given in the *Times* to people traveling to countries on the verge of revolution," he said. "I take my valuables with me." And he pulled out of his pocket his wallet, first edition of Hart Crane, and Louis's phone book.

"How are you, good evening, *bon soir, buenas noches, auf wiedersehen.*" Mister Lark smiled and nodded to the people sitting on the stairs as we descended the five flights to the lobby, which was now filled with excited men shouting in Spanish. Mister Lark kissed the tips of his fingers and fluttered them in the direction of the crowd. "Don't wait up!" Ned said, stepped down the three cement stairs onto the sidewalk, turned and waited for us. Even though it was snowing on this late March night, the stoop and walls of the hotel were lined with its tenants taking the air. "Hello Lulu," Mister Lark said with a smile, as one of the women in a pea coat waved at him. "Hello Stan, hello Bertha Mae." He turned and said in a lower voice as we walked to the corner: "Don't you think these people look *exactly* like the inhabitants of a small town in the Mississippi delta?"

"I'm sure they are," said Ned. "And they just got on the bus one day."

"Well," said Mister Lark, "they may be destitute, but they've got the two things that count—rhythm and a complete immune system! Taxi?" he said, turning when we reached the corner. "Or the IRT?"

"Taxi," said Ned. "My treat."

"You are," said Mister Lark, "a breath of fresh air."

Ned raised his arm and turned south, as Mister Lark cried "Get a Checker, get a Checker!" Minutes later we got into one, in a faint cloud of snowflakes, and began driving uptown. The streets were still so warm the snow was melting the moment it touched the asphalt. "Do you miss the city?" I said to Ned. "God! Yes," he said. "Terribly. Right now, it's just one big cemetery, but it still gets me so excited. When the plane started to descend, my stomach tightened and I began to shake."

"No!"

"And when I got *off*, I wanted to kneel down and kiss the tarmac, like the Pope. I didn't know *how* I was going to get into town from Newark. I was so impatient!"

"Next time," said Mister Lark, "you should have a helicopter lower you onto your apartment building. I never leave," he said.

"I used to walk this street every night on my way to the gym," Ned said.

"The McBurney Y?" said Mister Lark.

"Yes," said Ned. "It started to get yuppie by the time I left New York, it was filled with women in leotards doing yoga, and men taking karate, but when I first joined, it was a backwater. Dim and dingy, Puerto Rican boxers, sex in the air! You know?"

"I do indeed," Mister Lark murmured as we sped uptown; he was so frugal with what little money he had, taxis were one of the things he seldom allowed himself, no matter how sorely tempted; even though, he said, the IRT was something no man over thirty should go into unless in search of sex; and that was now out of the question. A taxi so enchanted him we might as well have been going uptown in the sleigh Ludwig of Bavaria used on snowy nights when he was bored and depressed, two things Mister Lark never was. He turned to us with a starstruck expression on his face, dazzled by the lights, the rushing, cold damp wind beside the window he'd left open at the top. "Boxers often do, you know," said Mister Lark. "Boxers *never* do," said Ned, "and never *are*. Just as homosexuals *never* wore rubber thongs into the shower, never boxed, and never played basketball."

"I knew one," said Mister Lark, "who did all three! Then he had his teeth filed down, and tipped with silver, and moved to Vermont to paint."

"Rick Satterwaite!" said Ned.

"Yes," said Mister Lark.

"He was divine," said Ned.

"But spaced out," said Mister Lark. "Though moving to Vermont when he did seems in retrospect, *very* sensible. *His* blood, no doubt, is pure as cows' milk!" He looked at Ned. "I used to see you at McBurney very late, on Saturday."

"That was my favorite time!" said Ned. "The last half hour in the locker room on a Saturday—there was something poetic about it."

"Now it's quite bustling, and busy, and renovated," said Mister Lark, "and some new director has increased the membership, and refurbished the weight and locker rooms, and it's full of copy editors learning self-defense. I don't know where I'll go when my membership runs out. Do you think there are still *seedy* gyms in Brooklyn? With old-fashioned swimming pools? The McBurney pool is—"

"A footbath," said Ned. "I used to wait an hour to get a lane. But the things I saw in it! I've showered beside creatures who could have—" He struggled for words.

"Persuaded the gods to come down from Olympus for an afternoon," said Mister Lark.

"Exactly!"

"But now the gods no longer seem interested in us as lovers," said Mister Lark. "Driver! Driver!" he said through the opening in the scratched plastic screen between the front and backseats. "Let us out on the next corner! There's been a change of plans!" The driver came to an abrupt halt, Mister Lark said to Ned, "I'll explain in a moment," and got out, while Ned paid the fare.

In a moment we were all on the cold, wet, and windy sidewalk across from the Fashion Institute of Technology. "Why did you do that?" asked Ned.

"There are two reasons to change taxis," said Mister Lark, his fine hair blowing about his head in the wind. "The first one I learned when I was taking drugs in the East Village—the feeling someone is following you. Now I think that's *why* people take drugs! To feel someone *is* following them. In my case, someone was. Because I wrote a somewhat nasty review of a novel by a man whose name I won't mention here. I knew I had crossed off our relationship with the article—I was young, and drunk on language—even though it was the truth. But he actually began to follow me everywhere. You remember Warhol was shot by that crazy woman around that time? I had a job with *Saturday Review*, I was taking cabs then. I used to change taxis five times in twenty blocks. Which introduced me to the second reason for changing cabs," he said as Ned held up his arm and shouted "Taxi!" at the one approaching. "And that," he said as it stopped before us, "is the driver." We piled into the backseat; this time there was no plastic panel between us and the front seat; the driver turned and smiled at us with big dark eyes, strong white teeth, in a pale olive face. "Julio," said Mister Lark, glancing at the information on the visor, "how do you do. And where are you from originally?"

"Ecuador," said the driver with a smile.

"Ah," said Mister Lark, "the kingdom of the Incas! Would you take us, proud descendant of Atahualpa, to the southeast corner of Madison Avenue and Seventy-fifth Street? Go through the park, please." He turned to us, and murmured: "The park is so lovely at night in this kind of weather. Gusty emotions on wet roads on autumn nights!" He put his hand between his teeth and bit it to repress the urge to shriek. "Now you were saying, dear boy, about the McBurney Y. Hmmmmm?"

Ned smiled and put his head back.

"The shower shoes? Hmmmm?" said Mister Lark.

"Just that after the gym," said Ned as we rattled north, "I'd go to the baths! I'd walk home from McBurney after being surrounded by these Puerto Ricans, down Sixth Avenue, and then veer over to Man's Country on Fifteenth Street to see who was standing in line," he said. "Or I'd go in and stand there till the urge went away. But the urge seldom went away," he said in a quiet voice. "I was in love with the two Cubans who worked the window. It was so cheap in those days, you could go in for three dollars. Three dollars! Movies cost five. And a night at Man's Country was infinitely more thrilling than any movie could possibly be. I think Man's Country killed Louis."

"What?" said Mister Lark as we stopped at a light on Thirty-fourth Street.

"He had a pass," said Ned. "He was a friend of the owner, and Louis could go there any hour of the day or night—it was only a block from his apartment—and check in. And get a room, unless they were sold out. They were never sold out. For some reason Man's Country never caught on—which is why I liked it. The Fire Island crowd, the circuit queens all went to the St.

Marks. Man's Country was utterly off the beaten path. *No* one I knew went there. Except Louis. We loved it! I used to see him there, standing naked in the doorway of his room. When he saw me coming, he'd put one arm up and another on his hip, and kind of *lounge* in the doorway—like Elizabeth Taylor in *Cat on a Hot Tin Roof*." He laughed. "One night Spruill saw him like that, and said: 'You'd better put that thing away, or people are going to throw peanuts at it.' "

"Put what away?" said Mister Lark.

"His dick," said Ned. "He had a gargantuan penis! *That's* what killed Louis—he came into his penis."

"Came into his penis!" said Mister Lark as we drove through Herald Square.

"You know the French saying," said Ned. "A woman comes into her beauty. Well, Louis came into his penis."

"But," Mister Lark spluttered, "he always had his penis! He didn't inherit it in midlife!"

"But he did," said Ned in a calm, reasonable voice. "I mean, of course his penis was always there between his legs, but it might just as well have not been. When we met him in the Pines in 1971, he was always in drag—of one kind or another. I remember one night Louis was coming up the stairs of the Sandpiper in one of his bizarre getups—torn fatigues, lamé tank top, and a towel, I think—and the man next to me said, 'Who is that?' And the person next to him replied: 'Some Jewish queen from outer space.' Remember? Louis used to stand outside the Sandpiper in a big red ball gown with black beads, black fan and a fake camellia in his snood, and curtsy to boys he adored. He was like a child. And he had, at that time, not the slightest inkling that he had a penis! I mean it was there, but he never used it. And then, toward the end of the seventies—he realized the . . . value of what he had."

"What value?" said Mister Lark.

"Why, everything," Ned said, "in the little world we were living in. That penal colony! The whole point, as it were. The central symbol. The Eucharist. What everyone, on some level, was looking for, what everyone would not pause in their search until they found."

"You mean the great, the distinguished thing," said Mister Lark.

"Yes," said Ned.

"Surely you exaggerate."

"I don't," said Ned. "A homosexual *is* his penis. A homosexual cemetery should have just three things on the gravestone: name, date, and dimensions of dick."

"You've grown bitter in Ohio!" said Mister Lark.

"There's nothing else to do," he smiled.

"And you've forgotten about the meeting of two minds and souls, the escape from loneliness, or what it really is. What Plato called it—the desire to be born in beauty."

"Oh, Richard," said Ned. "How many homosexuals even get to, much less operate on that level? Most of them are looking for a good firm cantaloupe. They find a dick they like, pitch their tents, and unharness the camels."

"Oh!" said Mister Lark. "And you're the great romantic!"

"You can be romantic, and still face facts," said Ned.

"I thought you couldn't," said Mister Lark.

"And the facts are these," said Ned. "Louis came into his penis. And when he did, he began having sex—because now all those famous models he used to faint over were now lying in the bathtub in the Strap waiting to be pissed on! If the penis was right! And his was. So in the middle of the night, if he couldn't sleep, or in the middle of the afternoon, if he had an hour between appointments, he would drop into Man's Country. It was like a harem he could drop in on. A harem. That's what it was. A family. A home. A men's club. A place of refuge. And *what* a place of refuge! Two things in life are as exciting to me now as the first time I experienced them—"

"The ocean, and autumn nights," said Mister Lark.

"Taking off in an airplane, and hearing the door of a bathhouse close behind me," said Ned.

"Oh dear," said Mister Lark.

"And Louis felt the same," said Ned, "though he didn't carry the guilt I did. He had that wonderful gift—the ability to enjoy life. Which is why he had so many friends."

We came to a stop in dense traffic south of Columbus Circle.

Ned looked out the window. "Do you think there's a car show at the Coliseum?" he said. "Or a health food fair? Or a convention of mind-control seminars? Should we just take the first right, and forget about going through the park?" But we could not even have done that at the moment: fenders, taillights, grilles enclosed us on all sides—we were trapped. "Something's going on," said Ned. Mister Lark leaned forward. *"Que está el problema?"* Mister Lark said to Julio.

"Qué es el problema," said Ned. Mister Lark turned and looked at him. "Spanish has two verbs for being," Ned said. *"Está* is impermanent, *es* is permanent."

"Ah," said Mister Lark.

"Qué es el problema," Julio said with a smile, and a nod, as he glanced at us in the rearview mirror, his large dark eyes glowing in the radiance of the reflected headlights bouncing off the taxi in front of us.

"Cómo está Usted? Qué es el problema?" murmured Ned.

"Cómo está Usted? Qué es el problema?" said Mister Lark. He covered his eyes with his hands. "Stuck in traffic?" he said. "Do facial isometrics, plan a party menu, learn to use the Spanish verbs *es* and *está*. Not a moment wasted in the life of a modern American maintaining a balance among all the elements of his split identity. Oh, darlings! When did the world become a microwave oven?" He uncovered his face, rolled down the window, and yelled: "Precious! Excuse me, sir? Hello! Darling! Cupcake! Pudding Face! Yes, I just wanted to know—has the water main burst up there? Is Mrs. Onassis going to the Opera?" Mister Lark held his head out the window to hear what a man on the sidewalk was saying to him. "There's been an accident," he said, coming back inside, "on the night of Louis's funeral."

"Let's get out," Ned said. "and get another cab on Fifth."

"No!" Mister Lark leaned toward us. "You'll never find another one like this, believe me! His voice is like a waterfall in a rain forest. He's got a *soul*."

"Richard, they all have souls," said Ned, still hanging on to the strap. "The question is, do they have immune systems?"

Mister Lark spluttered.

"The question is do we," said Ned. "And the answer is no."

"Do you think *you're* infected?" said Mister Lark.

"I'm sure of it," said Ned.

"But you haven't taken the test!"

"I don't have to," said Ned. "If *I'm* not infected, no one is. I was living at the baths."

"But you just looked," said Mister Lark.

"*Some*times I looked," said Ned. "Sometimes I touched."

"But—"

"You were at the theater," said Ned. "The opera, the reading. The rest of us were much lower on the ladder of love."

"You're turning bitter, aren't you," said Mister Lark. "You've been watching television, and shopping in supermarkets, and they've taken their toll. You're going to repent, like Saint Augustine, and turn against the past!"

"*You're* safe," said Ned. "Because I think of you as not having sex."

"This is hardly the time, or place, for *exposés*," said Mister Lark.

"I'm serious," said Ned. "You have the most precious gift of all! Your health. Your peace of mind. Your body, uninvaded. You are Sicily before the Normans. America before the white man. Mexico before the Spanish. Hawaii before the missionaries. You're intact. You're virgin. You're on fire." The taxi lurched. "You're even moving," he said as Julio, speaking rapidly in Spanish and honking the horn, suddenly floored the accelerator, sped round a car he saw, in passing, was broken down, flew past the police barricades, and on up Central Park West. "Thank God I'm not in labor," said Ned, lighting a cigarette. Mister Lark leaned forward to speak to Julio, then stopped, sat back and turned to us. "Would you say Louis *es* or *está* dead?"

"*Está*," said Ned. "*Está muerto*."

"But why?" said Mister Lark. "Surely his deadness is not an impermanent condition. He is dead forever."

"Not if you believe the psychic in the Beresford I used to see," said Ned, as the doormen and canopies and lighted facades of apartment buildings went by, "who told me I'm going to be a pediatrician in Bombay in my next life."

"You don't believe such nonsense," said Mister Lark.

"No, I don't," said Ned. "I believe Louis is dead, and we'll never see him again."

"So do I," said Mister Lark with a sigh, as he looked out at the buildings going by. "And at the same time I can't believe it. Quite. As I find it hard to believe your theory about his getting sick. In fact, I find it hard to believe anything about this nightmare except one fact—"

"What's that?" said Ned.

"*The wrong people are dying,*" he said, turning to us as we veered into the park.

"The wrong people?"

"You know how Louis always used to say the wrong people are having babies? Well, now the wrong people are dying. The germophobes, the anal-retentives, the small and mean and cold and ungenerous are going to survive. The ones like Louis, who loved life, will not. Because life's chief pleasure . . . is sex. And sex is what killed them."

"Africa is what killed them," said Ned. "Africa killed Louis. We are infected with a disease that got started in the garbage dump of a slum in Zaire."

He looked out the window at the skyline of Central Park South blazing through the dark trees. "And that's why it seems so awful," said Ned, "so out of proportion to what we were doing."

"And what was that?" said Mister Lark.

"Enjoying life," said Ned, "liberty, and the pursuit of happiness."

"Which you found twice!" said Mister Lark.

"Yes," said Ned. "Snookums, and Shithead." We went beneath a bridge and saw, when we emerged, the new wing of the Metropolitan Museum and the Temple of Dendur glowing pale cinnamon in its bath of golden light. "It looks just like an airplane hangar!" said Mister Lark. "I always expect to see the Spirit of St. Louis hanging there. *Eyes left!*" he said as we turned south on Fifth Avenue and the lighted facade of another apartment building loomed in the darkness. "*Mrs. Onassis!*"

"Have you ever seen her?" said Ned.

"Once, at the opera," said Mister Lark. "Her head is enormous. It just floated down the aisle in the glare of flashbulbs, like a spaceship." The taxi turned left off Fifth Avenue. "I have terrible news for you, Ned, about He Who Gets Slapped."

"What?" Ned said in an alarmed voice.

"On no, not that," said Mister Lark. He crossed himself. "You know how many happy days and nights we have spent in his flat, you know what teen tramps we have been there, what conversations, what pasta, what journeys downtown have all begun under his roof, when downtown was divine decadence and not dreadful death," he said.

"Yes," said Ned.

"Are you wearing a disposable incontinent brief?"

"Of course."

"The Whitney Museum purchased Curtis' building, and is *evicting* the tenants! They are going to tear it down to build an extension, an addition by Michael Graves that gives new meaning to the word 'silly,' " he said as the cab pulled up to the corner of Seventy-fifth Street and Madison Avenue. The driver turned to us with a smile. "Bravo, Julio!" said Mister Lark. "I would follow you across the Andes! In fact, if some evening you get off work and do not feel quite like going home, stop by. I have so many questions about Ecuador." He took a card from his wallet and handed it to Julio. Ned leaned forward to read the meter, paid Julio, and got out after me; Mister Lark stayed in the taxi to talk with Julio, as we waited beneath the portal of the Whitney Museum, which was still lighted within. Across the street, a showroom with mannequins in the windows was a brilliant cube of light.

"Have you ever *seen* a woman in a Givenchy?" said Ned.

Our host rounded the corner in a black chesterfield with the collar turned up, a paper bag in his arms, fluttered his hand in the air, and said: "Hi, where's Richard?"

"Still in the cab," I said.

"And here's my baby!" he said, embracing Ned.

"Happy to be back?" said Curtis.

"Very!" said Ned. "And to see *you*!"

Curtis went to the door of his building—a glass pane in the

door already shattered, graffiti on the wall beneath the mailbox —looked back and said: "Don't wait for La Gioconda! Come in and have a drink!"

"I can't believe they're going to tear this down!" Ned said as we went up the worn, shabby, carpeted stairs to the third floor. "It's ten years of our lives!"

"Twenty of mine," said Curtis.

"And what about the bookstore next door?"

"It's all going," said Curtis as he unlocked the door. "The Huns! Evicting us all," he said, "and everybody sick, or sick with fear. God, these are hideous times!" he said, hanging up his coat in the hall as we went past him into a white room with vases of irises and votive candles. "These be *real* bad times," he said. Ned turned around and took it in: the books that covered one wall from floor to ceiling, the clay horses on the mantelpiece, the long tiled table at which he'd sat so many evenings, the tall bookcase whose titles my eyes had played over often without being able to determine a theme among them, save the eclectic chaos of twentieth-century culture.

"The thing now is to gain weight," said Curtis, pointing to a platter of bread, cheese and roast beef on the table. "You're supposed to look healthy, and healthy is fat. I was with Louis and Spruill one day in an elevator in the D&D Building, when Louis was looking very gaunt. And a friend we all knew got on, saw Louis, and said, 'How are you?' And Louis said: 'I have cancer.' Which really shut the friend up—he got off at the next floor just to recover from the shock. When he left, Spruill turned to Louis and said: 'Don't tell them you have cancer. Tell them you've been swimming laps!' " Ned and Curtis laughed. "Can you imagine?" Curtis smiled. "So how does the city look?"

"Gorgeous," said Ned. "Driving across the park tonight was as thrilling as the first time I did it."

"With Louis throwing up out the window," said Curtis. "Wasn't that it? The night we met you at Marty Rowan's party?"

"How's Spruill?"

"Livid."

"He's being evicted too?"

"The whole building. The whole past is going up in smoke!"

"And Spruill?"

"He's going to the south of France with Martion Lafarge. To sulk."

Ned smiled. "Actually it's because he's even more terrified than we are," said Curtis. "He won't go to the funerals of his friends because he's afraid the germs are floating in the air." Ned sighed. He looked around the room as if he could not believe he was there. "I miss you all so much," he said. "My most important relationship now is with my Chevrolet."

"A Chevrolet can't give you AIDS," said Curtis.

"No," said Ned, "and it can't talk to you when you're driving home alone from the bars. Actually, my most important relationship is with the car radio," he said.

"How's your father?"

"Okay," he said.

There was a silence. Curtis lighted a cigarette. I went into the front room to see it again. It looked as if it had not been used in some time. On the mantelpiece were photographs, one of Louis in a ship captain's uniform, and another of him in a pale blue gown on the boardwalk on Fire Island. The windows were open an inch or two, and the room was chilly; a cold film of air stole over the sills. It was March—that strange, dead time in the city, when the season is not one thing or the other—when the nights lack the clarity of deepest winter, when cabs are warm and doorways magical. The apple trees in the park were not yet in bloom, or bodies shorn of their layers of clothes, or the buses running to Jones Beach. It was just March: when people were tired of winter, and everything they'd been doing; when life stands empty, like the squash courts at the gym, a month ago impossible to get on, and now brightly lighted, doors ajar. That odd time of desuetude and mud, bad complexions and soot, trash and litter blowing in the wind, and the whole town—as at the end of August—not quite functioning, for the same reason one cannot pedal a bike between gears. It was, in all its exhaustion and bleak mood and griminess a perfect time to consign Louis to the shades. "Would you tell me if *you* had it?" Curtis was saying when I returned to the other room.

"I—don't know," said Ned.

"You don't, do you?"

"Not at the moment," said Ned. "But I'm sure it's in me. along with the one thousand other things swimming in my blood. My sister says I was naive. Not to be more careful, suspicious, mistrustful."

"Of what?" said Curtis.

"Other people's hygiene."

"We didn't have any reason to worry about other people's hygiene! We had penicillin."

"But we didn't stop, even when we knew," said Ned.

"Knew but didn't believe," said Curtis. "For a while, there was a gap, you know. On Friday we were rational, and celibate. On Saturday night we were terrified, and in bed with someone. We didn't know Third World diseases. Doctors at the Ford Foundation knew about those. We didn't know some Australian flight attendant was going to sleep with someone in Africa on Monday, and then with David on Fifty-first Street on Tuesday. Would you have believed me if I had taken you aside on one of these nights you loved, with Mario and Raul and Umberto in the front room, with the candles lighted and their beards and mustaches black as coal, and said to you: 'Ned, don't fall in love with them, they're carrying a virus from Kinshasa that can shrivel you up to ninety pounds, give you cancer and kill you in two weeks!' You'd have looked at me and said: What science fiction movie did *you* see on Times Square this afternoon, dear?" He put down his cigarette and said: "We knew, but we didn't believe!"

"But why was I in love with Umberto and Mario anyway?" said Ned, standing up and turning around in a circle with his hands in his pockets.

"And Raul!"

"And Raul," Ned said.

"Because they were good-looking, nice guys!"

"But why was I *sleep*ing with them?"

"Because you wanted to merge your unity with their oneness," said Mister Lark as he came into the room. "There are thirty-seven dialects in the Andes of Ecuador," he said as he bent down to smell the irises, "and the word in one of them for potato is *yoringo*." He straightened up and turned to us. "Curtis, Ned is turning bitter. Like Saint Augustine in middle age, he has decided to renounce his past, his sensual youth. A typical reaction to middle age. Tell him the virus is merely a tragic accident that has nothing to do with either Africa, or our sex lives. Tell him it does not invalidate the thing which still persists in the midst of all this horror—I mean," he murmured, "the incalculable, the divine, the overwhelming, godlike beauty of the . . . male body. And then ask him about his bizarre explanation for Louis' death—not to mention all of homosexual life. He thinks, silly boy, it is all centered on the penis!" he said, and, looking back over his shoulder, disappeared through the kitchen doorway, to use (I felt sure) the telephone.

"Leave me some message units!" Curtis shouted after him. But all he heard in response was the noise of dialing.

Curtis turned to Ned. "He's right, you know," said Curtis. "You can't revise the past. There's no point in introducing a fact which was not a fact at the time."

"But we should have foreseen it," said Ned.

"Oh," said Curtis, tapping his cigarette against the ashtray and looking down at it, "there are lots of things we should have foreseen. But what did the man say? Life is understood backwards, but lived forwards. That's the problem, dear."

"You're *so* rational," sighed Ned.

"That's what I told myself when I fell down on the boardwalk one night this summer on Fire Island and started screaming: We're all going to die. We're all going to die!"

"Did you do that?" said Ned.

"Ask Richard," said Curtis. "He had to pick me up and calm me down."

"Richard," Ned said, glancing at the kitchen, "I don't worry about at all."

"Because he never has sex," said Curtis. "He just talks to them. Sex for Richard is having dinner with the driver of the cab you just got out of. Sex for Richard is learning the word for potato in Inca."

"There is no law in physics more implacable than the one in

New York which says the moment someone exits a room, he will be discussed," said Mister Lark, coming back into the room, with the scarf still around his shoulders, carrying Louis's phone book in his hands as if it were a breviary. Curtis and Ned smiled.

"It's only because you fascinate us," said Curtis. "It's only because we know nothing of your private life."

"That is because I have no private life," said Mister Lark. "I am entirely public. I spend my life in shower rooms and theater lobbies. Which is how I met Louis—sneaking into a matinee of *My Fair Lady* after the intermission. How many years ago." He sighed. "The last person I was to call does not answer," he said, sitting down in one of the cane-back chairs. "Have I ever told you how much I admire you all for not having answering machines?" he said.

"Why?" said Curtis.

"Because," said Mister Lark, "you maintain, by not having one, 'the pathos of distance.' Nietzsche." He sighed as he leafed through the little book whose binding was ripped and whose cover was gone—a book torn in half—and said: "Even Louis, toward the end, succumbed. Even Louis had an answering machine installed—"

"Because he was becoming very social," said Ned.

"Very," said Mister Lark.

"Curtis thinks Africa killed Louis, too."

"Unless tomorrow a scientist announces it was all caused by chicken salad in a restaurant on Forty-first Street," said Curtis. "Or fake fog in discotheques. Or the newsprint that comes off on your hands from the Sunday *Times*. The point is we don't know," he said. "The point is, we might as well be living in Beirut. Shall we go?" he said, standing up. "It's almost eight o'clock."

He and Ned went around the room blowing out the votive candles—as if extinguishing the decade—and Mister Lark turned off the Brazilian music. We paused at the edge of the room to put on our coats. "Take one last look," said Curtis at the door. "In another year it'll be a big white room filled with television sets showing video from Milan and L.A."

"God!" said Ned. "No wonder everyone who works at the Whitney is always at the Mineshaft."

And with a flick of his hand, Curtis plunged the room behind us into darkness, as if it too were just a theater set. We went down the worn stairs and emerged onto Madison Avenue, which looked exactly like what Mister Lark said it was after seven o'clock: The Gobi Desert. Nothingness stretched dreamily in both directions. Mister Lark led Curtis south into the darkness in search of taxis, and Ned, hands in his overcoat, his hair shining copper-bright in the light of the bookstore, surveyed the new titles in the window and then turned.

"This reminds me of old times," he said, "except, of course, we're going to Louis's funeral. But all our evenings began just like this."

"Were you all very close?" I said.

"Close?" he said. He looked at me. "We were the Four Supremes! And now Louis is the Dead Supreme. I still can't understand it."

"It must have been wonderful," I said. "You must miss it a great deal."

"Between you and me?" he said. "Not to leave this bus stop? I was very discouraged *before* all this began. I stayed in New York five years too many."

"Why?"

"Because the first five years were magic," he said, "and I kept hoping the second five would be too. But then you reach middle age, you'd rather have birds and trees and the sound of rain on the roof. That's all. Curtis and Richard belong here. Some part of them never ages. Richard is like the cockroach—he'll survive everything. When Curtis and I are gone, Richard'll still be going to the Opera, looking for Jackie O. But I was ready to leave before I did. I was listening to the radio one night in Ohio, some woman with a great voice began to sing 'More Than You Know.' Have you ever heard the lyrics to 'More Than You Know'?"

"Yes," I said. "Something about man of my dreams."

" 'Oh, how I'd die,' " he said, " 'oh, how I'd cry, if you got tired and said good-bye.' Well, when I was in New York those first five years, I used to hear that song and turn to mush. When

I heard it last fall in Ohio one night in my car, I thought: This is the clinical description of a masochist." He smiled. "For the *first* five years, it was fun being a masochist."

"And then? I said.

"Everything, including masochism," he said, "becomes a habit after a while. And once it does, you should go. No one should live in this city unless he's in a state of extreme romantic excitement. I'm no longer in a state of romantic excitement," he said.

There was a silence. "Why not?" I said.

"I can't romanticize this," Ned said, nodding south. "I can't romanticize taxicabs, or men with Spanish names. I . . . can't romanticize *me*."

"What can you romanticize?" I said.

"Budapest," he said, "in a light snow. Having wine in a café, with a pale, handsome waiter with very bony hands."

"So you *still* think you'll fall in love, somewhere else . . ."

"Though the settings get more and more exotic," he said. "In fact I'm happy just waking up in the morning. Louis, just before he died, was planning to go around the world."

There were shouts, a flurry of raised arms; we looked south and saw a cab, captured, and our friends getting in. My heart was pounding when I reached them, either from the run or that never-failing feeling of excitement that accompanies the entrance of any cab in New York City; as if one renews one's life each time a meter switches on. "Ah, Octavio," Mister Lark was saying in that priestly voice as we got in. "And what part of Buenos Aires?"

BAD PICTURES

• PATRICK HOCTEL •

IN A HUMPHREY Bogart biography, an interviewer asked Bogie why he'd done so many bad pictures when he'd had his pick of the good ones. Bogart answered that the good ones only came along once in a while, and the bad ones were steppingstones; he had to do them to make the good ones possible, to reach them. Without the bad ones, no one would've known he was still out there, and he wouldn't have been considered for his great roles. If you're out of the game too long, people forget you were ever in it, and after a while, so do you—I think.

Right after Anthony, I entered what I consider my post-slut, pre-nun phase, meaning I was celibate but still looking, still going out. Having been raised as a southern Presbyterian, I couldn't escape the Protestant work ethic, which carried over into my private life as well—work creates work; lovers create lovers. Not unlike advertising. If you don't advertise, then you won't get any business. However, if you get some business, good or bad, you stick with it until the right business comes along.

Anthony. He was so dark. Burnt brown. Anthony had a crushed-up nose and a mouth that had come out of an only partially successful harelip operation. He was a Latino Jean-Paul Belmondo, that same sneer for a smile, the right side of his upper lip curling back over his teeth. I met him in a bar in the dry heat of a Tucson July. He was wearing English khaki hiking shorts, the kind with no zipper, just two buttons at the top, a yellow Indian cotton shirt, and dull red Giorgio Brutini sandals. I was entranced.

I kept remembering *Breathless*, how I'd seen it at nineteen, high on 'ludes and poppers, wishing I could push Jean Seberg off the screen and take her place; how at nineteen, I wanted to be the cause of one man's downfall, to have one beautiful man say to me with his dying breath, "You really are a bitch, you know."

Anthony invited me outside to smoke a joint. When he found out I was new to Tucson, he invited me to "A" mountain to see the lights of the city. His invites were delivered formally; he even seemed to bend a little at the waist, deferring to any choice I might make. Something in his manner made me flash on those smooth Latin types from the late 40s, early 50s—the ones everyone mixes up—Cesar Romero, Fernando Lamas, Ricardo Montalban. Charming but a little oily, and even when they were being romantic, they seemed to be mocking you at the same time (probably because you were SO Caucasian and unworldly). "If you would like to see the mountain? Or if you prefer I take you home?"

I went to the mountain. I told him about my teaching. He liked English, he said. And he liked my name, which he pronounced By-ron, as in Lord, not Bri-an, like most everyone else. I liked his pronunciation better. I learned he worked at the copper smelter in San Manuel. End of first illusion. He was not the semi-gangster, or at least dope smuggler (we were only two hours from the border), that I'd imagined; however, he did make $15.71 an hour, which allowed him to indulge in the finer things: good dope, a new '81 Camaro with dark blue tinted glass, a stereo with speakers taller than either of us, and clothes off the pages of *GQ*.

After he pulled in front of my apartment, I got out and headed for the door, digging in my jeans for the key. When I didn't hear steps behind me, I turned. He was still in the car. "You coming?" I asked.

"Do you wish me to?"

At twenty-four, I assumed that certain things were just understood. "Sure," I said.

I had a studio apartment. Really, the only place to sit was the bed. We looked at picture albums, my family's history. The family was important, Anthony said. Over an 8″ by 10″ of my brother's ROTC Winter Formal, I kissed him. He kissed back. We kissed for an hour, exploring ears, the nape of the neck, shoulders. I bit his Adam's apple and he let out a shudder of breath. The next day my lips were chapped and bloody. I had a stain on my throat the color of violets. At one point when I had unbuttoned his shirt and was carefully rolling his left nipple between my teeth and tongue, he tensed and drew back. "Should we remove our clothes now?" he wanted to know.

We both then stood and removed our clothes. Suddenly, we were shy. Before his shorts came off, Anthony dimmed the light over my bed. "I'm fat," he said. He wasn't. Returning from the kitchen after a quick gulp of cold water, I tripped over his sandal in the darkness and he caught me, gently pulling me up, making sure I never touched the ground.

In the morning he turned the light on early, about seven. He had to go to work. He fished a cigarette out of his shirt pocket; he was one of those people you couldn't talk to until he had his first smoke. Then he spotted a poster on the opposite wall, a famous one of Marilyn Monroe, where her mouth is open so wide you can't tell if she's smiling or screaming, and her eyes heavy with mascara, the right one is winking, making her look like she's crying. "She's good," Anthony said.

He began talking about Barbra. Babs. How she was the greatest singer and actress today. To my amazement, Anthony was what was known as a "Barbra Queen." There were Judy Queens, Bette Queens, Dietrich Queens, Crawford Queens, and of course Liza Queens, but the Barbras were the worst. Had I seen HER version of *A Star Is Born*? *Hello, Dolly*? She was much better in that than the critics said, better than Channing. And why hadn't she got the Oscar for *The Way We Were*?

The moment I closed the door on Anthony I knew part of me never wanted to see him again, but the mechanics were already in motion. We had arranged a date for the weekend, which since he suggested it, meant that I would have to propose something for next time, and so on. The dynamics of dating are not unlike the old Domino Theory—once one goes, then all the others fall; one push is all it takes. Besides, the silent times were great.

So one night, many weeks later, driving in Anthony's Camaro, he brought up a friend of his who'd been at the party we'd just come from and mentioned what a terrific guy this person was, really funny. This terrific guy, after discovering I was an English teacher, had launched into a ten minute tirade, in a jumbled mixture of English and Spanish, about how he had not been able to get a degree because he never could pass freshman composition and why couldn't we all talk and write like we wanted to, anyway. Not thinking, too many Tanquerays past caring, I laughed and said his friend was a boor.

"Everyone bores you," Anthony exploded in that red-in-the-face way special to drunks. "You and your fucking English Department friends, always talking about books and movies like you were Rex Reed or something."

The Tanquerays were beginning to do their dirty work, because instead of remaining quiet or placating him, I snapped back. Maybe it was the Rex Reed comparison that got me. "All you ever do is get high," I said, "or tight. You and your friends sit around and get wasted. And when you talk it's about what's on sale at Goldwater's or what restaurant's best for Sunday brunch."

Anthony had been staring straight out the windshield, both hands on the wheel. He never looked me in the eye when he talked, fighting or not. The closest he ever came was about the middle of my chest. I'd thought it was another form of politeness, a kind of Latin deference, not looking directly at the person you're addressing. Now I wondered if it wasn't fear, a way to avoid whatever my face would tell him, or maybe I wasn't important enough to gain his full attention.

"If I didn't fuck you so good, you wouldn't even be here," he said.

He was right. The heat his brown skin pressed into mine and the sparks that came from his coarse, glossy black hair when we fucked, all around my fingers as I rubbed and scratched his head in the dark. Only in bed did we connect.

So now there was nowhere to go. We couldn't go back and pretend he hadn't said it, and sex wouldn't be fun after that nugget of truth. But secretly I was glad, already I could scent the end approaching, new prowling, fresh meat. I laughed out loud at my image of myself as some kind of great cat out for the kill, forgetting for the moment that I was with someone; I was drunker than I had thought.

How Anthony interpreted this laugh I don't know, but he reached over and grabbed me, kissed me, strangling the rest of my glee in my throat. I never saw him after that. Well, a few times in bars. He was always with a new boyfriend, always a Mexican: small, delicate, and pretty—black eyes, black silky hair (feathered bangs, sprayed back) and a compact, round ass. My exact physical opposite, I couldn't help noticing. Cha-Cha Queens. Anthony had a stable of them, all cloned from the original, like a master negative yields multiple prints. He'd also gotten heavier, or maybe he'd always been heavy, like he'd said, and I'd never noticed.

I couldn't remember Anthony's body that well later on, but I could recall our last session in his Camaro, and how the next morning, I'd caught a glimpse of myself getting into the shower, the bruises on my throat like a spreading amethyst necklace, his teeth marks still visible, a parting gift to wear till it faded to flesh.

A few months later, when my nun phase was in full force and I was on the verge of having my head shaved and taking the veil, I met Jack, one of Anthony's "fucking English Department" types. I knew his wife, a small, sharp-featured woman, before I knew him, but I'd seen him in the halls. He had a loping gait that shifted his buns rather nicely when he'd stride by my classroom. I was attracted, assuming he'd made an "academic marriage," but at the time I was still lighting votive candles and whatnot, so I limited myself to smiles and lingering looks.

When Jack and I were placed in the same office the following fall semester, we became fast friends. Jack's wife had, for reasons I had all kinds of theories about, left him, and Anthony was with his Cha-Cha Queens. Jack was a handsome man, not exotic in any fashion, except for his lips, which were a shade too full for such a classically American face, the lower one a little pendulous.

He was tall and thin of the body type coaches call wiry. He had an open face, dark brown eyes, short chestnut hair, strong jawline, good teeth, broad shoulders—a reliably good-looking man, nothing spectacular. A thin version of Joel McCrea. And just like Joel before he turned to Westerns, he was charming.

Lunch was what came first. It was the sexiest lunch I ever had. Cheese enchiladas awash in tomato sauce and sour cream in the university dining hall, hundreds of students milling around us, bumping our table. Jack could look at you in a way that you knew that your every last zit, protruding nose hair, or crooked, yellow tooth had disappeared. You were in bloom and that's all there was to it.

I don't remember the conversation, although it's not important anyway. The looks—the way he'd glance up from his plate as if you'd just said one of the most original things he'd ever heard, the way the light brought out the blond at the crown of his head, and the gestures—how he held his hands, the fingers stretching towards each other, elbows on the table, as if he could encompass anything in the space between where the fingers would eventually interlace.

He WAS like that young Joel McCrea of the thirties—earnest, smart (but not effete), and good. He was good in that he couldn't be touched, couldn't be corrupted, couldn't really be swayed. And goodness is the greatest seducer of all. I was like, well, Miriam Hopkins, at times—bright, energetic, perhaps a bit more savvy, a little zanier, but ultimately deferring to the security his earthy goodness provided. And at other times, I was Claudette Colbert: sophisticated, witty, gently mocking and, unlike Miriam, not entirely American; a suggestion of Europe in my background, something slightly wicked but enjoyable. I would educate him. When I wonder back on the first time, the first lunch, I see my mistake; I should've been Randolph Scott in *Ride the High Country*, then we could've been two ex-lawmen, just friends too old and too western for complications to develop.

For months we were inseparable—had our lunch together, dinners, went out at night. People noticed and began coming to me on the sly, remarking how glad they were about Jack and me. They'd known he'd come out in time. In the beginning, I was careful to keep everything on a friendly basis; he was legally still a married man, and I didn't want to get into something that would be great but a dead end. But Jack was affectionate, he proved his friendship with hugs, massages, and, occasionally, a kiss. We lapsed into something beyond friendship; I'm not sure what; I don't think it has a name. But whatever it was, it stopped just short of sex.

For a while, I liked the fact that people thought we were a couple or coupled when we really weren't, not in the way they meant. Then somewhere, in the back of my head, the voices started. One went: "Stick with him. He'll come around, it'll be like nothing you've ever known." The other one, the one that refused to be turned off, was along the lines of: "Ditch this asshole before the first good-looking woman comes along and he runs. Let him tease some other fruitcake."

I believed that second voice but made myself trust the first. That summer was a terrible one in Tucson. It had started getting hot in April, climbing into the low 90s. By mid-June, it was 104, 106, 108, every day. The hours passed in a stupor of white heat. Jack and I would stay up all night, then sleep until one or two in the afternoon. He'd call about four, then we'd decide where we were going for dinner—green salads, stuffed avocados, and gazpacho all summer long.

At night, we'd go swimming at a friend's house we were caretaking. After, we'd walk around the city until two or three in the morning, the only time it was cool enough to do so, fending off stray dogs with rocks we kept in our pockets. By August I was anxious and cranky; school would be starting soon, and I felt if something didn't give now, it never would.

On Jack's thirtieth birthday, we went to the Tack Room, Tucson's only four-star restaurant, to celebrate. I had good wine, Montrachet, not too much, but certainly enough. Jack didn't have a drop. "Liquor has never touched my lips," he used to say, mock serious but with pride. Like every other night, we wound up at the pool. I was, to my happy surprise, deliriously, delightfully drunk. For the first time in weeks, the weight of the summer had lifted.

I was on my back in the water, our friend's house was in the desert, close to the foothills, so there was nothing to block my view of the forest of stars overhead, so thick they were crowding each other for room. With my head in the water so that only my eyes, nose and mouth were above it, I could blot out everything.

I turned my head and watched Jack haul himself out of the deep end. Naked in the moonlight, he glowed, brown and hairless, so smooth like chrome. You'd glide off him, I thought. The only hair on his body was a fringe above his cock. His cock was long, sort of fat, and I remember his balls were uneven—the left one rode higher than the right, and they moved, fighting for position, like pistons, when he walked. He smiled when I looked at him a little too long, a little too obviously.

Jack jumped back in and swam over to me. "You're sinking," he said.

He put his arm under my back, and I rested my head on his right shoulder. Under my cheek, his shoulder resembled nothing so much as a nice scoop of caramel custard. I put my tongue to his breastbone and closed my lips over a fold of flesh, pulling slightly for a moment.

I let go and swung my body upright, slowly so as not to alarm him, keeping my head on his shoulder. I felt him receding, more water between us, when I draped my right arm over his left shoulder, but I wouldn't let go. Our bodies touched, and I moved against him, my shoulders to his shoulders, my chest to his chest. I was standing on his toes in five feet of water. He didn't move really, but I felt his body turn inward, away from me. Finally, I raised my head and looked at his face. He wasn't looking at me but beyond me, over me, around me, every way but into my eyes.

I let my free arm travel down through the water till my hand found his cock and balls and cupped them together. He instantly drew back, grabbing for them himself. I don't know if he thought I was going to steal them or twist them off or what, but for a moment, he held himself, clasping his genitals to his stomach.

He looked at me then. "I've got to change the filter," he said and walked over to the steps in the shallow end.

The good-looking woman the second voice had foretold came along two weeks later when school started, a twenty-year-old blonde in Jack's Chaucer course. Paula, Jack and I became a threesome, perplexing everyone, until I bowed out. Jack couldn't understand what was wrong, why we didn't have such wonderful times like before. But at the end of our group dates, he went home with Paula, and I went home to my studio.

After spending months with him and him alone, I found that my other lives were practically dead. Friends were either pissed at me for having neglected them or simply forgot to include me anymore—I'd been gone too long.

That's why, on Halloween, I found myself in the front seat of Jack's old Peugeot, squeezed between his girlfriend and his wife while he drove. As ridiculous as this foursome sounds, I didn't want to stay home alone on All Hallow's Eve.

The back seat was filled with friends from the department. All around me was the swirl of heterosexual small talk. My deskmate's mother had found out her roommate, Pat, was really Patrick, not Patty. Another woman's sister was having a first child at thirty-nine. Is that all they have to worry about? was all I could think. Living together and late pregnancies. Didn't they read *Newsweek* with a pretty man dying of AIDS on the cover?

Already I was regretting my decision to come. The four of us in the front seat had the makings of a very bad novel—HIS WIFE, HIS MISTRESS, HIS BEST FRIEND! I could easily imagine the lurid orange cover. Except on the cover the car was red and it was a convertible. Imagining what the English Department party had in store for me, I slunk down in the seat and rested my knees on the dash.

At the party I managed to lose Jack, Paula, and Jack's wife.

I danced three straight Stevie Wonder songs with Bitsy, secretary to the Liberal Arts Dean. She was fifty, a grandmother with great legs who looked swell in a red-fringed flapper outfit that perfectly complemented my scarlet taffeta choir robe. I had bought it because it looked like something Burt Lancaster might have worn in *Elmer Gantry*, absurdly flamboyant but riveting.

I found a bush a safe distance from the house and took a leak. After, I watched the dancers on the patio. Paula had come as a tree, her long blond hair, which hung to her waist, was spread out on the papier-mache branches around her head to resemble Spanish moss.

"She's beautiful, isn't she?"

I didn't know if it was my own voice or someone else's. A hand on my shoulder. Jack had found me. I shrugged him off.

His half smile became a pout of sorts, the lower lip curling even farther down. He turned his head toward the dancers.

"I thought you liked her," he said after the song ended.

If there'd been a large rock within my reach, he would've been dead. "I like her fine," I said. "That's got nothing to do with it."

"Sorry," he replied. Then, still facing the patio, he touched my elbow and repeated, "Sorry."

"You can look at me when you talk," I shouted, startled at the shrill alien voice, wondering what ventriloquist was playing a trick on me. "I'm not a goddamn Medusa."

He looked, along with the twenty other people outside, but his face was blank. What he dreaded most, a scene, was occurring, and what's more, his friends—and Paula—were watching. But he stayed calm, stayed himself.

"You don't have to yell," he said.

I was so mad I couldn't think; it was glorious not to be able to think. I struck out with one arm and hit him in the chest, my right foot already behind his left heel; he tumbled backwards into the bush I'd pissed in. Not waiting to check the look on his face, I walked through the backyard gate and headed for home, my scarlet taffeta bell sleeves inflating on either side of me in the evening breeze.

Lately, I've been feeling needy again. Three months after Jack. I swear I don't believe it myself. But there's this line in a Bonnie Raitt song: "And when you need a lover, nothing else will do." And it's true. After a while, my lust wasn't satiated by repeated dates with Mrs. Thumb and her four skinny daughters, no matter how inventive my fantasies. Of course, the next line in the song is "And when you need love most, it turns its back on you." But when blood engorges your capillaries, you tend to forget. At least I do.

After years of bar cruising, I found that I literally couldn't do it anymore. I'd get within sight of a gay bar and feel like I was going to throw up, or if I was able to make it inside, I'd get viselike headaches from maintaining eye contact.

Cruising in your own car is more fun. When you're behind the wheel, all locked in, you're in control, subject only to the pressures of your own hormones, which may tend to blur your judgment. There's a stretch in South Tucson I particularly like between Sixth and Thirty-Ninth. On the weekends, if I'm not going to a show or to dinner, I sometimes find myself in the vicinity.

There's even a man, Luchi, I talk to. He always has the same corner staked out and nobody bothers him. He's a punk Chicano, wears a black 40s Zoot Suit, rayon shot with gold thread, with a white undershirt beneath the jacket, a gold cross around his neck, black pointy greaser boots on his feet. He makes me laugh; he always tells me I have too much class for this neighborhood and wants to know when I'm gonna let him drive my car.

I play my scene with him, and he plays along. Maybe he doesn't know where it comes from, but he's a quick learner, never drops his cues. It's 1958, and I'm Lana Turner, or Joan Crawford, or Hedy Lamarr, and I'm "mature," slightly less glamorous than I once was, and I need love. And I have money, which I've managed to hold on to from more sumptuous times, and I just may dole it out to a man who can degrade me in the right manner. He's not Jean-Paul or Joel, he's more like Jeff Chandler or Cliff Robertson, or worse even, George Nader in *The Female Animal*. Eventually, he'll love me, although he won't be able to resist the temptation to exploit me, and I won't be able to resist letting him.

Luchi usually gives me a few bucks and I go to a taco place a couple blocks up and get him food. He likes to eat on the hood of my car, says I'm good for business, a pretty white man with a big car, makes prospective clients think he's worth the dough. I do see a lot of fat old hens nervously cruising him while shooting me murderous glares. He gets a kick out of this, holds my hand through the window, and sings me little songs. "Feliz Navidad" mostly. I suspect he doesn't know Spanish any better than I do.

Luchi has a tendency to get horny, especially if business is slow. I'm not sure if it's the lack of money or what; I guess even hustlers need their release. He'll come very close to the window, take my hand, press it against his crotch so I can feel his cock pulsing through the thin material. He'll moan then, low.

"You like that, don't you?" he'll say.

I do, but I don't tell him. I smile or nod, but I never say anything.

Then he'll slip my hand down the front of his pants between his silk underwear and his flat stomach. "You like me," he'll say, "I can tell. When are you going to open the door?"

"Soon," I'll tell him, already beginning to ease my hand out. "Maybe tomorrow."

But I'm protecting my options this time around. Up goes the window. He smiles from the other side. He knows what this means. We never finish the scene, but we enjoy doing it over and over again. Who knows when the next offer's coming our way?

NOTHING EVER JUST DISAPPEARS

• SAM D'ALLESANDRO •

I DIDN'T KNOW exactly what he meant by "accessible." He said he liked people who were, because he wasn't. He said a lot of things that I didn't exactly understand, or that seemed to carry connotations other than those most obvious. Or then again maybe they didn't. And often I would have asked for more information, explanation . . . intent, if he had been someone else saying the same thing. I didn't want to know him as much as I wanted to be able to be around my image of him. I didn't want things to get too difficult. I wanted to continue to be uncertain about him for as long as possible—to sustain the way it is with meeting someone new before a more thorough understanding brings comfort into the relationship. I did not want comfort. I did want to be comfortable with not seeking comfort or predictability in him. I wanted to be challenged but not in pain. All of these thoughts came to me some weeks after our first meeting.

I met him at the cigarette store. We just started talking. He seemed aimless, but not confused; unhurried but not unscheduled—we went to the park to see the ducks. We talked and smoked, smoked and talked. In fact he talked to me more than most of my friends do. That attracted me. He was interested in me, and that interested me. Here's what I found out that afternoon: He was a painter. He was a waiter. He was thirty. It was enough to know. We talked about other things, observations, an irritating little girl that kept screaming and splashing her mother, the duck with one leg, the cherry trees. They were in bloom. He had a camera with him and took my picture. Later, on the street he told me he'd had a good time. I took his number, it started raining, and we both went home.

"Do you go out much?"

"Not much."

"Where do you go?"

"Nowhere special."

"Do you like to dance?"

"Yes, but I don't like the dance places."

"I know what you mean. Sometimes you have to forget your dislike of them so you can go and have a good time."

"I know what you mean."

"I like small things, that's where my pleasure comes from. The big things disappoint me but there is always something small to enjoy for a moment, to look to for keeping life pleasurable. I like these cigarettes. I like a beer. I like the park."

"Sure, but it sounds like you're afraid to make yourself vulnerable to disappointment, so you miss the big things—it could make your life flat. I understand what you mean, but I think it's a mistake."

"Maybe so but then I'm not committed to living correctly at the moment either. It's hard for me to think about wasting my life when the alternatives don't seem much less wasteful. The way I see it we're all just doing things anyway. I'm not sure I think it matters so much how they're done."

"I know what you mean. I think it does matter, but I'm not sure how. Your way is not bad. I do the same thing. We're the same."

"No we're not."

"Maybe you're right."

In his apartment I always became very relaxed. I didn't do a lot of thinking there. When I entered I stopped makings plans, worrying, noting the little disappointments and triumphs of the day. Sometimes I would walk around the rooms while he was shaving or when I was there alone and just look at things I had seen before. Nothing seemed to really have a permanent location. The things that were scattered looked good wherever they had fallen anyway: books (serious books), magazines (frivolous magazines), canvas, cups, ashtrays, cigarette boxes, shoes and pens and brushes and tablets—a generally more attractive class of scatter than I found at many places of similar disorganization. There was a big pile of empty film boxes in one corner. The living room had good light. The bedroom had curtains covered with layers of thick paint, so that they resembled something out of *The Flintstones* where all the furniture is made of stone, even something seemingly pliable, like curtains. It made the bedroom seem like a cave. Artists do lots of things like that.

In some ways being there was like taking a nap for me. It was a pleasant experience, even though elsewhere I would have been bored. It was not uncommon, at times, for us both to sit in silence—smoking, occasionally commenting on something but with no real importance on talking—as if just being in the same room was as fine a way of visiting as another. But of course it wasn't always this way.

When I was with him I did a lot of sliding through the environments I found myself in: slipping through the air, exploring without paying much attention to the subject, sitting as if waiting but without thought of for what. Something more than hanging out but less than participating. That's what I was doing, or not doing. That's what was happening to me. And because this happened around him, it all seemed interesting. Away from him I was more productive, stimulated and stimulating, both volatile and quick to laugh—I had always been so— but around him things changed. The air got thicker. It seemed like an effort to do anything quickly, so I didn't and liked not doing so. He was a drug: a nice, soft, furry tranquilizer. And all of this is what I needed.

One day something lousy happened to me. Here's how we talked about it:

s: I was anxious, now I'm nervous—I can't stop thinking about it . . .

J: Don't try so hard. Problems have a life of their own.

s: Yeah but I want to forget this so I can go on to something else. I have more important things to be obsessed with. OK, this is it, I'm completely putting it out of my head. Let's just forget about it . . .

J: OK. What do you want for dinner?

s: I mean, let's just not worry about it. It's no big deal. I've done it, I've been through it, I'm sick of it. Let's just not think about it.

J: Right.

s: I mean what can you say?—it's like so many things that happen: I didn't like it, I gave it a chance, now I still don't like it.

J: Sure . . .

s: It's now, it's modern, it's dead. I think I'm starting to let go of it.

J: Yeah. I mean, to me it's always like the way everything I thought I would want to do twice turned out to be more than enough once.

s: Right.

J: How can we always be cool when we live in fear? Everything, really, is coated to some extent with a layer of anxiety . . . and that's not always bad, but still . . .

s: Exactly. It's a given we tend to discount.

J: Yeah, you can't really work too much with that one . . .

s: You're right. OK, what should we have for dinner?

J: . . . you did it, you saw it, you're sick of it . . .

s: Right.

J: I mean, it was now, now it's dead so . . . you know . . .

s: Let it dissipate.

J: Right.

s: Right.

J: What's for dinner?

My God, we'd become symbiotic I thought to myself. It was a small shock. It was in conflict with the uncertainty I'd always valued in us. It had been a long time since I felt like I was floating. My tranquilizer was becoming more real, more multi-faceted, more demanding. I knew that would happen, it always happens but I can never quite tell the moment it begins. If I could, maybe I could head it off at the pass, keep things vague. But that didn't turn out to be what I wanted after all. Even vagueness has its limitations. I don't know if there was a moment when I decided to let go and fall into the relationship, or if I didn't notice when such a moment could have occurred because I was already falling. I've never been one to take responsibility for everything that happens to me, so that makes it hard to always know whether a decision is a conscious one or not. After all, there is such a thing as the tyranny of fate. There is a feeling of falling.

What happened in the middle and the end are what stand out for me. I guess the middle is what drops out of a lot of our memories. The end points often define what we remember of what happens between them. So I'm skipping most of the middle part. Let's just say things were fine. Some usual things happened, some unusual. That's normal. We weren't too interested in things being perfect and they weren't. We learned from each other. We were starting to have dreams together. Then everything changed.

When the time came I wasn't waiting for him to die. I didn't wait. I wasn't really able to think about what was happening. I didn't think. I was just there. I got used to the sight of the tubes that sucked at his arms like hungry little snakes, trying to put the life back in. And I got used to hearing my nice, soft, furry tranquilizer talked about like some kind of textbook experiment. It was sometimes hard to trust that I was awake, that what was happening was what was happening. When I went in to see him for the last time it didn't seem like a last anything. At least not at the time. Later those moments, what happened in them and what didn't, would always stand out.

I don't remember driving home. I unlocked the door and closed all the windows. I took a bath. I sat. I listened to the phone ring. I went to bed. It was day again and then it wasn't.

This happened several times. I was born, I died, and slowly the night would seep back in. Sometimes I'd reach out as if to touch his face in the dark so I'd know I wasn't alone.

Later I made the calls. I tried not to listen to the people on the other end. I'd already said all of the things anyone else could say. After a while I just dialed the numbers, said my lines, and hung up. "He had to go. He's gone. I'm sorry. Goodbye."

When it happens it's like the film broke in mid reel, you don't expect it and you're still expecting everything you were before. Everything in my life except me was suddenly different. Eventually that would make me different too, but it takes a while to catch up. Someone said the pain would go away, but I'm not sure that's where I want it to go. It's how I feel him most sharply. Without it, every move I make echoes because he's not here to absorb me. I don't like bouncing back at myself. A dead lover wants your soul, wants your life, and then your death too. And you give it, it's the only way to feel anything again. Take the death as a lover and sleep with it and eat it and purge it and suck it back in quick. And finally it's no event, it's nothing that happened, it's just you: an anger and a beauty that never really goes away. Not something you can wait out as it disappears, nothing ever really just disappears.

Everything's OK now. I'm not waiting for anything. I shave and comb my hair every morning. I look fine. Nothing about me looks different. I change the sheets. I do the dishes. I pay the bills. Just like before.

Everything's OK. I spelled out his name with trash on the beach, poured the gasoline and lit it up. Pretty, but he didn't come back.

I'm OK. I was thinking: we were fine—some usual things happened, some unusual. That's normal. I wonder if there was a moment when he decided to let go and fall into it, or if he didn't notice when such a moment could have occurred because he was already falling. We can't take the responsibility for everything that happens to us. After all, there is such a thing as the tyranny of fate. I had wanted to be comfortable with not seeking comfort. I had wanted to be challenged but not in pain. I guess a lot of things seem to carry connotations other than those most obvious.

I went to the grocery store and bought everything frozen. Except for the freezer the refrigerator's empty. So I've been keeping the film for his next project in there. It looks really clean with just the yellow and black boxes against the white.

DAVID'S CHARM

• BRUCE BOONE •

From Carmen, *a novel in progress*

FEET: I HAVE little snapshots in my head of myself bent over, slavering. Why would I want to restrain myself? The feet ordinary, not dainty. Dealing with eros, a person has stopped dealing with facts, long since.

EYES: Eyes a lovely calm blue, changing in the light of a particular background, wherever we are—Noe St., Golden Gate Park near the autumn chrysanthemums, it doesn't matter. What gratified me was the slightest hint of animal terror I saw there. Oh, I tell you! My daddy's eyes held all of heaven's masculinity—cerulean, they were. A well-meaning Jove. A bit of a bumbler.

LEGS: hot. Just hot. Sometimes we'd do "pushup" contests, take long runs in the park in the athletic glow of weekends, late afternoons, and I'd show my daddy I was, of the two of us, the better athlete. Daddy would show off his legs. Would I notice, winner of so many contests? I'd pretend not to—though he'd catch me out of the corner of his eye. Great, strong, "golden" thighs he had, born for tongue-worshipping, I used to think. Then later, when we got back, that's what they'd get, while I groaned. Light blond hair of leg outlined against late afternoon light in shadowed doorway while I made loud animal noises. But the calves good too, I thought—and the thought would lazily buzz like a fly—like Jonathan's are they?

COCK: With your cock in my mouth I'd invent strategies by the hour to debase myself, submit myself—in an agreement I made with myself, not you—to your higher power. While you resisted. The world outside changed, the seasons went by. Nothing changed. David, the creep, deliberately tormenting me, tantalizing, torturing with this one hope, desire to lead me on—"maybe I'll change, maybe I'll come in your mouth this one time, sweetie." Such was/is a cock's logic—a mind of its own as in the phrase, "he thinks with his cock"—which stirs desire in me still. Logic of love, unfolding like a peacock's train, a burst of light.

SOUL: Of course Bruce's daddy *had* one, didn't he? But sucking daddy, Bruce realized you can't have it both ways—and daddy became a bisexual stud, just so many pounds of meat on the hoof. I swear! I never thought of David's soul once—only my own, and I'd see it reflected in the admiration of David's eyes. My soul/David's body—our fair, gloomy agreement.

OTHER (except nose): I've forgotten them or maybe I don't want to talk about them anymore. To jerk off, I remember thighs, blue eyes, and a big fat dick in my mouth.

I guess daddy's gone to work now with his new white shirt on but of course Brucie realizes he'll not be gone for long cause he's gonna be back at the end of the day isn't he and uh huh such a nice surprise is it oh yes it is a nice surprise for Brucie flowers which he always liked so much and does while you are gone daddy I'm always a good boy you'll see I'm a good boy I've been making your favorite for you what daddy's boy knows daddy likes isn't it it's fried eel and drenched in tomato sauce doesn't that sound good and these cute little dim sums I got in Chinatown don't they look good they're made of haricot beans oh and for dessert daddy I know you'll love it a flan daddy a flan oh oh and now daddy is getting so happy he's patting my ass I think he's getting me ready for it I think daddy doesn't give a damn about the goddamn flan at all he's making me turn around while I stand at the stove with this stupid wife's kitchen apron on me frying up the eel while daddy the animal the brute the fuckin pig has got his hands all over around me patting my little ass good kneading and playing with it until my heart starts going faster, it's going faster and fluttering now my heart has leaped to my throat in terror I feel the terror of it oh daddy wants it from his boy uh huh daddy's gonna get it uh huh daddy's such a bisexual stud isn't he and his ex-girlfriend Margie is going to be so jealous when she finds out isn't she isn't. (faster and faster)

Then another time daddy gives *me* the daddy position—but it could only be for a little while, can it? (yes and no)

Sitting in the Guerrero St. kitchen, not the one on Noe St. I just described myself in—and there's this knock. Landlord, Rich wants to come in, OK, OK, Rich—though I make sure to show Rich lots of teeth, so he'll get the point he's intruding. I think he has snooping in mind. Can he look at the paint job on the bathroom floor he did a couple days ago? Push push push with my pushy middle class politeness and I've got Rich to the bathroom and back again to the door of my apartment before he can do anything (ANYTHING) about it. Bruce glows with modest self-assertive pride. Not bad, huh? David looks up at me open-mouthed. Working class David. He can't buh-*lieve* how these middle class people know how to boss everybody else around by using so-called politeness, language, to their own ends. It's astonishing, David feels. I've spun around and caught these emotions registered on his face and—thud!—there's a pit in my stomach as I see David transparent with admiration for me, envy for the ability to *compel* people by using language a certain way —the skills he's attributing to me. My dick gets hard. I want to turn him over my knee, paddle him hard—real hard—till he cries. Fuck him then and there. David, if you were here with me now, I'd be trying to get up inside you—doing everything I could to get your pants off. Alas!

Postscript: Later that night I remember fucking David's face. He's giving me head with so much energy and willingness to please and submission written across his face I lean over to kiss his forehead like a puppy's. I'm so moved I hardly manage to hold back a tear from forming—a single tear. To feed David's face is to be a poet, I decide—and I know that sometime in the future (who knows when) I'll write of this. To his credit and mine. (what I'm now doing)

Here's something else. The story of how we met. David, the working class activist, straight man for ten long years, now coming out as bi—or maybe, maybe gay SOMETIME—tells me he's gonna be a therapist. David—I protest—then you'll be middle class! You won't be *working class* anymore, I tell him fretfully, scarcely knowing myself whether I mean what I'm saying. David crossly reminds me of how we met.

We met at the baths. What was I looking for? It was undefined, because it was taking place in an orgy room. I was perplexed and frustrated, since I usually go for some detail or details in a person that suggest that person's history, something about them besides just the basic equipment. The visual's as important for me as the sense of touch—so I was wandering in this darkened orgy room seeing only shadows, unsatisfied with the only exchange values I could see. Let something happen! I don't want to have sex with just ANYONE, you know—so how about a clue?

Then I see a silhouette across the room, a nose. It has some character to it, it's a good one, I decide. And the man *behind* it— I continued—what would *he* be like, I wonder? I decided there could well be an interesting story behind that nose; since, as I always believed, for those who know how to read them rightly, noses can be the very map of the soul, and this particular nose strongly intimated the INTELLIGENCE and PERSONALITY of its interesting-looking owner. Go for it, Bruce, I tell myself, go for it!

The other men in towels part easily before me as I push my way across the orgy room to the man's side. With his eyes he gives me unmistakable permission, acceding to the liberties I've begun to take with him. Then I'm down on my knees, giving him a great blow job. But when I look up I don't seem to see any particular emotions registering. Why isn't the guy reacting? What more does he want anyway? I continue—and slowly, slowly he seems to relax, get into it more, enjoy it. That's OK, he's into it now and showing it and I decide that all's well that ends well. Now the handsome stranger seems totally at ease and happy. He reaches down and lifts me slowly to my feet, then starts to return the pleasure-giving attentions I've just showed him. I become a rose blooming—a cherry tree in spring with white blossoms, a young apple tree and supple brimming over with all the tingling sensations and pleasures you can imagine. I get hotter and hotter. I feel like I'm in a novel—aren't these the proverbial bells they talk about starting to go off and ring inside me now? Rockets they describe go off in the innermost parts of my sensitive inner ears, I'm THERE. WONDERFUL!—I think. This guy's got POSSIBILITIES—that, for sure.

Then we go find a place to be quiet, talk. Small world; it turns out we have a lot in common. So you know Fred Wasserman then? Well we're just roommates, David says, not lovers—but we live together. And then we talk about people from the old gay lib days, turns out David knows them all! We discuss theory next. David likes Guy Hocquenghem's—I prefer Mario Mieli but have an increasing partiality for David Fernbach. We talk about our pasts, his family of very "modest circumstances," mine not so. Futures—we'd both like to see money there, the question is, *how?* After a while David starts looking antsy. What's the matter? He says he'd like to see me again, but right now wants to go back to the orgy room and play some more. I think I probably reacted with some shortness. If we had as good a time as it seemed like, why doesn't he play with *me!* An odd person I decide, telling him—a transparent lie—it doesn't make any difference to me, since I gotta get home anyway, since I have to get to bed early, then get up early the next morning. He says he'll walk me to the door. At the last minute grabs an "introduction" card from the counter near the checkout window, writes briefly but furiously on the back of it, gives it to me with a kiss. I pocket it without looking at it, give him a friendly kiss, the attendant buzzes me through the closed door—and then I'm gone. The stars look great that night as I leave the bathhouse. They're all wispy and delicate, traceries, doilies for heavenly confections. If you have to decide one way or the other—I tell myself—never trust your emotions or you'll be sorry. You'll just get into worse trouble. Never trust them. Men are beasts.

Later: I'm looking at the card David gave me at the checkout window. It says, "21st St. Baths, 3244 21st St., San Francisco." It shows a drunken-looking street sign, cartooned, just above. One arm loops crazily one way and says 21st, the other says Barlett—and the two arms look like they're embracing (staggering?). On the back I read David's tentative, vulnerable handwriting. "We discussed ambition, Hocquenghem and I gave you a great blow job. David Miller 387-8454 (M.F.C.C.)." The initials stand for David's projected therapist credential—by implication, a middle-class berth in life, no?

The Princess phone has put on its Hula-Hoop, shaking itself, a Hawaiian lei, started to dance like a cartoon cutout. R-r-r-i-n-g, r-r-r-i-n-g! all festive like the illustrated brochure the phone company sends, price list—somewhere between Trimline and Touch-tone. 9:30 in the morning, too early, isn't it?

Hlo? Groggy with sleep. A philodendron at the end of the room telegraphing infectious enthusiasm and waving its leafy green arms.

Hi dear, I just got to work and don't have time to talk. I'm calling to invite you to a party tonite at my friend Naphtali's.

Ng ng ng and inarticulate glugging noises.

So you wanna? We'll get a chance to unwind a little know what I mean?

The glottal stops now indicate Bruce might be on the verge of a choking attack, hysterical fit.

Sweetie? So think it over sweetie and I'll call you again at the end of day OK?

The hysteria's now definitely set in.

Sweetie? There'll be lots of food, I'll call you again at the end of the day OK? . . . Hello? Anyone there? Dear?

3 Dreams

In the first I'm running up a heath, above me roll the ominous thunderclouds. I've got to reach . . . it. "It" turns out to be Northanger Abbey, on account of a conversation I've had

with Dodie about the vampire novel she's writing. As I reach
the door, I wheel around to face my pursuer, a famous ex-San
Franciscan who's into s/m. This person happens to be a lesbian
and she's in her full leathers. I know she intends to go for my
neck, but it's too late. The languor seizes me as she pins me
against the huge medieval oak door of the Abbey and I give up.
I can't fight this anymore. I've reached the end of my resources.
She starts to rub up against me and I can feel her cruel metal-
studded bracelets bruising my delicate flesh. Too late the realization dawns on me—this is what I'm made for, this is what I'm
born for. I groan, ineffectually resisting the pleasure I've started
to feel. I allow her to take her will.

Also: I'm at home at my family's house in Portland, Oregon.
It's late in the afternoon, since it gets dark early here in the
North country. So I turn on the lights in the bedroom I've had
since I was a child. My mother comes in quietly and just stands
there. For your punishment (but what was the fault?—I can't
remember) I'm going to have to *ground* you—and a little tremor
scurries down my spine. Brass gleams in the late afternoon twilight. I think, I *must* remember to get off my article for the *Poetics
Journal*. Is there a deadline? I can't recall if there is.

In another I'm visiting my friend Martin at his pied-a-terre
in the Silver Lake area, L.A. He's teaching a class in art criticism
there and has rented this cottage temporarily. The warm evening floods us. Outside, banana trees are spotlit, L.A. style,
wonderful yellow green against night. Where the traffic is down
below, the streetlights make a frivolous diamond necklace. We're
waiting for Martin's friend Tom to come by and take us to the
bars. Why isn't he *here* yet? I demand. We're horsing around,
then take off all our clothes so we won't be encumbered. It's
obvious where all this is leading to, I think—I'm going to get to
suck Martin's cock, why has it taken so long? But Martin suddenly changes the whole scenario. He spreads my legs and tells
me quite calmly he's going to fuck me. The proposal enrages
me. What about AIDS! I tell him indignantly. Martin is very
self-possessed. He remarks casually that I must be a very re-
pressed person if I let a few vague fears stand in the way of a
good fuck. I fall to the floor immediately and start a temper

tantrum—Martin isn't taking me seriously as a person, I'm just a sex object for him. "I'm *not* your little boy and you *can't* tell me what to do!"—I protest disingenuously, hot salt tears in my eyes. The L.A. light goes cool, as in Raymond Chandler. And suddenly I think, but really—why not? My eyes narrow to slits. I'm a hot little bitch. I give Martin my ass, maliciously.

I want to add a note about sex as power. During the whole time I was with him, David was still crazy for women. He couldn't get enough of them. One part wanted to be gay of course. The rest was obsessed with what David called pussy. When we went out walking and saw women and he'd say stuff like "Nice tits huh?" I felt hopelessly outclassed, outmaneuvered. I realize I should have said something sarcastic like, Nice for *you* don't you mean, David? But I didn't, and maybe this was part of our dynamic. I was getting trade, straight dick. Should I stop loving them because they're shits?

David used to tell me how he beat off to the pussy mags or how he'd meet some nice woman at work and sneak off with her, they'd do it in her car or maybe in one of the empty conference rooms. Big deal. Then one time he told me about going to the Sutro, a local bi bathhouse, men and women both. David really likes bathhouses. When he turned the corner, there was this big guy, barrel-chested and macho, standing there, legs akimbo, arms folded across his chest. A couple of demented-looking women were at the crotch, sucking and licking and carrying on all over him. The trio was the center of interest of a larger circle of men around them, watching what was going on, beating off, and looking like hicks who'd never seen anything like this. The big man demanded of the women more and more insistently—this is what you want isn't it? Huh? Isn't this what all women want huh? According to David's story this had got the watching men so hot their tongues were lolling out and they were jerking themselves off like mad. "So what were you doing, David," I ask him. David looks at me like I got a screw loose. "I was jerking off too, what do you think?"

You just can't tell what, if any, of our sexual systems are going to survive. That's what I say. On the one hand, who wants terrible things happening to women? Not me; I identify with them too much, it'd hardly be in my interests to allow for stuff like rape battering etc. One thing I do know is I want hot sex, and that for me presupposes a power imbalance. Maybe the future will figure a way to put all this together. I dream of hot sex. I want it. My life depends on it to be happy. For the rest, don't ask me. I don't know.

Here's a snapshot. David and me are trading stories, we're talking about the history of socialism like we often did. He tells me about his political work, the relatives he found later in life who'd been stalwarts in the old CP. We're little boys in the 3rd grade again—trading baseball cards. I tell David about this wonderful/terrible quote I found from Max Eastman, when he'd gotten back from some conference in the Soviet Union (this is all in the 1930s). He'd discovered "scientific socialism in the process of verification." We both have to laugh. Such generous hopes betrayed by such stupid language. But the fact that David could laugh at this and is laughing with me, and is one of the few people I know who knows all the levels of hope and disillusionment and then hope again that this laughter means for me, kindles hopeless desire in me. It makes me want to conclude every story of David I ever tell with just one conclusion. Seeing me grow pale with desire, David decides to seize this opportunity to treat me like a thing, an object, takes me defenseless and sticks his big dick down my throat till I choke on it. That's the fantasy. Like I told you earlier, if I could reduce David to so many pounds of meat on the hoof I'd do it.

Onward, but to where. The news is, they come and they go. I haven't heard from David for at least a year.

Last time we talked, he said he had a girlfriend. A *girl*friend, David? He was at this dance and told her, I want to be completely honest with you—looking straight into her eyes and holding the glance to show sincerity—so I'm gonna have to tell you I'm a gay man. But if David was expecting to *epater les bourgeois*, did he ever get a surprise. The woman looks back at him equally straightforwardly and says brashly—well, I'm a dyke! And apparently that was the beginning of a very happy relationship. They're going steady now. They both really like getting it on; and what makes it all the more exciting is that, since one is a gay man and the other is a gay woman, obviously they don't have to feel boxed in. You are who you are, and they're not heterosexual. All the fucking in the world won't make you who you aren't. When David tells me this, he slightly averts his eyes. I like that actually. And really, I like David a lot. Just the way he is. With that slight gleam of animal terror in his big blue eyes. Don't change, David.

THE MOST GOLDEN BULGARI

• FELICE PICANO •

From Men Who Loved Me, *a novel in progress*

No one has yet determined who can be loved and who cannot.
Old Yiddish Proverb

IF EVER IN the gloomiest moment of yet another broken affair I wonder if I was truly loved, I always stop and recall a certain Bulgari watch given to me by Djanko Travernicke.

For years, I'd forgotten the watch even existed. Then, in 1972, my apartment was burgled and the thief caught. Even more surprising, the watch reappeared ten minutes later, draped over the midnight blue sleeve of a big blond cop. "I figured it was yours," he said, "because of the F. before your name on your doorbell." He flipped the glittering object to its golden back which read:

> *Carissimo Felice*
> *Oro per L'Oro*
> *Mai domenticar—Djanko*

"What's it say?"

I translated: "Dearest Felice. Gold for the Golden One. Don't ever forget me. Djanko. That was his name," I added.

He looked me in the eyes and said right out. "My partner says that watch must ta' cost plenty!" On his lips, unsaid, fluttered the questions he wouldn't ask, that I wouldn't answer: Who was this Djanko, and how had I merited such an expensive gift?

"I should thank that burglar," I said, hoping to forestall his questions. "When I sell this, I'll have more money than I've had *all* year."

The next morning I went down to the Sixth Precinct to reclaim the watch. I did sell it, two days later, wearing my best suit and tie, using my copy of the precinct claim as an ownership i.d. It brought me several thousand dollars, although less than its value, and in fact got me through the rest of that year, including rent, food, and utilities. And, as the elderly Hasidic jeweler on Forty-seventh Street looked it over for flaws, I sighed and said, "It's 24 karat gold, throughout," remembering with a pang the day that Djanko put it around my wrist in that plush first floor lounge of the shop on the Via Condotti and whispered in my ear, "As I promised, no? The most golden Bulgari of them all!"

Djanko was not the handsomest, the sexiest, the most emotionally intense nor the most intellectually gifted of my lovers. He wasn't even the richest, despite his munificent gifts. He was my only European lover and the most sophisticated human being I'd ever encountered. Ten years my senior, Djanko was in the manly glow of his early thirties when I met him in 1966, but already as wise and loving as a centenarian. A Yugoslav from the mountains of Croatia, he'd moved to Rome in time for the movie-making boom at Cinecittà, and there had directed dozens of films from low budget science fiction to costume and muscle epics to "spaghetti westerns." He even managed to find the time, energy and money to shoot a few serious films in the Croatian language, starring some of his Rome-based ethnic colleagues. I later learned that he'd received a Golden Bear at the Berlin Film Festival.

Djanko never had the least illusion about art or love. The first time we separated, he kissed me in the front seat of his silver Maserati, overlooking the flats of the Ostia seaplane port at dawn, and said in his own brand of English, "One of us shall break the other's heart. If it must be so, I hope it is my heart.

You are too young." His prediction would come true, though he never actively did the least thing to make it happen. In truth, I would have had to be as perfect as Djanko thought I was to not have hurt him. But in the instant that policeman held out the watch I knew that while I hadn't thought of Djanko for years— so concerned with the petty madness of my own life—he had probably never ceased adoring me. His adoration was neither pure, nor idealistic, nor unneurotic, yet oddly enough for about a year I made him happy, and I'm sure if, as old men, we meet somewhere, he will agree that I was his finest lover.

Given the fact that Djanko's earnings in those mid-60s years were enormous (according to one Italian magazine), it made sense that I would be kept by him. There was always more than enough spending money left around for my jaunts and lunches out. Everything else was charged or else somehow or other paid for. In addition, Djanko periodically dragged me down the Via del Corso to buy me things. In and out of Ginori, Ferragamo, and Cerutti we would go, with him insisting that I dressed like a *Provo* when I should be dressing like a marquis. I would try on a silk shirt that I sort of liked yet not be certain of the color: Djanko would buy all six colors the shirt was made in—that way I would have a choice and no excuse not to get it—or three pairs of a particular kind of shoe, or a half dozen bathing suits, or three linen suits.

A modest if fine dresser himself, Djanko adored gold jewelry and would stop and stare at ridiculously expensive pieces in Bulgari's windows, while I tried to pull him away. He owned almost no gold himself—which I attributed to residual guilt over his having become a world-class capitalist, given his socialist upbringing. This he hotly denied and I came to another conclusion: Why should he wear anything to detract from that 24-karat head of hair.

But if Djanko didn't wear gold, he certainly insisted that I wear it. I spent hours in shops with him, fending off bracelets the size of manacles, rings thicker than my fingers, neck chains too lavish for a Byzantine empress. In the end, of course, he got his way.

How was it that I went from being a social worker living on

the Lower East Side of Manhattan to being a film director's lover
kept in a suite in the most exclusive hotel in Rome, hobnobbing
with aristocracy and movie stars? In retrospect, it appears to
have been utterly accidental. If any two people are to be thanked
they are my Department of Welfare co-worker Phil Koslow who
got me to Europe in the first place, and an Italian citizen whose
name I forget who smashed my motorcycle against a rock cliff
outside the Genoa city limits and thus made sure I would have
to take a train to Rome—the train on which I met a handsome
fellow named Orazio who worked for the Ministry of Finance
and who promised to meet me and show me around the city.

Those first days told me a great deal about Rome and why it
was as it was in those few years. My pensione overlooked the
Piazza della Repubblica; my windows in front, so I could sit
there an hour at a time looking down seven floors to the enormous train station or the National Museum or the Baths of Di-
coletian. It was a late sunny afternoon when I got off the train
from Genoa and ascended to my rented room. An hour later,
washed and cool, I noticed that the sunset rush hour traffic
appeared unusually congested in the piazza. It remained that
way for the next day and a half: the longest traffic jam I've ever
witnessed. I found it difficult to believe that it had required that
long to untangle mere traffic. Then I realized how Italian, how
specifically Roman, that madness was—like the unexpected, instant closing of museums and shops and restaurants and even
churches anywhere in the city, without rhythm or explication,
like the sudden drenching rainfalls which came out of cloudless
skies, like the incomprehensible system of streets and piazzas,
like the winding of the Tiber itself, and the decision where to
place bridges across its sluggish waters.

Still, I was free: free, impatient, bored and horny.

Orazio arrived and with him the expected brother—no, he
was a friend—only a shade less handsome, named 'Cesco, also a
worker in the Italian Treasury Department but with about sixteen more English words. Could Orazio have guessed my interest in him for what it was? Better still, had he found 'Cesco for me?

No. It turned out that both men were engaged. After many

months in Rome I would discover that every unmarried male over fifteen considered himself engaged and that even if he were, in fact even if he were married, this hardly meant that he wasn't open to a little hanky panky, hetero or homoerotic, depending upon your charm and generosity and his whim. At the time I was still untutored and the two of them seemed far more interested in their Camparis, and in the various women strolling by along the Via Veneto, or using narrow makeup mirrors to check their appearance in low-slung pearl-gray sports cars, or sitting in the abutting sidewalk restaurants—especially three females at a table separated from us by a large, noisy, four generation family. Even so, during a lull in my conversation with 'Cesco and Orazio I decidedly heard two of the three girls talking excitedly, saying in English, "I'm *certain* he is." To which the other replied, "No. No, he *can't* be."

Until the first one declared, "I'll *prove* it to you."

She wove around the family and came to sit right next to me: a short, pretty girl with light brown eyes so large they shone through all of her eyeshadow and lashes, a close cut "Italian boy" haircut, the palest pink lipstick. She wore a lacy long sleeve blouse that revealed as much as it hid, and skin-fitting shiny ebony slacks, all of which showed to great advantage her extraordinary physical development.

"You're not Italian, are you?" she asked. "I mean Italian Italian?"

The others at the table didn't know what she was talking about. I did.

"No, I'm American."

"See," she said to her table of friends, slowly, nasally, and I wasn't at all surprised by her next question: "From Noo Yawk, right?"

"Right."

She stood up to face her friends. "I *told* you!" she said in a loud stage whisper. Then to me, "I told them you were one of us. One of us, and American. Not that there aren't tons of Americans in Rome. But they're all tourists and other icky things. Hey!" to the other girls. "What are you waiting for? C'mon. C'mon!"

The girl she'd been arguing with earlier leaped up from her chair to join us. "Hi guys! Are you really from New York? Where? East Tenth Street? Where's Cicely? Oh, by the way, I'm Tina Ledger. That," pointing to our first visitor who was now back at their table trying to convince the reluctant third to join us, "that's Donna Slattery. And our friend," pointing to the svelte, ash blonde who had stood up and was allowing herself to be tugged over, "is Cicely Bowen. We're actresses."

If Donna was short and stacked and Cicely taller and slender and quite surpassingly Beacon Hill in her tweed tailored suit, then Tina was the Corn Belt personified, a flame-haired, curly headed Wisconsin farmerette, wearing yellow toreador slacks and a frilly paisley-patterned off-the-shoulder blouse I never expected to see outside of a Wyoming saloon.

Without a doubt, separately the three were the best-looking women in the area. Together they were a spectacle. At our table, befriending me, they were an event. My Roman companions were more than pleased by the sudden company: In response Orazio and 'Cesco were sweet, they were attentive, they bought us drinks and coffee and dessert and they sincerely wished they knew more English for the *"belle attrice Americane."*

I almost wished they did too. Primarily because once comfy, the three women treated me as though we'd known each other for months rather than for two minutes. On and on they chatted, Cicely remaining the coolest, but Tina and Donna going on as though they were home in Flatbush or Dubuque, flirting, outrageous, throwing their arms around my shoulder, feeding me dessert on a fork, slipping a hand inside my shirt (three buttons open to my sternum like all the young men in Italy) to play with a nipple, turning to whisper to me, "I've had Dago men up to here, but these two seem sweet."

And I still couldn't for the life of me figure how I was "one of us" as they kept saying. So when Donna and Tina got up to greet some pals at curbside in a super fantastic Ferrari, I looked at Cicely and in the style of our encounter so far, asked her point blank.

"You know," she responded offhandedly, "you're not *bouge*."

I decided this was slang for bourgeois. "How do you know?"

"Pre-cious, we can tell. You're off. Just like we are."

"Off?"

"Off. Daft, Daring. Dangerous. An artist or writer or laya-bout or . . . God, Donna," she suddenly tried to get the others' attention. "It's Angel! There in that awful Principessa's La-gonda. We've got to rescue him!"

She jumped up and the others joined her in being lifted over the restaurant fence. They dashed into the slow moving traffic on the Via Veneto, and stormed an enormous pre-World War II sedan, pulling out of the backseat a giant young muscle builder —so pale blond he might have been an albino Samson—clad only in a pair of yellow skivvies, obviously borrowed, far too small for him.

To shouts of *Putane!* from some female inside the car, the three girls hugged him, jumped all over him, then skipped over auto bumpers and had him lift them back into the restaurant.

Close up, Angel looked exactly like his name. He was smash-ingly good-looking, tanned to a fare-thee-well, and didn't seem to speak a word of Italian other than *ciao*.

"Well, howdy there," he drawled, sitting in a chair next to me which the girls finagled from another table. "These sweet thangs told me we wuz having a purty."

'Cesco and Orazio were nonplussed by the arrival of this most competitive apparition. My eyes almost popped out at the sight of his pinwheel periwinkle blue eyes, his astonishing ex-panse of flesh, pectorals like dinner plates, waist-sized biceps, tree trunk thighs upon which Tina and Donna perched, explain-ing that Angel was a movie actor—he'd been in three films which had opened in the past six months, with *dozens* of lines, and he was another "one of us."

They introduced me, Donna saying, "Isn't he cute, Angel? Couldn't you just eat him up?"

Angel reached around her back to deathgrip my neck in greeting. "Ain't these wimmin fine, huh? They're lak sistuhs to me since I came to Rome."

His arrival had not gone unnoticed. Several women from various tables came over, mostly middle aged and overweight and giggling shy, asking for autographs, which Angel provided, slapping one suddenly freed knee (it resounded like a side of beef) at his celebrity.

A uniformed chauffeur pushed the last of Angel's fans out of the way—evidently the abandoned Principessa's driver—and stood arrow straight, saying something in a low voice and barely restrained fury, to which Angel replied, "You tell her Princess-hood I'm all blown out, ya hear! Take me at least another hour or two to churn up some more stuff for her. Ya hear!" To which the chauffeur looked frigid with shock and homicidal mania, but merely snorted and stalked away. "Now where wuz we?" Angel asked, all innocence.

He ordered and gobbled down a series of rich desserts ("building up my strength—and my virile liquids") then promptly dozed off in his chair.

This relaxed Orazio and 'Cesco who'd been quietly discussing leaving. But though they remained, it was soon made clear to them in Tina's much accented and Cicely's superb Italian that the girls were not to be had—at least not that night—and that in fact they were off to a party, late even by Roman standards, at some Count or other's palazzo south of the city, near EUR, that fascist monstro-city Mussolini had never completed building. After a courteous period of time, the two men begged off and left, Orazio swearing up and down, complete with fraternal hugs and leers at the women, to call me the next day.

"Don't you leave too!" Donna warned. "You're coming with us to Contino Eddie's."

I wouldn't have dreamed of getting up. Partly because I liked them; partly because I didn't have to get up the following morning; partly because in his sudden sleep Angel had flung an enormous tanned arm across me, his giant hand landing precisely in my lap, under which my erection throbbed like a dangerously infarcted heart.

The girls talked on, shouting *ciaos* at friends, suddenly falling into instant whispered conclaves when someone important from *Cinecittà* arrived—"We live, breathe and sometimes even *work* there," Cicely confided. "Don't look left," Tina would quietly say to Donna, who of course couldn't resist looking and would reply breathlessly, "It's Piero"—or Mario or Enzo or Luchino or

Claude . . . In less than an hour I knew everything about Tina and Donna's Defoe-like fortunes in the Roman movie business over the past year and a half and, despite her reticence, a bit about Cicely's too. And as we kept drinking wine, I became so at ease with them I slurred out a slip of the tongue: I called them "Stollywood Harlots." Instead of being insulted, they loved it so much the name stuck for all four of them.

Angel reawakened as suddenly as he'd fallen asleep, looked around, promptly found a waiter and ordered a *zuppa Inglese* which he accompanied with a plateful of cookies and three cappuccinos. When he lifted his hand off my crotch, he shook it a bit, saying "Dang near burned it!" Before I could perish of mortification, he leaned over to me and whispered, "Boy, you'd best do something about that thang." He asked which of us had a car to get to Contino Eddie's.

None of us did, but Donna remembered a former boyfriend of some weeks before who worked in some executive capacity at the night desk of the nearby Excelsior Hotel, and talked the other girls into going with her to help convince him to loan his cap to them—an offer with so much acting and mischief potential, they couldn't resist.

As soon as they were gone, Angel paused in his destruction of a massive chunk of chocolate cake to say to me, "Now I wasn't kiddin' back there, boy. You ought to get into the jakes and whack that thang before it breaks through your trousers," his periwinkle eyes fluttering through naturally long lashes Sylvana Koscina would envy, a smile on his lips stained foamy white from the cappuccino.

"I think I could use the bathroom," I said flushed and flustered, attempting to gather together the remaining shreds of my dignity.

"Nuthin' to be 'shamed of," he said as I stumbled away. "Only natural."

When I managed my way through the tables into the restaurant proper, I promptly bumped into someone. Still embarrassed from the talk with Angel, I blushed and murmured *"Scusi."*

The man I'd knocked into stood back to let me by. The jacket over his shoulders, a la mode that season, made his shoulders even larger. A shock of straight straw-colored hair under an askew bone-white fedora was wetted or oiled so that every thick strand was visible. His forehead was high and wide, a single deep horizontal line creasing it suggested much thought and not a little suffering. Heavy brows and shaggy honey-hued eyebrows shadowed his Slavically angled sea-green eyes. A brush of wheaten mustache hid most of his top lip—the full lower one suggesting both—and cradled his short, asymetrically squashed prizefighter's nose. A cleft in his chin completed the perfect jawline.

"*Va!*" he said, in a mellifluous baritone. "*Prego,*" he added, gently, somewhat amused. I'd been so stunned by his golden looks I hadn't moved. "*Per piacere,*" he now insisted.

I finally got together enough sense to stumble toward the john; but once arrived at the door, I couldn't resist turning around to look at him again. He was stopped, talking to a vampirical-looking black model. What held me was how completely he filled some idealized portrait of The European Man I'd developed, without ever being fully aware of it. It had happened over the years from various foreign films I'd seen, from glossy, glamorous full-color ads in *The New Yorker* and *Esquire*, where men exactly like him stood aloofly, a slight smile on their faces, as someone held their polo pony or a mannequin stepped out of an expensive automobile. Despite the fact that I'd been in Europe a month, in Italy a week and had seen my share of good-looking men, not a single one had so utterly encapsulated this particular cosmopolitan persona. Without having spoken more than a few pleasantries with him, I knew he was cultured and kind, pensive and provocative, sensual and considerate, deeply intelligent and yet caring. In short, I arrived at a terrifying, exhilarating, Aristotelian recognition that he was devastatingly attractive to me: the first male who had been attractive to me in more than a decade. Then he noticed me staring at him and glanced from my face down to my crotch, which sent me quickly inside.

The Slavic god was gone when I got out. No, there he was, at a table not far from ours, sitting with the needle-thin model and a bald, fat man wearing an unseasonal knitted sweater and

Ray-Ban glasses, despite the fact that it was now past midnight. I looked at my heartthrob and he looked at me as I managed my way back to where Angel was once more snoring, rejoined by the girls. As I pulled up and sat down the Stollywood Harlots were chatting away. "Kit was right there in the Excelsior bar," Donna said. "He'll be here in a min. Who *are* you glaring at?" she demanded of me.

"He's glaring back," Donna said, angling to get a better look past other diners. "Now he's raising a glass of wine. Cis, isn't that . . ."

"Djanko the T," all three girls said at once and in a somewhat hushed tone.

"Who?" I asked. Like a fool, I'd also raised my glass to him. Maybe not like a fool, as he smiled and I saw a row of strong white teeth peeping out of that bushy mustache and those thick lips. I was erect again.

"Djanko Travernicke, *the* hottest director in Cinecittà!" Tina murmured. "Do you know him?" she asked suspiciously.

"I bumped into him."

"Angel, wake up!" Donna said, "Djanko the T is toasting our new pal."

Angel not only instantly woke up, he also stood up, then did a most amazing thing: raising his clenched fists, he began to ripple his muscles at Djanko. Up and down they bumped and thumped and rolled along his arms, chest, stomach and back, until I thought I would collapse from overstimulation.

Applause and shouts of *Bravo* greeted this display, and Djanko now raised his glass to all of us in a toast.

"I believe we got his attention," Cicely understated it.

Angel sat down again, smiling, and reached forward for more food.

Seconds later an insistent car horn turned out to be Kit, picking us up. Before we'd paid, gotten out from the mess of tables and onto the street, the fat man with dark glasses who'd been at Djanko's table managed to take Cicely aside and speak to her. I didn't hear what he said, but she replied in Italian numbers.

Kit turned out to be an Australian sheep heir, a playboy

who'd lived in Rome almost twenty years—"long after he was still new or cute," Donna confided—who seemed delighted to have our company in his flashy chrome and acid-green Buick convertible. Tina and Donna jumped in front. Angel, Cicely and I in back, and Kit revved away from the curb despite the slow, tight traffic, with much shouting from the girls and burning rubber from the rear tires.

Once we were on the road Kit took every curve as though he were driving in the *Mille Miglia*. This either tossed the beauteous Cicely into my arms, or more often threw me into Angel's huge outstretched curved arm, where I finally ensconced myself, Cicely's head in my lap so the wind wouldn't mess her hair. With each sharp turn, Angel would holler out a bloodcurdling "whoopie!" and hold me tighter. Contented as I was at that moment, I still couldn't stop thinking about the man in the restaurant. I was certain he was attracted to me if by no means as bowled over as I was by him. But how could I meet him? And what if once I did meet him, he turned out to be as densely heterosexual as Orazio?

At the huge barococo gates to the palazzo, we met others driving out again. The party was a drag, they told us in four languages, even Eddie had left to go to Ulrica's place in the Alban Hills.

"Where?" Kit asked.

"Follow us," one carful of revelers shouted.

During the ride, I fell asleep. Once we'd arrived (Cicely later told me) Donna and Tina thought I looked so "darling" they convinced Angel to carry me inside and put me into a small bedroom on the second floor of this seventeenth-century country villa, a palace built by a Pope for his Cardinal nephew and their mistresses. I must have napped about two or three hours. When I awakened, I wandered through rooms full of people, a rather disorganized, slowly-ending party. I found a bottle of cognac but no glasses and sipped from the bottle neck as I searched the large old chambers, looking for the people I'd come with. Outside one room I heard laughter, and the door opened to reveal Tina—quickly pulling up her paisley blouse—with two men. One of them turned out to be Contino Eddie, the other an

Austrian Olympics ski champion. They invited me in and offered me a pipeful of burning hashish. I smoked and left again when all three began to undress each other. Finally, in the library I spotted Cicely who took my arm, pointing us outside where an enormous flagstone terrazzo wound around the palace. The night sky was beginning to pale. It was still too early for birdsong.

We strolled silently past French doors ajar upon rooms with people sitting, talking, or sprawled sleeping in chairs and on beds. At one window-door I saw Angel flat on his stomach, snoring away, his yellow skivvies pulled down to his ankles, Kit fully clothed astride those giant calves, his hands separating those large, hairless buttocks, Kit's tongue about to dart into Angel's unsuspecting rectum. Casually, Cicely pulled a curtain, and murmured "I swear, that boy could sleep through an earthquake," and we sauntered on. We stopped where a double stairway broke the terrazzo's length of balustrade and descended to a tiny fountain where a travertine satyr was ravishing an alabaster nymph in graphic detail.

"Would you believe me if I said I was still a virgin?" Cicely asked pensively.

"Why would you say a thing like that?" I asked back.

She stared at me, then giggled. "Donna was right about you. Well then, would you believe me if I told you that I was a fat and hateful little girl. And that I want more than anything to be a famous actress just to spite all the people I grew up with back in Marblehead?"

"No. I think you were a beautiful little girl. Your burning ambition to be an actress is to prove to yourself that you're worthy of all the attention you got."

"You clever thing! That's exactly right! Now, your turn. Go on. What's your burning ambition?"

"I don't know. Sometimes I think it's writing. But first I have to live, I guess."

"You should write for the movies since you're here," she said.

"I couldn't possibly do that!"

"Well then," she temporized, "you should at least try your

hand at translations. You know they make scads of films here of all sorts, then sell them all over the world. You could help translate them into English. That's mostly what I do in Cinecittà, except of course for fending off lewd offers. I'm the only one of the three of us who works steadily, you know."

"Well, maybe. But I didn't come to Rome to work in the movies."

"Don't try to tell me you came to look at the Vatican and all that trash?"

"No." Then it just blurted out of me: "I came to fall in love."

She looked astonished then giggled, but instantly stopped herself. "Pre-cious! What a lovely idea. I'll help. Do you have a clue who it is?"

Now I hesitated. "Someone I met tonight."

"Please don't say it's me," she begged.

"No," I said, but didn't know how to say more. "I'm not sure, of course. But I think," I went on, checking her aurora-lighted face for reaction, "I think it may be that man in the restaurant. The director," I explained.

Both of her perfect eyebrows went up a bit. "So *that's* why the Pig wanted our telephone number. So Djanko could get hold of you!"

I thought that was rushing to conclusions and said so.

She shushed me. "Djanko is *perfection* for you, Precious. Rich, powerful, restless, temperamental, unfulfilled. I couldn't have chosen better for romance if I'd tried."

"Except," I had to say, "What if he's not . . . interested," I added lamely, not wanting to reveal myself as the *bouge* she thought I wasn't.

She seemed not to hear me. She went on to tell me I mustn't breathe a word about it to the other girls, who would mess it up trying to get jobs through me. "Leave it to me," Cicely concluded, rubbing my cheek ever so softly. "This *will* be fun!"

Not too many years later, under a different name, Cicely became quite famous as an actress. She made a dozen films, went on to some plum roles in West End theaters, even had a longish run in one Broadway play and was nominated for a Tony award.

Then she disappeared; married—I guess—to a young man from Marblehead, Mass., having proved to herself that she was indeed worthy of all the attention her regal looks had brought her. Of the three of them, only Cicely fulfilled her acting ambitions—if only for a decade. In fact, of all the young Americans at Cinema City I came to know, only she got what she wanted.

So, you can assume that such a small and easy thing as matchmaking would be a cinch for her.

I awakened on the floor of the girls' flat about noon, the phone ringing in that particularly insistent way of Italian telephones. I wondered if I could negotiate my way over Angel slouched next to me in a dead sleep. Cicely was already up, dressed in a little wraparound smock, her hair freshly shampooed and done up in a pink towel turban. She spoke into the phone, then shooed the other girls away until they'd retreated into the bedroom they shared and closed the door. She looked to where Angel and I were sprawled—him out of the yellow skivvies—and turned away, then began speaking again in a somewhat haughty tone I'd not heard from her before. After several minutes of exchange, her tone of voice softened considerably. When she turned into profile, I could see her smiling. Still smiling, she said, "*Si, si. Certo!*" and then hung up.

"All right you two," she said loudly. "Get up. I've got jobs for you."

Tina and Donna tumbled out of the bedroom doorway from where they'd remained, unsuccessfully trying to overhear the conversation.

"Not you two," Cicely said. "*Those* two."

"Oh, Cis! How could you?" the girls whined.

"I didn't do a thing. It was a foregone conclusion. I merely pretended I was their agent so the Pig wouldn't screw them too much. Wake up, Angel. Flexing time!"

Tina and Donna stormed off into the kitchen, a room separated from the rest of the flat (*eighth!* floor walk-up) by a long sky-lit corridor. Once there, they could be heard making fresh coffee and loud rude comments on American boys taking the bread out of American girls' mouths.

Angel was awakened enough to hear, and shouted, "Hell! I

gave you all eight hundred dollars worth of that there Monopoly money they paid me for my last movie, didn't I?"

Immediate apologies ensued all 'round, and kisses to make up. Sitting around the living room, we had a breakfast of coffee and day-old Italian bread smeared with apricot preserves. It was a most informal affair. Angel modestly pulled the sheets in which we'd slept up to his midsection, and when I tried to put on my clothing I was pushed back onto the floor, and so wore only my underwear. Tina and Donna wore bras and panties, their hair in curlers, and sat near us on the floor. Cicely had the only chair, poured coffee, jammed our bread and played mother.

Once we were all settled and fed, she quietly and effectively explained what she'd set up for us. As we all thought, Angel's impromptu exhibition of the night before had been noticed by the film director. Angel was to be screen tested for a small role in a Medieval historical film Djanko the T was in the middle of shooting. And if he worked out there, he would be tested for a much larger role—that of Hercules in the future *Jason and the Argonauts* production. This latter role was a co-starring one, third name down on the credits, with lots of action and not too many lines to learn.

"When you go there today," Cicely warned, "pick up something heavy in the room and swing it around. And Angel, wear a jockstrap, will you. Portions of your genitals have been seen in every screen test you've done in Rome."

Under Cicely's special recommendation, I was to be personally interviewed by Djanko for a position as dubbing translator.

"Whatever you *want* to do," she warned, "resist the impulse and keep to business. I've given him a complete rundown on you. All lies, of course. He thinks you're a Whitney or Rockefeller or something. I told him you're a brilliant writer and just trying your hand at this for what you may learn of the film business for a novel you're planning. He's prepared to treat you like the crown prince."

"But I don't even know if . . ." I began to protest.

"*I* know. He's willing to pay you _____ lire per hour (here she named some outlandish amount, which even when translated into dollars was a stiff tariff)."

"The real trick," Tina said, "is to *always* make them pay for it." She was eating the sesame seeds off a small rotund St. Anthony's roll, biting them off the hardened crust one at a time.

"It's true," Donna agreed sagely. "In fact, it's absolutely expected. In Rome if you get anything for nothing, you consider it worthless."

"Oh, come on," I protested.

"Ask anyone."

"I've never been paid," Angel said with dignity, "except for work."

"Pre-cious!" Tina laughed. "You arrived home this morning with a *sheaf* of lire *shoved* in your underwear." She reached for the skivvies and daintily holding them at a distance, shook them. Italian bills fluttered to the carpet.

"Well, I'll be . . . Where did that all come from?" Angel wondered.

Cicely and I exchanged glances but kept quiet. She took the bills and doled them out to us, tucking a few into her towel turban.

"Carfare," she said succinctly. Then to me, "In principle, the girls are right. However there are always exceptions. I don't for a second doubt that you'll continue to be your pre-cious discerning self and know which is which."

Angel stood up to go to the john. He reappeared wearing not the yellow shorts but a tiny pair of sheer black panties he'd obviously found hanging in the bathroom. It looked like a posing strap and fit him spectacularly.

Cicely groaned, "It's ruined!"

"Don't it look good?" Angel asked, turning all around in front of us. "Hell, this better than a nasty old jock, ain't it? Ain't it?"

What I had told Cicely about coming to Europe to fall in love was true, although I'd certainly never expected it to happen quite so quickly.

The past half-decade or so had been romantically sterile for me. I hadn't had a steady girlfriend since my junior year in college, when I stopped seeing Beverly because she was getting "too serious." For the following three years I watched, slightly on the sidelines, as my college friends went into a series of unbelievable contortions over their women. Alex would fight with Barbara, then arrive at my apartment sodden drunk and threaten for three hours to join the army instead of going to Stanford Law School. Matthew would break up with Christa, and actively attempt suicide when she announced her engagement to Kenny. Horrified yet fascinated, I observed all these goings-on—and wondered. I'd never once felt possessive, jealous, suicidally depressed, or furious enough to smash an apartment door over a girlfriend's words or actions. Something was clearly wrong with me.

I tried discussing the problem with Billy Lee, a sensible fair-skinned black co-worker who came from Springfield, Mass., and who shared with me an "interest" in eventually being a writer. It was Billy who logically if offhandedly suggested that I try out men. "Maybe," Billy said between ordering draft beers for us at Stanley's, our crowded Avenue B hangout bar, "just maybe, you'll discover you can only become emotionally involved with another guy!" Despite my distant memories of preteen sex with a neighborhood boy, I doubted if Billy Lee's solution was the right one. But I also thought I felt an attraction to some men, so I decided to give it a try.

In the following months I allowed myself to be picked up by men maybe a half dozen times. These brief encounters always began most promisingly, with both of us sexually aroused—that is, until we got undressed and into bed—at which point I suddenly became completely turned off. I wasn't nervous or frightened, I wasn't in the least bit concerned with what someone "might think." I was bored; or at least put off in some other inexplicable manner. I wouldn't take his cock in my mouth, would barely touch it, and the one time a man tried to fuck me it hurt so much I almost punched him out. A few times I let myself be sucked off—but even this wasn't always possible if I couldn't stay hard. In most cases, less than five minutes after we'd strolled in through the apartment door, I'd be up, dressing rapidly, mumbling asinine apologies, leaving some poor frustrated guy to wonder what he'd done wrong, how he'd turned me off, and why he would have to jerk off alone, again.

The sixth time it happened, I promised myself would be the last time. I'd been told both by close friends and by Beverly that I was cold and unfeeling, incapable of love. Fine. I'd accept that judgment. It wasn't the worst thing that could happen to me, was it? Anyway, I was still young. I had time. I could still fall in love. It happened when you least expected it. Happened to the most unexpected people. The right person would still come along. Not the right man, mind you, or the right woman, because by this time, despite my brave front, I was unconsciously so desperate that *anyone* would do, regardless of gender.

When I decided to give up my job at the Department of Welfare instead of being promoted to supervisor and to go to Europe, one of the items on my unwritten agenda had been "Fall in love." Even so, I hadn't expected it to happen.

Despite that, and given all of Cicely's buildup on the telephone, the first thing I did when I arrived at Djanko's apartment-office suite at the Hassler was to tell him

1. I didn't really want a job.

2. I wasn't a Whitney or Rockefeller—obvious I thought from my name—but merely a middle-class New Yorker.

3. Cicely wasn't my agent, but she was a wonderfully talented actress and surely he had some small part for her.

Djanko wore no hat inside, had no jacket slung over his shoulders. He did have on a sexy waist-pleated pair of white linen slacks, a royal blue polo shirt, and two-toned aerated wing-tip shoes.

At the time I thought he looked like a fashion plate from *Gentleman's Quarterly* on current International Style. Years later, I would be leafing through our family photograph albums and come upon photos of my father taken in the late thirties when he was still single, and I would groan, seeing him in a virtually identical outfit. Djanko spoke in a deep voice, in not terrible English: "Then that's why you came here?"

"Pretty much," I lied.

"You could have told me that on the telephone, no?"

"Yes."

He stood up from behind the desk and came over to where I sat in the office and to my complete astonishment, knelt down in front of me and took my hands in his own large, golden-haired hands. His perfectly combed hair glittered golden in the afternoon light, his eyes dancing green. "You came here, why? To make love?"

"Yes," I said, and immediately wondered that those words had come out of my mouth. *"Certo."*

"You have done this before? In New York?"

"Not really."

"Nor I too much. I was married to a woman. But a little bit, yes."

He kissed my hands lightly, looked up at me again, and I felt like a heroine in a Jane Austen novel receiving a marriage proposal.

"My father, in Jugo-slavia, belongs there to the Party. You know what I'm talking about? There he is a very serious Communist. All the time I was growing up, he would say to me 'Djanko, remember the Americans are your enemy.' At the same time, while I was a small child, he would read to me stories of the old Greeks, their legends and their myths—Hercules, Theseus, Andromeda, Perseus.

"But when I came here to Rome, everywhere I looked, I saw Americans. They were not devils, as my father told me. Yet . . . Yet . . . they were not ordinary people like the Italians, like the French people. No. Those girls, that boy Angel, and you, especially you, you are all to me like those people in the Greek legends my father told me. Some Italians make fun of you, call you the new conquerors of the world, despite yourselves. But even they wonder how it is that even the most innocent of you come among us as though . . . as though you *know* something."

"Know what?" I asked confused. He was getting it all wrong: he—the European—possessed all knowledge, all culture, not I the barbarian American.

"I can't say what. None of us know. That you are better maybe. That we are all small and old and ridiculous, maybe."

"I never thought that." He smelled faintly of cologne, an

odor more insidiously disturbing than any after-shave I'd ever inhaled; it inflamed me like an aphrodisiac.

"It's true!" Djanko said. "But what is most puzzling to us is that you want so very *little* from us, and we wreck our minds to wonder why that is."

"I want you," I said, boldly, waiting for him to stand up and laugh, tell me the charade was over, and I could go—fool that I was to dare aspire.

Instead, he continued to astonish me. "Caro. Since last night in the restaurant I am already yours," he said, thrillingly. Then we went into the bedroom and I understood what it was like to be with a member of my own sex whom I adored. Without a thought, without a jot of the awkwardness, distaste, or free-floating boredom of the months before, I did everything with Djanko that all those men had expected from me in New York. Loved it, and excited, panting, sweating, loved him.

That night after dinner (sent up to his rooms from a restaurant below) we made love again. During an interlude, Djanko said, "I spent all of last night trying to think who of you five were lovers with each other. Then I thought, 'Wait, Djanko. These are Americans. It won't do to think of them in the usual way.'"

"Well, you're right about that. We're all just friends."

"Tonight I fly to Cannes on business. I'll be back tomorrow afternoon. You'll stay here, of course, from tonight on."

Later, we were sitting in a Via Veneto cafe watching the Kessler Twins singing *"Danke Schoen"* on the Scopetone—a movie and jukebox duo that never successfully crossed the Atlantic—and Djanko told me more of his childhood as a Young Communist, one of twenty boys and girls in the local party division who'd gone off on a combination summer camp and history/geography jaunt to Dalmatia.

Djanko spoke of the basalt barrenness of those skyscraping rocky shelves, so cleanly broken they might have arisen out of the earth's restless mantle the day before. He told me about the storm-swept sunsets observed from what had once been an overdecorated Grand Hotel. Magyar Princes and Italian revolutionaries, the principal residents of the previous century, had preferred their bit of nature unpredictable and few experiences could equal a piano recital in the glass-enclosed conservatory, lightning crackling to punctuate someone's attempt at "Reminiscences of Norma."

In his eleventh summer, Djanko's group had stayed a week at a People's Summer Resort in a shell-shocked Romanesque abbey. Somewhere among the warren of tunnels and vaults was inlaid an icon of St. Stephen, a local patron, who, Djanko swore, looked like me—preordained me: "Greek, Italian, Spanish, Lebanese, *echt* Mediterranean." During one of the many organized activities, young Djanko had run off and hidden in the vault. Discovered, he had been slapped across the face by his leader and dragged back to the others and later on censured for dawdling so long in front of the icon-studded wall with its un-Leninist religious connotations.

Long after midnight, we drove out of the city, past the airport to the Ostia seaplane basin. There, Djanko told me one of us would hurt the other and that he hoped I would be the one who left first.

Coming so soon after eight hours of complete bliss, his statement was highly unnerving to me. "Why? Why even talk like that?" I asked. "It's so fatalistic. So negative."

"Why? Because I'm a European. What choice do I have?"

"Just get to and from Cannes safely, will you?" I demanded.

Once the seaplane had buzzed off over the Tyrrenian, I started up the Maserati's engine and left. Speeding back to Rome through a fog that shredded into mist and turned into a soft warm rain, I luxuriated in a new emotion compounded of jealousy, anxiety, longing, desire. I became angry, sad, terrified, hopeful, content again, all within seconds. Jesus, I remember thinking, this is *weird*.

"I count only the sunny hours" reads the inscription on a bronze sundial I'd come across in a chateau garden in the Loire Valley. Were I to tell of mine and Djanko's affair for the following months, it would be counting mostly sunny hours which are virtually alike and frankly more interesting to experience than to read about. So, I'll pass over the idyll. Yet in the midst of our newfound romantic and sexual happiness, we also had problems, larger and smaller, and conflicts, which at the time didn't seem at all irreconcilable. It was following what probably was our most outspoken argument that I came by that expensive Bulgari watch.

Djanko's housekeeper and cook, Mafalda, a squat barrel of a woman just past middle age, yet still black haired, had been with him since he'd been in Rome. That is to say, all through his early difficult days of living in a dingy flat in the Pincio—where she'd slept in a closet—right up to these palmy successful days in their seven-room Hassler suite, with hotel help to overlook for all the heavy work. That is to say, through Djanko's earliest love affairs with waitresses and actresses and film students through his two-year marriage to Jocelyn, an Anglo-Irish magazine writer, right up through the separation and divorce, to me.

At first, she assumed I was a toy, an affection of the merest moment. But as the days devolved into weeks, the weeks to months, and I was more in evidence than ever, Mafalda began to stare at me when she thought I wasn't noticing, as though wondering if she really had miscalculated and must now take me far more seriously—as seriously say, as his secretary Valentina, known as La Bernakovka, or his producer, known to all as the Pig, or as his friend and screenwriter, Jiri Bernakovka, one of the most persistently masochistic humans alive.

These three were to be found inside the Hassler suite at any time, day or night, whether Djanko was present or not. At first, I would be surprised to step out of the shower in the middle of the afternoon to encounter Jiri asleep on the bedroom chair, or come home from lunch with Djanko at Cinecittà to find the Pig on the phone in the office. After a while I became accustomed to them. Valentina, of course, had a key, and was, after all, working there, but Jiri especially seemed to be underfoot at the oddest times. On a late Sunday morning while Mafalda was off to Mass with her sister's family, Djanko and I would fuck and eat breakfast in bed and fuck again, then hear a timid scratching at the bedroom door, and in would creep Jiri with newspapers, wine and a smug look on his face. I'd be upset. Later on I would say to Djanko, "But he was out there all the while! All the while!" and Djanko would shush me and say, "Be kind to Jiri. He's a tragedy." But how could I be kind when I saw his pale blue eye through a crack of bedroom door as Djanko sucked me, or when I came home from shopping to find Jiri on the master bath floor, his head in our hamper, sniffing our underwear?

Djanko and Jiri had met about a decade before when they were film students in Budapest, studying under the great Russian director Kozintsev, on loan from Mosfilm. The two youths' shared interest in American popular movies had brought them together. In fact, of the two of them, it was Jiri and his deftly witty slices of Communist life on sixteen millimeter which had the greater success; Jiri who'd held the more promise. It was because of one such film that the two friends had gone to the Bratislava Film Festival, where Jiri had met Valentina who soon became his wife, and where his film won an honorable mention.

That day had been the apex of Jiri's life. While he'd been accepting homages, Djanko had been busily getting drunk with an Italian film distributor who'd promised to make him rich and famous. The man's promise turned out to be good. Less than a year later, Djanko was in Rome, assistant director to an aging Italian has-been. And Jiri, who was still in 'Pest making fifteen-minute fragile wonders, was now saddled with La Bernakovka's considerable clothing bills.

As soon as he was able to, Djanko sent for Jiri. The Berna-kovkas arrived in Rome just as the Italian Film Rennaissance was getting going. Jiri dreamed of making his own *Cabiria*, his own *Rocco and His Brothers*. Instead, he went onto Djanko's growing payroll, helping to write and direct films with names like *Theseus and the Cyclops*, *Messalina's Last Gladiator*, *Invasion from the Red Star* and *Bad Afternoon at the Broken Corral*, where his knowledge of the idiom of American films added to Djanko's already encyclopedic background, resulting in a chain of spectacularly re-created, often quite bad, movies.

La Bernakovka instantly assessed the situation and left Jiri's bed for Djanko's; then when it was clear he was only being friendly, and not a meal ticket, she leapt into the flabby arms of the Pig. By this time Jiri's incipient Peeping Tomism had fully developed—for if he couldn't possess his wife, it was just as well that his buddy was doing so. Yet when Valentina moved out, Jiri remained. Unable to watch his wife, he now peeped on his friend.

In vain did I attempt to convince them that all Djanko's lovers—myself included—were obviously mere props for their own unfulfilled affair. Jiri protested. Djanko's nose wrinkled in polite distaste, and he pointed out that Jiri was flaccid, pale, ugly, and balding, whereas I, I was a golden tan, firmly molded, trim, and "pretty as that young tailor in Battista Moroni's portrait."

If Jiri was so much fouler and more perverted than his inoffensive mien suggested, the gross Pig turned out to be a great deal healthier and nicer all around. His name was Bruno Tratano, and as a boy, he'd worked in film in every conceivable job —grip, gaffer, gofer—until his breakthrough making a documentary for Mussolini about the war against Haile Selassie. To his credit, the film was both good and useful as political propaganda. But the sight of pasta-chewing soldiers with machine guns leisurely mowing down hordes of spear-throwing natives had turned Tratano's stomach. As soon as the film was successfully screened, he left for Paris, then London, and finally to Brooklyn where he worked in the Navy Yard during the entire Second World War. Either despite of or because of his superb ethics, he was reinstated in the film business in his native land following the American occupation and was instrumental in getting some of the classic films of the time produced.

After I'd gotten over my own initial fear, repugnance and distrust of Tratano we talked one long afternoon on the set and afterward he called me "The Manhattan Kid" and would sometimes make me sit on his fat knee and would feed me sweets, talking in a garble of Bensonhurst and Calabrese that I more or less understood.

Despite all this largesse, I was soon bored and wanted to work. I'd seen enough aging courtesans of all genders in Rome by then to know I didn't want to be one of them. So, after weeks of nudging Djanko, I was allowed to translate scripts into English, with the considerable aid of a vast Mondadori Italian-

English dictionary: the work I'd ostensibly been interviewed for months before, the job which the Pig claimed I'd been doing all the while to get me a temporary work permit.

Watching British and American actors lip-synch my words onto audio tape as the film started and stopped every minute was both thrilling and profoundly embarrassing to me. While half of the films made by Tratano were dubbed into English to be sold overseas, few of them were ever shown in the United States. Instead, Hong Kong, Singapore, Bombay, Capetown and Sydney were all larger markets for *Creatures from Rigel IV* and *Silver Spurs* than were L.A. or New York. I had to find some sort of recognizable transliteration of the Italian dialogue (which itself had often been lifted directly—purportedly in homage—from John Ford's and Raoul Walsh's films) into an English which a Parsi or Aussie or Balinese might easily comprehend. Westerns were unstoppably the most problematic given the formulaic dialogue—"Get em up pardner"—but Sci Fi films and costume epics were often more malleable, especially the latter. I brought in all of my years of reading and gave these less than paper-thick film characters new words and phrases to speak which their historical counterparts wouldn't have gagged on. "Unusually literate," reported the film critic of a large Melbourne daily of my work, "One might almost call the language dubbed-in Marlovian." One might well call it Jonsonian, Shakespearian, Beaumontian and Fletcherian too: as I rifled English Lit. for rhythms and meters.

It was thankless work, but the Pig read (or more likely had Valentina read to him) reviews of the films as well as box-office takes, and he told Djanko that he believed I was now ready for on-screen work. This meant spending long, coffee-drenched afternoons before shooting began with Djanko and Jiri and the Pig going over endless revisions of screenplays they'd put together.

At first I was shy, but soon I began to ask questions no one had considered before: If common water really did kill the seventy-five foot rhubarblike Beta Centaurans, then wouldn't they have all melted in the first substantial sun shower, rather than having to be spectacularly spray hosed by our hero? The others would stare at me in horror and disgust, then the Pig would laugh—"You've *ruined* us!" And we'd start all over again. I called out the word *consistency* so often in these meetings, that Jiri mutteringly called me that, addressing me as Signor Consistency.

All this naturally swelled my young head a bit and led me to believe that I was more than a useful, I was a needed, part of their team. I now know this was what I've come to call *A MAJOR AVOIDABLE MISTAKE.* I didn't then, and it all fell down around my head with a film project that Djanko had been planning for years.

One Greek myth that Travernicke Senior had told and retold his son back in Croatia was that of Jason and the Argonauts. A later reading of Apollonius of Rhodes's second century B.C. *Argonautica* in college had confirmed Djanko's belief that this tale would make a great adventure film. Why, I'm not certain. It was loose, episodic; its love interest was spotty (Medea, but she came and went) and none of the adventures were terribly unique—perhaps Hercules' labors the most exciting and those were a longish digression in the epic anyway. Still, the idea of a group of heroes—including Castor and Pollux and Hercules—out in a boat cruising around struck some idealized Communist chord in young Djanko. He was determined to see it in full color, lavishly produced, with the best special effects that the studio's money could buy.

Because I soon knew of its background, and because the project seemed "in development" so long after Djanko and I had met and become lovers, I assumed it would never require my attentions. However, about eight months into our affair, as we lolled upon a sunstruck terrazzo at Ravenna, the Pig suddenly pulled out a script I didn't recognize (they were coded by jacket color for easy identification) and asked were we ready for a script session.

Jiri and Djanko were; they'd been at the script for years. I said, sure let's go, I would read it later.

"No," Tratano declared. "You'll read it now. We'll have a session tomorrow."

"What's wrong with the script?" Djanko asked.

"Who said there's anything wrong? There are four of us. All of us should know it."

"For consistency," Jiri said.

"That's right," the Pig agreed, "for consistency."

As soon as I could, I got away from them, drove Djanko's little Maserati roadster to a restaurant *sul' Mare* overlooking the parti-colored Adriatic, and for two hours drank wine and read the script.

It was a beautiful screenplay. It was full of Mediterranean light and nobility, the sweetness of Herodotus and the legendary quality of Homer, filled with the brisk spanking of an Aegean wind and the mysterious monstrousness of Thracian mountain clefts. These Argonauts weren't a pack of idiot teenage boys on a fishing trip; they were demigods driven to know their world in all its terror and wonder, to seek love and enmity, no matter the consequences—to seek knowledge for its own sake. The script was almost perfectly Hellenic and quite filmic.

That night with Djanko, as the floor-length lightweight muslin curtains fluttered a sea breeze into our bedroom, I told him how marvelous I thought the script was. I quoted Ulysses' lines about his final, fatal, 'til then unrecorded voyage from Dante's *Inferno*.

That convinced Djanko that I understood what he'd been aiming at in the script. But I'd also found a few small inconsistencies and typos, and we carefully corrected each copy of the script we could find.

"Ah! You see!" the Pig said triumphantly the following day in our first work session on the script. "Already we have more consistency." He'd spotted the revisions instantly.

In the next two months, the script was cut apart and put back together again. *Jason* became *Jason II* then *Jason IV* and *Jason X*. Meanwhile, preproduction began in earnest—sets were designed and built, costumes designed and stitched, locations sighted and checked, story boards laid out and relaid out to accommodate script changes. All in perfect order.

Angel and the girls now arrived to rehearse. He as Hercules,

Cicely as a statuesque blond Aphrodite, with Tina and Donna (one line apiece—my doing) as two of her accompanying Graces.

It was an unusually springlike early April day when principal shooting began on Jason. The first day's scenes were easy and fast and went down well. That night we all celebrated with champagne.

I'm still not sure what fatal impulse led me to pick up a copy of the script—*Jason XV* by this point—to reread it. Ennui perhaps, or a desire to be moved as I'd been when I'd first read it. But lift the script I did, and read it through. It was tighter of course, less episodic, the love story spread throughout most of the film now, and all of it less lavish of settings, costumes and special effects. But it was still quite grand. I had almost reached the end, when I came upon a short new scene which I didn't remember seeing in the last version—*Jason II? Jason IV?*—I'd read.

In this scene, the goddess Aphrodite, offended by the kidnapping of her favorite priestess Medea (now completely enthralled by Jason), not to mention the theft of the Golden Fleece from her temple in Colchis, demands a sacrifice from the ships' crew before allowing the Argonauts to arrive safely home. Aphrodite gets her wish from the council of the Gods and in the next scene set in her grotto on Cyprus, she spins herself into a tornado. Cut to a long shot of the Argo sailing along a still, moonlit sea, all of the crew sleeping on deck: with Hercules and Pylades, Castor and Pollux, and of course Jason and Medea entwined in each other's arms. Only the helmsman, Turnus, is awake. Suddenly the little silver tornado approaches the deck, spins around Turnus, gagging him into silence, and lifts him off deck. We see him drowning, then cut back to the Argo, where all are sleeping as before and where invisible hands now guide the ship. A final cut to Aphrodite's grotto: The tornado enters, slows down to become the goddess, who—satisfied—smiles.

I was appalled. The scene had been directly lifted from *The Aeneid*. Granted it was plagiarism, wasn't the entire story stolen from Apollonius and Hesiod in the first place? What bothered me was that the scene derived from a completely different sensibility altogether, too modern for this rather primitive tale. In Vergil, Turnus had become an exemplar of destiny, and of its absurdity: a sad grace note that a Roman stoic could appreciate for what it said about his turbulent age. In my mind, the tiny scene grew and grew, threatening to capsize the entire project.

Getting Djanko alone was impossible and when we went to bed that night he was so horny—as he always became when freshly into a new film project—that I was tickled into passion and kissed into forgetfulness. Indeed, I might have forgotten the scene completely. But at the next general business luncheon, held in the afternoon after morning filming had already taken place, Jiri spoke up.

"So, Signor Consistency," he began with unaccustomed effrontery, "we haven't heard any criticism of illogic from you in a while."

"Jiri," La Bernakovka warned. She looked ravishing as an Amazon that day and expected the obedience beauty ought to call forth.

"No, wait, Cara Valentina," the Pig spoke around a slab of bread soaked in olive oil he'd pushed into his mouth. "This is important. Have you read the final shooting script?"

All eyes were on me.

"I saw him reading it last night," Jiri said.

"I read it," I admitted.

"And it's perfect. *E vero?*" Jiri asked.

"Of course it's good." I turned to Djanko, "I really think it will be your best film."

He accepted that and went on reading the copy of *Corriere* he hadn't gotten to yet.

"Partly," Jiri said, "thanks to you. Your friend makes a splendid Aphrodite. You've noticed how much we're using her? We've even written a new scene especially for her," he went on, clearly baiting me. Two beats passed, then, he added, "You read all of it?"

"I said I read it."

"All of it?" he insisted. By now La Bernakovka had stopped fooling around with the spaghettini straps on her sundress, and the Pig was done swallowing. Both were surprised by the ordinarily obsequious Jiri's insistence. I felt I had to say something.

"Are you referring to the scene you stole from Vergil?"

Djanko looked up from the paper.

"Vergil, Caro?"

"The new little scene with Aphrodite and Turnus." To Jiri I said, "You might at least have changed his name so the plagiarism wasn't so obvious." Plagiarism is nothing new in film scripts, so the others weren't yet alerted that something was happening. But Jiri's face glowed as though I'd actually and not merely verbally slapped him.

"Still," he said, "it's a beautiful scene."

I knew I was out of my mind to be making a fuss over such a small point, one that I really didn't care about. But the fact that Jiri had misguidedly chosen to make a power play riled the hell out of me. Since the battleground was selected, I'd stand and fight there.

"It's fine." I said. "It's plagiarism. It's Vergil. It has no place in the script."

Jiri leaned over the table, savoring each sentence, avid for more punishment.

"And, since you absolutely must know, Jiri, it's *totally* inconsistent!"

Jiri could have undergone orgasm under the table for the sudden relief he showed at those words. He sat back, pleased and humiliated.

"It's not from Vergil, Caro," Djanko said, less gently than before. "We wrote it ourselves, Jiri and I. It was an inspiration, something to give an edge, a flavor of *tristesse* to their homecoming."

"It works exactly as you planned it," I admitted. "But I'm sorry, it's from Vergil's *Aeneid*."

"Where?"

"I don't know. One of the middle cantos. I haven't read it often enough to know exactly which canto and lines."

"So you could be wrong?"

"I'm not wrong. Look, let's drop it, huh?"

Djanko was up at the library bookshelves, searching. Now both La Bernakovka and I said, "Djanko, sit down. Forget it. It's not important."

But no, he continued searching, bellowed out for Mafalda, berated her for moving his books around (she'd arranged them by the color of their spines), then asked where his Vergil was. She shrugged and walked back to the kitchen.

"Help me look," Djanko pleaded. None of us would.

Finally the Pig said, "Djanko, don't doubt our *ouaglio*. We know he's always right on this sort of detail."

Djanko flung a look at Jiri—by now shrunken to the metaphorical size of a mouse in his chair with shamefaced secret glee —then Djanko glared at me.

"So," he said, "Signor Consistency. You don't think my script is any good. My film will be a gross failure!"

"I didn't say that."

"No. But you *think* it. Which is worse."

I stood up to leave the room and made it as far as the doorway from which I could see Mafalda down the corridor in the kitchen, at a great distance from the stove, where she stood stirring a pot with a long-handled wooden spoon, evidently listening. She darted out of sight.

Djanko grabbed my arm, stopping me. "The scene stays in," he shouted into my ear.

"Fine. I'm going to take a bath."

"It stays in," he growled at me.

"Do whatever you want, Djanko. It's your goddamned movie."

"Do you know *why* it stays in? Because it's beautiful. That's why."

"It may be beautiful, but it's not true. 'Truth is beauty, beauty truth.' " I quoted Keats' most mooted dictum at him.

"It's beautiful, therefore it *must be true!*"

"It's untrue and therefore it *cannot* be beautiful," I said, in small, flat, hard little words.

The color rose up his neck, chin, face rapidly. He let go of my arm and hauled off and slapped me so hard I fell against the bookcase with the impact. Stunned, I crumpled to my knees.

Valentina and the Pig leapt up from their chairs and grabbed Djanko before he could strike me again. Jiri remained ice quiet in his chair, whimpering just a little. Mafalda rushed into the room, took one look at me, helped me up, muttering *"Barbaro! Barbaro Slavo!* at Djanko and half carried me out of the room with amazing strength and dexterity into her bedroom where she found rosewater to mist on my face and spirits of ammonia for my nose.

Two minutes later, I stalked out of the Hassler suite. The others were in the library loudly arguing.

I didn't get back until almost a day later, but I doubt if a lover has ever had a better excuse for the old question "Where *were* you?"

Angry then sad, after I'd left the hotel I wandered around the city until I found myself in a piazza that I seemed to recognize—no wonder, the Stollywood Harlots lived nearby. It had been a few weeks since I'd seen them, and while Cicely was away in London, Tina and Donna were home and more than willing to commiserate with me about "those rotten European men" and to offer advice and cheering up. It was early evening when—following cocktails—we went off arm in arm to Ruggiero's, our favorite haunt on the Via Veneto, for dinner. Within an hour of being in their company I'd almost forgotten about Djanko and our problems.

Kit dropped by and said he knew of a party outside of Rome and we all hopped into his convertible to get there. By now I'd been to a score or more of these international jet-set shindigs and knew the people and the scenes. I was far more comfortable than I'd been wandering around Ulrica's villa. This party proved to be more boring than usual, but getting back home was a true adventure.

I left the party with Tina and Donna in the fire-engine red Triumph TR-3 Contino Eddie (in "Alex" for the weekend) had given Tina. We were all stuffed into the small front seat of the sportscar, all astonishingly high on vodka and hashish, which had been available in huge quantities during the party.

Tina drove wildly and badly. The Autostrada sobered her

up a bit and she began an animated conversation about their roles in Djanko's film, detailing how Djanko and I would make up later on. "No nookie," Donna declared, "until he apologizes publicly. In fact, I think we should *all* go on a nookie strike!" which somehow was hilarious beyond recounting and caused the Triumph to slither across two lanes at a time.

A minute later we were driving off the ramp, but it was a ramp for cars coming *up*. We just missed a car coming at us— horn blaring indignantly, the driver purple-faced with ire—and Tina shouted, "I've got to turn around or we'll be killed."

Going fifty miles an hour downhill on a curved ramp, Tina executed a U-turn. She'd raved about the Triumph's handling before and I guess she actually expected the car to succeed in this farfetched maneuver. In fact, we spun around neatly, then promptly stalled. Just in time for another car coming at us—and now behind us—to screech out of control to a stop, tapping our left rear bumper, and adding precisely enough thrust to propel the Triumph into and through the meshwork guardrail.

All three of us screamed going into the air and then screamed again as with a rude swoosh of branches we tore through the forest of trees on the side of the Autostrada. Lucky for us the Triumph had stalled or I don't know where we would have ended up. After some fifty yards or so we slammed neatly between the trunks of two stout trees which reverberated like elastic bands with an accompanying rustle of leaves and branches— one of which ripped off the TR-3's back plastic window.

We'd braced ourselves for the thump of stopping and so none of us were hurt when we did stop. We were wasted perhaps, shocked out of our highs unquestionably, but unhurt. We were also fifty feet up, the TR-3's front fenders stuck between two chestnut trees.

It took hours, several local farmers with ropes, much persuasion of Tina who was afraid of heights, melodramatic, tearful good-byes between the girls (in case one of them didn't make it), and a great deal of swearing and screaming whenever the car shifted under us, to get safely down. When all three of us were safe, the car slid almost vertically, cracking branches beneath its ton-and-a-half weight, until it stopped, its headlights still burning but pointing now at the sky through what was left of the tattered tree cover just as the police pulled up, whistling sirens and blue roof lights aglitter.

Ten minutes later, the reporters and *paparazzi* appeared and bribed the police to allow them to photograph Contino Eddie's sportscar wedged upright between two trees, its gleaming fenders illuminated by arclights.

Feted by the farmer family, snapped by the *paparazzi*, questioned by the reporters, written up in all the morning papers (and later in a weekly magazine), questioned more officially, if with ultra courtesy by the local police—after all we were miracles to be alive and Italians have a true respect for the Hand of Destiny—I arrived back at the Hassler at almost eleven in the morning, newspapers in hand to provide me with alibis.

Mafalda seemed to be out, probably at the Friday morning fish market, and at first I didn't see Djanko. I made myself a cup of coffee and walked through the suite, finally deciding that he'd gone to the studio. Only when I sat down to look at the photos of me and the girls and the TR-3 did I notice him.

Djanko was sitting on the little balcony off the living room, wearing a jacket against the still cool morning air, his head in his hands. I'd never seen a more forlorn human being.

He greeted me as though I were a ghost: utter disbelief, then with wan smiles, and finally a big hug and mumbling into my shoulder. I dragged him inside and tried to show him the newspapers. They didn't seem to register upon him, and I realized that he'd reverted to Croatian in his speech and so probably made little sense of the Italian printed words.

"Don't you even want to know where I've been?"

"When you walked out," he finally managed to say in English," Bruno said to me, 'Idiot! Italians you slap, they swear a vendetta. Slavs you slap, they start a revolution. Americans you slap, either they kill you on the spot or they go away forever. It's a big country, America. Every day the newspapers there tell about men who wake up one morning and instead of going to work, they go away forever. They go west, all of them, to Wyoming, to Nevada and are never heard from again.' I thought that you'd gone away to Nevada forever," Djanko added, making the name sound as exotic as Katmandu.

"Without my passport? My visa?"

"You could always get new ones."

"It almost seems like you wanted me to leave."

"No, no, never." He placed his head under my hand, as if I were to give him benediction, and while there he mumblingly promised never to strike me again.

I extracted a few other promises from him—among them a trip to the Dalmation coast of Yugoslavia he'd always talked about once the new film was in the can. So we made up, and despite Mafalda's scandalization, we went to bed for the next three hours, letting her answer the phone and listen at the door. Where the Pig or Jiri or La Bernakovka had disappeared to I never discovered, though they returned after the weekend in full force. When Djanko and I finally did decide to get up that Friday afternoon, I turned from pulling up my trousers to see him still on the bed looking at me not as a fond lover three feet away but as though I'd just returned from a lengthy vista of plains and Rockies.

When he read the papers, Djanko was angry and thrilled and fearful, all too late for my safety. "How close it came to being true," he mused.

Naturally he promised to take the disputed scene out of the script. I tried to get him to agree to write a new scene in place of the one cribbed from Vergil which would contain more lines for the girls, but he shushed me: the radio was on, playing a tenor aria of great mellifluousness and poignancy. We listened to it rapt, almost afraid to release our breath until it was over. The announcer identified the singer as Fritz Wunderlich whom I'd never heard of. The aria was from Ambroise Thomas' *Mignon*, and was titled simply "Adieu Mignon" (or in his German rendition, "Leb Wohl Mignon").

"I wish he'd play it again," I said. And as though he'd heard me, the announcer did: Djanko and I moved into a silent, immobile embrace to listen.

Later on, I joked about the incident, saying, "I've never even been to Ne-va-da."

Our argument never came up among the others. But on Monday morning, when we were all gathered for lunch at the studio, Djanko pointed to my watch. "Look Jiri, Valentina, Bruno, all. Lovely, no?"

The day after my return, Djanko had insisted upon buying me the ridiculously expensive gold watch. The clerk at Bulgari had opened up the back to show us how every gear and cog and wheel inside was either a gold alloy or pure gold.

I've mentioned before how much gold Djanko had already foisted on me. My keys to our suite at the Hassler Hotel had been put on a golden keyring; he had Ginori take all the brass fittings off the forest-green Gladstone weekender I'd picked out and had them replaced with gold. I had to have *one* gold ring, he insisted (I didn't even wear a school ring), and he found a slender ancient white-gold one I couldn't be too offended by. What, I owned no watch? I'd never be on time: I must have a watch. Soon watches in all sizes and shapes—from vest pocket pointers to standard wristwear—had filled my little leather visa kit. My cigarettes were always getting broken, so I had to have a metal cigarette case—gold again. I was always losing my Zippo lighters, always asking for a match, so naturally I had to have one, then two, then six, gold lighters. And a gold-plated fountain pen, of course. Once he'd broken down my resistance, I was inundated in the stuff: I hadn't known how heavy, clanking, clunky and awkward all that gold could be. Finally, I put my foot down: I had nowhere to put it all, it was ruining my leather kit. Naturally Djanko had a solution to that too: He bought me a silver and gold jewelry case. The Stollywood Harlots had taken to calling me "Our own little Danae" every time they saw me with some new bauble, a not so subtle reference to the imprisoned mortal woman in Greek mythology wooed by Zeus who slipped into her bedroom window as a shower of gold.

With the Bulgari upon my wrist being admired by all, I began to realize that what I'd taken merely for a reconciliation gift was far more than that. Djanko bought me gold because the Pig bought Valentina gold and that was how one treated courtesans, no matter their gender or upbringing. The watch and all the other gifts he'd given me were still fetters attaching me to Djanko so I would not dare go off to Nevada. I also realized that the jewelry amounted to the same thing as Jiri sniffing my underwear—for what? the Elixir of Youth? the Holy Grail? some uniquely American alchemical secret? The Bulgari was supposed to be compensation, but could I ever be compensated for Djanko introducing me to strangers as his *fidanzato* (fiancé) *Americano*, and answering me in sweet desperation, "But Carissimo . . ." as though every statement was grounds for dispute. "Let him wait," he'd once told an assistant director when I'd appeared on time at the studio to drag him off to a business dinner he'd wanted to—said *he had to*—attend.

But although all these little betrayals and Djanko's need to chain me to him, to cover me in gold until I was too weighed down to breathe, could be kissed away temporarily, my principles were another matter.

It would take months for the poison of the Bulgari to fully seep into my system, months while *Jason* went before the cameras and occupied all of Djanko's time. If the script writing had gone easily enough, except for that one hitch, the shooting seemed to take forever. The two stars—an established Italian leading man for Jason and an up-and-coming starlet as Medea—turned out to have an almost chemical dislike of each other and held up production while their arguments were settled. In addition, the Jason became intensely jealous of Angel, who, as Hercules, earned applause on the set and whom everyone was sure would emerge from the film as a new Lex Barker. Once they'd filmed all they could in the studio, they went on location and everything went wrong. Storms at sea held up shooting. Locations selected for crucial outdoor scenes proved completely unsuitable and had to be altered. There were mishaps and labor strikes. Djanko was gone days, then weeks at a time. When he returned he went into the editing room and remained there, fighting with the editor and the Pig over every scene. He had La Bernakovka call to tell me not to hold dinner for him, then not to wait up for him at all. He would arrive home long after I'd gone to sleep, and would be vague, annoyed and anxious during breakfast—most of which he spent reading the film trade dailies or yelling into the telephone.

One day, La Bernakovka told me that although she hadn't yet seen it, nearly full edited rushes of *Argonautica*—as the film was now being called—were being shown to distributors, publicity and advertising people connected with the studio. I thought it would be a good idea if I went to a viewing where Djanko wouldn't be present, so that night I could tell him that I'd seen the film and encourage him to persist in his vision.

The film was good: grand and wild. Angel was a god as Hercules—his blond crew cut grown out, the tips of his hair, mustache, and beard frosted bronze like a living helmet. The Italian Jason wasn't half bad. All the Argonauts were scrumptious, especially the two Greek twins who played Castor and Pollux. Medea was a bit too Martha Graham for my taste, but Tina and Donna were fine in their small parts, and Cicely was magnificent, beautiful as the goddess Aphrodite.

Indeed, I got a chance to see more of Aphrodite than I'd expected: I saw her in the scene where Aphrodite turned into a whirlwind and drowned the Argo's helmsman. Djanko's one concession had been to change the doomed steersman's name from the Vergilian Turnus to the more Hesiodic Actaeon.

I remember sitting in the deep velvet upholstered chair of the studio screening room, watching the scene stolen from *The Aeneid* and thinking how curious it was that it no longer seemed as inappropriate as I'd been certain it would.

It wasn't until I was driving back to the Hassler that I realized that the screening manager had called the film we were viewing "as close to complete as we'll get short of the premiere." Djanko had never for a second dreamed of taking the scene out of the film, despite our argument, despite his fears that I would run away, despite our reconciliation, despite his promise.

I was shaking so badly, I had to pull the car into a sidestreet; and finally get out, walk around. I even stopped at a café to have a cup of espresso to calm down.

A week later I left Djanko and Rome. I've never been back.

The afternoon I unpacked my bags in my West Village apartment, I discovered the gold Bulgari watch folded inside my navy turtleneck sweater.

For three or four days I thought of wrapping up the watch and mailing it back to Djanko in Rome. Then I thought of all those jewelry boxes probably still sitting atop the dresser in the Hassler suite and of the unintentional slap he'd get receiving the watch. So I put it away, behind socks and underwear, with my passport and birth certificate and college diploma where I'd never see it. Without a qualm, I'd already sold the single gold cigarette lighter and case—the only other of Djanko's golden gifts I'd kept. But with the Bulgari's reappearance I was in a quandary; although I was desperate for cash and knew it would pay expenses long enough for me to complete the first novel I'd begun to write, I was sure that selling the watch would also be a symbolic act, finally cutting all ties with Djanko. Did I really want that?

I was wrong. Even now, having written about him, hoping I'd exorcised him, I still see Djanko Travernicke on a set, hunched down in his director's chair barely containing his fury and frustration as something impossibly wrong occurs; still see a pencil tapping his teeth at our script sessions, listening impatiently just before he bursts out "No. No. No!"; still see his golden shock of hair reflecting like an ancient Athenian's plumed helmet in the illumination of some luxurious Via del Corso shop and his sea-green eyes light up as a salesman places upon my neck or wrist or finger something expensive and glittering and gold.

BACKWARDS

• RICHARD HALL •

THE BEGINNINGS ARE always the hardest. Learning how to walk when your legs are weak, how to run when your breath comes short, how to go to the bathroom without soiling your clothes. Of course, there are people here at the Happy Village to help you. I don't always remember their names, so I make up my own. The Purple Blimp, who wheezes when she pushes my wheelchair up the ramp. The Angel, a young man who gives me my bath every morning and whose cheeks are as firm and round as nectarines. The Illustrated Man, whose tattoos change color according to the time of day. Mighty Mouse. The Piston.

Of course, the boredom is the worst part. Nothing happens. Sometimes I wheel myself out to the veranda to watch the sail-boats on the Bay. I try to imagine what it might be like to sit in the scuppers, one hand on the tiller, the canvas beating over-head, the gulls crying. Yes, what will it be like when I'm younger—forty, thirty, twenty? It will be a world of excitement I can hardly imagine now.

Last week Bradley brought me the recorder into which I'm dictating these remarks. He delivered it in his usual flat, hostile way. "Here, Morley, you can yap into the microphone and you won't have to drive everybody crazy." He deposited it on my lap, making his usual joke about Morley the Trombone. My last name is Trumbull and it's a joke I don't much appreciate. I scowl but he sits on the foot of my bed and pretends not to notice. Still, I can see the familiar expression on his face. Kind of tight and squinched up, as if he'd just swallowed a turd. I call it Bradley's Hating Look. Yes, hate is the dominant emotion between us, though I like to think it's more on his side than mine. And why shouldn't we hate each other? Two old men who know too much. Who know all the necessary truths, in fact. Trust no one. Resist dependency. Love is a fiction. Violence lurks everywhere.

And yet we go on—don't ask me why. Bradley returns each day—he's very spry, heredity, I guess—and sits on my bed. He tries, unsuccessfully, to disguise his squinched-up look and we discuss the future. Where we will live when I am discharged from the Happy Village. What kind of careers we are to have. How to manage the changes that lie ahead of us.

I have a vague idea of what I want to do, but I don't mention it to Bradley. Only trouble will come of that. It's something I have to hold inside, allow to unfold in solitude. He's too full of hate to let me have it happily.

It has to do with the theater. Yes, the stage. I have felt faint stirrings at night, when I lie in my bed and listen to the snores of my roommate, old Harbison. I want to make something beautiful of my life. I want to make it an emblem of a better world. And one night I had a vision that convinced me my choice was right. I saw myself in tights, magenta tights that showed off my handsome legs. (No director would ever have to put me in boots!) As I paced the stage, handsome as a god, embracing a whole series of heroines—Juliet, Mary Stuart, Saint Joan, Millamant—the audience roared with admiration and delight. Morley Trumbull, the handsomest pair of legs in show business!

How Bradley would scoff if he knew. ("It might help if you could act instead of showing off your calves.") But of course, his real emotion would be jealousy. Watching him as he sits on the foot of my bed, talking about companionship, I know that his deepest fear is that I might succeed where he fails. He needs my ailments, my inadequacies. They make him feel strong.

And yet, we go on. We both know there is no alternative. It will be Bradley and Morley for the foreseeable future, as if each of us were softened, molded, to receive the imprint of the other. And—to be honest—I need his weaknesses too. His impracticality, his impulsiveness, his ready anger. I want to be cool for both of us. And so we interlock at all levels, good and bad.

My discharge has come through! I am to leave next Tuesday. Bradley helped engineer it—he has found us a little house in Pacific Acres—and the authorities believe I can manage. For the first time since my arrival, this place seems attractive, almost appealing. I can wake up, eat, walk, use the potty, sleep—all without the slightest effort. Everything is done for me. Why must I try for more? What is the urge that makes me light out for the greater world?

The night before my departure I have a terrible dream, more hurtful than any I can remember. It was quite simple—merely a conversation with the grass. But it comes back to me, insisting, as I pack in the morning. "Listen," the tiny green spears whisper as they wave in a long sweep, "listen." And then a sigh runs along that emerald harp and they cry, "Every centimeter of new green costs us an agony beyond measure." The message shudders along my spine as I snap my bag: *The grass does not want to grow.*

By the time Bradley and I reach our new home, that message is forgotten, thank goodness. More important things come up—how we are to furnish this little house of weathered shakes, what rooms we will choose for this and that, who our neighbors are.

He has begun to question me about my plans too. Several times I almost let it out—my secret dream of a career onstage. But each time I catch myself. It will come in time but I want to be sure, first. I don't want Bradley destroying it from the very beginning.

I've chosen an attic room for myself. Bradley sleeps on the second floor. There's a skylight right over my bed, so I can see the clouds wandering—wisps of gauze that change color every hour. I love to lie flat and stare at them as they cross my little square of glass. I prefer that to reading or listening to the radio. Bradley, by the way, is a fierce reader. He buys several books a day—books on the most diverse, arcane subjects. I don't believe he'll get around to reading all of them for years.

We're a little awkward with each other. There seems to be so much to protect against—as if behind our sharp bones and scored flesh, contoured like relief maps, there were other, sharper dangers. We know too much. We were born that way. But sometimes, when the clouds above me are particularly soft, when I imagine I am in a glass-bottomed boat turned upside down on the sea of the sky, I wonder if we really know too much or if we merely know the wrong things.

Sometimes at night I can hear Bradley turn over in his bed just below me. His groans strike me as the saddest human sound there is—the charges leveled by the flesh against gravity or God. One night, after hearing him groan, I got up and went downstairs to look at him. Even though I tiptoed, the stairs gave off little squeaks of alarm, like an emperor's canaries. Something was pulling me down—something I hadn't felt in the six months I'd been in the house. I stood over his bed for a long time. I saw a grim little man, peeled down to bone, his hands balled into angry fists by his head. But even as I stood there, something trembled in me. I felt—what? Not desire, exactly, but the hint of it. A brief image of how that skin will smooth out, the muscles expand, the endoskeleton flex into postures of grace. Another night, during my secret visit, he woke up. Perhaps he heard the stirring, the trembling, in me. "Are you spying on me, Morley?" he hissed, sitting up suddenly, eyes aflame. I left, murmuring apologies. I was guilty, confused. What did I really have in mind? Suddenly it seemed better to stay in my attic bedroom, not to explore our future, not to change. *The grass does not want to grow.*

Bradley has slipped and broken a small bone in his ankle. He is immobilized in a cast for six weeks. This happened early in the second year of our life together. I had made my first attempt at a career—acting class with an excellent teacher downtown—and had to tell Bradley. He seemed to take it well, perhaps because he was launched on his own training as a librarian. It seemed both of us had found pursuits that satisfied us. But his fall, his broken bone, changed the status quo somewhat. We had remained as before—I in my attic scanning the sky, Bradley holed up in bed, staving off the world with tight fists and angry groans—but now I had to bestir myself. Carry food, help him to the bathroom, find new books and magazines.

One day, bringing him a washcloth, I suggest I wash his back for him. Our eyes meet—his a delicate hazel, the color of aspens in fall—and I feel a slight gap in the hatred between us. A hint that better times, better feelings, might lie ahead. It seemed that we might expand our list of necessary truths—not yet, but soon. It was only an instant, and we didn't talk about it, but as I washed his back (skin so white, tendons so long and fine), I thought that we did not have to keep faith with what we had learned so far.

But after drying him, sensing his withdrawal—almost a physical shrinking of his skin under my fingertips—I put away the thought. Men hate more steadily than they love, I reminded myself. Why should Bradley and I be any different? Besides, hatred is as strong a bond as love. I shouldn't complain, after all. Don't we have each other's company? Don't we have this little nest under the visiting clouds? What more can I expect?

My career has taken a turn for the better. John Hauser, director of the Neighborhood Thespis League, has offered me a nice part in an upcoming production. No magenta tights, alas, but a very nice scene with a dragon sister-in-law. John heard, or saw, something in my audition (I did a soliloquy from Richard II) that excited him enough to cast me. His instincts are very sound because *Another Language* couldn't be more different from Shakespeare. Absolutely plain, no fancy language, no breast-beating or melodramatics.

I give a lot of thought to breaking the news to Bradley. At last, after an especially delicious breakfast of sausage and French toast (his favorite), I let it drop casually. "John is thinking of casting me in *Another Language*." Not much reaction—an encouraging sign—and I continue. "A small part, not too taxing." A hypocritical sigh follows. "I guess I'll find out whether I have it or not."

I know perfectly well that I have it in spades, but I'm not about to announce it to Bradley. My speech floats around the sunlit kitchen and lands on the sugar bowl like a fly. He nods and continues reading the newspaper. A little gust of relief goes through me, compounded with disgust. Why do we circle each other like this, stepping around our pettiness and egotism? Why don't we take pride and pleasure in each other's efforts?

A useless thought. I choke it off by getting up and washing the dishes.

Bradley came to the opening. I willed him out of my mind, blocking the thought that he was in the audience, as I went into my big scene with the monstrous sister-in-law and was rewarded with the best hand of the evening. If I had thought about Bradley I'd never have been able to get out a word. Of course, I am instantly at the height of my powers.

He came to the green room afterwards. "You were good, Morley," he said in his flattest, most uninflected voice. I looked at him. We had both changed in the years we had been living together but his alterations were suddenly very visible. His head was straighter, prouder, on the column of his neck, his chest was fuller and thicker, his hands were free of the speckles of age. Middle age was settling on him with a massive grace. But did he mean it when he said I was good? I peer into his eyes. No information there. A wave of guilt sweeps over me—quite unwarranted, I know. Has my success diminished Bradley? Have I failed him in some way? He seems to be scrutinizing me angrily. Will I ever know what goes on behind those stern features, those eyes the color of fallen aspen leaves?

Two nights later I'm awakened suddenly. The moon is down. Bradley is standing over me. My first reaction is pleasure, but when I hear his voice I freeze. "Damn you, Morley, damn you." He seems to be speaking automatically, from some blind, dead part of himself. I whisper something reassuring, try to plead with him—as if I'd done something wrong!—but my words are puny against the wall of his anger. And then I see the gun, blue-black in the haze of the descended moon. "Bradley!" I scramble back, clutching the blankets as if they were armor. But it isn't physical fear that destroys me. No, it's the realization that we are both weapons pointed at each other, living affronts, avengers. I hear a click. The safety is released. A vast passivity seizes me. So this is the way it ends.

The next minute there's a strangled sob and the sound of

steel clattering. I see his form bending under the eaves as he moves off. He goes downstairs quickly. A moment later I retrieve the gun. It is heavy with hatred.

The next morning Bradley comes down with a raging fever. The doctor can't help, nor penicillin or mycin. He is in the grip of some vast, incoherent malady. For two weeks he lies on the couch in the living room. At last, pale and thin, he rallies.

Bradley's brain fever—that's what it was—seems to have cleared the air. No mention of his visit to the attic. I've dropped the gun in the Bay. And then, to my surprise, a month after recovering, he urges me to audition for another part, a bigger one. "You can do it, Morley, you're better than any of them." I can hardly believe my ears. Or my eyes. Because Bradley is looking at me with something like humor. He puts out his hand and rubs my arm. Not long, not hard, but enough so that a new necessary truth pops into my head: the true lover says yes. An absurd notion, but it comes again in expanded form: the true lover says yes over the noisiness of your own no.

Is our solitude, our shared loneliness, about to end? Is our hatred exhausted—a hatred bred in brittle bones and scored skins and disillusion like a grey sheet drawn over the face of the world? My arm still tingles where he rubbed me.

Bradley stands up suddenly, as if he too were perturbed by this new possibility. He says he's going out for a walk. I sit silently, my hand on my arm. I feel lost amid a sea of books. Our living room is awash in volumes, the detritus of Bradley's endless curiosity. And then, picking up one of them, I realize what has fed my attraction to Bradley. It is that he knows things. Knows why the sea is salt, what keeps an airplane up and why computers remember things. Knows the names of the stars and the roadside weeds and how all that naming started. The power, the sexiness of knowledge! The realization bursts through the surface of my mind and I am aware of a new lustfulness. Not the placid desire, tinged with melancholy, which has filled me until now but something fiercer, more dangerous. I imagine Bradley's body as it might look under my sky-window, crossed by shadows of clouds. The world, our customary world, seems to recede slightly. New bodies, new hopes.

But old habits don't die easily. After my next show, in which I get to wear tights, though of a somber black, I find Bradley's sullenness has returned. Maybe we are moving too fast. Several nights I sneak down to his room and stand over him, only to find him watching me through slitted eyes. What do we want? What do we expect? A midnight visit to his bed no longer brings an accusation of spying, thank heavens, but there is still fear.

And then one night, climbing back to my attic, I realize that we prefer the ill will, the discomfort, to newer and stranger feelings. To explore is to cast off, to be swept away. Who wouldn't cling to shore? And so Bradley's sullenness seems a signal of home, and I stop my midnight visits.

But our evenings have taken on new excitement. Bradley talks to me of scientific marvels and the wonders of the ancient world and the habits of birds. I forget where I am, in the delight of that learned recital. And then, after a few months, my seducible heart starts to buzz again and I feel my veins sizzle and bulge. Once again I know there is no escape—not for Bradley, not for me. We are imprinted on each other, each visage the one behind the many. Bradley has told me about Plato and I think that clever Greek might have been right about the Ideal, though I can never think about it too long or I get muddled. I never had a head for abstractions. Detail is what I love—the whorl of a petal, the brush of an eyelash, the gleam of a saucer. If I stare into space too long my head fills up with the emptiness of great ideas. Still, as Bradley expounds Plato and I watch his face, fuller now, burgeoning with a hint of youthfulness, it seems that there is a grand design, a single plan, and that Plato knew it before anyone else.

And then one night it happens. After a cast party for an Ibsen play. We'd been drinking but that wasn't the real reason. In point of fact, we were ready.

We got home after midnight, but instead of separating as usual we moved to the kitchen. I had just suggested a cup of tea when Bradley moved toward me. Suddenly he was hunkered down in front, his arms around my waist, his head on my lap. I touched his hair—no longer grey and crinkled but a soft chestnut glinting here and there with gold.

And then it came to me how little we had said over the years. Silence had enclosed us, broken now and then by some trivial remark. Nothing important seemed worth the bother of putting into words. What difference would they make? How could they possibly bridge the gap between us? But now, with Bradley's lustrous mop under my fingertips, I am possessed by the desire to talk, to tell him everything. How I love his nighttime lectures, how I am terrified of a certain emptiness, how the mystery of the world can be parsed, explained, solved. Why did I ever believe such sentences were useless?

And so I start to say the things I'd never bothered with before. Bradley raises his head and looks at me. He is, I know, seeing me anew. Seeing past my smooth skin and clear face into an interior which he did not know existed. His hazel eyes lose their focus. He is forgetful of self as he listens and I know we have passed some old barrier for good.

At last he puts his mouth to mine. His tongue is fierce against my lips. We pull back, breathing hard. "Let's go inside, Morley." He motions toward his bedroom, where I have passed so many midnights trying to read our future in the twists of his torso, his balled fists, his groans.

A moment later we're peeling off our clothes, blood pounding, eyes starting with new sights (when had he sprouted all that chest hair?) and a new necessary truth pops into my head: trust somebody. As we tumble onto the bed I say it out loud: trust somebody. He doesn't hear me and it doesn't matter.

We're new at this but there's a natural order that asserts itself. Why did God give us parts if not to use them? As we experiment, we go off into giggles. Who would have thought we could discover so many wonderful fits? Bodies are full of interlocking parts. At last the giggles subside and we help each other to the high plateau where, I am suddenly convinced, we will spend the rest of our lives.

As we settle down for sleep, neither wanting to leave the other for the night, I marvel at the fact that this happened only after so much waiting. Why had I believed in the end of things before I saw their beginning? Why had I thought we would be strangers forever when I had only to reach out and touch? Feeling Bradley's body nestled into mine I can only wonder at the partial vision which obscures each stage of life, at the truths which appear to be necessary but may only be convenient.

And so a new existence begins. Bradley has forgiven me—or decided to overlook—my professional success. At the same time he is having great success of his own. Some of his free lectures at the library—given to growing crowds of admirers—have attracted the attention of publishers. He is invited to write some books. An encyclopedia board offers him a chair. A TV crew comes to town; he will appear on a game show called Information Bowl.

The years seem to be perfectly balanced, at work and at home. Bradley has his elite, adoring public; I have good parts in important productions. In the season when I triumph triply as Macbeth, Trigorin and Ernest, he is invited to the White House for dinner.

Our happiness abroad overflows at home. We sleep together in the attic now, under the sky-window, where we scrutinize each other for hours, by lamplight and moonlight, noting details which give new pleasure: the hollow of a throat, the little valley where the thigh locks into the trunk, the drifting eddies of hair. There is nothing we cannot do together, no fear which cannot be shared, no joy which cannot be celebrated. The swirl of our blood matches the swirl of the world. We are often invited into homes just so people can observe us together.

And then, little by little, the excitement of my career begins to pall. Maybe the enthusiasm of starting out is gone. But one night I have a clear vision of a future filled with boredom. Why am I dressing up in other people's words and lives? Why do I need all this acclaim?

When I tell Bradley this he nods quickly, the tossing shake that signifies he has been thinking about the same thing. "Sometimes I think if I have to answer one more question . . ." he doesn't finish, just sits glumly. He is slimmer now, lighter. It occurs to me that we are mutating from hard-working grubs to butterflies, from husk to flower. Perhaps our job is merely to bloom.

One night, soon afterward, he tells me that the brain secretes a substance that makes us forget. This fluid, whose name I can't recall, saves us from the past, wipes the slate clean, so that we can only look ahead, plan, hope. When he says this I cast my mind back, trying to remember. What did I call that heavy black woman at the Happy Village who pushed me up the ramps in my wheelchair? What did I speak into my tape recorder? What was Bradley's nickname for me? Everything has faded. Another memory nudges at me, something about a gun. Did Bradley really hate me to the point of murder once?

I don't know who suggested the trip to Europe, but we both knew that the time had come for our honeymoon. A long trip— we plan to stay away for at least a year—means the end of our careers, but neither of us cares. We haven't really cared for several years. We have both begun to forget our skills, preferring to spend time dreaming or walking or running, our heads as empty as the sky. I have no idea now how to hold an audience, how to charm the people who give out the parts, how to walk quietly into a room and hold every eye. And Bradley doesn't seem to be sure of his facts anymore. Last week he got two of the pharaonic dynasties confused. He didn't even care. A few years ago he would have sat up all night rememorizing the list, from Hatshepsut to Ptolemy.

And so the day of our departure arrives. It's going to be a grand tour, a dazzling procession of palaces, ports, galleries. A journey of wonder and discovery, the climax of everything.

It is in Paris that we have our last and greatest quarrel, proof (as if we needed it) that we live more intensely in each other's company than anyplace else on earth.

It started in a restaurant, Le Chien Qui Fume, where a new friend, name of Chester Maynard, had joined us for dinner. Chester was staying at our hotel, a fleabag near the Sorbonne (we had reached the age of youthfulness and insolvency). He was a southern boy, with a poorly defined chin, squinty eyes, airbrushed hair. I thought of him as a walking pudding.

At one point during dinner, Chester made a pass at me. It wasn't unusual, of course—I had grown into a handsome young man—but for some reason Bradley took it very amiss. After Chester had drawled out his double entendre and squeezed my knee, Bradley picked up the carafe of wine and poured it down the front of his shirt. Chairs were overturned, waiters aroused, punches exchanged. We were made to pay for a meal we hadn't eaten, ushered to the door and told never to return.

Bradley, striding beside me through the leafy streets, refuses to speak, but I don't mind. In fact, I am full of a throttling joy. Bradley is jealous! I recall, with an effort, his earlier envies. This is very different. In the old days he'd been acting from an empty heart; this time his heart is full.

When we get back to the hotel we have a shouting match. The usual accusations—we have read about them in cheap novels, but now we let fly with a melodrama that is new to us. It seems that strangers are screaming at each other. A few minutes later we're on the floor, tearing, hurting, punishing. But it's a warm anger, a fury hiding love, and the inevitable happens. Before long we're grappling with passion on that filthy carpet, our supple bodies reflected in the giant *armoire à glace* alongside. Even as I maltreat Bradley's slender body, I adore it. Only once, near the end, am I aware of a paradox: how the body invites and then prevents true union. By the time we finish, the awareness is gone.

Bradley remains on his back. Loss and death are all around —in the grimy mirror, the tattered chairs, the wet spots on the dirty rug. We have plated the room with gold for a few minutes but now it's uglier than ever. Bradley's forearm is over his eyes and it takes me a few minutes to realize he is weeping.

"What's wrong?" He doesn't answer. His chest heaves. "Don't cry, Brad."

And then I know he's right to cry. Why not, after all? I roll over on my stomach, wondering if it hadn't been better when we were old and full of mistrust. Those were minor pains compared to these.

"Don't you see?" He sits up, his nose red, his eyes bloodshot. "Don't you see?"

I try to reassure him but without conviction. Our mutual need, our hopeless dependency, lies on us like a deformity. We are both cripples at heart. I see it as clearly as he does.

At last, exhausted, we burrow into the bed and sleep. When

I wake up, I discover that a new necessary truth has blown into my ears: the whole world is my home. The notion took up residence while I slept, the shining residue of our struggle on the floor.

It's hard breaking the news to Bradley. In fact, I wait until we get back to tell him he's been replaced by something larger, more general. He feels betrayed, of course—at first, anyway. It's only later, when his own changes come, that he accepts it.

I begin to look at children more closely, at the fierceness with which they feed on life, at their greed in eating, sleeping, speaking. Sometimes, watching an infant grasp a toy, I am struck by the simplicity of it all. One day I shall be as old as a baby.

Of course, there are times when I resist change, remembering my dream in the nursing home, clinging to Brad and the old comfortable love. But these resistances become fewer. Not long after returning from Europe I insist that he move downstairs, out of the attic room. I don't want to be interrupted in my progress. He doesn't mind. He too is exhausted by our years together. He wants out of that slavery as much as I.

As the years go by I see him less and less. Most of the time I'm outside, playing in the street with new friends. Sometimes, in the middle of scrimmage, or a game of hide-and-seek, I reflect on the long voyage now coming to an end. Its purpose, I see now, was only to bring me here, to this field, waiting to be tagged or raced or wrestled. It was for this I mastered all the changes of mind and spirit and gland. A shudder ripples through me as this discovery expands. I have passed through solitude and doubleness in order to merge into every particle around me —the trees, the dirt, the bricks of the school, the dresses of the girls, the flashing faces and quicksilver forms of my teammates. I am at the peak of existence, closer to birth than ever before.

And then, as more time goes by and I move forward into the rapid changes of boyhood, I marvel at the peculiar progress of my life. How brilliant is the plan that moved me from disillusion and disgust to the playgrounds of youth! How subtle the hand that steered me from wheelchairs to marriage to games! How terrible it would be the other way around. How, I wonder, could the human race ever handle such diminution, loss, decay?

And then, as my frame fattens and shrinks, as my fingernails shrivel into tiny half moons and my ears into the most delicate shells, as people appear who hold and rock and tickle me, I am filled with increasing joy. It won't be long now! Bradley has disappeared, but it doesn't matter. Nothing matters except the changes ahead, the voyage home, when I shall kick off my booties, wriggle out of diapers and pins, and pierce the membrane that separates me from my mother's womb.

At last the day comes. There is much excitement all around but I pay no attention. I do not need them; my course is charted. And then it begins. I enter and dissolve. The warm fluid surrounds me. I start to glide upstream, propelled by spasms and waves. Gradually I dissolve into my component parts, ovum and wriggle-tailed sperm, molecules, atoms, shudders of electricity. The warm core waits and I am deconceived, unbegotten, at the very moment that I marvel for the last time at the richness of life, at the beauty of the world. And then, on the edge of eternity, I am possessed by the last necessary truths—truths that have arrived too late to be of any use: Love is eternal. Death is an illusion. Trust everyone.

HARDHATS

• ETHAN MORDDEN •

As THE SON of a builder I spent high school spring vacations on various construction sites in and around New York. It was my first experience of absolutely impenetrable men, not only tough but emotionally invulnerable. Ironworkers—the men who lay a building's steel skeleton—are a class unto themselves. Passing someone while carrying a load of material, they don't say, "Excuse me," but "Get the fuck out of my way"—yet they say it in the tone Edmund White would use for "Excuse me." Challenged by their own kind, they can be vivacious; challenged by an alien, they are fast and lethal.

It's an intolerant class, racist, sexist, fascistic yet patriotic about a democracy; almost the only place to see the flag these days, besides outside federal agencies, is on the trucks serving construction sites. (They also mount a flag atop each building as the last girder is placed, as if they had climbed rather than built a mountain.) Ironworkers are not merely proletarians; they are proletarians without the barest internal contradictions, without ambition, pull, or PR. They are the cowboys of the city, skilled workers who are also vagabonds with nothing to lose. They have one of the toughest jobs in America: exhausting, permanently subject to layoff, and extremely dangerous. The raising of office towers routinely claims a life or two. At least bridgework is worse. The Whitestone Bridge was regarded as a life-sparing marvel because only thirty-five men were lost on it.

There is one major contradiction in the ironworker, his endless enthusiasm for street courtship. What other set of Don Juans ever went out so unromantically styled—casually groomed, tactlessly dressed, unimaginatively verbal? "Got a cookie for me, honey?" they will utter as a woman strolls by. Of course she ignores them; it wouldn't get you far in the Ramrod, either. Sometimes a group of them will clap and whistle for a ten, and I've seen women with a sporty sense of humor wave in acknowledgment. But there the rapport ends.

So why do they keep at it? Has one of them ever—in the entire history of architecture from Stonehenge to the present— made a single woman on the street? There are the occasional groupies, true: a few days ago I saw a young woman with the intense air of the bimbo about her waiting outside the site next to my apartment building just before quitting time with a camera in her hands. But this is the kind of woman these men have access to anyway, not least in the neighborhood bars where they cruise for a "hit." The ladies of fashion who freeze out these lunch-break inquiries are a race of person these men will never contact. After all, women like being met, not picked up, especially not on the street.

One of the workers next door eats his lunch sitting on the sidewalk in front of my building. Men he discounts or glares at; women he violates in a grin. The pretty ones get a hello. I was heading home from the grocery when I saw a smashing Bloomingdale's type treat his greeting to a look of such dread scorn that, flashed in Ty's, it would have sent the entire bar into the hospital with rejection breakdowns. But the ironworker keeps grinning as she storms on; "Have a nice day!" he urges. Emotionally invulnerable, I tell you. Yet are they really trying to pick these women up—sitting on the ground in a kind of visual metaphor of the plebeian, chomping on a sandwich while ladling out ten or twelve obscenities per sentence? This ironworker at my building is young, handsome, and clean-cut; but he's riffraff. Sex is class.

When I started working on my dad's sites, I saw these men

not as a social entity but as ethnicities and professions. There were Italians, Poles, Portuguese, and the Irish, each with a signature accent. There were carpenters, electricians, cement people, and the ironworkers themselves, the center of the business, either setters (who guide the girders into their moorings) or bolters (who fasten them). They were quiet around my brothers and me, not respectful but not unpleasant, either. We were, as they term beginners, "punks." Still, we were the boss's punks.

My older brother Jim fit in easily with them and my younger brother Andrew somewhat admired them; I found them unnervingly unpredictable. They were forever dropping their pants or socking each other. They'd ignore you all day from a distance of two feet, then suddenly come over and bellow a chorus of "Tie a Yellow Ribbon 'Round the Old Oak Tree" about two inches from your nose. Surpassingly uncultured, they were nimble conversationalists, each with his unique idioms, jokes, passwords. One might almost call them sociable but for their ferocious sense of kind, of belonging to something that by its very nature had to—but also by its simple willfulness wanted to—exclude everyone who wasn't of the brotherhood. Their sense of loyalty was astonishing—loyalty to their work, their friends, their people. Offend that loyalty and you confronted Major War.

Most of them were huge, the mesomorph physiques expanding with the labor over the years so that even fat wrecks sported gigantic muscles under the flab. Strangely, ironworkers don't throw their weight around, don't try to characterize themselves the way gay attitude hunks so often do. Ironworkers don't care whether you're impressed with them or not: they are what they are. *They're* impressed. And just when you think you've figured them out, they'll pull a twist on you. My dad built the Louisiana pavilion at the 1968 World's Fair, an evocation of "Bourbon Street," and one of the setting crew, a tall, silent Irish guy who drank literally from start to finish of every day, impressed me as being the meanest bastard on the site. "Hey, you," he said to me, on my first hour on the job, "what the *fuck* are you *doing*?" I had been sorting material so bizarre I don't think it has a name, and I said as much. He stared at my mouth for a moment, then said, "Fuck *you* and fuck your *college*." I avoided him as much as was possible. And it happened that one day, some weeks later, the wind blew a speck of dirt into my eye while I was on the roof, and before I could do anything about it, he had come over, pulled out the bandanna they all carry, and was cleaning out my eye with the most amazing tenderness. "Okay?" he asked. It was, now. "Thanks," I said. He nodded, went back to what he was doing, and never spoke to me again.

The younger ironworkers had a certain flash and drove dashing cars, but my dad warned us not to take them as role models; they spent their evenings getting drunk and came home to beat their wives when they came home at all.

"Is that what you want to be?" he asked us grimly.

"Yeah," said Andrew.

The superintendents on these various jobs were supposed to keep an eye on us lest we get into trouble, but they seemed to delight in posing us atrocious tasks, such as climbing rickety, forty-foot ladders on wild goose chases. Sometimes they'd give us a lift home, whereupon we'd be treated to an analysis of the social contours of the business: "Doze Italians, now, all dey wanna do is make fires. De niggers are lazy good-for-nothings." And so on. Once, on lunch break, Andrew told my dad about this. "That idiot," was my dad's comment. "Look," said Andrew, pointing to a group of Italians who had just made a pointless little fire so they could watch it go out.

Unlike the rest of us, Jim stayed with it. After a year of Rutgers he abandoned college forever and joined the ironworkers union, an unthinkable act for a building contractor's son, virtually a patricidal betrayal of class. Yet I doubt he could have gotten his union book without my dad's assistance; The building trade is harder to get into than a child-proof aspirin bottle. By the time I reached New York he was living in Manhattan. We ended up a few blocks from each other in the east fifties, and tentatively reconvened the relationship. My dad's "Is that what you want to be?" ran through my head when I first visited Jim's apartment, nothing you'd expect from a birthright member of the middle class. It was somehow blank and gaudy at once, rather like a pussy wagon with walls. Mae West, reincarnated as a blind lesbian, might have lived there. No, I'm giving it too much texture. It was the house of a man whose image of sensuality was a nude photograph of himself, his torso turned to the side to display a tattoo of two crossed swords. The photograph hung on his wall, and when I saw it I said, "If that thing on your arm is real, you'd better not let Mother see it." He pulled off his shirt, smiling. It was real.

"Girls like a breezy man, sport," he told me. No one else in my family talks like him.

I don't understand this craze for tattoos among working-class men. Permanently disfiguring oneself falls in with that hopeless flirting with inaccessible women and other self-delusory acts of the reckless straight. At least Jim's tattoo was high up on the arm, easily hidden even in a T-shirt; his pal Gene Caputo had a tattoo on each biceps, forearm, and thigh. Colored ones, no less —snakes and eagles and murder and paranoia. Socially, Gene had one topic, "layfuck." For the first three beers and two joints, he would expound on the attracting of "my woman." Four beers and another joint along, he would outline the various methods of layfucking them. By the eighteenth beer, he'd get into how to dispose of them. Then he'd pass out wherever he happened to be.

Plenty of ironworkers are happily familied, jovial, and intelligent. I even knew one who was—on the quiet—a Dickens buff. But it is not a settled life: the work wanders, the schedule is erratic, the weather can freeze you, boil you. It's not for anyone who has the chance to do something better. So ironworkers tend to be roughnecks—and in this Gene was the essential ironworker. He was a fabulously uninhibited slob. He was also one of the largest men I've known. The flow of beer bloated him a bit, but he had something like six shoulders and a chest that could cross the street. A good man to have on your side, if you've got to be in the war.

He was hard company, the sort who expresses his *joie de vivre* by putting headlocks on you. He also laced his endearments with threats of sexual attack, a typical ironworker anarchism.

When I asked him to stop mauling me, or do it more gently, he said, "I could screw your butt. Would that be gentle enough for you?" Of course, one doesn't take any of this literally. They like to shake up the taboos. Jim would say, "I don't know why I'm so exhausted," and Gene would reply "Because I was fucking you all night and now your fucking asshole's all sore." Imperturbable, Jim would observe, "Yeah, that might be it," and they'd proceed to other matters. After a number of these outbursts, I began to wonder if something genuine might be pouring out of Gene.

He was often at Jim's when I was, elaborating his theory of layfucking, and, out of loyalty to Jim, would attempt to draw me into his philosophy. Or perhaps it was just because I was there; perhaps he would have polled Eleanor Roosevelt for dos and don'ts of layfuck had she been in the room. He would be deep in the depiction of a pickup, acting out the parts, even filling in passersby who, he once said, were "huffy and out of date." Then, he told us, tensing, showing us how it felt, "My woman spots this briefcase dude and she is traveling. She is traveling away." Now he showed us Rodin's *The Thinker*. "But what she don't know is, see, those guys in suits don't spend money on my woman like an ironworker does! Am I wrong or what?"

"You're right, my man Gene," says Jim; and I'm trying to figure out where all this lingo comes from.

"What about you?" says Gene, to me.

"What about *what* me?" I respond, trying to look about six foot eight.

"What do you think of my woman dodging me like so?"

I took up my beer can, swirled the liquor thoughtfully, and offered, "I read that as an uncanny act on the part of my woman." Had I made it, passed? Jim was nodding, but Gene was just looking at me. I looked back.

His face a puzzle, Gene asked me, "So like tell us why you didn't join the union like Jimbo here."

"Jim already knows," I said, backpedaling.

"So me."

"The punk's a writer," Jim put in.

"What kind?" asked Gene, his brow clouding. "Novels, fiction, stories?"

"All of the above," I answered, for they already *were* all of the above.

Gene looked dire.

"Fuck me and fuck my college," I said. "Right?"

"How come you could have joined the union and instead you're being a writer?"

"Well," I said, "every family has its black sheep."

Gene looked over at Jim, digesting this comic flattery, and I believed I had scored the point. But there was one more test.

"So tell us," said Gene, "some of your unique procedures in the enticing of my woman."

Jim smiled. I hadn't told him I was gay, but brothers always know. Sometimes they care; not Jim. Gay neither irritated nor interested him. It was like water polo or raising sheep: someone else's fucking problem.

As it happens, I am bent toward the analytic. I love codes, theories, lists. So, despite our differences, I easily fell in with Gene's taxonomy, following—and sometimes leading—him into theoretical situations calling for the most finely honed expertise in layfucking. And I laid one concept in particular on him that struck vastly home: the wearing of shirts with a college insigne, I had noticed, encourages people to talk to you. "It's a mark of class," I concluded. "Especially if it's a snappy college."

Gene thought it over. "Girls like college, don't they?"

"They admire a college man."

"Yeah," said Gene, slowly. "I could be the fucking football hero."

Well, rougher men than Gene have attended school on jock scholarships. Jim remembered a Rutgers sweatshirt in some closet at my folks', and I retrieved it the next weekend. It was early spring, a nice wind up—excellent sweatshirt weather, and apparently Gene did score a social coup in his new accessory, though he had had to cut it up to fit into it. He didn't win any woman over to a date, but a few actually replied to his addresses; according to Jim the most popular remark was, "Did you *really* go to Rutgers?"

From then on, I was Gene's main man, after Jim, and he took to dropping in on me for confidence and advice. He called me "little brother." I put up with him, at first because I was trying to straighten out my standing in the family at that time and I thought it politic to tolerate Gene as a favor to Jim. After a while, however, I began to like Gene himself, for under the perversely insensitive behavior he had a rather touching sweetness, a Dostoyefskyan idiocy, maybe. Too, there was that amazing ironworker loyalty, something I've never encountered in members of the leadership classes, gay or straight. There was this as well: though his days were filled up with labor and his evenings with pub talk, he was a very lonely man. Jim and I were his only friends; the women he took to bed, I gathered, were whores of small quality. He disposed of them not because he was heartless but because there was nothing between him and them but a hit. One night he turned up at my place in his Rutgers shirt, drunk and sorrowful and inarticulate, but clearly heading toward something. The subject was love.

"When you got a buddy, man," he said. "Then you can show him how you feel about him, right? It's *radical*. Because when you really like a guy, and he trusts you, you *know* him . . . you know him right down to his cock, know him like a man. You get a buddy like that, you can do anything with him. *Anything*. You could ask him to lie down on his stomach because you're going to lock him up and ream his cherry out for him, and he'll do it. That's what love is. Loving your buddy." He gazed at me as if measuring my ability to understand what he was saying. "You hear me, little brother?"

I nodded.

"Now, your brother is really solid. That is a fucking solid guy, and there aren't many. You better know that. Right?"

"Right."

"Sure. Because if you don't know it I'll kick your butt in. Shit, he's solid. But he doesn't like to let a guy show him how he fucking feels. Know what I mean?"

"You're hurting my arm."

"I'll be good, little brother," he said, releasing me. "Because listen. This fucking city is filled with buddies. And they trust each other. Sure they do. But there comes a moment when you got to show your fucking buddy how you feel about him. You got to. There's no words. A guy just looks at his buddy, and he loves him. He *loves* him. Not just as a friend but as a man. He's got to show him, don't he? Put his arms around him, show his buddy. Am I wrong or what?"

"You're right."

"Say my name, too."

"Gene."

"Okay. I like to hear it. So, like all this time there's buddies together, and there's this one fucking moment, and they both feel it. They know it's true. It's fucking true. So one guy just takes his buddy and shows him how he fucking feels, whatever it fucking takes. That's how they know they're buddies." Finally he slowed down, took a deep breath, and shook his head. "I can't do that with Jimbo, little brother. Do you know what he's like?"

"I grew up with him."

"A rubber band. You can stretch it *just so far*, and then . . ." He pantomimed an explosion that almost blew me off the couch. "I just wish there was a place you could go and find a buddy. You know?"

A thought hit me.

"There is one, Gene."

"A buddy club, like."

"Listen, there is one!"

I had been going to the Eagle, and it occurred to me that what Gene needed and couldn't quite name was a man to take home. Or was I making the mistake of taking him literally?

"What is it?" he asked. "A gin mill?" Their term for a pub.

"Sort of. Potential buddies stand around and try to meet."

"Then what happens?"

"They go somewhere and show how they feel about each other." That didn't sound right. "No, they . . . try to like each other."

"How?"

"That's hard to say." Then I added, "It doesn't always work." The greatest understatement in Stonewall.

He took a last swig of his drink. "I don't fucking care anymore. Let's go."

Thirty seconds after we entered the bar, I decided I had made a mistake. The Eagle, then in its heyday, was the showcase for tough men, and I knew Gene would never have taken it for a gay bar. It looked, in fact, like what he had asked for: a buddy club. Still, Gene may have been too authentic a buddy for this gang. There was always a lot of leather and muscle, and bar discounts for shirtless men encouraged a trashy savor. But that impenetrable invulnerability set Gene off from the others, and the tattoos, when he pulled off the sweatshirt, were a shock. After all, this was the place where I once saw two incredibly ruthless-looking hombres intently conversing in low tones, and innocently sidled over to eavesdrop. One of them might say, "So we stripped the kid and secured him and then . . ." The other might say, "Belts are kid stuff, just makes them giggle. You have to whip those butts." Lo, this is not what I overheard, boys and girls. One was saying, "Barbara Cook could play Sally and Angela could play Phyllis," and the other replied, "What about Liza?"

In fact, I couldn't have blundered worse if I had set up Ozma of Oz on a blind date with Leo Tolstoy. This was a place of sculpted hunks; Gene was lewd. They were practiced; Gene was improvisational. And they had polish; Gene was basic. He'd find no buddy here. A partner for the night, maybe: but he would have been repelled by the idea. A man has one-night stands with women, not men. Anyway, Gene didn't want a sex partner. He wanted a buddy he could like so badly he would be bound, almost incidentally, to fuck him. That particular stylistic riddle he could only solve among his own people, where tattoos are not exotica but a convention, and where loyalties fiercely combine. Sex is class.

Dimly, through the liquor, Gene realized this. He said he liked the place, and energetically approached a few men, yet nothing panned out. "Let's blow," he said; once we got outside, he didn't want to go: "Let's just talk." We leaned against a car on the corner and watched the others saunter back and forth between the Eagle and the Spike. We didn't say much, and, after a long silence, Gene put his arm around me. I looked up to cheer him with a joke and saw that he was crying.

We stood frozen like that for a long while, till he put his arm down and said, "I don't think those guys liked me."

"Maybe I should have—"

"I couldn't fucking understand half the things they were saying. And one of them called me a fucking *Bulgarian!* I never even been there! I never been out of this country!"

Hell, I thought, if Gene is a vulgarian, whoever called him that, *you're* a Firbankian!

"I want to deck somebody. Anyone here you don't like? Point him out."

"Let me call Jim."

"Huh?"

"He's your best buddy, right?"

"Yeah, but . . . look, does he ever come here?"

"No. But let's see what we can arrange."

Jim, roused from sleep, was annoyed till I explained the delicacy of the case.

"Shit, the fucker's on a crying drunk, that's all," said Jim. "Everyone does that now and again. He can stay with me tonight."

"Jim's coming to get you," I told Gene.

He mauled me in relief.

I must say the Eagle–Spike parade had picked up notably—but for all the lingering stares, no one actually dared to cruise Gene. Is it possible that there's a man too authentic to be hot?

Gene was still crying when Jim's cab pulled up—it is, as they say, a jag. I thought, everyone likes my brother except his family, as Gene threw himself at the door. Suddenly he turned back.

"Gotta thank little brother," he said, and, staggering back to me, he planted a huge wet kiss right on my mouth.

"The fucking meter's running, man," said Jim.

After they left I noticed that Gene had left his Rutgers shirt on the car with me.

Later, when I told friends of this incident, they invariably turned against me, one of their favorite activities. How did I dare bring one of those violent homophobes to a gay bar? What if he had wrecked the place? Or me?

Rubbish. I was protected by ironworker loyalty: your buddy's brother is *your* brother. As for ironworker homophobia, Gene would never have taken the Eagle for a gay bar, because ironworkers don't believe in gay. Males are men or faggots; men are solid and faggots are weak. A husky leather dude who beds his own sex is even so a man. A little *New Republic* nerd who proudly bangs his wife and sneers at gays is still a faggot. This is why ironworkers casually throw around what we regard as gay references, and why they can climb into the sack with a buddy without regarding it as a sexual assertion.

No doubt all Gene got out of Jim was the chance to sprawl in his arms all night. There are buddies you fuck and there are buddies you only love; and I think Gene loved Jim. And sometimes I think there are hardhats and there is everyone else, because in looks, worldview, and behavior they are unique. I have been wrong about one thing: they are not invulnerable. When I pass a file of them, I look for Gene, but he is probably working some other part of the country now; they move around a lot.

However, they never change, whether in their habits, dress, loyalties, or patriotism, though their fix on love of country is at times comprehensively ignorant. Just a few days ago, as I walked by our local gang lounging out the lunch break, I heard one of them casually call out, "Hey, traita!" Accustomed as I am to New Yorkers' public speaking, I paid no notice. About a block later, I began to wonder what the heckler had seen to inspire the epithet. Jane Fonda? La Pasionaria? There were only a few shoppers and businesswomen walking with me.

Then I realized that he had been speaking to me. I was wearing my Yale sweatshirt, and ironworkers regard the big eastern schools as hotbeds of Stalin-loving treachery. Inadvertently, I had challenged an ironworker's loyalty to his kind, and probably baited his sense of class as well.

Anyway, it proves my contention that college-logo sportswear encourages people to talk to you.

STREET STAR

• WALLACE PARR •

LESLIE'S MOTHER WANTED to raise a daughter in a lovely home and when she was in her teens take her to Hollywood and let the producers see her. Instead she had Leslie. Before she had a chance to try for a daughter her husband, who was a demolition contractor, was killed by a falling plate-glass window. With the insurance money and what she earned as a mental hospital night nurse she was able to give Leslie many advantages her own childhood had lacked—disc-jockey music and nonstop TV, backyard blanket parties with a portable record player, popcorn and Dr. Peppers. She taught him to pin up her hair and do her nails as she read aloud from *Photoplay*. As far back as he could remember they went to the movies every time they changed. *Gone With the Wind* came around every year and they took a picnic basket and sat through it twice. They watched the Late Show together and worshipped the stars—Judy, Lucy, Marilyn. They both had little hillbilly faces like Marilyn's and thick, light hair. She laughed at the church-work ladies who <u>read *Gone with the Wind*</u> and said they'd never get anywhere. She went everywhere—Memphis, Nashville, Louisville—and Leslie rode his bicycle through the colored town to where there was a town the Yankees had shelled and burned. It was overgrown with brambles so he could hardly tell where the streets were and the center where the church and cemetery were had flowerbeds tended by a woman who smoked cigars. She lived in a dugout and Leslie had the idea there were corridors between the graves and the dugout, as though death were a continuation of life conducted under the cemetery surface with visits and parties and lace dresses which would crumble away if sunlight touched them, like dreams or the images on the screen in the movie theater when somebody opened the balcony fire-door, or the way his face faded in his mother's bedroom mirror as night fell. After he was too big for his bicycle he went in his mother's room when she was away and smiled and talked in her mirror. As he grew older he leaned closer to it and with his eyes nearly closed and his mouth puckered whispered what a wonderful person he thought he was and kissed it. He made friends with the cigar-face movie projectionist who told him there was a Marilyn movie coming with men with women's clothes on in it. The morning the stills for it were up Leslie went in his mother's room and tried on some of her Revlon Combination. That afternoon the TV said Marilyn was dead. That night they went to her movie and laughed through their tears and came out feeling as though they'd been watching *Gone With the Wind*. They got home and saw her casket on the late news and listened to sidewalk-interview people groping for words for their feelings. Leslie made up his mind he'd do anything to be loved like that. He began cuddling the yard and kitchen cats in an attempt to make himself more magnetic and taught the parlor cat to sleep on his bed. He bought his own makeup and secretly practiced reshaping his eyes with shadow and his mouth with lip- and makeup-sticks. He told his mother gangster movies and westerns irritated him and got him in too many fights. That fall he took *Photoplay* to school to read during lunch hour and when anyone teased him he hit him in the mouth. If anyone said anything about the stars themselves he'd just as suddenly and as though in a manic outburst get him down and sit on him until he took it back. One morning the parlor cat had kittens and on the way to school he walked by the theater and the projectionist was out in front changing the stills. He told him the cat that slept on his bed had just had kittens and the projectionist took the cigar out of his mouth and said he had just the thing. He gave him a shipping box such as distributors send the reels of a feature in. When Leslie got it home that afternoon the TV said the President was dead. He decided to go through his *Photoplays* and clip out all the things on Marilyn and put them in the feature box. By the time the President was buried the box was full.

When he went to college he took his box and his thirty-threes and *Photoplay* write-ups on all the stars. By then he wore his hair in a feathercut and spoke in a sound-stage love-scene whisper. When the students rioted and went to smoke-in rock concerts, he went too. Wasn't it part of growing up? And yet by the next spring he knew there'd be no one on campus he wanted to be loved by and decided to go to New York. He liberated the cat and bleached and set his hair like Marilyn's and put her write-ups and pictures in the cat carrier. I guess a little air won't hurt her any, he thought. All the other stars he sealed up in her old box and got on the Louisville bus, changed there and in Pittsburgh, and when he got off in New York felt like he was stepping into a movie. He'd seen the city on the screen already, with a xylophone trilling while a muted trumpet made a sound like a car skidding and thick sidewalk crowds were shown. He got a job working in the cashier's booth of a conventioneers' hotel and smiled through the glass as though his mouth were overpainted with strawberry and fluttered his lashes. When he spoke he sounded like Marilyn and laughed at how he could make people think they were seeing her. One morning he was on his coffee break and went back to the kitchen, got his coffee and walked back to the corridor to the service entrance and stood by the door. The coffee was too hot and he leaned his head back against the wall and shut his eyes. When he opened them the corridor was full of what appeared to be businessmen. One nudged him and said here's your chance to meet your senator and air your views. Your senator's anxious to meet you. He's coming this way now. The crowd parted and the senator took a step toward him and stopped. Nice to see you, Senator, Leslie whispered. The senator turned away and the crowd followed. One of those weird things, Leslie told himself. In the days that followed he brooded. Hadn't Judy, in one of her movies, come to New York and had all the key people say she was what they'd been waiting for? He wondered if people might not be the opposite with him and laugh when he talked and when they saw how he walked. One evening he walked up to a policeman and hit him in the mouth and was in Bellevue before he heard the senator'd just been shot. In a few weeks he was released and put on welfare. and given a room in a hotel at the corner of Barrow and West. It was a truck-driver's hotel and his window opened onto a fire escape and faced a blank wall. He bought a Jap battery record player and listened to his thirty-threes and sorted through the stars. When it got hot he walked up Christopher. All the other kids were on welfare and with his southern manner he quickly made friends. They turned him on to doctors who'd write ups and downs, told him they all found their drags in the garbage and took him to the Silver Dollar and introduced him to Jackie and Candy. Candy'd just had a sex change and was taking hormones. Leslie wanted some too but you couldn't get them without cancer checkups and you couldn't get the checkups on Medicaid. Anyway he found falsies and cocktail dresses in the garbage and in no time was a street-star—walked around thinking he looked like the big studio product while wearing things he trashed or 'twenties drags he bought on credit, soon terminated, in the Christopher Street antique stores. Sometimes he had his record player cradled in one arm like a viola playing Judy. He decided to go on the stage and Jackie promised she'd write a part for him in her next play and took him around to the factory and Andy said he'd use him in his new movie. He chose Fuschia for his stage name. Ultra Violet was then big and too much originality puts people off. It had all been so easy. Here he was nearly a star already and he hadn't taken any acting classes or been in a road company. He thanked Marilyn and the Senator. In a way he brought them together again and now they were opening doors. The President, too. From the other side they singled him out, found him capable of carrying out their wishes and rewarded him. He thanked them by remaining true to Marilyn's taste, stuck to barbiturates and said they did for him what ups did for the rest of the kids: took away his inhibitions and gave his mirror-smile that big studio look. When he got a script filled he liked to take twenty and walk around the halls wearing a bedsheet or go up and down Christopher in heels with a pinch-toe 'forties walk. A year went by and a new element moved into the hotel, drug derelicts, mental hospital fodder, colored winos. Garbage and broken bottles accumulated on the fire escape and even on hot days he kept his window locked and the shade down. It isn't hard to make people think I'm looking the way I want to look in my shadowy room, he said. When he had no more downs he reverted to the feathery-voiced nice guy who had James Dean-type speed-cadets crashing with their boots on on his bed.

When a fairy's favorite movie star dies or when a fairy's mother's favorite movie star dies he goes into a trance—an image worshipped from afar becomes accessible in death. That summer when Judy was laid out at Frank E. Campbell's he waited in the line of mourners, cradling his record player in his arm playing her thirty-threes. When he got to the door he turned it off and when he was in the deadroom turned it on and stepped back out of line. The attendants said nothing. In a few minutes someone from the office came in and asked them to help him find his way out. Outside some reporters thought the idea'd been ricky-tick and snapped his picture and took down his name. The next morning he was in the centerfold of the *News*. He sent a copy to his mother, saying he had a new kitten and had named him Arithmetic. He began wondering if Judy'd been appointed to carry on Marilyn's work. Marilyn had given him the Senator's frightened glance across the service entrance corridor. Judy'd given him a news camera shot. Maybe Judy and not Marilyn was the one. He reminded himself his news pic looked like one of Marilyn without makeup and in other ways struggled with doubt. Hadn't the paper said Judy's final interment place was as yet undisclosed. Lying on a mortuary or cemetery shelf she'd be powerless. Without a grave or a tomb the body can call its own the spirit can no more wander around doing favors than undeposited money can earn interest. He got a letter from his mother, mentioning Judy and groping for words for her feelings. After thinking it over he wondered if she could be induced to send money. He called her collect and said he'd found unhappiness in love and it had caused him to—he hesitated in the phone booth—become a little addicted to something. After a silence she said, "Addicted to what, Leslie?"

"Oh, I don't know. Scag I guess." "Oh, Leslie." "Oh, well I think I can get off it all right if only I have a little help." "Well what do you mean, help?" "Money, I guess." "Well how much, Leslie?" "Oh," he let half a minute go by. "Well, you see I owe some people something and if I could pay maybe they'd stop coming around because when they come they always have more and I could get off it." "Well yes but how much, Leslie?" "Well not a whole lot. I guess fifty'd cover it and leave me something until my next check." "Well all right, Leslie," she said, and in a moment hung up. In fact in the next few days he did borrow from the cigar-face who ran the hotel, saying he was expecting something in the mail. When her letter came there was a dollar folded in it. The kitchen cat had had kittens and after a page of what she'd gone through trying to think of names she said she was sorry to hear he'd been driven to the use of his own medications. They could only lead to further heartbreak. The cigar-face running his hotel said he could work off his debt doing the graveyard shift on the desk.

He soon knew the colored winos' names and made them his audience. He's always imagined the nitty-gritty was like show-business movies—Busby Berkeley girls braving it through bankruptcy or war, backstage heartbreak followed by self-destruction by the poisons. When he got a prescription filled, he liked doing a scene where a showgirl who was on the brink of stardom when she hit the skids and got fired goes back to the theater one evening, doped-up and moved by reminiscence, and wanders along the corridor behind the third balcony and comes to the head of the stairs when the orchestra goes into her old dance number. Her eyes widen, her mouth sags open and she tumbles down the stairs to her death. When the winos saw Leslie wandering around the halls in a bedsheet they clapped their hands and said show us how the old showgirl went when they played her number. And Leslie, full of tuies, always obliged, rolling down the staircase and lay at the bottom wearing a mortuary smile. The winos always chuckled and offered him a pull on a pint. One night Fat Mary, the junkie on the top floor, copped it and after the police went the morgue wagon came and as she was too big and stiff to fit in the elevator and too heavy to carry they pinned a sheet around her and rolled her down the five flights. When they were gone Jackie called and said she was having tryouts for her new play. It was cornball Busby Berkeley with blood and guts thrown in and Leslie rehearsed and appeared in it and as other cast members dropped out enlarged his part and took other parts but satisfaction eluded him. He got his first big break when Sophia, who was shooting a New York movie, chose him and Candy to do cameos in her jailhouse scene. His was scheduled after Candy's, just before lunch. Sophia, who appeared in the background, had a camera and crew scheduled out in Brooklyn that afternoon for the trial scene. Leslie blew his lines all afternoon. At five Sophia hit him in the mouth and walked out. The director said they'd splice his scene together from the footage they already had. Leslie wondered whether Marilyn, watching from the other side, had envied him. He'd always believed Marilyn's was the wrath and late that night, behind the desk in the lobby, he touched his bruised lip and wondered if Marilyn couldn't be induced to make Sophia sorry. He closed his eyes and pictured her kissing Sophia's knuckle joints and then, holding both her hands, leaning closer and whispering what a wonderful person she always thought she was. He imagined Marilyn's eyes closed and her mouth faintly puckered. One of the lobby winos came in and started toward the telephone and fell and broke the window. Leslie screamed at him to get out and the wino pulled a knife. When he tried to put him out the wino slashed him. He beat him with a windowshade roller and the wino stabbed him in the arm. He shoved him out the door and called an ambulance. The ambulance men found the wino on the sidewalk. There was a lot of blood. When they picked him up his head rolled off. They came in and called the police and the police asked Leslie what happened. He said there was a fight and the wino stabbed him. He shoved him out the door and he apparently picked a fight with somebody else who got hold of his knife. The police drove Leslie to St. Vincent's and had him sewn up and took him down to the Tombs and booked him for murder one. The others in the gay ward were in for loitering or soliciting or possession and when they heard about his murder one count looked up to him. His legal-aid lawyer said it looked bad and he spent the days and nights in a trance. Depression-days' movies in which a beautiful rich girl is on trial for her life were big on 'fifties TV and he looked forward to the trial scene. He imagined the thousand things they'd say—that he was from the south and did dragshows and had hit a policeman. He imagined the wino's body being taken apart by wise-cracking medical students, the strands of arm and leg muscles separated out in fan shape and held with pins and labeled, the nerve casings cut lengthwise with scalpels and the nerves themselves viewed, the brain and eyeballs sliced for cross-section examination. He pictured the hands and feet flayed so the bone and muscle structures were visible. Little by little at first, then in larger amounts the skin, the fat layer under the skin, the musculature and finally the tendons and nerves and bones would be deposited in the garbage, the teeth, the shapeless gobs that had been the vocal cords, all of it smelling of formaldehyde and in a while, in plastic garbage bags mingling with parts of other bodies being dumped in the ocean or buried in a trench. The trial itself was disappointing. There wasn't enough evidence, as there were no witnesses and the knife was never found and it was known there were methadone Nam veterans in the building who'd cut anybody up without a thought, for a verdict of guilty of anything to be brought in. Leslie went back to the hotel for his things (Arithmetic was gone) and took most of it over to Jackie's apartment. He only stayed a few days. It turned out the cast had abandoned the play and Jackie'd closed it. Leslie's arrest had frightened them, Jackie said, though each cast member seemed to have had a different reason.

He took the bus back to visit his mother. Her father, a virile man in his sixties, had moved in and Leslie saw he wouldn't be able to come back again so he told her everything—the time in Bellevue, the speed-cadets on his bed and what he wore on certain occasions and on the stage and his stage name, the hotel work and the fight, jail and the trial. His mother embraced him and cried and said he was braver than she didn't know what. The next morning his grandfather came downstairs with a shotgun. Queer, he screamed, women's clothes. Now you get out and never come back again. Leslie's mother cried again and said she'd go too. Her father said all right he could stay until the afternoon Louisville bus. He stomped out of the house and the mother and son spent the morning packing. Leslie said he'd get an apartment and she said then he'd have to have another cat. He said he couldn't take one on the bus and she said she'd give her something to make her sleep and he could take her in a wicker picnic basket. How could anybody think of an apartment without a cat? While she was getting her he went in her room and put some of her costume jewelry in a lunch bag and put it in his traveling case—'forties dimestore stuff, summer white wooden beads, clamp earrings that looked like flattened beads (the purse of white beading he didn't have room for), other necklaces of cut or molded glass, some plastic cameo pieces. When he was on the bus he opened the case and she'd switched lunch bags on him, this one had only his rubber baby pants and baby shoes. He left it in the garbage and when he got back and found an apartment on east Fifth, got his things from Jackie and began trying out for parts. Everyone said he had talent though of course he was no longer a discovery. Candy had inoperable cancer by then and as she wasted away did the things the kids all dreamed of doing—did Williams's plays uptown, appeared on German TV, had plastic surgery on her nose so she looked like an old-fashioned movie star in the hospital when the drugs calculated to kill the cancer were killing her. The vogue for Late Show drag queens was dying with her. Andy'd dropped them and when an open casting call went out for Ruby's Busby Berkeley show, Leslie and Candy and Jackie all said they'd go. But that morning Jackie was crashing and Candy felt too weak and Leslie was walking on with a line of girls when the cigar-face calling the steps said, "Ah, miss, I'm sorry, you're too tall." Down in the dressing room when the girls saw she was a he they giggled and asked if it was part of a fraternity initiation. He got evicted from Fifth Street and moved into a cockroachy place down on Ludlow. The cat played with the roaches. He'd hoped she'd eat them. He visited Candy in the hospital, having heard she was dying this time. In the midst of flowers and chocolates and imported tidbits she couldn't swallow she wept. "I could have had a TV series and been like Lucy," she said. "I know," Leslie said. "Tennessee said I could play anything." "I know." "What have you been doing?" "My check didn't come so I've had to scrounge." "You can take all this stuff Andy's friends keep sending." "Maybe I will. Listen, don't think about dying. You'll be out in a few days. Just like the other times." "Look at me. I'm like a skeleton already. And the smell." "It goes away. It went away the other times." "I could have been loved like Lucy." "She's retiring, you know." "No. Where'd you hear?" "On the TV I guess."

That winter the cat found a way in and out and had kittens and on the day Lucy retired Candy died. Though by then the kids were scattering they showed up at Campbell's for the funeral. Leslie wore the sari-material cocktail version of Chanel's last afternoon dress, the one with the jacket with the three-quarter-length sleeves. All in basic black with a sleeveless white blouse, elbow-length black cotton gloves, two strings of jet, 'twenties' pointed pumps and a cartwheel black gauze hat. No stockings, no makeup. When he got there Judy's room was occupied by the son of one of the Revson brothers, automobile accident, couldn't have been over twenty-nine if that and not bad looking. Just what Candy'd have wanted. He thought it was sweet of Judy to go out and get him for her. In Candy's room the flowers were piled to keep anyone from getting too close to the coffin because of the cancer smell and though Candy looked as glamorous as ever Leslie could see the wax on her throat covering the emaciation. And he could tell the dress was padded. There was a crowd and all the kids' faces shone with excitement. Jackie asked how his kittens were doing. He said they were nearly full grown. It took all his check to feed them. He wished they'd eat the cockroaches. They all slept on his bed though he left the window open hoping they'd find their way out. Jackie said she'd heard they were going to bury Judy soon. "Bury?" Leslie said. "She's been dead all these years." "Yes but they wanted a mausoleum or couldn't agree on which grave or something, I don't know, it was something, anyway the attendant told me they've had her on a shelf and this year they'll bury her." After the service there wasn't room in the hired cars and Leslie started back downtown. The flowers and flesh-colored lights had dazzled him so he felt as though he were just coming out of *Gone With the Wind*. He was full of yearning and gnawed by envy. Though they'd buried Candy the real Candy lived on, nesting in the plastic coils of her videotapes and films. Once he'd have done anything to be one of those smiling creatures in a headdress and tutu made of ostrich feathers and carrying a big ostrich feather fan around in a circle on the stage and when the number was over being picked up by a gangster in a long car, a man she's trying to drop from her life and who in the end dies for her. Now he stopped trying out for things. His thirty-threes stayed out of their jackets and covered the floor. At night the cockroaches walking on them sounded like rain on the window. Like a lot of the kids he went only to Jackie's wine and speed and popcorn Late Show parties. On the first day of a cold snap Jackie said she had the use of a camera and crew tomorrow out in Brooklyn and wanted all the kids to be there. "What do you want us to do?" they all said. "What shall we wear?" "I want everybody to do shtick," she said. "And wear antique lace." She gave them the address and said eight o'clock. "It's way the other side of Brooklyn so take taxis," she said. "I'll pay when you get there." By daybreak Leslie had on his dress and shawl and white satin dancing slippers, had washed his hair and found a taxi. They drove for half an hour and came to a marshy dump. The driver said this was the address and one of the kids waved. The wind took away Leslie's breath when he got out. As the other kids arrived there was talk of a mistake and the drivers talked among themselves and when it began to snow drove away. The kids thought of building a fire (none of them had a coat) then made a dash for a place where they saw cars. It was an expressway on the other side of a fence in a ditch. Someone said this was how Jackie was getting back at them for abandoning her play. Someone else said no, it was Candy'd got hold of her mind from the other side so she made a mistake. She's a lot further into Candy than you think. They started walking back the way the taxis went and reached a place where they caught a bus and when it left them off caught a train. Leslie had a fever the next morning and couldn't get out to borrow money for food and died a few days later. The kittens were faithful to the end, devoured his genitalia and entrails and worked their way up through the stomach cavity, tearing away liver, lungs and heart. They ripped away the skin and swallowed it and ate the muscles and tendons of his arms and legs and hands and feet and gnawed away at the bones until they were dry. The scalp they ate, leaving the hair scattered in gobs, also the eyeballs and tongue. The cockroaches got the brain. The kittens fought over the bones and, fighting, scattered them through the three rooms. They ripped open the kitchen garbage bags and scattered the garbage around so the place looked like the sort of welfare hotel room in which often as not an old widow or wino is found decomposing. That spring the cigar-face landlord came for the back rent, unlocked the door, took one look and went and hired another cigar-face to empty the place out. On the day a cortege of a few automobiles behind the hearse wound their way through a Westchester County cemetery to Judy's mausoleum with her coffin, Leslie's bones and hair in a dozen black plastic garbage bags were stacked on the sidewalk.

LIFE DRAWING

• MICHAEL GRUMLEY •

From Life Drawing, *a novel in progress*

IN FEBRUARY OF my last high school year, I came home from wrestling practice, went straight to my father's liquor cabinet, and finished off half a bottle of Old Crow. My parents were out, and my younger brothers were at a party with their grade-school chums; I was alone, and got drunk and headed for New Orleans. Liquor was fuel for my impulse, and it kept me warm through the wet afternoon and evening. I recall I started out down by the railroad tracks, imagining I'd be able to find a boxcar that was headed south. Prowling among the ice-encrusted railway cars, I soon realized they were locked in for the night, if not the season. The local freight train I'd heard all my life didn't make a full stop in Lillienthal as I'd always imagined it did—it slowed but continued its rattling journey at a nonnegotiable clip, and running along beside it, I cursed its speed and heedless girth. I had to leave town, would leave town, though I couldn't say why. The whiskey kept me chuckling to myself as I trudged along the tracks. It was warm in New Orleans wasn't it? That was reason enough.

From the tracks I followed the curving highway till it came to the river. Down on the levee at night, the men who worked on the paddle-wheelers heading downriver to Memphis and the Gulf would congregate. When we were younger, our parents had taken my brother Franklin and me for walks along the levee, holding us up so we could look out over the loading of boats, the movement of winches and barges. My friend old Don Hammer sometimes worked on the levee, and when I was delivering newspapers he'd tell me about the accidents he'd seen, when a bale had fallen on a man and paralyzed him for life, about a novice struck with a baling hook, a captain knocked overboard and nearly swept away. His accounts were gleeful, filled with the blood and thunder of a catch-as-catch-can life. The levee in winter was bleak—truck drivers collected around a drum fire: half a dozen men with dark faces, walking up and down, stretching their legs before they crossed the bridge and took the highway south through Illinois, down into Missouri, finally Arkansas, Louisiana. The river was open, and a barge was drawn up at the end of the loading pier. How long it had been moored there was hard to tell. Next to it stood the *River Queen*, and as I moved closer to it, I could see light in its cabins, and men moving along the passageways and decks. The *River Queen* churned up and down the Mississippi during the summer months—once I'd gone for a ride on it with my girlfriend Sammy. A band had been playing, and it was great fun slipping and sliding on the dance floor as the current changed and the band changed with it. But I'd never thought about where it went or what it did during the winter when no pleasure-seekers queued up at the dock, no wedding parties waited to be carried away.

It must have been about nine o'clock at night now, and the damp winter rain was beginning to put a chill in my robust traveling plans. Steam rose up from the water, or a kind of fog. Laughter came from on board, and the smell of soup and cigarettes drifted out of the portholes.

I stood on the dock, watching the mysterious motions of the figures in the dark as they passed back and forth. Cigarettes lighted up like fire-flies, lengths of white rope were tossed here and there.

The door of the cabin nearest the gangplank burst open then, and out of the swirl of swearing and yelling and the clank of pots stepped a figure I was sure I recognized. Not many black men were in my acquaintance—hardly any black families lived in

Lillienthal—and so for a moment I pictured the faces I knew, or had only seen. With the light behind him it was hard to see his features, but after another second I was sure who it was and called out his name, Horace!

He squinted down the gangplank. "Who's that calling my name?" he demanded, stepping closer to the edge. He looked at me curiously—hundreds of caddies must have worked at River Hills Country Club the same years I did, and just because he worked upstairs in the locker room, why should he remember me after all?

"Are you Horace?" I asked, suddenly unsure of myself, and at the same time feeling dizzy. The smell of kerosene and of the muddy river came up from the space between us, and I put my hand on a timber that stood next to the gangplank to steady myself. Whiskey flowed through me.

"Horace Olibanum Jefford, that's right. And if you know my name, you might as well come on inside, and tell us what you're doing, wandering around this old levee looking like a half-drowned river rat. Come on, step lively now!" He reached over and pulled me across, and I stumbled a little, and then was inside the cabin he'd stepped out of, amid tied-up bedrolls and wicker trunks and pans hung on a long trestle.

"This here is Sneezewood McKenna, and Ralph Scott. And this nasty looking creature is my son James—don't you call him Jimmy—and somewhere or t'other is Curtis Stringfellow."

The men, who were seated around a table in the middle of the cabin, looked up from their cards, and mumbled howdy, all except James who just stared at me close-mouthed. They were smoking and the smoke was like a canopy over the table. Next to it was a stove as big as a sofa, a sink, and vegetables and fruit in baskets, all in what seemed like one pile against the wall.

"Well?" Horace raised his eyebrows, finally put out his hand.

I came to myself enough to mumble my own name, and to tell Horace I'd seen him at the Club. I said I was going to New Orleans.

At this the other men looked up again from the table, and one of them, I think it was Sneezewood, said: "People all the while dying to come up north; what do you want to be heading the other direction for?" There was a pause. "Of course," he continued, going back to his cards, "some folks have more trouble traveling than others."

Horace said, "Now now . . . ," and I suddenly felt foolish, and thought what *am* I running off for, me so white and comfortable and all?

Then the boat gave a heave, as if the barge had bounced against it. "Current's turning. Better get at it," Horace said and gave me a quick look. "You want some coffee." He took a cup from the trestle and a pot from the stove and put me off to the side to drink it. The boat moved again, and the men lay down their cards and together moved out the door.

"You, Caddy . . . you stay here, and when we get back we'll talk about New Orleans!" He winked at James, who hadn't got up with the other men, but stayed at the table, his face rocking in the light, looking at me out of the brownest eyes I'd ever seen.

James was eighteen, which meant he could drink and work on the river as a dealer. He was on his way south "to do a little business." When I knew him better, and kidded him about the phrase, he'd laugh back at me, his laughter coming out from behind one of the cheroots he was always smoking. Cards were his business, and had been from an early age.

He got up from the table, and I could see he was taller than me by an inch or so, but rangy and wide-shouldered, with long arms. I thought of a spider.

"My papa doesn't know I'm in the life, so don't say nothing." He was rinsing out his glass at the sink as he said this, not looking at me, and his words fell from nowhere, floated in the thick sweet air. He was shaking his head, and after a moment he did turn. He came back and took another look at me.

"You know what I mean?" he asked.

I didn't, exactly—but I was excited in a way I hadn't been excited before, and waited to hear what else he might say.

"Forget it," he finally said, and sat down again.

Then Horace came back in and put on a yellow slicker over his jacket, and said the river was rising.

"So what about it, young bub? What's waiting for you in New Or-LEANS?" He stood at the door, expecting an answer.

"I'm going to school down there—college," I said, getting ahold of a lie by the tail and starting to twist it. "I go to Tulane University, and I had to come home for a while—and now I'm going back."

Father and son looked at one another, and then looked back at me.

"Well, that sounds right," said Horace.

James had pulled out a nail file and was moving it across his nails, frowning down at his hands. I couldn't take my eyes off him.

Horace said, "James here is headed down that way himself. You sure you're not running away from something? No officers of the law after your little tail?"

Sneezewood came back in the cabin and, hearing Horace, made a loud guffaw. Then he put his lips together and shook his head.

"What do you think we got here, a convicted felon?" He and James laughed.

"You never do know," Horace put in mildly, and seemed satisfied no trouble would come sniffing his way. He sat down at the table and picked up the cards: "All right, then. When that barge gets done bumping up against us and knocking off my brand new paint, it's going down the river. And James is going to be on it, and the captain—he's a real bulldog—can surely take along another boy if I say so." He pulled a card out of his hand and flipped it on the table. "And I guess I say so." He looked at James. "That all right with you, James?"

James spread his hands apart, shrugged his shoulders, said "Makes me no never mind," and then giving it up, showed me a wide grin.

The cabin rocked once more, Curtis Stringfellow made his appearance, blocking the doorway, as big and important as the night itself—then James and I were down the gangplank, and across another one, and on our way.

The river was wide and long. By the time we got to the

Missouri border the next day I felt like I'd been on it all my life. We kept out of the way of Captain Eugene, who regarded us as no more or less interesting than the cargo—soybeans from Clinton, wheat and alfalfa.

We slept next to the boiler that night, and nothing we said could be heard over its clanking, the repeated stanzas of iron grating against iron. I woke up once and saw James watching me —we weren't very far apart, one bunk space between us. He offered me a drink from a little silver flask he carried in his jacket, and I took it from him just so I could touch his skin. I couldn't go back to sleep then; we both were half-sitting up, with the early morning light slipping in, and as long as he was looking at me I was looking at him—like we were both laughing, but neither of us was even smiling. The boiler chugged on, leaving no room for words; I sat up all the way and leaned across to him to hand back the flask. He took it, and kept hold of my hand with it, and the current ran through both of us until we bounced toward each other, and that was that.

I saw I knew nothing at all about giving somebody pleasure, and I tried to do better, again and again. James was pleasure. Hot, snake-smelling skin, knots of muscles hitting me like snowballs, breath like gin and jasmine—he was everything at once.

Whatever I'd been going to New Orleans for, I'd found by St. Louis. When we finally got out on deck—which wasn't a deck at all but a big flatiron field moving through the water, lines looped all across it, and nowhere to walk but along the gangways —the captain grunted good morning, and the ugly little river towns spilled out their undersides like bunting. I was ready to take on the world, whatever the world happened to be.

But by then I was also thinking about my family, wondering what they were thinking. James told me he lived off and on with his mother in Chicago, and didn't see his father but once or twice a year—he'd been staying on the *River Queen* with him for a week, before starting downriver to ply his trade on the gambling boats there, and he had older brothers that he never saw. He was so out in the world, compared to where I was, that it seemed the world was written all over him. He glowed with it.

We stood behind the lines. The wind coming up from the south had a chance of spring in it, but the day was cold, no matter the clean white clouds snapping overhead, the bright blue tunnel of sky.

I took a breath and told him that I wasn't actually going back to school at Tulane, that I was just going to New Orleans plain and simple.

He let out a long low whistle.

"And your mama? She know that's where you're bound? Or did you just happen to run off without telling anybody where?"

As pleased with me as he had seemed in the cabin, now he seemed as angry. He moved away from me and walked along the gangway, and I followed after him.

When he turned around, it appeared the dark of his eyes had spilled over into the whites, they were so somber, so full of hurt.

"I thought you and me were going to be a team for a while," he said. "I thought you were your own man, but now I see you ain't even dry behind the ears."

I was confused, reached out for his arm, but he pulled it away, stood there looking at me with so much reproach I felt I'd fallen overboard and was drowning. Then he relented some, said in a milder tone, "Nobody goes off and leaves their family, less they have a reason. Nobody lets them worry and carry on and wonder if they're dead or alive. Nobody I want to meet."

The softer voice did not ease the weight of his disapproval. I was wretched—my brave freedom, purchased at the price of my parents' anguish, hadn't been such a grand thing to achieve after all. Wouldn't they be calling the hospital and the police by now?

I must have looked as bad as I felt, for he pulled me to him.

"Don't think I want to let you go; but seems like I'm going to have to." Then he turned me around and pushed me back toward the cabin.

"Time's got to be right," he said, and went to ask Captain Eugene how long before we tied up in St. Louis. And that was how long we stayed in the cabin, pressed together, pulling the future out of each other, sweating and moaning and making sure each of us remembered.

When we stepped off the barge together, he walked me to a Greyhound bus station and we sat drinking awful coffee till it was time for me to go. I'd got my dad when I called home, and though he was angry, it wasn't as bad as James being angry, and I didn't have to talk to my mother at all. Dad let me know he was relieved I was all right. That was the main thing, he said.

The waitress behind the counter kept her eye on us while we sat there, and I finally realized we were in the South, or nearly. People looked at me more than they looked at James it seemed, and I thought of what Sneezewood had said. I wondered suddenly if James would be all right. I had already made up my mind that I'd come to New Orleans after school was out—then I *would* be my own man. He had given me his mother's address, and I had given him mine.

The bus north was called—I couldn't understand the announcement, but James could—and we got up and walked toward the gate.

"I'm sorry," I said to him.

"Well, maybe it's all right," he said, smiling, and put his hand on my shoulder. "And I'm sorry, too, for thinking you was in the life . . ."

Then I laughed, and said I guessed I was in it now, and he liked that, and that's how we said good-bye.

The bus rolled out and I watched him through the window as he got smaller and smaller. We turned the corner, and he was gone.

The trip down the river stayed with me. I was moving through Lillienthal in fits and starts, waiting for graduation. It was as if I'd been inflated with a gas that had me bobbing through the streets like a circus balloon. New ideas and new faces kept coming to me, rushing down like meteors, littering the front lawn and the fields around me. My parents had been surprisingly philosophical about my running off—my dad blamed it mostly on drink. My brothers thought it odd of me, although Franklin had, a few years back, been discovered with his sheets tied together, ready to step out through the window on Oak Street. We were all prepped for departure: Dad always said he didn't want any of us living at home once we were grown, that two adult males were too many for any one house. Thinking of this, I wondered if I'd been too sentimental about coming back.

Drinking was a sporting endeavor in Lillienthal, and many stories worked their way through its boozy depths. My father had a scar on the back of his head from one night in Peoria—I remember him sitting at the kitchen table, and Mom standing behind him, swabbing it with iodine. He told us he'd been in a bar with some other men—on a business trip—and he'd been sitting in a chair with his feet up, and somebody had come by and knocked them down. We were outraged that anyone should have laid a hand on him; who would dare? But drinking, we knew, had come into it. Drinking had come into it when Mrs Maxwell had her hysterectomy, and when Mr Maxwell didn't come home, and drinking had most certainly come into it when Mrs Ryan's brother Willie had been arrested. And now, drinking had come into it with me.

Part of being an artist was drinking—and part of being a man. It wasn't good that I had run away from home, but it would've been worse if I hadn't been drinking. Drinking was a net that descended and caught one, a familiar bugaboo that kept other bugaboos obscured. If drinking wasn't exactly patriotic, it was a long way from being un-American. The boys who'd come back from the Korean War were notorious drinkers; we'd see them coming out of Mizlo's Tap, weaving down the street, hollering, their arms around each other's shoulders. Their Korean silk jackets bobbed along; the villages north and south of the famous 38th Parallel shone like small white blossoms on their backs.

Franklin drank, up at school, where he had joined a fraternity. He told me how one night he and the other brothers drove off with a whole houseful of furniture they'd carried out of a model home on the edge of town, carting it back to the fraternity annex in a pickup truck. He told me about how they'd all got drunk one weekend and had an "orgy" with two girls who were in town with Shipstad and Johnson's Ice Follies. I went up to see him that spring, and got as drunk as the rest of them, but no orgies or burglaries transpired, only a Saturday night of endless dispassionate necking to Ray Coniff albums—me and somebody's sister, who disappeared at midnight.

The fraternity house was an inappropriate setting in which to tell my brother what I'd really done when I took off for New Orleans, but I did tell him. He listened, and said I should do whatever I felt like, but I could see he was perplexed. What about my girlfriend Sammy? he asked.

I couldn't tell him any more than I knew myself. I told him what had happened, without going too far into the details—I realized the details weren't what he wanted to hear. His listening had the effect of making it matter-of-fact, and for that I was grateful. I had begun to be afraid of the future, afraid of it tilting and sliding back on me—not exactly afraid, but unsure. I felt myself getting more and more attenuated, and sometimes thought I might blow away entirely. His calmness kept the freak in me at arm's length—a weird nocturnal specter like the hermaphrodite on the midway, its leering face half-rouge, half-stubble—and I was able to drive back down to Lillienthal with my equilibrium restored. I saw, though, that to keep my self-image from getting too garish, I had to keep the externals neat and wholesome. You could do what you liked, so long as you kept it your own affair.

I dreamed of James, and woke to take finals in History and Natural Science. I called information in New Orleans late one night and tried to get his number there, but they had no listing. I tried to write letters to him, but they didn't sound like me at all—or, rather, they sounded too much like me. I couldn't write in anything but breezy, and breezy wasn't at all how I felt about him, about us. But I sent him a letter anyway, written on a Gauguin note card I'd got from the Art Institute, saying I missed him, saying I wanted to come get a job in New Orleans that summer. I drove down to the levee at night, and sat in the car: I saw lights on the *River Queen*, but never went on board. I listened to Johnny Mathis and Elvis Presley records and played Laverne Baker's "Jim Dandy" till even my brother, Dennie Lee, complained. And lifted weights and did a hundred sit-ups, and wondered how I'd look with long hair. The summer got nearer and nearer.

Finally, I heard from James. His letter came the day after I received word that I'd been given a scholarship to art school at Iowa City. I had, in the twenty-four hours between letters, nearly convinced myself that an Iowa college was what I wanted. It was what my parents wanted for me—a career that would successfully blend creativity and practicality, talent and cunning. I had no trouble seeing myself as an advertising man. But then my enthusiasm abruptly jumped the track. James wrote that he was staying in a rooming house in the Quarter, and that I could come and stay there, too. He said he had been lucky with the cards, that he was working on the river weekends. He said he would be happy to see me! It was all I needed to change my plans, my life.

My parents didn't want to hear about New Orleans. Dad had arranged an interview for me with an advertising man across the river. If all went well, I was to work as an apprentice in his small agency, learning paste-up and copy, getting the jump on my college classmates. It wasn't the summer I saw before me now. I saw James and only James. I was coming on fast toward my eighteenth birthday, and was as full of myself as a tree is full of sap. If I could just get away and live a more romantic sort of existence, I would become the person I wanted to be. Nothing could have stopped me from getting out of Iowa. And nothing did.

New Orleans in early summer, with the sun shining through the balconies of the French Quarter, creating blocks of swirling Arabic letters on the brick and stucco walls behind them, mixing chirping Patois and languid Gulla with the broad flat vowels of Texarkana, confounding the eye and ear at every corner—New Orleans in June is a sweet chunk of marzipan one could chew all one's days. In late summer, that same sweetness will cloy, and produce what are known locally as the vapors, the aversion to all things warm and honeyed. Women will put a dash of vinegar in their soups and bathwater; men will sprinkle cucumber and lemon into their handkerchieves, and decorously mop their brows. But that is later. June is a dream, crisp and clear and golden.

On Borchardt Street, where James' rooming house stood, the trees on either side branched up and met in a thicket of green and scarlet, and the light that came in through to the street and sidewalk below was dappled—at midday it was like walking through confetti. The flowering bushes that spread out along the fences and sent purple and yellow vines up along the clapboard walls contributed all the more to the festive effect. Small birds darted in and out among the blossoms and white butterflies hovered over the small vegetable patches that crept around from side gardens, thrust themselves up next to the gate.

James had gained some weight that spring, his spidery frame now more that of a man than a boy. And his hair, which had been coarse and unruly, had come under lye and pomade and lay back from his forehead in soft shining waves. When he met me at the station, he was wearing a hat, and rings on his fingers I didn't remember—but his smile was the same, and led me to him like a beacon.

We took a streetcar from the station, and walked the last bit to Borchardt Street. I had brought a suitcase, stuffed with summer clothes and drawing-pads, and we took turns carrying it. I was going to be a real artist that summer, justify my impulse, and everywhere I turned in those shining streets and alleys I saw sketches and paintings, quick bright flashes of color.

"So now you're on your own," he said as we walked along, and he looked at me sideways, appraisingly. "And nobody's going to be worrying about you but me . . ." It wasn't a question, and I didn't need to answer. The way he talked and the way he looked at me made me feel I'd been stitched on to him, like the sleeve on his jacket, or the band around his tan fedora. We walked slowly, stopping once to ᴗ ɪy shaved ice and syrup, but I was already in bed with him pressed against his broad black chest, inhabiting his New Orleans life and my future.

The boardinghouse was painted a dull mustard color, and

the windows were framed in a deep green. Inside, it was dark and cool, and smelled of candles and frangipane. Someone rose from a chair.

"This is Mrs Odum. Mrs Odum, this is my friend Mr McGinnis."

Mrs Odum was a big woman, but delicate. She offered me a tiny warm object—her hand—which I shook, and she moved to the side of the room on two other tiny objects—her feet. Elsewhere, she was vast. There was something pleasing about the odd conjunctions of her frame, and also about the disharmony of her costume—it seemed she had left some of herself behind, or sent it on ahead: her hair was tied by a purple scarf, and her smock was orange and blue, beneath it trailed a hem of vivid pink. She was here, but not here, tentative as an unfinished sketch, present only as an idea of herself.

"Pleased to meet you, Mr McGinnis. Make yourself at home. You're just off the second landing there"—she waved her bird-like hand upward—"and Mr Jefford here will show you"—she bent to pick up a bit of lint, straightened with a sigh—"what's what."

She smiled, fluttered through to the hallway.

We mounted the stairs, turned past doors that opened and closed, dark male faces smiling out, around toothbrushes, with circles of shaving cream—towels adjusted, coughs interrupted, somewhere a gentle insistent swearing.

A sign on the landing read: No Ladies Above the First Floor. James pointed to it as we passed, shook his finger in mock-warning.

"Mrs Odum doesn't much take to other womenfolk. But she surely does love the men," he said, chuckling and raising his eyebrows.

We stopped, and he pushed open the door of one room, put my suitcase inside it, then closed it and opened another directly across the hall.

"That's yours, and this is mine," he said, pulling me after him across the threshold. "And this"—he indicated the great big four-poster bed in the middle of the room—"is ours!"

And didn't we ramble. The months between us fell away, and we were back on the barge again, the boiler pounding. The churchbells in the Quarter rang every hour; they took us into the night, past vespers—like the bell before each round in a prizefight—punctuating the long sweet hours of give and take, the tolling reminding us that we were somewhere in the world.

He liked saying my name, and I liked saying nothing at all, not having to say anything—just holding on. There was a sink in his room, and from time to time we splashed each other with the cool water from the tap. His lips were so sweet, and his long educated fingers so tender. From outside, along with the ringing of the bells, came other music. Musicians who played in the bars and the clubs of the Quarter stayed in the rooming houses of Borchardt Street, and Petaluma Street beyond it. We heard an olio of music up in James' room, thick and overheated, simmering through the afternoon and evening. We had clarinets for robins and saxophones for bobolinks, and a big bass fiddle somewhere sounded like a bullfrog on a pond. And the children yelling and making mischief, men pestering and women eluding— all contributed to the vines of sound that rose and flowered in our window.

The first few days had no demarcation, eased into one another. I had to get a job, that was the condition of my being in New Orleans, but for the moment I had no obligations. We spent our days and nights getting reacquainted (acquainted, really—what we knew of each other from the river was only the fundamentals) and prowling through the streets and alleys, looking in on James' friends here and there, stuffing ourselves with hush puppies and gumbo and warm greasy crullers from the Cafe Dumond. James decided I had to have a hat, and bought me one—a white panama that was years older than I was, and I resolved to grow a mustache to go with it. Nobody seemed to notice or care that we spent all our time together, that my bed stayed flat and unrumpled while his was a sea of wrinkled linen. Or that we kept hanging on each other and poking and cuffing and finding any excuse to keep flesh on flesh. Once we stopped at a bar, and never went back. He said people had been real friendly when he'd been there by himself, but the two of us

together bottled up that good feeling—we got cold looks from
the crowd and the fish-eye from the bartender. It was all men in
the bar, all of them older, and shrill voices and elaborate gestures, and a kind of hissing noise when we left.

Nobody minded if we drank in the boardinghouse; we kept
beer in the refrigerator and whiskey in our room. Mrs Odum
never asked me how old I was—I believe she thought that if I
was old enough to be away from home and out in the world, I
could do what I liked. She cooked up some spicy stews, and a
lot of beer and wine went down with them. There would be six
or seven men at table—one other white face complementing
mine, belonging to a Mr Chough, who had bad teeth and seldom
smiled. I caught him once or twice watching me while his jaws
moved up and down on the shrimp and peppers, something
quizzical in his gaze, but we had no conversation. More talkative
faces hovered over the blue and white crockery, the checkered
cloth—Mr Mulkin and Mr McBride lived on the first floor, and
kept up a lighthearted exchange on the events of the day; both
worked as bus conductors and had plenty to say about the comings and goings of the human race. Mr Mulkin was heavy and
wore his hair cropped close to his skull; he had a thick warm
laugh that we sometimes heard bubbling up from his room
below us, joined by the higher, more ethereal notes of Mr
McBride. Mr Harrison lived on the same floor as these two, but
was irregular at table. He was younger than they, but older than
we, lean as a rail, with dark hooded eyes and nervous hands.
We'd see his light on when we climbed the stairs at night, with
always a sweetish smell coming from under the door. In addition
to these guests there might be a suitor of Mrs Odum's at table.
Insubstantial as her spirit seemed, her fleshly appetites were
down-to-earth, and considerably varied; the numbers of cousins
and old friends that passed through was high. She had a blood-
nephew named Thomas who helped out in the kitchen, and on
weekends Thomas' mother might come to call, but no other
Odums appeared. Humming and fluttering by, our landlady
moved like a burgee in the breeze; she kept house, cooked and
cleaned, and managed still to look as if she lacked the authority
even to boil water. She took some pride in her cuisine.

"Hand Mr McGinnis over those beets," she directed Thomas. "We want him to appreciate our New Orleans cooking."

"Do I taste coriander in this stew?" Mr Mulkin wanted to know.

"Yes indeed you do—you do know your spices, Mr Mulkin," she replied. Her broad face was fresh as a young girl's.

I found I didn't have to initiate much in the way of conversation, only let myself put in a few words now and again, smile, and eat my fill. I'd paid out for my first two weeks' lodging, and had enough for the rest of the month, but after that I was going to have to earn what I needed. I wasn't worried. I'd already started doing some sketches, down at the end of the street in a tiny park where older women sat and sewed, or just sat, where tinkers and fishmongers stopped for a cigar and a taste of something cool. A chipped statue, whose inscription and dates were nearly rubbed off, stood in the middle of pigeons: a French hero whom James told me had routed the pirates when they threatened to burn the city. The park was where we'd stopped for shaved ice my first day in town, and I soon thought of it as someplace personal and special. It was best at dusk, and if James was taking a nap, I'd slip out of the house with my pad, and come down.

I watched the women at their stitching, and the youngsters jumping rope; at first they all watched me, but after a few days I think I blended in. After I started work at the ribbon factory, I only got to the park after it was turning dark, or on the weekend. Sometimes it was just the old white hero and me in the gathering darkness. The more sporting collection of people would come later to take their ease, after supper and beyond. I noticed how the aroma of the flowers, and all the other smells of life—the horses on the street, and even the wash still hanging from the balconies on either side; geraniums and cobblestones—all became stronger at dusk. That dark grainy mist that fell on the park seemed to make all sensations more vivid—you could hear farther, breathe deeper, at twilight.

James was used to sleeping for an hour in the afternoon; he said it gave him an edge on the night, when sometimes he'd play right through till dawn, stepping off the dock on Decatur Street as the rest of the city was waking up. He worked on the *Belle* and the *Avalon* mainly, where he knew the crew and where card games were arranged as a matter of course. I tagged along the first weekend I was with him, partly because I was curious about the life, mostly because I didn't want to lose sight of him. He stood by our big bed, pulling on his rings, and putting himself into his sharkskin trousers, humming whatever snippet of melody had chanced to appear at the window. Watching him dress was almost as exciting as watching him undress. When he was set to go, I walked with him down the stairs, carrying his little valise. It smelled of Florida water and talcum, and always a little half-pint of whiskey in it, in case somebody needed a drink.

We boys had played poker at home when we were growing up, and Dad had tried to teach us pinochle, but I was never much for cards; the stakes we played for in Lillienthal were like no stakes at all, toothpicks and pennies.

The brand of cards James played was a universe away. I stood off to the side of the *Avalon* saloon, and watched him, marveling at the sleek ease of his movements, the concentration on his face as he calculated and bluffed, then reached for the kitty. To have him so close and not to have any contact with him—no quick glances, no wide smile flashing across the table —was disconcerting.

"Twelve on Ruby," said the dealer, and the men at the table grunted or nodded or were still.

And then, "Opal takes it over the top"—and a sigh. The players were known by their gems. James had earlier told me this was the local peculiarity, and no one sat down to the gambling table unembellished.

"Eighteen on Tourmaline," the dealer went on, then "Twenty-one!" and a belligerent chorus, a scraping of chair legs, and the refreshening of drinks.

"Tourmaline shining tonight," remarked a fat catfish of a toff, helping himself to the bourbon from the tray beside me, throwing it back, returning to the fray. Tourmaline was James.

I watched them play, and felt a swell of pride when he won, and disappointment when he lost or folded early. They played and drank, and I simply drank, and no one noticed me at all. I went out on deck and looked at the stars, and it was quiet on the water, the blackness all around thick and soupy. I could see across the river to Algiers where a few lights still shone. I sat down in a deck chair to watch the lights for a while, and fell asleep.

When I woke up, James was standing over me, smiling.

"Looks like you don't find it all too exciting," he said, poking at my shoulder till I grabbed his hand. I felt guilty for having walked out and fallen asleep.

"Oh, no," I said, protesting. "It *is* exciting."

But he was right, and we both knew it, and without saying it out loud it got resolved that I wouldn't tag along any more nights on the *Avalon* . . . I imagine I didn't much like being outside the frame, with him and the others so suave and dark and beautiful in the middle of the canvas. I caught a cold from sleeping out on deck, and was sneezing and wiping my eyes for the next few days, and he was bringing me up honey and lemon from the kitchen, and one way and another the balance got restored.

James was the youngest of seven children, and all his brothers and sisters were spread out across the country. Two of the sisters were living in Chicago with his mother; the brothers were in Kansas City and Atlanta, and his father had for ten years or so been working at River Hills, living here and there around Lillienthal, and on the river. His mother worked two jobs in Cottage Grove, on the south side of Chicago, and he had lived with her till he finished high school, then stepped out on his own. He was a year older than me, but had collected authority in ways that made him seem more than that—he had a cousin who was in and out of reform school who had taught him all about his own equipment. James told me about how he and Rudolph would hang out together, and how Rudolph had an older white friend who used to take photographs of the two boys playing with each other and whatnot.

"Used to go down on us too," he said, stroking my back as we lay together in his big pink bed, drinking bourbon, spreading out our past.

It was the first time I'd heard the phrase, and it could've meant so many things, I was a little disappointed when he told me what it did mean. Putting a phrase on a thing didn't enhance it much I noticed. There weren't two others like us in the world, we were unique and fabulous. All the rest was nonsense. I found I didn't want to hear about him and Rudolph, not how they shot craps together or engaged in this and that bit of petty larceny in the Loop, or how they worked up the photographer, or salesman, or deli man together.

Besides, I hadn't much to tell him about my own experiences. I knew that I felt proud of myself when I was with him in a way I hadn't before—easier to be proud of what you are when you have someone to be proud of it with. Walking down Bourbon Street, sitting at the dock on Decatur, or calling on his friends on Esplanade—anywhere we went something seemed to follow us, a kind blue light that made us glow. The music of the streets was high and tender, and it rang us up and down the streetcar lines. Women reached for us out of their open doorways as we passed; whatever it was we were demonstrating, people wanted to buy.

Mrs Odum would remark, "You boys look mighty spiffy tonight," and add one of her quick sighs. I loved wearing my hat when we went out in the evening. James had picked up eye-catching items of apparel that he wore with style: a velvet vest with little pearl buttons that was as smart as anything on the river, a pair of deep red suede shoes with Cuban heels. He moved through New Orleans with a graceful lope. It seemed he was always scooping up the air as he passed—he had played basketball, he had known how to run through the streets—and his smile was like his armor. His spirit and his body were one, and that to me was magical. Remembering his long, lean authority is remembering the night air, the river and the honeysuckle, the smell of his skin that was like all of it together. When I was drawing in the park, or just sitting on the dock and watching the boats go by, I was thinking of him, and the sense of rightness and fullness that came from what we had together carried me along.

Then the second week I got a job. Little Mr McBride knew someone who worked at Regalia Manufacturing, a ribbon factory in his old neighborhood, and he had heard from him that they might be hiring. He presented this fact at dinner.

"Taking anybody," he said, "even Northern boys, I expect . . ." He liked to have his joke about northern and southern, by which I guess he meant white and black. I got the feeling that the men at Mrs Odum's were all somewhat enamored of James—Mr McBride included—but they never said anything outright that let me know they were jealous. McBride was good-natured, and handsome in his small impish way. He had learned from Mrs Odum to make sweet potato pie, and for two nights we'd had it for dessert.

"Printing ribbons for prize winners and for the County Fair. You go talk to Darnell Weeks." He said he'd take me out on his bus line the next day.

I had another slice of pie, and considered, and looked to James for his opinion.

"Young ar-teests do have to eat," he said.

So I rode out with McBride on his lurching blue and tan bus, and got off twenty minutes from Borchardt Street. I spoke with Mr Darnell Weeks and he said they'd try me out. Then I started taking that bus every morning.

The factory was on three floors, and the top floor was where I worked: white and black boys together, women sitting at their spooling tables, winding and winding. Below us, trophies were boxed and the grey cardboard boxes of PRIDE OF PLACE and CHAMPION and RUNNER-UP got labeled and dispatched.

The spools of color hung from the wall—blue first, red second, yellow third, white then pink, finally green. We got our work orders from Louie at the type table, whose hands moved over the drawers absently; grinning and chewing gum with his eyes always on the ladies. Louie was a Cajun. He sang in a high-pitched whine over the sound of the machines and the chatter. His thing was taking out his dick while he was setting type with the other hand, keeping a conversation up with the woman roller at his side, the high desk acting as a screen between them. From where we six or seven men stood against the wall, on his other side, we could see him pulling on it, spitting in his hand, shooting us a sly wink. I had to be cool and not too fascinated when he first did it. Roscoe to my left said it happened once or twice a week, I should pay him no mind.

Roscoe was my age and already married with two children; his wife worked down on the second floor, and the kids stayed home with her parents. She's only going to work another month or so, he told me, or, another week or so, or, sometimes, just till the end of summer. He was disgusted with Louie, and expected me to be too. When Louie took it out, Roscoe would set his jaw and glower at him, as if all the women on all the floors were being demeaned by him, not just the roller of the moment. The other men on the line were unperturbed.

The work wasn't difficult, but we were on our feet all day, and the bending and pulling tired me out. The air was thick with the smell of sizing, and bits of gold leaf that clung to every stationary surface; it was under my fingernails and in my hair when I came home every afternoon. An old white man named Harris was the foreman, and walked among the workers frowning and complaining and blowing his nose in his grey handkerchief when he was especially upset. The years of surveillance had dropped his chin low on his chest, and his back rose behind his neck in an odd hump. He was a short man, with no authority in his bearing, and the workers generally ignored him.

I came home flattened out, but James would cheer me up. I tried to do some drawing in the evening, but it seemed there was always something else going on. It was a job, and I was glad I had it, but it taxed my body more than I imagined it could. It was like the first days of football back in Lillienthal, when you practiced early in the morning and then in the early evening, and in between, lay around the house trying to consolidate your strength.

We went to Tipitina's club the second weekend after I started at Regalia, and I was still feeling sluggish and heavy-limbed. My shoulders and back hadn't yet got used to the pulling pressure of the press handles. A knot had developed on my right shoulder near the neck, and at one point in the evening

James leaned across the table, smiling through the welter of Dixie beer bottles and fried peanuts, and massaged it. It made me feel proud and happy that he didn't care who saw. The club was smokey, and the man on the piano had a round mouth and the songs came out like bubbles from a fish. Everything was underwater. James moved like a shark, coming up close and then fading back; the waitresses danced like waves. We were crowded into the tiny room with a hot Saturday night crowd and the music was pumping up and down:

> And when you come to New Orleans
> You will see the Zulu King

coming through the sweet sticky air. They called the piano player Professor, and he kept on squeezing the notes: they flew out of the piano like squirts of lemon, hit the walls and the ceiling and happy faces. He rode the piano, and the young broad-shouldered men behind him slapped at their drums and guitar, all of them nearing the finish together.

The music was the closest to the earth that I'd been—the swaying, bouncing crowd kept my face right against it. The sort of music you could smell and taste, the kind that swirled you around in its vortex, pulled something out of you that you didn't know was there. James stood behind me when the tables got too crowded, tight in the middle of a netful of shining arms and faces, white sleeves rolled up over muscles of midnight blue, men with their women standing pressed against them, women in scarlet- and mustard-colored dresses, in terry-cloth halters and pedal pushers, a crowd coming out of its shoes. The Professor would throw his notes toward one or another of the couples, and they would shout them back, and the rinky-tink sound of it all was something thrilling.

Hard and fast, like a storm at sea, and the music rose up in higher and higher waves, with James rocking and sweating behind me, and then things all tilted sideways, and were quiet.

I came to in what must have been the manager's office, the photos of this and that jazz great slowly coming into focus over the couch where I lay. James was bending over me, concern all over his face, and his brown eyes as big as I had ever seen them.

"Giving me a turn here, Mickey," he said, and I saw there were some other men standing behind him, waiters probably, and as I started to sit up, one of them came forward and motioned me to stay where I was.

"Too much heat," he said in a low rumbling voice, and gave James a wink. "You all right now—but you better have your friend carry you home and put you to bed."

He was grinning so hard that I had to sit up to prove I wasn't just some little pastey-face. James wasn't crazy about his smirk either, I could tell.

"That's all right," James said, exaggeratedly polite in the midst of innuendo. He asked was I fit enough to get up and come home and naturally I said I was. The man still stood over me. I recognized him as the bouncer. He was taller and heavier than James, with a smile that you might call nasty, but you would not call unattractive.

Get me out of here, I thought.

The next morning, I felt embarrassed, as if I'd behaved badly, gotten drunk. Maybe I had gotten drunk. People did, after all, pass out. But the guilt I felt wasn't so much to do with what I'd done as what I hadn't. It had to do with the big slick-looking bouncer at the club, with wanting him to crawl right on top of me while I lay on that couch. This was something new, something I hadn't had to deal with before now. Up until that moment, I hadn't seen anybody but James. Up until then, I'd thought I was set for life.

I got back to drawing in the park again the next few days when James went overnight on the *Avalon*, up to Vicksburg and back. I was drawing the white statue, giving it more life than it had, filling up the paper around it with oleanders and dark faces, getting it wrong and starting up again. One of the sketches I produced looked like a real drawing when I finished it, and I put it up in James' room, stuck under the rim of the mirror. When he came back, he professed to like it a great deal, and that made me keep on. I got the idea I'd like to draw him sitting in the park, and I couldn't tell if he thought that was an especially good idea or not, but he agreed. Next afternoon, when I came home from Regalia, and after his nap, I sat facing him on the wooden bench, and tried to get his fine dark features down. Trying so hard, I made a mess of him again and again; a lot of other faces began to peep through the smudges of pencil and conte, but none of them was his. I wouldn't let him see my little stack of failures, wadded them up and threw them into the backyard trash can before dinner. But the next afternoon I tried again, and finally something came through, which *might* have been his brother or his cousin. But he didn't even see that resemblance when I relented and showed it to him.

"Why don't you just use your imagination," he suggested after wrinkling and unwrinkling his nose, giving the sheet of paper a long look of disapproval. "I know your imagination's a powerful thing."

But that's not what I wanted to do. I wanted to draw him from life, not memory. I got short-tempered and said I'd do it my way. I drew something ugly and beady-eyed the next time, and finally decided that was enough of that.

James was proud of his looks, and me not doing them justice must have been like denying the veracity of that handsome charm. You look into a mirror that gives you back a distorted image, quick enough you look away. I felt something lacking in me, in not being able to catch his likeness—not so much a lack of talent as a lack of affection. I had to get him down.

Work at the factory plodded along, the July heat becoming steamy and uncomfortable. Roscoe disappeared for two days in the middle of the week, mumbled about trouble at home when he came in again. Darnell Weeks fired a girl in the trophy department because she was taking home as many pieces as she engraved—little bitty things she stuck in her purse, like statuettes from a midway: she just had to have her own collection.

The presses wheezed and sighed and clanked, and at night it took me a good number of drinks before I felt my ordinariness slip away, and my sense of uniqueness return. The more time I put in, away from James and away from my drawing, the less I felt I inhabited an adventure that was mine (ours) alone. The pattern I was setting for myself at Regalia seemed decidedly humdrum.

James was a glamorous figure, but was I? Could glamour rub off? If it could, I was. Otherwise, I had to admit, as the 4-H streamers passed beneath my fingers and the other Regalia workers spat and swore, glamour was elsewhere. I might as well have stayed in Lillienthal, and gone to work across the river at Hamilton Beach. It was only when I brought James into the picture of my life that it brightened, took on colors other than the glossy blues and purples of the ribbon factory. Through him, I was learning things about myself, about the life of the senses, and at a rapid clip. That, I knew, was what an artist was obliged to do. And I was earning my own way in the world, which was a not inconsiderable satisfaction to me. Most of all I felt the pleasure of spending my emotions, emotions hoarded so long—and delighted in the fine soaring freedom, the solidifying of my amatory intent.

Lillienthal was hundreds of miles upriver, with tiny figures going about tiny chores. Here in New Orleans I was larger than my previous life. My younger brothers, Dennie Lee and Chris, sent me letters; they were now working as caddies the way Franklin and I had. I realized how quickly they were coming up behind my older brother and me—and that, too, augmented my feeling of freedom, as if, by filling our shoes, they let us step up out of them, move on. James asked me to read these letters to him. He was enthralled with the idea of having younger brothers; being the youngest himself, he'd never had the chance to baby any of his siblings—had never expected from but always been expected of. And he wanted to counsel, to help; he often talked to me about doing this or that with my life, using my imagination, fulfilling my potential. No doubt his expectations were too high. Sometimes he sounded like Mr Adams, the guidance counselor back in high school. All I had in mind to do was soak up life, become in turn all the vivid colors that came my way, never mind about potential.

What resolve I had hardened into a determination to see all I could, to do all I might, and worry about putting it to use, sorting it out, later. If I was lucky, I deserved to be lucky—wasn't that the way it went?

It got to be a Sunday afternoon in late July, with James upstairs asleep, and me down on my park bench, thinking about my brothers, making a series of desultory passes with my pencil, wishing I could be a little bit more inspired. Usually I would have been in the boardinghouse at this hour, or out with James calling on friends and players. But he was exhausted from running up and down the river and he hadn't done too well at the tables either, so he was sleeping off Mrs Odum's pork roast and his discontents, and I was marking time.

Women who usually sat in the park on weekdays were home now with their families; children who played kick-the-can next to the entrance gate were drowsing on their daddy's knee. Everything was still, except for the blue jays who kept on with the usual disclaimers, contending with the church bells and the notes of a listless piano that came from the direction of Bufort Street.

"Well, now, you look recovered."

Some familiar voice coming low and wet from behind me; a man standing in a patch of speckled sunlight beside the bench. Big and powerful looking. Smiling in a way that said he knew something I didn't, but that I'd find it out soon enough.

"Mind if I sit down?"

It was the bouncer from Tipitina's.

"Make yourself comfortable," I said. Suddenly I was alert, roused from my torpor. I felt the presence of sex and danger at once, cool air flowing over me, tingling my flesh.

"You all by yourself this afternoon, hunh . . . seems like I'm in the same situation. My lady doing her social duties today, letting me fend for myself, so to speak."

He was leaning back against the bench, blue serge slacks pulling tight over his thighs, a polka dot shirt gapping here and there down the front. His hair was slick with pomade, and he had a gold-capped tooth that shone in his smile. Around his neck was a chain hung with small charms, amulets. The smell of peaches, of sharp cologne, talc.

He looked down at my drawing pad, then around the park.

"What sort of drawing you do? Not much here to look at, that's the truth. Draw some of this night life here in the Quarter, get some of this here local color." He laughed, a low rumbling sound that got inside you, made your skin dance. I felt his magnetism, his sexual energy. He leaned a little closer, lowered his voice, let it boil slowly, confidentially. I was feeling fidgety, uncomfortable, stuck to the moment like a fly on flypaper.

"Too hot out here by half. What do you say we take a walk over to my crib. It's not far, just over toward Jackson. Get us a little re-lax-a-tion." He winked as he articulated each syllable, and my face got hot, and he laughed to see the color there. Maybe, if I didn't say anything in compliance, it wouldn't be my fault. Maybe I could just drift along . . .

His crib as he called it was a basement apartment, small and dark with a dressmaker's dummy in the corner and sheets of paper stuck with pins on a big red upholstered chair. He switched on an electric fan that had little strips of ribbon hanging from it, got out a bottle of gin, and poured two glasses.

"Here's to it," he said, and drained the glass in one motion, then reached over and pulled me against him.

"Feel that?" he wanted to know, his lips moving against my ear . . . "That's what all these women wanting hereabouts . . . gonna give you some today, see what you can do with it."

He pulled back, and I took as much gin as I could swallow. He looked at me till I looked away, and his trousers came off like the skin off a banana. I got scared for a moment, but that passed, and then he took charge and I just let it happen, getting hotter and hotter the guiltier I felt. His joint was like a forearm and a fist, the kind you see drawn on rest-room walls, in eight-page bibles, never expect to see in life. Not up close.

"Bigger it is, the easier it is," he was saying, stretching me out on the carpet. Some little fluffy yellow cat had come out of the shadows, and stood watching; I stared at its face as mine bent backwards. With James, sex was give and take and a lot of caring. This wasn't anything to do with that, this was winding me and unwinding me like a top, seeing how much and for how long, playing with a rag doll that didn't protest.

More gin, and more. I was learning about life, taking a good long drink at the well of the senses. And hearing the bells of St. George's, closer than on Borchardt Street, so close they seemed to come from inside my own head. Feeling they might crack the walls of my skull wide open, keep me crazy and freakish, for good and always.

It was late when I finally pulled away from Leopold and out of his sticky lair, so late the stars were out and the moon was filling up with light, the night birds busy in the trees. It might be James was still asleep, and I could keep mum. Maybe you did something like this and just walked away from it. Dad once said that a man has to take his actions upon himself, and keep them to himself—that telling all and whining for forgiveness only put the burden on somebody else. Was that true?

Back at Mrs Odum's the supper plates were still clean on the table in the dining room, and the sound of Thomas watching TV in the kitchen seemed to me reassuring, calming. I crept up the stairs, but caught the glances of Mr Mulkin and Mr McBride who were sitting in the parlor playing checkers. I felt they could see everywhere my body had been and everything it had done in the last few hours. But they were gentlemen, and, seeing me creeping in so furtively, pretended they didn't see me at all.

Upstairs, the light was off in James' room, and that was when I should have left well enough alone. But I was in a state, and had to be *sure* everything was as it was before my adventure —that was a good word for it—and so I pushed his door open and peeked inside.

"Mickey? I been wondering where you all got off to. Come over here . . . come on . . ." He was propped up in bed, with no light but the moonlight coming through the window and I couldn't tell how long he'd been awake.

In that light, there was something catlike about his eyes, the deep brown shining with a milky blue. I came to him and lay down beside him.

"I'm sorry I've been outside so long, just drawing, out in the park, trying to get something done . . ."

He didn't say anything in reply, and I pressed close against him. He'd thrown off the sheet and lay smooth and naked in the patch of moonlight, and I thought, this is a painting, this is art, just this.

In a soft voice he asked, "Where's your drawing pad?" His hands weren't moving on my body the way they usually did. He was waiting, hanging in the moonlight.

I'd left my pad at Leopold's. Thrown in the chair with his old lady's dress patterns. Left behind, forgotten.

"Gotta get a new one," I said, in my squeaky little voice. "Used it all up."

"I bet you did," he said, slow and deliberate. He sat up, facing away from me on the other side of the bed. "Better take a shower," he said in a flat voice I'd never heard before, "cause you be smelling like something out of a whorehouse."

He was up and pulling on his slacks and shirt, bending over to lace up his suede shoes.

"James . . ." I didn't know what words would come out of my mouth, but the panic I felt was something I had to cover.

"I don't want to hear it. Whatever you think you gotta say, you go tell it to the wall."

He was standing by the door now, and I jumped out of bed and tried to put my arms around him, but he pulled away. I guess he saw in my face the fear and panic and shame. Maybe he relented a little, and for a minute let me hold on to him. Then he was out the door, and down the stairs. And I wasn't half of something glorious anymore. I wasn't sure and proud and invincible. I was shivering and cold in an overheated room in New Orleans, somebody small and insignificant and alone, somebody who's just thrown away more than he knew he had.

Next morning, I got up out of that pink bed and went to work as usual. Crying through the night hadn't done me any good, and waiting for James to come back had made the minutes seem hours. I decided I would go off to Regalia, and when I came home in the afternoon, he'd be there again, and he'd understand I was miserable about going off. He'd forgive me, and everything would be fine.

It was a humid morning; the men at the factory had their shirts off by ten o'clock. The Louisiana State Fair had sent in a rush order for cattle and poultry rosettes and badges, and old Harris was running back and forth, exhorting the women to clean it up, clean it up.

Just before noon, when there was a temporary lull, I saw out of the corner of my eye that Louie had leaned back in his chair and was giving his nether self an airing. He looked over at us, to make sure he had a gallery, but only Roscoe and I seemed to be aware of him, busy as all the rest were lining up their Firsts and Seconds and Honorable Mentions. And I saw that Roscoe was in a state himself, as if the steam coming off the type was rolling off his head and shoulders: as if he was some kind of animal about to jump.

The clack-clack of the presses covered the words he was saying—I could only see his mouth working and the muscles of his jaw clenching and unclenching. He turned to look, and abruptly turned back to his press, letting the length of red ribbon he was printing fall beside him. He leaned forward for a moment and pressed his forehead against the wall, and I could see a tremor moving across his shoulders.

Then he wheeled around and came at Louie with his line of type, brandishing it above his head like a hammer. He was yelling and swearing, and Louie stood up so fast to ward him off, his pants stayed in the chair. He twisted away, his joint slapping one thigh then the other, and thrust him off. Roscoe was scrambling over the type table, Pica and English flying all around him, and I was suddenly in the middle of it, trying to pull him back. Beets, the man on the other side, was pulling at me, and it was as if Roscoe was made out of iron himself, he was so powerful. Red-eyed and furious he fought back—the letters in his type stick were like hot, glowing teeth. All the women were screaming, and the girl just on the other side of Louie's desk was looking across at him with an expression of horror and disbelief.

Harris scurried over from the far end of the long workroom —I had my eye on him as much as on Roscoe, thinking now it would all come to an end, when Roscoe turned and caught me across the stomach with his smoldering stick.

So hot it didn't burn at first, the type left three letters on me

—when I looked down I saw the S E C burned into me, and was outraged, and I slumped against the table. My strength drained away. The pain came fast enough, and then I was flailing at Roscoe, with Harris and Weeks standing over us, and the other printers finally getting Roscoe's arms behind him.

The pain and the heat made me nauseous. Beets helped me out of the press room, into the lounge where there was a ratty old couch I could lie down on. I could hear the loud voices, Roscoe's yelling, almost weeping, then a woman's voice—which I guessed was his wife's—rising and falling, and gradually the noise of the machines taking over again. Weeks came in, tight-mouthed and stiff, and said they couldn't countenance brawling, and that I had better pick up my check and call it quits. Just then the door to the nearest toilet stall swung open and Louie came out, shaking his head and grinning, but looking worried when he saw the blisters on my stomach. He told Weeks it wasn't my fault, that Roscoe had come after him, and that he was surely indebted to me for helping him out. Weeks looked dubious but grudgingly accepted his words, and I came to understand I wasn't fired after all. Louie got some salve from the office and patted it on the burn, and wrapped gauze around me, humming his bayou melodies all the while. His tobacco-stained fingers were softer, gentler than I would have imagined, and his scratchy song was like a lullabye—it was all his fault of course, but I felt my anger coming undone as he patted my skin. He leaned close enough that I could smell the tobacco on his breath, his solicitude easing the stinging pain that ought to have been his.

They told me to take the rest of the day off. Louie walked downstairs with me, and said again how sorry he was, and we shook hands. I said it wasn't his fault, really. I wondered whose fault it was. Roscoe was clearly out of himself, and you couldn't blame craziness, could you? Blame evaporated in the air, along with the smell of sizing and gold leaf. And there was in the pain I felt something almost ennobling. I felt the sweet sanctity of the victimized.

I wasn't fired, but I knew I wasn't going back to Regalia. I sat out on the back porch, listening to Thomas in the kitchen as he chuckled and snickered at the dancers on "American Band-stand." A blond girl named Franny Giordana was striking atti-tudes on the Philadelphia dance floor, part jitterbug, part twist, being cute and oblivious. Living for the camera. The sound of Sam Cooke's high clear tenor came out to me as I sat waiting for James—*Bring it, bring it on home to me*—ringing out lustrous and lyrical, floating over the hydrangeas and the sweet peas. I leaned against the rickety balcony and knew it was over, all of it: the summer, my life in New Orleans, the spiraling freedom that had tossed me around one time too often.

Through the screen door I watched as Franny's blond curls and smug pout gave way to the face of Dick Clark, and I looked away, and wondered, in the fullness of my disillusion and self-pity, what was to become of me, after all.

SEX STORY

• ROBERT GLÜCK •

BRIAN UNDID THE buttons of my Levi's one by one, pulled down my pants and Egyptian red cotton briefs; white skin and then my cock springs back from the elastic—"hello old timer." A disappointing moment when possibilities are resolved and attention localized, however good it's going to be. So it's going to be a blow job—that's nice. So it's going to be sex—nice, but less than the world. That blow job defined the situation, then a predictable untangling of arms and legs and stripping off shoes and clothes, my jeans, his corduroys, lighting sand candles, putting on records, closing straw blinds, turning back sheets, turning off lights. Brian has a way of being naked a few minutes at a distance—he politely averts his eyes so I can study him unselfconsciously.

"From his small tough ears, his thick neck came down to his shoulders in a long wide column of muscles and cords that attached like artwork to the widened 'V' of his clavicle, pointing the way to his broad, almost football padded shoulders and then down to those muscular arms, covered with blond hair. The tits were firm, and never jiggled, though the nipples were almost the size of a woman's, and seemed always to be in a state of excitement. A light patch of blond hair was growing like a wedge between them, and a long racing stripe of blond hair led the eye down over the contour of his rippling stomach muscles, past the hard navel, and streamlined down to a patch of only slightly darker pubic hair. There, in all its magnificence, hung the 'Dong.' Its wide column of flesh arched out slightly from his body, curving out and downwards in its solidness to the pointing tip of its foreskin where the flesh parted slightly exposing the tip of a rosebud cockhead. The width of the big cock only partially hid a ripe big sack behind it, where two spheric globes of his balls swelled out on either side of it. The cock hung down freely, without the slightest sign of sexual arousal, and still it spanned downward a full third of the boy's young strong legs.

" 'Turn around slowly,' Cliff said to Rags, unbuttoning his own shirt and pulling it back off his torso . . ."

That was from *Fresh From the Farm* by Billy Farout, pp.20–21. I want to write about sex: good sex without boasting, descriptive without looking like plumbing, happy, avoiding the La Brea Tar Pits of lyricism. Brian is also golden, with a body for clothes, square shoulders, then nothing but the essentials decked out with some light and pleasant musculature. He carries his shoulders a little hunched—the world might hit him on the head —which goes with a determined niceness that can become a little grim, like taking the bus to the LA airport to meet me. But if he has his blind spots, Bruce, Kathy, Denise and I said philosophically in various combinations over cups of coffee—well, who doesn't. It's that this one doesn't correspond to ours. Five years ago Brian painted a picture of a house and had many delusions about it. Finally he went to live in the relative safety of its rooms. I can understand that. Brian looks like anyone. Rags looks like no one; he's an alluring nightmare that reduces the world to rubble. Really, I could never grasp Brian's looks, a quality I admire. When I understand his face, solve it into planes and volumes, factor in blond hair and green eyes, then he turns his head a little, the essential eludes me and I must start all over. Sometimes he's intact as a fashion model exuding sunlight. Sometimes he's a fetus, big unfortunate eyes and a mouth pulled down, no language there, his fingers and toes waiting to be counted.

I knelt and returned his blow job, his body tensed toward me and his cock grew in my mouth according to his heartbeat, each pulse a qualification that sent me backward to accept more. I was not completely in favor of his cock—it seemed indecisive —but he didn't care about it either. When I complimented him —"the fineness of its shape"—he shrugged and the compliment didn't register. It was his ass, full and generous, that we concentrated on.

He more or less pushed me onto the bed and tumbled after me, raising our exchange a level by blowing me while looking into my eyes. He's giving me pleasure and looking at me, keeping me focused. I'm acknowledging that. There's no way to dismiss this by saying I'm lost in a trance, by pretending I am not myself. Still, I make up an escape clause—I say: I put myself entirely in your hands and what I know you desire is to put yourself in mine, so I demand what I know you want me to want. I stood and commanded him to blow me, to do this and that: crawl behind and rim me while I masturbate myself. Brian replied, "As James Bond used to say, 'There's no mistaking that invitation.' " A tongue in your ass is more intimate than a cock anywhere; I receive the sensation inside my groin, in my knees and nipples and wrists. Now this was like a porno movie, or the sex ads in the gay newspapers:

Top (Father, Cowboy, Coach, Cop) wants Bottom (Your prisoner and toy)—and conversely.
29–34? Small waist. W/M, Fr a/p, Delicious tongue worship your endw. Lean back & watch yr hot rod get super done, Sir. Don't any of you with long poles want to be shucked down and get some down-home Fr?
EXHIBITIONISM, j/o, facesitting,
Close Encounters in Venice.

What made it sexy? Probably the posture that isolated sex, isolated fantasy. He blew me and I took one step backward. He murmured, loving to crawl forward. The gesture, economical and elegant as a hawk's wing, pointed toward a vista that was not geographical.

I lifted him and we kissed passionately, our first real kissing filled with deep tongues and assy fragrance, running my tongue over his lips, each tooth defined by a tongue, our saliva tastes the same, he played with our cocks and I carried him to the—no, first he knelt and licked me, licked my feet and legs, tongued between my toes. "I don't like pain but I don't mind a good spanking." I obliged, spanking him on one cheek, then the other, while he blew me and masturbated himself. Then I had to piss and Brian made coffee. What if friendship and love are extras tagged onto sexuality to give it a margin of safety, of usefulness based on repressive goals, and the relations between subject and object, usually dismissed as a set of perversions, were the heart of sex? Brian slipped into the bathroom while I was thinking and pissing. To my surprise he knelt and drank from my cock, looking at me. I wonder what I'm getting into, I said to myself, getting into it.

Still in the bathroom: "I sit on your lap and you talk to me like a father." What if desire and power take the form of "Law" as we experience it, whether as the "father" or the "cop." "Have you been a good boy?" "I have a special treat for you." "Are you going to do a good job of it?" Whispered while tonguing his ear and raining kisses on his neck and cheek—all the language of blackmail and instrumentality, its context shifted to pleasure. Brian dutifully replied to his father's cock, not daring to raise his eyes. These few phrases established father and son, where desire is accumulated and forbidden, yet we remained animals exploring pleasure, teasing prostates with inserted forefingers up to the first and second knuckle, learning by heart each other's cock better than our own, needing to touch all his skin with my tongue: the tonguing of nipples until erect and then little bites accepted resistingly, tongue around the ears inside the head, his curls of blond hair a county line for a tongue going out of town, down the backbone, pause, into the crack, pause, testing the asshole—clean as a whistle, tidy boy—tapping with the slightest pressure, knocking again and again to produce a moan, the straining backward, the gasp of a penetration. Caressing him there satisfied me as though I were touching all of Brian at once.

That got old and the kettle whistled. We settled back in bed with the coffee. There was no way around it, he loved me. It was plain to see in his melting eyes. More, in the steadiness of that melting gaze: he made me more naked than without clothes. I hadn't been loved that way for years; my relief was so fierce you could call it passion. Brian loved me quickly and thoroughly, without a credit check on my personality. I felt abashed.

Responding to my thought he told me the story of his falling in love (which I fill in):

Brian and two women friends traveled from LA to San Francisco to spend Halloween with me. Brian wanted us to portray Earth, Wind, Fire and Water, and accordingly made costumes and masks which he brought along. They were brown, baby blue, scarlet and royal blue, with matching sequins and feathers. I forget which was mine but I rebelled when I saw the scanty muslin toga. "I'll make my own costume," I said, and so we went as Earth, Fire, Water, and a bumblebee. I drank—scared and belligerent. A blur of emotions. In a bar: "I'm a BUMBLEBEE, asshole." We returned home; the scenario indicated passionate happy lovemaking for hours and hours. I dreaded it. Instead I drank a half pint of brandy on top of the evening's beverages. That was October. I hadn't divested myself of the summer's construction project in LA, an escalating nightmare of fraud and anxiety. Ed and I formally separated in June; I desired him in the same way that I still require a cigarette, a physical call. I hardly drink, I never drank. Depressed, I ate Viennese pastry. Ed said he knew when I was upset because I left doilies around the kitchen.

I drank myself into a crying jag. I peeled off my sweaty cigarette-smelling bumblebee outfit and cried on Brian's hot skin for hours. Sometimes I paused, then a stronger wave would submerge me and carry me up. Crescendo. The pain registered as isolation. My body really hurt, my skin hurt, so I decided I'd better eat bread to absorb the alcohol. Besides, crying had made me claustrophobic. It was five in the morning. I got up feeling like Monday's wash, put on one of my abject T-shirts and sat down in the kitchen, wearily sniveling and cramming saltines down my throat. "And that," said Brian, "is when I fell in love with you."

We were on our sides more or less tangled up. His free hand meditated on the slimness of my waist, the power of my shoulders and chest. I basked in his general radiance. I loved his waist and the gold of his skin, I wanted to fold myself into it. Then he slid down and kissed my cock the way you kiss lips. He said, "I love your cock." He said it with more fervor than customarily applied to a sweet nothing, and so lapidary that I assured myself I would remember it during that amount of "forever" which is to be my portion. I've been reading Jane Austen. He said it to my cock's face, and I thought Oedipally, "A face a mother could love." "How's your mother?" And, "How's her emerald collection?" I liked to hear him recite her stones. I think Brian felt he betrayed her a little, that my eagerness and the question itself was not in the best taste; "Gimme a break," he would say. And here I am justifying his fears. But really I viewed her collection as a victory, a personal domain wrested from so much that was not hers. I liked its lack of utility and sexual shimmer. I liked the war that each piece represented, complete with siege, ground strategy and storming the fort. Her collection was an Aladdin's hoard, not an investment. She had: (1) A diamond and emerald bracelet, groups of four each alternating around. (2) A diamond ring that Brian says doubles as a Veg-a-matic. (3) A diamond and gold brooch set in an inch-wide gold bracelet (Brian's favorite). (4&5) Two pairs of diamond and emerald clips. (6) An emerald brooch, geometric design within a rectangle. (7) Many pearls. (8) A large emerald ring. Plus opals and a few token stones.

She has a few things. Is she ruling class? A question at this point is a double one: Who stands to gain what? Brian's mother merely angles back a little of her own power in the going currency of charm and attractiveness. She's not the Enemy.

I met the enemy at a gay resort on the Russian River. It felt strange to be there, surrounded by money and its attendant— available and well-groomed flesh. Until that day I spent my vacation at a small neighborhood beach where nakedness was not so much a declaration. Each morning I took Old River Road to about five yards from the Hacienda Bridge, veered right and coasted down a steep grade that carried me back to an older level of houses and crossroads beneath the bridge. Like a dream: there is a world underneath this one and it's here now. I parked at

the end of Hummingbird Lane, stepped over a barbwire fence
and its PRIVATE sign, took a darkly congested path—maple trees
and blackberry bushes—which became sunnier—manzanita and
buck brush—opening out to the hot sun and an arid span of rock
and sand bleached white right up to the river's channeled cool-
ness. Naked people lay as far from each other as possible. The
air was white and deadlocked from reflected heat, it made the
sunbathers look like quick sketches. When I wet my lips I almost
tasted the remote breeze that stirred the tops of the laurel and
Douglas fir growing up the opposite hillside. I couldn't hear the
river; a loud buzzing sound came from the spellbound air, the
inactivity, the heat, my own breath—I either submitted to it or
felt anxious.

That stretch of river held a special attraction for me. A few
white alders grew on a little island. Next to the island there was
a small rapids with an alder overhanging it, and someone had
tied a rope around a branch. A swimmer could grab hold of the
rope and be carried up by the water—lithe and quick—legs,
belly, everything washed and washed. Buoyed up like that, if I
submerged my head a giant roaring surrounded me. It was so
pleasurable I could endure it only a few minutes. I was bored,
alone, diffused—there was no ground to be me pursuing my
aims, no margin for the anxiety of perspective, resolution into
categories. Gradually I spent more time dangling from that rope;
finally I tied myself to it although I feared drowning. What a
pleasurable agony each moment is as it dilapidates into the next.
The water rushed, brought my body to a point, it felt good.

My friend Sterling came up from San Francisco and stayed
at a gay resort, which is how I found myself lying nakedly with
him beside a swimming pool along with fifty other men. I was
comforted by the smell of chlorine and hot cement. We looked
like a David Hockney that had gotten out of hand; the sun was
spinning ribbons in the water and also cooking eight thousand
pounds of shellacked gay flesh. Sterling introduced me to suntan
oil. His friend Tom, the enemy I mentioned before, had joined
us. We repositioned ourselves to the full sun. I was on my stomach, drowsy, and Sterling absentmindedly put his hand on my
left asscheek, he put his hand on my ass, he put his hand on my

ass and he kept it there, he kept it there—I didn't move a muscle and basked in his hand more than in the sun, pleasure spread to the back of my legs, my lower back and my nipples—not a muscle, he'd think I was uncomfortable, his hand was hotter than the sun on my other cheek—somebody said, "Bob's got an ass like a peach." Sterling, who's black, said, "Not that much color." I suggested wintermelons. "What?" said Sterling. *"Wintermelons."* "What did Bob say?" asked Tom. "He said *wintermelons*," Sterling answered.

Tom gazed abstractly down at his unformulated body, master of all he surveyed. The afternoon passed and much conversation got said and forgotten, but information about his wealth gathered like nuggets or objets d'art set mentally side by side on a mantel. Instead of ormolu clocks and Chinese epergnes, I counted three houses—mansions—in San Antonio, a farm in upstate New York, two houses in Florida, a ranch in the Panhandle, three houses in San Francisco, and condos in New York City and Palm Springs. These were his proud investments; he'd made this million on his own, not resting on the laurels of his inherited millions from Gulf Oil. Answering me, he said, "My watch cost $8,000. Look, it's a twenty dollar gold piece with a diamond nob, set in a gold case."

Tom furnished much food for thought. It shocked me that he was so undefined. At thirty he still had his baby fat, aimless good will. He wore the most conventional plastic leather outfits. Never in his life had he voluntarily read anything more detaining than a magazine. Was *this* the Pomeranian Earl of Rochester, his overbright eyes leering subnormally under his peruke? I expected manners, Jane Austen, nice debates as to who takes precedence at dinner, fine points. How else do you know you're different from the servants?—and the people who run your farms and rent your apartments? When I returned from the toilet he joked, "Did everything come out all right?" And later he asked it *again*.

How could all that wealth be condensed in this fatuous presence? The answer: it wasn't. The wealth stayed where it was, intangible. Maybe Tom's character grew vague by way of response. Tom doesn't live on top of his servants; his property remains as abstract as the money it equals. Even the fifty Persian carpets he treasures wait in constant breathless readiness to be traded or sold. So manners might be beside the point, the tweed and horses of his seniors a tip of the hat to feudal wealth. But how can I attack Tom's life and still defend his sexuality? When Sterling, Tom and I walked back to my car we passed a bunch of "youths" whiling away the day lounging on their pickups, and despite Tom's bank account they started yelling: "Death to Faggots," "Get Outta Town," "Kill Queers," etc.

Tom became vivid for me in one passage that afternoon. Is it surprising that the medium of his transformation should be pleasure? We were cooling off in the shallow end, watching the suntan oil slick make marbled paper patterns on the pool's surface. We acknowledged a passing physique, a body that summed up what's happening these days. Tom attempted a joke about fist-fucking that included a reference to a subway entrance. I said that I could understand the erotic charge of bondage and discipline, of water sports and so on, but I could never grasp fist-fucking's sensuality. Was it homage to the fist and arm, that masculine power engaged, taken on because inside you? Tom responded with patience and expertise, accustomed to making things clear to laymen. He said that most fist-fucking is beside the point because it stops at what he called the trap. I think that's a plumbing term. He said that the colon makes a right-hand turn and then loops up all the way to the diaphragm. He drew the arch on my torso with his forefinger. If you negotiate that turn and forge ahead, your hand is a membrane away from the heart—in fact, you can actually hold your lover's beating heart. More than that, after a while your two hearts establish a rapport, beat together, and what physical intimacy could exist beyond this?

I let out a long breath. I was a little stunned. Until then, being naked, I felt naked. Facing this vista of further nakedness, I felt dressed and encumbered as a Victorian parlor.

I joined Sterling; I lay face down on an orange plastic cot and dozed. Troubling images: We're on top of a pyramid. The Aztec priest holds a stone knife in one hand and in the other he lifts the still-beating heart above its former home, the naked warrior, whose lower back balances on a phallic sacrificial stone. He's held by half-naked priests at the hands and feet, his body still spasming and arching. That from the eighth grade. There were no undressed white people in my textbook. The compilers felt that Indians, like animals, did not possess enough being to be capable of nakedness. If I were that picture everyone's cock would be hard as the stone knife.

And this from Anne Rice's *Interview with a Vampire:* "Never had I felt this, never had I experienced it, this yielding of a conscious mortal. But before I could push him away for his own sake, I saw the bluish bruise on his tender neck. He was offering it to me. He was pressing the length of his body against me now, and I felt the hard strength of his sex beneath his clothes pressing against my leg. A wretched gasp escaped my lips, but his bent close, his lips on what must have been so cold, so lifeless to him; and I sank my teeth into his skin, my body rigid, that hard sex driving against me, and I lifted him in passion off the floor. Wave after wave of his beating heart passed into me as, weightless, I rocked with him, devouring him, his ecstasy, his conscious pleasure."

The vampire's erotic charge consists of just this meeting of heartbeats, yet our hero consumes the life he is experiencing. Rice weaves homosexuality into vampire society. Does she think it will make the dead deader? "The pleasures of the *damned*," "the *pleasures* of the damned"; in "Carmilla," once Le Fanu underscores his vampire's grief, you are free to enjoy by proxy her lesbian embrace: "She used to place her pretty arms about my neck, draw me to her, and laying her cheek to mine, murmur with her lips near my ear, 'Dearest, your little heart is wounded; think me not cruel because I obey the irresistible law of my strength and weakness; if your dear heart is wounded, my wild heart bleeds with yours. In the rapture of my enormous humiliation . . .' "

So death accompanies this heart stuff. And some would say, do say, that Tom's journey through the anus is a trip to the underworld. Yet this is all very far from the harmony of Tom's description, far from the particular realm of pleasure that expresses the urge to be radically naked. Tom isn't dead, neither are his partners. The construction on their pleasure comes later. As Tom and his friend get dressed, culture, ideology and conflict all enter simultaneously, telling us we are supposed to be alone, discontinuous. We experience this as safety. We experience as transgression the penetration of our boundaries, fusion with another, and they warn us that this transgression is fearful as death. Naturally the vampire always wears a criminal half-smile. This guilt, even if slightly embraced, even if an inch stepped toward, becomes a sexual apparatus increasing the pleasure it decreased, a second ego becoming its own opposite.

I woke up on the plastic cot in the sunlight and shade, looking at a grid of sun the cot stenciled on the cement, thinking over and over *Orfeo ed Euridice, Orfeo ed Euridice*. I forgot who I was; the music and sunlight seemed more real. It was not a Freudian pun on the composer's name, nor—I think—the trip through hell motif. Not even the "Dance of the Furies" to which I did my situps every morning. It was the following band I recalled, "The Dance of the Blessed Spirits," so limpid and noble that I would lie back exhausted and just float.

Sterling was by my side; the rest of the pool area was mostly deserted. He told me a story about his mother which reminded me of Brian's mother and her emeralds. While Brian's mother operated in that middle-class locus of power, the parents' bedroom, Sterling's mother went outside of the house, changing the terms. Sterling grew up in San Antonio where his father, a gambler also named Sterling, had married in his forties a woman twenty years younger. Along with other business ventures, Sterling Sr. ran a "buffet flat." He usually had a mistress but age brought respectability, and now he confines himself to real estate and Adele. Sterling recalls only one fight from his childhood. He can't remember why, but Sterling Sr. slapped his mother. They were in the kitchen; Adele stood in front of a stove filled with a complicated Sunday dinner. She yelled, "You want a fight, motherfucker? I'll give you a fight!"—and she systematically threw at her husband: muffins, potatoes, roast, salad, peas, collard greens, gravy and peach pie. Sterling Sr. stood uncertainly for a moment, weighing the merits of an advance. Finally he broke for the front door. Adele followed. She continued throwing the household at him, including, Sterling said with a pang, a cranberry glass lamp with lusters. Sterling Sr. jumped in his car and started to pull away but Adele got a rifle and blew out his tires. He skidded to a service station, changed tires, and spent a few days in Dallas. This affair triggered in Sterling's mom a meditation; its theme was power and it signaled a change in her relations with Sterling Sr. At that time she worked for a travel agency. Her employers, an alcoholic white couple with liberal views, absconded to Mexico with the advance receipts for a tour of the Holy Land, leaving the agency more or less to Adele. She moved it to the black section of San Antonio and became financially independent. On one of her guided tours of Los Angeles she acquired a lover; they met there for years. All this strengthened Adele's marriage. The two went past the inspirational bitterness of events to the events themselves, and now they are enjoying their sunset years, closer than ever.

"What's a buffet flat?"

It's a railroad flat, a long maroon hallway with many rooms: one room had two men doing it, another had two women doing it, and really each room had anyone with anyone, doing it. It's a sexual buffet. You paid an entrance fee to watch or act. I like the town meeting aspect of this. Also there were stars whom the audience egged on; 1910—big hats and skirts—or the twenties, a little tunic of dark spangles. Against that antique clothing nakedness becomes more naked.

What if I am a black woman who propositions one of these talented big fish. What a smile I'm capable of, I flash him one of these. I'm wearing a black beaded tunic I mentally refer to as my star-spangled night and the streets aren't paved. Want some tequila? Just a splash. What if we're naked together, clothes tossed over a chair and he only fucks me in the missionary position. What if I ask after a while if that's all.

What if he says, "Baby, I'm just warming up, just giving you a taste." I am the bottom man and this river is the top man, lithe and muscular with two handfuls of flesh. I am a bottom, the person who really controls is the bottom and sex is the top and I arrange for it to take my streaming body and clear me of names and express me and bring me to a point. This is pleasure and I'm no fool.

Brian said, "Jackie Kennedy made the pillbox hat famous. She made Halston famous, she made sleeveless dresses famous, she made Valentino famous. She made Gucci famous." "Thrilling words," I said, "I can only add that the discovery of the individual was made in early 15th century Florence. Nothing can alter that fact. Don't you think that's interesting? I do." Brian laughed at me and said, "You're like $e = mc^2$, always brimful of meaning." Then he asked conversationally, "Don't you think your cock is more interesting? I do." I thought it was a likely topic and finished my coffee. "Or am I putting words in your mouth?" he continued, taking my cock in his mouth and laying his head on my lap, still looking up at my face. I replied, "I reckon I'll just kick back and get me some old-fashioned, down-home French." Brian looked like a fetus. Then he sat up and said, "We boys in the back room voted you Mr. Congeniality." "What makes me a great catch?" I asked, falling into his arms so he'd have to catch me. "Looking for compliments?" "I just want to see if our lists tally." Then, seriously, "You know, I have a very beautiful couch." By way of response Brian tickled me, which escalated into wrestling. I lost because I wanted to see what he would do with an immobilized me; he held me down and started licking my torso while I mock resisted even though I was hard. "Want a frozen Reese's Peanut Butter Cup?" he asked my extravagantly arching neck. I pictured them stacked neatly in his freezer. Coffee, Kools and peanut butter cups were Brian's staff of life. I followed him into the kitchen, past his new room arrangement that I had just admired upside down through the bedroom door.

Brian lived in a bungalow in Venice, CA—a bedroom, living room and kitchen. He furnished the living room with a mattress, a box spring, a large palm, a poster-size print of a sepia photograph of women in long skirts carrying rifles in the Mexican Revolution, and another poster of the Hiroshige woodblock print (*36 Views of . . .*). The room was spotless and these five elements constantly found new spatial relationships. I followed him: a small deco kitchen with a total of four dishes, three cups, two one-quart stainless steel saucepans, mismatched flatware for two and a half, and a knife. I liked the cups, Mexican enamel with a decal of an innocent nosegay.

We stood in the dark kitchen kissing; that got old. He wanted to sit on my lap. I was so aroused I was wide open. We mutual masturbated like that and kissed—I was gasping. I caught our reflection in the window and it was funny to see us so localized inside these giant sensations of pleasure, my hips and muscles permanently cocked.

That got old so I carried him to the kitchen table where he squatted like a frog and I fucked him. My own body knows what his experienced: each time my cock touched a certain point hot and icy shivers radiated outward. I burn and freeze. If you have a man's body that is what you would feel. A cock's pleasure is like a fist, concentrated; anal pleasure is diffused, an open palm, and the pleasure of an anal orgasm is founded on relaxation. It's hard to understand how a man can write well if he doesn't like to be fucked. There's no evidence to support this theory; still, you can't be so straight that you don't submit to pleasure. Ezra Pound claimed his poetry was a penis aimed at the passive vulva of London. Perhaps that's why his writing is so worried, brow-furrowed. We dallied with coming for a while but decided no. Brian loved to be carried and pleasure made me powerful, sent blood to my muscles and aligned them. I lifted him from the table and fucked him in the air.

It was great sex—not because of the acrobatics, not even because he loved me and showed it and showed it, but because we were both there, very much of us, two people instead of two porno-movie fragments. Brian knelt in front of me, sucking the cock that fucked him. That's one—among many—of the things I wouldn't do. Don't do too often. It's not so bad, but all I think is now I'm doing this and what disease will I get. I quickly brush the cock with my hand like kids sharing a bottle of Coke, certain that no germs are killed, just so something besides my lips touches it first. I admired Brian's range and mobility; his sexuality makes little concession to the world. I contrasted him favorably with myself. Brian is more sexually alive than anyone I know. A shower of sparks spills off his skin like inside a foundry. I'm a little more cautious, a little less generous. Let's say I had to avert my eyes.

I had to piss, Brian smiled, I laughed—a light went on about all the coffee he kept feeding me. Ed, whose dream life still seems definitive, described pissing into epic Busby Berkeley waterfall fantasies, erotic masterpieces of technical know-how. I presented to Brian the difficulty of pissing when hard, but in the spirit of the great director he assured me that when there's a will there's a way. All the same, these particular golden showers were intermittent. Kneeling, he put his head between my legs —I piss on his back, then slowly in his mouth. Because the temperature was all the same I couldn't tell what was cock, mouth or urine, like pissing in a lake, just feeling warmth and a pressure outward. I envied Brian the clarity of his position.

Not sex, but my concern for you makes this story vulgar. You see I named it before you could. Brian and I were both so powerful, admiring each other's power. Surely power and sexuality seek each other out, even if ultimately they are held in a suspension. But our force was opposite to the kind that oppresses and controls, so it engendered permissiveness and generosity. Like the strategies of the two mothers who wanted to reclaim their lives: on the one hand, power lies in understanding the given terms and using them as leverage; on the other hand, power changes the terms. In literature, the former is *technique*— I wanted to create beautiful things (precious stones); the latter, *tactics*—I want a dynamic relation with my audience (my husband).

I scooped Brian up, kissed him and carried him back to bed. He asked me if I'd like to hear about his confinement in a mental institution. He asked so politely that I understood he wanted to tell me about it: "You have to understand I repeated the story about 498 times during the first two days—doctors are even more curious than *you*—but I'll try to make it fresh." (It's true he talked as though he were composing a letter.) He began, "Well, Bobbo, it's like this:

"I'd been whittling my life down so that smoking a cigarette became an actual activity. I just broke up with a boy named

Aaron who lived about three blocks away. I used to visit him in his new apartment and model for a painting called *The Junkie*. It showed me sitting in a pile of garbage with a needle in my arm."

"You sat there with a needle in your arm?"

"After I went nuts, Aaron told me he never found anyone who could hold the pose as long. I was taking a visual perception course taught by a woman named Edith Hammer. She was a great teacher; she'd show different works from different times and compare their visual components. After my second class I had an acute guilt attack, rushed to an art supply store and bought a large square canvas, paints and brushes. I rushed home to the apartment I had shared with Aaron but now occupied alone, and started painting.

"At first the idea seemed lyrical and intelligent: to make a cross section of reality in the form of a house."

"Sounds like an idea to me. Meaning and Safety."

"The windows were shaped like coffins and corresponded to gravestones above. The windows opened on a blank horizon. Above was a cemetery scene illustrating a story from my mother's childhood; it showed my grandmother and my aunt sitting under a tree, my mother as a child running to them, and my uncle as a baby watching the whole thing from behind the tree. It was done in mottled brilliant colors and I was very excited about it.

"I would wake up every morning and *see* something else and keep working, drawn deeper into it. I saw duality in everything; the painting helped me break down reality into its basic components and I thought if I saw past the duality I'd get to the nitty-gritty. Meanwhile it was getting a little scary. I titled the painting *The Conception and Evolution of Brainchild's Unity Theorem*, and when I printed that on a piece of paper and thumbtacked it to the lower corner, the gesture completed the delusion. I thought I had brought the symbol to reality—that some presence came from my painting through the white of the clouds which were unpainted, thus being a void. Then I had the terrifying conviction that I somehow evolved myself through the painting to be God.

"The more I tried to reason it out, the deeper I got. I tried burning the frame I had made in my bathtub, thinking if I partially destroyed the painting I could save myself. I was afraid if I burned the whole painting I might die or the world might end. I started schlepping the painting. I took it to school—'nice' —and then to Miss Hammer—'spiritual.' I wanted to throw up.

"Finally after a visit to my friend Mary Dell (with the painting)—no one seemed to be able to deal with what was going on with me. I called Mary Dell back that night and she drove me to the hospital where I lied and said I had insurance and committed myself. The admitting shrink thought I was tripping."

Brian had finished. I felt trapped by his story: his years felt like a graph with sadness as both scales. It struck me that the same qualities—generosity, emotional presence—that paved the way for all this distress also made him good at love. Should I charge in and set up squatter's rights in his experience? He wasn't dejected, didn't call for support or even sympathy. Just because of that, he seemed to test my aptitude for sympathy and support. I feared Brian might want to be saved, and how could I do that? Then I realized he just wanted me to pay attention. With tremendous exertion I asked him some interested questions. How long was he in? Nine months. Jesus! Did they try to cure him of being gay? (I squeezed his cock.) Yes, although they didn't succeed. (He squeezed my cock.) But in the end the violence of Brian's story was so much a condensation of dream to me that I was falling asleep; sleep was a cliff that I fell off, drifting slowly as a parsley flake in a jar of oil. Did he have to wear a uniform? Yes. They sedated him most of the time.

Our bodies had turned around. We looked up at the ceiling, absentmindedly playing with our own and each other's cocks, which enhanced my detached response to Brian's story. As a postscript he added: "Aaron embraced the Bahai faith and swore himself to celibacy. He now lives in a trailer in Champagne, Minnesota, and calls me occasionally to ease the Way. The painting ended up in my shrink's office closet. I moved to Los Angeles and found a job as the manager of the toddler's department at Saks." (I see him looking like the sun in his linen suit. He's saying—with his hand over his heart—to a bullying child, "Hey, gimme a break.")

In the silence that followed we applied ourselves to each other's body more creatively; we dribbled on some Vaseline Intensive Care lotion while Brian speculated that probably gay men have younger cocks because of the oils and lubricants. Truman Capote wrote that we also have youthful necks and chins, I added, because of all the sucking. I recalled an Isherwood quotation: "Of course it would never have occurred to any of them to worry about the psychological significance of their tastes." I copied this passage on my journal page after three recipes for potato salad.

I don't think "disturbed" people are more healthy than "normal" ones, but sometimes there is a fine line, or no line at all, between "disturbed" and oppressed. Driven crazy is more like it. And the psychiatrist's couch turns this oppression to profit. Are oppressed people more sexual? Other forms of discourse— languages of production and ownership—have been denied us or disowned. By default we are left with sex and the emotions —devalued as a Cinderella at the hearth. And then we become —maybe—Cinderella at the ball. Then we are blamed for embracing sexuality and we will be a bone in the throat of people who don't. It's the same with the popular cultures of gays, people of color, women, the working class. They are feared because they draw energy away from "productive goals." And they are colonized, neutralized and imported into our stagnant mainstream culture. Sex is a sign of life. If sex is relegated to gays as a sign of our devalued state—becoming the shimmer of jewels— it's strange to me that the Left hasn't broached the topic of pleasure. You could say the Left leaves it to Freud, but where is pleasure in all his systems and epi-systems? In all that dominant where is the tonic, the home key?

Brian asked, "What would you like?" A thought sailed by, "It would be nice if you . . ." Here inspiration failed—I was dejected, couldn't grasp the rest. It was growing light. I felt a little scared to be doing this for so many hours, a little "disturbed." I thought of the Marquis de Sade, the business of being perpetually feverish, energy spiraling out because it's mental, disconnected from physical rhythms, busy, busy, busy. I wanted my borders back; I wanted to curl into myself intact as a nautilus shell and let my sleeping mind group and regroup to absorb and master this experience. I said, "Masturbate me as slowly as you can." We lay on our backs, side by side and head to foot. This is really a solitary activity for two in that your attention equals your sensation, and the hand on the other's cock requires as little care as the hand that grasps a branch in the Russian River. We masturbated each other slowly, achingly gathering up skin into folds which were meditative and inward turning as the mantle of a 14th century Madonna; then in a reversal that we experienced as a huge change from night to day, or the turning in some great argument, we brought our hands down. It made us gasp. The pace was excruciating. We were permanently aroused, erectile tissue flooded and damned up, and so we enjoyed a kind of leisure and Mozartian wit based on invention. I knew from the first with Brian that we would continue. Love and friendship aside, you can tell on a first meeting the number of exchanges it will take to accomplish the various sexual permutations—know by the way he touched you rather than by positions and tastes.

I could just see the top of Brian's sunny head over the horizon of his chest. Silence, gasps—out of the blue he said, "You would have looked like dynamite in that toga."

What if I'm fucking on the grass in ancient Rome like we always do on Wednesday night. Is it Thursday? What's one day? Nothing—you turn around and it's dark, the tick and tock of day and night. What if I'm the woman? I'm languidly stretched out on the grass fanning myself with a spray of flowering myrtle. When he enters me I'm spread open as a moth, I'm all colors. What if I'm the guy when I feel someone on me and wham!—I've got a cock up my ass—I never saw the guy before and I *still* haven't seen him but I ride his cock—why not? —I'm riding it across a continent of skin. I feel like a sandwich, the pleasure's in the middle because no one has had or knows this much—I can't see, I'm bellowing and I start to come, it begins in my ass as a pinpoint of light a thousand miles away. I move closer to it with a religious sense of well-being and when I come I shout a little prayer—I shout *Je-Sus!*

What if I'm fucking this boy and his orgasm is so absolute it

leaves me gasping. What if I'm watching the three of them calling on the gods and gasping their extravagance—their arms and
legs, their skin filled with rosy orifices, they look like an anem-
one. First I'm the woman, then I'm the man, then I'm Catullus,
then I'm an observer remembering a poem, the distance becoming erotic.

He's going to make us into a poem, I've heard better lines.
What if he takes us to his villa and merely to pluck at my nipples
he feeds me olives pickled in caraway, dormice dipped in honey
and rolled in poppy seeds, sausages, orioles seasoned with pep-
per, capons and sow bellies, blood pudding, Egyptian and Syr-
ian dates, veal, little cakes, grapes, pickled beets, Spanish wine
and hot honey, chickpeas and lupins, endless filberts, an apple,
roast bear meat, soft cheese steeped in fresh wine, tripe hash,
liver in pastry boats, oysters and hot buttered snails, pastry
thrushes with raisin and nut stuffing, quinces with thorns stuck
in them to resemble sea urchins, because I'm handsome.

Some people like sex, most men don't. What if I'm blowing
him, I look up as he brings down a knife—I either die or don't
die. I'm alone at night in bed, someone's moving silently up the
stairs—this was to be a sexual rendezvous but instead he intends
to wrap a wire around my neck. I don't die but my erection's
gone. I must begin again: what if he puts his hand under my
tunic, his finger up my ass and I squirm down on it, why not?
My girl's laughing—dildos shaped like birds and fish. He's
moaning *Nostra Lesbia, Lesbia illa, illa Lesbia*—what is this, Latin?
This guy's obviously educated.

Orioles must be aphrodisiac or maybe it's the situation because all we want to do is fuck, we can't keep our clothes on, we
go to it, showing off for him. I love how our eyes go blank and
then we think with our bodies. She licks it like a cat with her
rough tongue, or like licking ketchup off your forefinger—one
two, that's all. Then men come and lift me and hold my legs and
body while he fucks me and I'm blowing somebody, it's fantastic, all I ever want to do is this.

Brian and I were working ourselves around to coming; we
enjoyed the sense of absolute well-being and safety that precedes
orgasm. But now we are on our knees kissing urgently and mas-

turbating ourselves. Our cocks felt a little ragged and wanted the master's touch. Masturbation can *feel* better, although I favor a penetration for emotional meaning. Still, that was hardly necessary since we filled up the house to overflowing, and besides, we weren't planning to have a baby.

Orgasms come in all shapes and sizes, sometimes mechanical as a jack-in-the-box—an obsessive little tune, tension, pop goes the weasel—other times they brim with meaning. And other times, like now, they are the complimentary close that signals the end of a lengthy exchange. I recall a memorable climax, a terrific taste of existence in the summer of 73. I was with Ed; we weren't doing anything special but the orgasm started clearly with the fluttering of my prostate, usually a distant gland, sending icy waves to my extremities. Then a hot rush carried my torso up into an arc and just before I came a ball bearing of energy ping-ponged up and down my spine.

Brian and I curled into each other. Our semen smelled faintly of chlorine. Sunlight glittered off or was accepted by the domestic surfaces. On our way to falling asleep we exchanged dreams.

BOB: I dreamt that an alligator lives in my kitchen wall; it cries brokenheartedly on the weekends. A cannibal rabbit with sharp teeth lives there too. A pathetic shabby man who looks like Genet keeps beckoning to me, appearing at a distance everywhere, even on the Greyhound bus I take to escape him, standing up the aisle and beckoning. These characters fill me with dread. I know they can't hurt me in themselves—they are intensely defeated, already claimed by death to such an extent that I writhe backward rather than associate with them.

BRIAN: I dreamt this while I was nuts. A group of nuns in black and white floated on the surface of a foreign planet. They were only heads, like that creature in the space movie. In their hands they carried candles that vibrated colors and gold. Everything on the nuns' side was gray and dead, but where the candles were, the light created moving patterns of color and electricity.

BOB: One day Denise, following a recipe of mine, made baked apples in wine. But something went awry and they turned out hard and sour. That night I dreamt there was a new kind of elephant called an Applederm, and its babies were called Apples.

BRIAN: I was at a party with my father. Our hosts—a family —were noticeably absent, which made me angrier .nd angrier. I followed my father into the dining room to placate myself with some food and as I looked up I realized it was my parents' apartment. There was laughter from the other room and someone said, "All our hearts are the same here."

BOB: I dreamt this around puberty. I was making love with my little sister on her bed but the springs squeaked and I was anxious because my family in the next room might hear us. So we became bumblebees and hovered above the bed, buzzing and buzzing, and when we touched stingers I came. (I never told anyone my bumblebee dream, had forgotten it for years. I felt that now Brian could know me in one piece—what wasn't in the dream he could extrapolate.)

BRIAN: I stood in a room that was all black and white and because the dream was in color it was beautifully vivid. Black and white tiled floor, white walls, black and white solid drapes. As I looked around the room I saw a black bed from classical Greece, white sheets and in the bed a boy, sun-tanned with platinum blond hair. The contrast between him and the black and white setting filled me with joy; I moved closer passing through veils of black and white (remember duality?) and as I kissed him I awoke with the overwhelming erection that only dreams can provide.

Brian and I sometimes exchange letters. In the latest, Brian told me he is moving in with a lover. I felt a pang that I had no right to turn into any claim—the pain augmented by the fact that Sterling moved out of my life without leaving a forwarding address. I had been curious about the story Brian painted from his mother's childhood. He answered:

"The image was based on one of my mother's frequent outings with my grandmother, my great aunt Kate and her uncle Ollie. Kate's husband, Hugo, died young and on weekends my grandmother and Kate would pack a picnic and make a day of visiting Hugo. I'm not sure why this is so peculiar to me. Maybe because that's my mother's impression of it. More likely it's that Be-Be (our name for my grandmother) and Kate were so unaware of the irony of taking children to play in a cemetery. I made my mother the embracer and my uncle the observer. Later, Katie was institutionalized along with both her daughters, who somehow were not in on these trips. I met Katie when I was six and she would definitely win the most terrifying-person-I-ever-met award. She had straight black hair cut severely across with straight long bangs. She sat hostilely on my grandmother's sofa, barely acknowledging our family's presence. She also scared the shit out of my father. She eventually died in a hospital singing Irish lullabies to herself.

"My grandmother held her own in the strange department. In her sixties she had to have one of her eyes—including the lid—removed. Instead of wearing a patch, Be-Be opted for glasses with a large plastic artificial eye attached to one of the lenses. It had a bizarre effect, particularly when she napped. What can I say about riding the subway with her —that people stared? that I got angry? It made me dislike the world and love her. She would call and invite me to lunch. 'We'll go out!' she'd say expansively, as if The Acorn on Oak were the world. I gave her a feather boa one Christmas and we were thick as thieves after that. She loved to dance, drink. She would come out of the bathroom with hair she had just bleached platinum, make a 20s pout in the mirror, say, 'Your mother and I are both blondes,' and giggle. She was great.

"When Be-Be died, she presented a unique problem to the undertaker. My mother insisted that the coffin be open in the Irish tradition. The undertakers were perplexed—should they put Be-Be's glasses on her and create the disconcerting effect of a corpse with one eye open? In the end that's exactly what they did, and dressed in her favorite red beaded gown, Be-Be said goodbye.

"Moody in her earlier years, Be-Be became senile later. I'd go to her apartment and cook dinner. I loved her very much. In the hospital she suddenly became lucid and rose to the occasion of her death. She said, 'You always learn something. Now I'm learning about tenses. How long is this going to take?' Then she removed her rings, one by one, and placed them on the nightstand for my mother."

SECOND SON

• ROBERT FERRO •

From Second Son, *a novel in progress*

AFTER SOME TIME he realized the house was speaking to whom-ever might be listening: this was Mark. He heard it in the wind through the porch, in the boom at the end when a door slammed, in the whine of the furnace when first engaged; sounds that held images the house reminded him not to forget, images of moments fractured in air as when, turning at the bannister at the top of the stairs, he saw his young niece tilt her head to listen to her vanity and adjust a gypsy earring—a languorous, emblem-atic moment of her magic childhood, in an older safer world. The house made this possible. He could see it still in the air.

—Images also, besides his family, of the two strangers who long ago had built the house and lived in it and died upstairs: the Birds. *Captain* Bird, it appeared. The childless Birds had never struck such chords, while the numerous Valerians, occu-pying every room, adding others, had changed the house into something alive and hovering, a huge pet that engulfed them, vitally interested in the goings-on. Captain Bird however had seen to it that everything about the place was nautically and astronomically sound. It faced exactly East, on a line drawn up the middle, like a keel, that passed through the center of the hearth and out the bay window into the heart of the sea with the sudden precision of the speed of light. The sea, visible from every room, was in some rooms a wall; in others a picture on the wall. From the upper windows it seemed you were on a river-boat, and in winter, with the furnace, as if the whole place was under way, moving through a delta perhaps; approximately. From the long deck over the porch, leaning into the wind, he could see the sharp edge of the planet he was on.

Mark was ill, dying perhaps; say no more. He stood at the window downstairs—the window toward the pond, as opposed to the one toward the ocean, or toward the lighthouse. Its view contained a wedge of sea on the right, high after a storm and figuratively rushing across a bight of beach as if to flood the house. A man with a metal detector was invisibly weaving a herringbone pattern across the sand, feathering back and forth along the beach, now and then scooping up small amounts of sand with a long-armed basket. Within the ranging intimacy of his binoculars Mark could almost hear the electronic *ping* of the metal detector as the man suddenly stopped.

This small drama: the man drops to a crouch. After two or three diggings in the sand, the little metal scoop proves inade-quate. Only the human hand will do. The man is young, dis-tantly handsome. Through his binoculars Mark can see the cold, downlike glow on his cheek. Fingers touch something which then is held up. It glints. Again the young man takes up the scoop and detector, glances for an instant up at the house, per-haps sees Mark in the window, and resumes the inferred pattern along the beach.

Mark's heart is thumping. What had he seen? Someone searching for valuables on the beach. His beach. Taking a deep breath he calmed himself. His sister Vita, had she been present, would have an explanation. An obvious metaphor, she would say, considering his illness, but useful. Mark might feel that much of his life lay buried on the beach—things of no conse-quence to anyone else—to be found and pocketed indifferently. This could be it, he thought. Or was it that the man with the metal detector was handsome? Perhaps Mark, being alone and frightened, merely wanted company—to talk—but wanted it as a pale vestige, in all its dimmer configurations, of the desire to make love.

Like the Birds before her, Mark's mother had died upstairs, eclipsing those two earlier, less-felt deaths, and claiming the house at last and utterly from its builders. Their two transparent shades faded further and Mrs Valerian's presence took over, as had been her intention. Her death, from a series of hemorrhagic strokes, had overlapped in an ironic but intentional way with an extensive restoration of the house—two processes sharing themes and schedules along similar though reversed lines: an Egyptian way of death, in which a place for the abiding comfort of the spirit is prepared. Mrs Valerian had theorized that the house would bind its occupants—her family—to her after she was gone. She had concluded that she herself would be similarly bound, an intention to be evoked with her name and memory by whoever entered the house.

Restoration had required a lot of money, thousands every week for months. This was regarded as a medical expense by Mr Valerian, who on the surface appeared to be rich, and who on the surface was, and he willingly gave whatever was needed because doing so assuaged his helplessness and grief. You could do nothing about a stroke, but the roof could be changed, and even the roof-line. On the ocean side windows could be cut to improve the views and lighten the interiors, with the immediate effect of liberation, as if something trapped inside the house, the Birds themselves, were at last released. Ten rooms of curtains, a dozen new rugs, every stick of furniture restored—the house emptied into a huge van and hauled to a penitentiary in New York State for refinishing. This had been arranged by Mr Valerian, a person not averse to pursuing a bargain across state lines. Mark asked if this meant their furniture would be stripped by convicts with guns held at their backs—the sort of question his father found surprising. Outside, the garden was also reconsidered, spaces around the house pushed back so that new sweeps of lawn were created where sea-rose and masses of creeper and honeysuckle had stolen up over the years nearly to the porch. A different curve was cut for the drive, as if Margaret Valerian, in her imagination, had flown up above the house and looked down to see at a glance the ideal line. These improvements went on all at once with a number of different crews and loud machines. After the broad strokes came the smaller, meaningful ones—with outside the new garden, a dozen trees, a fence —all corresponding to the different phases of Mrs Valerian's decline, in which every day some new deficiency appeared or matured. As she deteriorated she rested her ruined mind on the new stability of the house, its lovely air of completion and bounty. Each day she went in a wheelchair room to room to see everything in its place, fixed by rules of association and design. Beyond regular use of the wheelchair, she lay propped on clouds of pillows, regarding the sea through the big window in her room. On the best and dwindling days Mark read to her from a pile of cookbooks—recipes like short plotted stories, with twists, nuance, surprises, and uncertain endings, success by no means assured. To these details she listened closely, as to the chronicle of mysterious events. And when finally she died, it was with everyone around her, after a long and decorous farewell commensurate with the many months of the other sort of preparation. Light played over her face. Mark kissed her cheek and felt her spirit swirl into an angle of the ceiling, like perfume seeping through the house, a faintness of scent relative to its distance from her room—all of it lingering behind as planned.

He could not then agree, precipitously, to a plan to sell the house. Odd that all her labors and intentions, her clearly expressed wishes, should now be used against her. For no one could bear the accomplishment: that she permeated the place. For months everyone but Mark avoided it. And the expense, coupled with an obvious enhancement of the site, made its sale an ongoing temptation that grew. Someone approached Mr Valerian with a blank check, willing to pay anything, anything at all. Here would be life's financial truncation of the dilemma. To mitigate the issue further with a suggestion of the practical, Mr Valerian offered to divide the proceeds among his four children. The house, their legacy, would thus be converted to the means for a still easier life. To counter this, Mark threw his mother's memory in their faces. What weight, now that she was gone, did she have over such decisions, when in the past—with a glance—her least whim would have carried? The house, he protested, was the legacy; not the money but the house.

"I say sell it," his sister Vita announced suddenly—hers being, for various reasons, the pivotal vote. Betrayed, in speechless amazement, Mark fled the room.

At forty-three, Vita Valerian was three years older than Mark, similar enough to understand his reactions to any event but not enough to share them. Vita was more objective about life and held back her feelings in favor of a cool look at circumstance, while Mark surrendered immediately to an emotional response, believing this to be the natural way through difficulty. Cumulatively, in the end, these two systems had worked in Vita's favor and to Mark's detriment—for a practical approach is invariably rewarded, while the emotional often fails and only leads down. Beginning from the same point, Vita constantly adapted and would survive, while Mark plunged through life like a pet in jeopardy.

Some weeks later Vita met him at the beach house. On a late fall morning, the same as a summer day but for a faded difference in the light, they sat with coffee on the enormous porch. Up and down, the beach lay empty for miles. Boats in the offing, gulls and the changing light, the blue-hammered sparkle, the broad planes of sea and sky—these bright pictures were framed by the porch supports. Vita spoke first. Given the weight of his feelings she had changed her mind: she would not now agree to sell the house. For this was the most important thing, that if a person felt strongly about an issue in life, it mustn't be ignored by others; for if it was, everything subsequent to it would turn out badly, even though there should seem to be no direct connection.

"Then why did you say you would sell?" he asked. "Because I was tired of Pop's games," she replied. "He thinks we're beyond his control down here." Mr Valerian, since being widowered, had not again set foot in the house. "I think," she said, "he believes that if it's sold we'll all spend more time with him."

In the morning light, regarding the female version of his own face, he said, "Is it as simple as that?"

"In a way. But even without your objections they couldn't sell it now." *They* meant the two Georges, father and brother. "Until other things are settled nothing will be done."

George junior, the oldest, was forty-six. As the first to encounter their father, he had in many ways responded predictably. Three or four years of unallayed approval and praise had set him up as a prince of expectation, and by the time Vita, Mark and Tessa arrived, he was obviously indomitable. *They* always meant George and his father because the two of them, far from being merely similar, were each other's invention. Neither could have been what he was without the other, except that now George Jr might easily go on being what he was, unassisted. Their relationship formed the new axis of the family.

Tessa, the youngest, had seemed from the beginning to respond to them all, and to Mark in particular, as a person to be protected—not simply as a helpless baby-girl creature of great beauty, which she had been, but as an idea: that she was the youngest, smallest and last, and in her doll-like beauty somehow the least. This idea had served her personally through her first fifteen or twenty years; after which, Tessa suddenly saw, it had been everlastingly transmuted into a liability. As the youngest she never felt a sense of protection so much as a feeling of standing fourth back in line, as if buffered, with three other people between her and life. And now, also in near middle-age, she found herself still fixed within an order of precedence established at birth. Only to Tessa did this seem entirely unnatural.

Their father, George Valerian, was the wild card. His life had brought him as from one planet to another. His own siblings —who all lived in New York City—hardly knew him for what he had become, a kind of magnate, rich and apart. To these sisters and brothers George Valerian represented all that seldom occurs in life, or that occurs only to other people. Here, in him —and their view of him was greatly exaggerated—they were themselves lightly touched by success. Dreams of extrication from want, of the glamour of finery and excess, of fearlessness in restaurants and flight to sunny beaches, they associated with him. They envied him, seeing him as richer and happier than he was. He in turn remembered them as what he had left behind, witnesses and proof of what he thought he had done and become.

None of it had ever changed, as none of it ever does. The weather of their lives swirled around them randomly; and it seemed that if you could go from the beginning to the end, you would find innumerable distractions and surprises along the way but ultimately nothing in any of them that had not been there from the start, in a way, fixed and waiting. George Valerian had gone as far as altering the name by which the world knew him: Giorgio Valeriani. And even this had not mattered, except to be considered good advice by a business superior in the Forties. Mark—named for his maternal grandfather—thought the name euphonious; he felt that Marco Valeriani showed through like pentimento, which it did. It meant the world took them for one thing while they were quite another—not wasplike and cool, but beelike and quick to anger and perhaps unpleasantness. When he lost his temper or suddenly fell flights into depression, he thought this is my blood which can't be changed.

After Mrs Valerian's death, alone in the beach house, Mark moved into her room and slept in her bed. This felt peculiar only on the first night. Margaret Valerian's room, with its large bay window on the ocean, was long and handsome, running the width of the house, with fine views up and down the coast. It was blue and white, with white taffeta curtains, Indian rugs and white lacquer furniture. Through the line of windows the horizon stretched around like the true walls of the room, making it immense, bringing in the sea and the sky with all its light. It was a room to wake up in. At sunrise the lemon, red and orange colors of the sun revolved over the white curtains like flame, drifting down the wall as the sun rose, as in a stateroom on an enormous slowly listing ship. Outside the sea slapped the beach resolutely, but he would be awakened by the clamorous light. Next to the blue room was a green room, and then a pink—no longer pink but referred to as such after so many years. The green room had been Mark's. Now he slept in the blue.

He felt that nothing was more important to him than this house, now that he had saved it, and since no one else stood in this relation to it, they would not have understood the degree to which, day by day, the obsession grew. Having blocked its sale, he saw himself as its custodian and protector, its Mrs Danvers, the connection coming through the blue room, '. . . *the loveliest room in the house, the loveliest room you've ever seen.*' Like Mrs Danvers he was proud to show it to anyone who called, though callers were not likely to be interested; alluding in a fond, crazy gaze over objects and views to a special, mysterious, nostalgic association with the past, never specified. Mrs Warden, a neighbor passing by, had been brought into it on a bright sunny morning, when all the white and blue seemed edible, and had said excitedly that if this were her room she would never leave it. Exactly, Mark thought; a woman skilled in noisemaking. And in fact his mother had never left. Sometimes it seemed he might suddenly turn and catch a wispy glimpse.

But the others did not love the house in these terms; why should he so care?

Its beauty, no doubt; its canopic aspects regarding his mother, and now regarding him; the memory of thirty years there together. This, while enough, overwhelmingly enough for Mark, was insufficient to them, to whom it remained a pretty house by the sea with associations. They might say to him and to all this emotion: why and so what? Were it not for Mark, things would be different—simply the profit really, instead of the expense and upkeep. He had no firm answer for himself or them, for whom beauty and recollection—like danger, glamour, greed, hunger (everything but disappointment and desire)— were concepts belonging to other people. In fact, he thought, they might not see themselves for what they were, since what Mark saw and what they saw were not the same—when they should have been. House and mother had belonged to all. All had been children here; he and Tessa practically the same age, Vita just three years older, only George very grown at fifteen.

They had peered in at the misted, dusty windows. To one side Mark saw the dead, startled Birds withdraw backward through a doorway. His father signalled disapproval by keeping his hands in his pockets. Furniture lay in the middle of the vast room before a bulky fieldstone fireplace, stacked like expensive

fuel. Mark had dreamed the room many times, though of course
never in such a state: the same overlooked, nearly but not quite
forgotten room, off a corridor of his mind—dusty, unrealized,
unlooked at. He stood and turned toward the sea, which tilted
over him at a slant like a picture, the line of the horizon that day
blurring higher into the sky than might seem normal—it was all
so important. "Only on the ocean," Mrs Valerian had instructed
the realtor. Downstairs the ancient furnace spread itself across
the cellar like the roots of a banyan tree, funneling huge fat limbs
along the ceiling and up through the house. Mr Valerian shook
his head, Margaret shuddered. She wanted to see the bedrooms.

He was ten, Tessa nine, the first summer, living like the
Birds. Mr Valerian was not yet so rich and they camped out at
first. It was necessary to replace all the windows right away.
They were fake. Margaret Valerian repeated this unbelievingly.
How could they be fake? The cost of sixty windows was thus
added to the mortgage. The air then blew through it—as long
ago Captain Bird, besides saving money, had feared the sea
might someday enter at the portholes—and the long front room
behind the porch became a deeper verandah in itself, open to the
cool blue breeze. On the dune beside the house Mark built a
network of sand channels down the incline, encouraging a pink
rubber ball to travel from up there to down here as if under its
own power, to fall with a satisfying plop into a pit at the end:
the top, center and bottom; the beginning, middle and end; up
coming down, from there to here. As a metaphor it seemed to
fit for a long time. Most things in life, including life itself,
seemed to have sections, discreet and separate and straightfor-
ward.

Now when he entered a room or suddenly turned he encountered himself and his family, his siblings and nieces and parents,
as if he had been mistaken in thinking them gone and himself
alone. How could he be alone there again, except for a few
moments at a time? It had become, besides, actually the sort of
house that attracted people to it, in a daily ration of deliveries,
the maid, plumber, carpenter, furnace man, the painter who
never finished and seemed to work on his own; the alarm man,

the gardeners. Mark would hear them on the gravel, or the too-loud bell would ring and he would see again the futility of thinking it was a house to be alone in. The others asked what he did with himself, knowing to themselves that he did, simply, everything and was endlessly busy. It was large, with every nook of it developed into something to be maintained. He would sit for a moment and realize the hatch at the top of the tower was ajar; when it was open the covers of magazines on the table by the fireplace, three floors below, lifted and gently settled on the coil of updraft swirling through the rooms. Or some quadrant of the lawn was being watered, or a storm the day before has misted the north-facing windows to a blur that must be squee-geed; or a drain at the back was loose, or moss had begun in the outdoor shower, as it did every year, a furry lime-green that called to mind the baroque grottos of overachieved Italian villas. He was half-inclined, scrubbing it away, to let it this year take hold.

With his mother gone the house, far from being ever empty or complete or perfectly in order, was, beyond being a house, a place and monument. This is what the others did not see except in the passion with which he explained the undertaking of yet some new repair or project. For it was big enough never to be finished, and everything that was done to it—had been done to it—seemed to call up in him a progression of further things, as if it now itself kept a list for itself, a list far more deeply ambitious than his own. When he tried to explain this to Vita, she characteristically voiced her opinion: that he liked to think this was true, yet of necessity you would have to say it did not come from the house. "These are your standards and ideals," she said. "Within the process, *you* decide." She was no doubt right. Her field. But the *impulse* she described in him was met by something in the house as palpable as its present shape: the shape it would have in the future. When Mark looked at it in a particular way, he saw it suddenly as it eventually would look. He said to Vita, "It's not imagination. I imagine different features and improvements all the time. They don't occur. But sometimes I see something already done, all its details at once, and after that it's a matter not of imagination but of recollection of the actual thing."

Vita shook her head, willing though temporarily unable to

follow. "You mean the imposition of your will . . ." she suggested. But he had meant that with the warp of experience folding back on itself, as did time, it was all on a great tape—racial memory, the Collective Unconscious her colleagues had been talking about for so long—history itself, the future, the larger flavorsome bits: the house had a soul, it had a history.

"But not a destiny," she interrupted. "It could be sold tomorrow, and then who would interpret these—visions? Who would have them?"

This was precisely the point, he pointed out. No one would. That was his department. She did not doubt the potency of the scheme, as it inspired him, as it affected them all. Four or five weeks a year she basked in this perfection like Princess Grace in the Monaco of her dreams. The rest of the year, with her children and their commitments, with her job and career, it was as with the others, a question of the odd weekend. They might have held on to the house because the original investment was so eternally dwarfed by modern value—this was the Monaco of everyone's dreams—or now because of Mark; but without him keeping track none of it would have worked. Mrs Valerian had managed it alone for thirty years. Now he did, in his own way. They all saw his reasons overlapped with their own in letting him.

Odd that four such people should turn up in the same family; or odd that he should be among them, it being himself who made the collection strange, who set the curve with his inverted sexuality, sensitivities and thin skin, his standards and thoughts from some other, different place. While they seemed or were strange only in these comparisons with him, which threw them to the opposite ends of all these spectra—George Jr, practical and cunning; Vita, evolved and cool; Tessa the winning, excitable wife and mother, still young, steeped in the details of her children's lives—all so different from Mark and now abundantly clear, after years when it had seemed otherwise. The gallant struggle to convince themselves and the world that Mark was merely another sort of Valerian—rather like Mrs Valerian, whose instincts in all of this had been unwavering—this struggle in the end had been incorporated into the great Filial Wars, pitched battles between Mark and his father which had dragged on for a decade, and in which the heaviest losses had seemed as usual to be innocent civilians: the family itself. It seemed to him his mother had given her life as part of this prolonged struggle, the only evidence at first of how deadly such things became if not settled early and wisely through ambassadors. They, he now supposed, were the ambassadors. He felt the exhausted truce lately reached between his father and himself represented the world's last opportunity to avoid catastrophe. It was, as Vita said, a question of not denying something vitally important to someone else. If you did, it more than harmed you; it destroyed you and your world to the extent it was itself destroyed. Now his mother was dead, his father already old, and he himself apparently dying, although you could never, he had learned, be sure who would die before whom.

Vita did not in the least cavil, or hesitate. Like many of his conclusions this came out in conversation with her. She thought the force of Mark's will, being thwarted by this immovable object—his father—had been turned back on himself with devastating results, and that evidence of this effect would subsequently pull his father down.

They were making a turn around Rittenhouse Square, within a stream of joggers all fleeing a devastation to which only they remained obdurately oblivious. "You must cure yourself," Vita said, going right to the payoff—these were not office hours with a stranger, he thought. Meaning that if he could turn the process off he might neutralize its effects in time, and so at least slow the disease, or convert or divert it elsewhere. This was the idea, to buy time.

The stupendous news of his illness abruptly ended the Filial Wars, like a smothered blaze. In the driveway of the beach house, where Mr Valerian came to discuss it and see for himself, they embraced and wept. It no longer meant a great deal that Mr Valerian could weep, although there had been an era—most of their lives—when the idea itself represented a kind of doom not to be envisioned; while Mark had been, in compensation, always a person to weep as easily and effortlessly as an actor. Together they wept in each other's arms in a way that might have obviated all unpleasantness, if only, if only; the unfortunate misapprehension of one person, meaning well but getting it wrong, by another; he and his father weeping beside the gleaming automobile that now, a moment later, slid across the white gravel and carried his father away.

———— • ————

Parents feel that in the huge unnaturalness of the world the most unnatural thing is the death of a child; which is to say death out of order. In Mr Valerian's mind his son's illness sat at the top of a pile of problems that appeared to constitute this last segment of his own life. It took stepping back, but from his point of view it seemed, as he would presently say to Mark, that if they could only change places all this nonsense would be resolved, beginning with the medical thing which, of everything, was most beyond his control. The other great problem in the pile concerned the collapse at the last moment of the greatest deal of his long and profitable business career—the sale of Marval Products itself, Mr Valerian's life work, to Court Industries. This collapse, coming only hours after he learned of his son's illness, had transpired with equal force, like a second bomb dropped on rubble. In a long moment of realization Mr Valerian had thought the two events to be in some way connected (as subsequently did Mark) beyond the usual compounded coincidences of life; as if, had you thought in astrological terms, which Mr Valerian did not, you might find that on this day and at this hour several planetary masses had aligned themselves toward his specific ruination.

But that it should happen now, and so quickly, in this mad, last-minute upheaval of his life; that here at the top of the monument you found not a statue, not the figure of Victory poised for flight, but instead pigeon shit and disappointment—Mr Valerian's disgust at this was less effective as a demonstration against life than it had been against his mortified children over the years. He was a man who had always intimidated people. He looked at them and dealt with them until he saw a light of defiance go out in their eyes. He kept on until he saw it—

minutes or years. At last, in the driveway of the beach house, he saw it in Mark's eyes. Help me, they said: it was all Mr Valerian had ever wanted to hear.

Strength is what he told himself he'd always had; strength is what would see them through. But here, at the age of seventy-five, at the end of his life, here now were larger problems than he had ever faced—with the exception of his first great insoluble: his wife's death—more problems than even he could see his way, decently, to solving. It made his unhappiness resonate with loneliness but he was glad Margaret had missed this. How little, now he saw, it had taken to make her sicken and die. The most important distinction between them was that he had coped so easily and expertly with forces that had quickly done her in. To Mr Valerian it seemed she had died just when everything was about to come together for the stretch; and perhaps, had she lived, it would have—instead of this. But then surely this would have killed her, if that hadn't.

With something extra in her voice, due to the fact she was discussing her own father clinically, but also for what she considered the endless resourcefulness of the subject, Vita described Mr Valerian as "very heavily defended." The fortress of their father's mind, Mark thought, thinking of something rocky and impregnable by Baldasare Peruzzi. "If such a structure collapses, it comes down all at once," she said. "At the end the mind is ruined. Much better if somehow it holds together."

Mark's opinion of his father in these later years had thus been based, he felt, on this other resident expert—for what was Vita but court psychologist, the best money could buy, right there in the family? rather like the best legal advice from their brother. Bolstered by the respect he felt for Vita's mind, Mark applied these opinions to his own situation: the Filial Wars. It was from Vita he realized he would never convince his father of the legitimacy of his cause; quite simply because Mr. Valerian saw homosexuality in religious terms—as a sin—which then threatened the great buttress of his own defense system: religion. The top third of all widowers, Vita reported, meaning in health and adjustment, survived with the help of strong religious beliefs. Thus the establishment of Mark's orientation as a viable

mode ran in conflict with his father's own concept of survival.
Not simply a question of live and let live, Mark saw with dis-
may. It meant he must think of his father's generation as en-
trenched and lost—as of course they all thought of his.

For he *was* different from them—from his own father and
sisters, especially different from his brother. He had something
of his mother in him but this was because he realized that in the
end only her love was unconditional, and in gratitude he had
emulated her. Only that much of this appropriation did not sit
as gracefully on him, the strapping male, as it had on her. And
perhaps he had chosen some of her more problematic traits—the
tendency to catastrophe for instance, of immediately expecting
the worst in an unpleasant situation, hardly important but negative, and which seldom turned out as badly as she expected.
He heard a variant of this in himself and recognized it as surely
as an old piece of clothing that fitted him but belonged to someone else: his mother's sense of catastrophe. This had stuck.

Ah, the victim. This too she had allowed, had encouraged in
herself until too late. She had proved to him that the victim
creates and perpetuates himself. This was the embarrassing part
of being ill. The metaphor here was also too tellingly clear: the
homosexual as victim. Unfair perhaps to pin it on his mother,
who would be indignant to be thought of in these terms. But it
was Vita's point that this was the cycle to be interrupted if he
would break the pattern and save himself.

Yes, Vita, but how? And for a long time—most of his life,
and often even now—he'd thought of this difference between
himself and his family as evidence of *their* failings, not his. Was
not the absence of beauty the ugliest thing in life? (Vita would
say no.) In the general scheme of things among the Valerians
he often felt that wrong choices won out over right—wrong
ideas, wrong directions, wrong fears. From an early age he had
spoken up, feeling that in this small crowd was room—the dimensions—for more than one opinion; or even two. After all a
family might advance, as in certain quiz programs on TV in
which a whole generation, sometimes two or three, put their
heads together to define reality, and for their efforts won a car.
It seemed the diversity he offered might be of use to them as a

family, if they could only see it that way. In this his mother half the time had been his ally; half the time, with a gimlet eye, not. In matters of taste at least—of form, aesthetics: the usual homosexual metier—they had long since looked to him for quasi-professional guidance; so that George Jr was legal, Vita psychological, Mark . . . artistic—though it might be argued that this end of things lay otherwise vacant of opinion for cultural, sexist reasons.

—Different too in that he was alone. This was it. Each of them had a unit of their own, while Mark clung to an order that had outgrown itself, whose vestigial remains could be found only in his father and himself, and in a ghost of the enmity between them, now laid to rest by . . . by It. The occasions on which the five of them might collude had been reduced to those of state—the meeting about selling the house for instance—or perhaps when Tessa, whose instincts, though less developed, ran along similar lines, might suggest a public lunch on Father's Day—just them—which however George Jr would be too busy and overworked to attend.

It was not that they thought any less of the idea than Mark; if anything they thought more. Simply that family meant their own brood and not the abstract enshrinement, as if in retrospect, of the Valerians as they one day might have been but were no more—something in Mark's imagination. He might make every effort to impose this vision on them—the fight for the beach house had been one such effort—of a caring, interlocked group of siblings. But the exigencies of their own broods made this unavailing, except at intervals, or when a flare of need went up over the life of one of them. It was not that it didn't exist, this idea of family, but that it did not seem to exist always, and never as Mark saw it; or if it did, which he saw it did, it was really only among each of them and for their very own.

Meaning that he was not a member, in each case, of their *very own*. Here we had musical families, like musical chairs—life was nothing but quiz programs and time-passing competitions—and when the music stopped he alone stood in the circle of upturned, satisfied faces. None could feel this sense of estrangement, apartness, because all of life's institutions had seen to it that they didn't. Mates, children, parents and other siblings all fitted into arrangements laid out for this specific accomplishment: to belong. So much easier, he thought, for them to go along—unnatural for them not to—because for them it was stupefyingly enjoyable, one small triumph of legitimacy after another.

He had slept with women but not many; or again with the one woman with whom he might have fathered children of his own (a luscious *of his own*); for that's how it had been with the others. He liked the children to whom he was related, loved them; was tolerant or not of others, but suspicious. Nothing was so unpleasant as the sound of young people having a good time; nothing so haunting as the same sound from your own people. He did not want children, except perhaps impossibly those of a certain age, when the sensibility either was there or not; then yes he would want them, for his own; but *after* the rapids of parentage. In their infrequency of visits, in the intensity of rituals, they all took on mysterious outlines of themselves in which they assembled and arranged their own imaginings.

But did he really expect family life to be arranged around the requirements of spinster aunts and bachelor uncles? Freud would say Grow up. The burden of neurosis added to the weight of history was too great. Darwin would call Mark's kind a mad biological experiment teetering on the edge of extinction and doomed to failure. Both privately would shake their heads, though Freud, being Jewish, would wonder. Vita, their avatar and spokesperson, who contrarily considered, among others, the twenty-six million Americans extrapolated from Kinsey to be homosexual—one in ten—would say that some people slipped through history without ever reaping its rewards.

It did not do to complain, but to understand. The analogy was in this case the primeval tree of primitive man. Mark knew it as a two-story tree house he had built at an early age with Donny and Brock. It popped so immediately into mind that he knew she was right.

"But can we not provide some other service? Is it all just the timely impregnation of females?" he asked indignantly.

"You may of course sound the alarm," Vita replied. "But life is not that simple, and sometimes sounding the alarm only arouses passions and causes trouble. In the commotion branches are broken, people fall and hurt themselves. The leopard grabs one of them . . ."

"But without the alarm . . ." Mark said weakly. He would never be convinced.

In these conversations Mark was aware of this same weight of respect coming across the line from his sister. What was it in *him* that held her interest? Creativity, he thought; the position engendered by a combination of male egotism—the inculcation of centuries—and feminine passivity, rarely mixed in those days, openly; or at least in her Philadelphia suburb. Only later did he see she had realized her professional luck in finding, in her own family, a fine, pure example of something they were alluding to at school: Freud's obsessional neurotic. She of course made no effort to inform him of this conclusion, and he went on thinking she saw in him, at least potentially, the artist he wished to be. In any event, it would be one or the other; this was perhaps a matter of opinion, and too soon to say. Art, he thought too, was nothing but obsessional and neurotic. And what might have alarmed the sibling of another shrink seemed, to him, to be evidence of some sort of artistic progress not otherwise obvious.

He was less different from Vita, perhaps because they had in their own way each been made to follow their brother George, with Mark's version matching hers in certain cross-gender ways; as if their parents, the Valerians, having thought just so far, had put everything into their first child, and made do with the remnants of parentage for the other three. George and Tessa were easier—not that *they* were similar—for being obviously the first and the last. But Vita and Mark, appearing as if unbidden or at random, seemed to share the burden of catching their parents unawares, unprepared or bereft, even though never in her marriage had Mrs Valerian made love without the thought of conceiving a child. How for instance did a little girl differ from a little boy? Why then was this second son, who had come from the same people and in the same way, so shockingly different? The Valerians, smug, oblivious and proud, did the best they knew how, making an awful mess, Vita thought; Mark thought. But then in those days, who hadn't?

Tessa could not be simply defined, even in part—like George, by his superb professionalism; or Vita, by her lift from inadequacy into something like personal power; or Mark, by his existence within the hyperbole of an *artistic* temperament. Tessa herself had each of these things—the professionalism, force of character, the hyperbole—but she had them without their objects: a profession, a firm idea of herself, or art. Perhaps she was an emulsion of all of them. Mark didn't know. She didn't know. She seemed after her mother's death to be more like Mrs Valerian, as by an effort as conscious as the revival and preparation of Mrs Valerian's favorite recipes, or the use of a favored nail color; measures matched by others too subtle or obscure to recognize. Perhaps the strongest instinct enhanced in her was that of motherhood itself, and only a year after Mrs Valerian's death Tessa gave birth to a third child, hardly anticipated but made welcome nonetheless, yet another little girl; and the devolving questions of her life, reemerging as her original two children had grown, fell back again, receding before the flooding instincts, the revived priorities of motherhood.

When artists die the value of their work increases, perhaps because a scope of talent is established, perhaps because that's the end of it. This same thing happened to Mrs Valerian. With no more mothering, what was remembered was emulated in any way appropriate. Such was the fate of Tessa's little girl, to be reconstituted along all the precepts and philosophies Tessa could recall, in the way that we allow ourselves to remember without actually recollecting, by instinct, guess and impulse. She did several things differently from the beginning with this pregnancy, including the luxury, some would say the indulgence, of gaining fifty or sixty pounds; until, on his weekly visits, Mark sensed a kind of insulation gained both for herself and her fetus by the manly, the piggish intake of food. He heard his mother say, Eat. And Tessa ate. Being so near in age they were, with each other, unencumbered by what had transpired before their arrivals. Perhaps this was why they always ate in each other's company, as if—as at six months and older—that's habitually what they had done together.

Within one of several overlapping first memories, Mark held Tessa's hand at the water's edge. They had a photograph of this, at four and three—as young as it is possible for a child consciously to hold another's hand, and only thus is catastrophe averted, of the watery kind, before which even the gorgeous lifeguards must be unavailingly, distantly helpless: protection in the abstract. Tessa had been of a delicacy to inspire this feeling in all living creatures. Now her grown son was himself a lifeguard, forming the chief reason for her pride in the matter—that her son had grown to be a lifeguard on the spot where Mark had held her hand at the water's edge. This symmetry pleased both in the same way, and represented perhaps their strongest bond. It had been added to over the years, and elaborated on most especially after Mrs Valerian's death—that much more to divvy up between them—but this early memory lay at the center of the way they saw each other.

Regarding the concept of protection, the irony of Mark's illness might have caught Tessa unaware, were it not that in puberty and thereafter they had changed places. Tessa reached several given points before him, had in fact taught him to smoke cigarettes at fifteen; dated first—although the delay in Mark's case was compounded. For years a single year's difference in their ages was more than canceled by her feminine precociousness, a faculty of worldly sense that often eluded him, if as often not; so that they were able with almost equal opportunity now to draw each other up short. In many situations they might predict each other's feelings. "Mark is not going to like this," she often reported herself, rightly, as saying. Or if they did not agree at the beginning of something, they did at the end. Without her, as much as without Vita, he would not have been able to save the beach house.

Tessa had felt at a loss for *something to do*. It had been her children, she always said. And now this last child meant more for coming after her own mother's death. Into this devotional object she would both pour and find a superb professionalism—motherhood; a power—over life and death; the power also of the art of exaggerating emotions, the hyperbole of being alive. And when someone said they thought it ironic that Margaret Valerian, a famous grandmother, knew nothing of this subsequent, tenth, final grandchild, Tessa smiled her ironic smile and said, "She knows."

Because they knew, she and Mark. Together they built a nursery that involved the addition of an entire second floor to Tessa's otherwise modest house, thereby doubling its size, with the baby arriving the day after the curtains went up. If Mrs Valerian had left the world from the liner-like luxury of a Cape May beach house, little Margaret came down into a delicate confection of nursery allusions, not one lacking, and all executed in tiny Laura Ashley-ese: sprigs, rose buds, two different patterns and a stripe, the deep protective rug, little lamps—the miniature boudoir of a miniature princess, ready just in time.

———◦——

Mr Valerian stepped from the car and shaded his eyes from the sun. Perhaps he had been weeping on the drive down. Expecting him to the minute and hearing tires on the gravel, Mark came slowly out the door and through the garden, hands in his pockets, footprints blazing up behind him in tiny, sickle-shaped fires: his pockets spiritually picked, his life up in flames. Flowers in the border flashed dots of color at his feet, drifting by in focus within a long green blur. As he approached his father, they each wore the same ripening expression, of remorse and reproach, of colossal disappointment; this overlapping response paired their display—a sad caving-in of their feelings—and like two fine dynamos reaching tandem, they embraced. Mr Valerian pounded once, twice, on Mark's shoulder in an excess not of tenderness but anguish. He said into Mark's ear, "Believe me if I could change places with you I'd do it in a second." It was what on the drive down he had decided to begin by saying. Holding his son by the shoulders, and at last seeing all defiance gone, he added, "We're going to go through this together, and there's nothing we can't do if we want." This sent them back into the vortex. Mark felt infantile, helpless. He was ill: something between the two of them had shifted into something manifest on its own, against which both were helpless; a third, evil thing set loose. Now an alliance of his own resolve coupled with his father's was meant to bear some force against—this, which coming from within, must be pursued from within; though it appeared now, even in the abstract, beyond spiritual, intellectual, even emotional measures. Perhaps only the medical remained. Strength of intention his father meant to give him, not realism or facts but something to use in the coming fight, something abstract to fight something real, against which as yet no real weapons existed.

They came through the house into the sitting room. Being alone, Mark had ordered it with the precision and flair of a photo stylist. The vast blue plane of sea stretched around. Mark could almost feel the little hop his father's heart took, of pride, recognition and pain at the purity of sudden association with Margaret. Mr Valerian looked out over the beach, nodded his head, but sat in a chair with his back to the view—a gesture that meant here again were reasons why, with one thing and another, he was unable to enjoy this house further. They sat quietly. The waves squandered themselves. Two brown rabbits appeared on the lawn to feed, ears ruby sunlight. Mark watched them over his father's shoulder.

"Well," Mr Valerian began. "Tell me about this . . . Tell me what the doctors said, what—y'know—what you know about it."

Put me in the picture, Mark thought his father had with a certain delicacy refrained from saying. The terminology of a business meeting seemed appropriate to the situation, certainly automatic. He saw that sometime in the next few minutes he himself would say, "The bottom line is that there's no cure."

"Look," his father exclaimed when in fact this remark had been delivered, "that's where you're wrong. It's not the bottom line. You mustn't think that way. They'll find a cure. They're all looking . . ."

"Utter bullshit," Mark interrupted. "It's not a cure they're looking for, it's a vaccine. Protect the healthy, let the sick die off."

"But Mark . . . ," Mr Valerian protested, shaking his head.

"It's what they did with polio, and they were *children*."

"Well, you've got to think of yourself," his father said. "You've got to be positive. You'll beat it one way or another. Either they'll find something or something will happen."

They regarded each other.

"And," his father went on—these are the things he had driven here to say—"I have a feeling this is a light case."

"A feeling?" Mark said.

"I just don't think it's as bad as you think."

"Dad, it's not what *I think*."

". . . And there's experimental things," he went on. "I read yesterday there's a guy in California immune to everything. They're studying his blood . . ."

"I don't think this is something we'll be able to buy."

"Why the hell not?" Mr Valerian demanded, then sat forward and went on in a fresh tone. "But you see, Mark, this is what I mean. You mustn't say, 'No, no, I can't, I can't, this is impossible, it won't work and I'm going to die . . .' You've got to think something will happen. Some goddamn clever Swede or Frog will find the answer . . . And you'll see, it's not as bad as you think—in your case."

"You say that only because you can't face it."

"Then what the hell are you going to do!" his father snapped, "lay down and die? Is that it?"

"I'm not going to kid myself because you want to hear it."

"And that's where you're wrong, my friend," Mr Valerian said derisively. "Why not a miracle? Open yourself up to the idea that anything can happen, and you're going to get through this in one piece."

". . .Faith," Mark said quietly.

"Faith," Mr Valerian repeated, adding a slight though unmistakable measure of reverence.

Mr Valerian turned and they looked out the window together, each backing away from the idea just raised—Mark because he wished to avoid an argument about religion; Mr Valerian because, while relieved to have hit on something *tangible*, he was not prepared to pursue it further. He knew prayer and hard work were the answer—had already begun his own program along these lines—but not until you came to it yourself. And Mark thought it time to say something about his father's other great problem: the collapse of the deal to sell Marval.

"George told me," he began—out to sea two small sailboats took different tacks on the same wind, sails pinned to the opposite reach, the one crossing the other's wake. Mark thought of the currents as invisible streets—". . . about the rest of your day. I'm sorry this happened all at once."

"I don't want you to think twice about that," Mr Valerian replied. "It's a disappointment, that's all. It means more hard work when I would've been retiring. But I can deal with that sort of thing. I've been doing it all my life."

"All in the same day . . . ," Mark said wonderingly.

"Yes, well . . ." His father turned away from the window.

They put together a lunch of odds and ends and ate on the porch in front. Here Captain Bird had most seriously contrived to duplicate, on dry land and for the enjoyment of his dwindling days, the unique commanding experience of a ship's bridge. An end of the porch came around and finished in a circle topped with a pointed cone, like a gazebo jutting from a corner of the house. With the arrangement of a sand dune, a trellis, and the eastern orientation of the house, Captain Bird had created the illusion of being actually at sea, within a wheelhouse. If you sat or stood in a certain spot the horizon stretched three-quarters of the way around, the beach fell below the level of the porch railing, and all land disappeared, leaving the sea. As they ate, a net of diamond shadows fell through the trellis, drifting over their shoulders and across the floor.

"What about George?" Mark said, to stay off It for a while. His father looked up. "What about him?"

"Well, he's disappointed isn't he? He's worked hard on this, for a long time."

"Yes, he has." Mr Valerian had thought to learn something about George. Sometimes his children told each other things which then he heard secondhand, as intended. "He's got his practice to repair. This thing took a lot of his time."

In conversation, as otherwise, Margaret Valerian had been

their connection, the buffer between them—in a way demonstrated by the damage she herself had sustained; by the worry, never clearly stated, that the wrong person being right, the right person wrong—and she herself never sure—not enough had been said or felt for either. Instead she worked hard to make them comfortable, knowing mere comfort was never enough. They seemed only to disagree on principle, the principle of sex. This she held to be impossible, for love alone mattered, not principle. In fitting and tailoring their disparate responses to each other, she managed for years to fend off the implications and disasters of the Filial Wars, saying to one what the other could not. "Your father does not mean what he says. He loves you very much," and vice versa. So real was the need, any transparent effort worked. After her death the connection devolved through necessities surrounding her funeral and burial— the plot, the monument—for if the beach house meant the survival of her memory and spirit in Mark's mind, even in her own, in Mr Valerian's a cemetery was where such things naturally came to rest. To him the beach house was not so much a reminder of his dead wife, or the dying one, as it came to be his sole connection with Mark. Some months after her death, at the change of seasons—when fifty steps to wintering an old mansion on the water suddenly presented themselves—Mark had automatically taken up the job, interpreting this as an extension of his mother's wishes; while Mr Valerian saw it as an opportunity both practical and wise. Several years into the arrangement, it had become and remained their subject. And now to Mark, being ill, it seemed he might belong there as much as his mother. In every conversation, one or the other of them brought it up.

"How's the house?" his father said now, sociable over the food.

"That depends," Mark replied, "on where you look."

Mr Valerian waved his hand in agreement. It was endlessly expensive, unfinished, yielding to salt air and sea. They were still compensating, thirty years later, for Captain Bird's economies. "That Bird," Mr Valerian would say, "had an anchor for brains." It had been some years before they discovered all the drains simply stopped below grade. All had to be dug up and connected. In his own mind Captain Bird had been constructing a boat. Nothing except her moorings must hold her. She must be free to sail at any moment, in the dead of night or day, straight to sea on the course so carefully drawn through the hearth. Now, Mark thought, the place was locked in—by water main, sewers, gas lines, TV cables, telephone wires, even the thin lightning rod of copper braid twisting from its height off the tallest chimney and down the sides of the house like a package tied with cord.

In Mark's mind, as opposed to Captain Bird's, in the moments before setting sail, someone must sever these new connections one by one. Where possible over the years he himself had felt inclined to keep the boat idea in mind. An innovation of his own had been to shape the ocean-side lawn into a bow, with a low, white, chevron bulkhead pointing east into the waves. He thought that if this bow-shaped piece of earth were included, giving her deck space all around, it would be easier to hook the severed connections to a life-support system, all within a clear crystal cube containing the earth's atmosphere—on a fresh morning, the sun still on the water, or a starry night for sleeping, dreaming—a crystal ship of lights that silently slips her lines and sails away.

THE OUTSIDERS

• DENNIS COOPER •

From Closer, *a novel in progress*

GEORGE LOOKED AS though he were sleepwalking, whether he knew it or not. Something was wrong but he "wouldn't know how to describe it." At first taking LSD three times a week helped. Then he'd relied on our little talks. Now there was nothing between him and "it," as he called what he currently felt. "It's getting worse," he remarked as we strolled hand in hand through a city park.

I understood what he meant. "It" was as vague as that sentence. In other words, I'd never see it. Saying so wouldn't help. Friends were just light entertainment at best. I kept my ears open, exaggerated my interest and hoped compassion would strike him as sexy at some point. "Let's sit," he sighed when our eyes met.

His hand was cold. Otherwise I might have thought I was walking around with my shadow. One time I turned and examined his eyes on the off chance he'd started ODing. I wanted to read his mind but all I saw was some dry leaves get larger and larger then crush like miniature fireworks beneath his shoes.

"I'm feeling totally weary for one thing," he said. We'd situated ourselves on a grassy slope. The day had cooled. A light breeze came up from the parking lot. His eyes were so shadowed they looked like dark glasses. His lips were so full and red they seemed magnified. His chin was balancing atop one knee, his arms wrapped loosely around that particular leg.

"George, stay at my place tonight." I knew that sounded too matter of fact. I wanted to fuck him. That was my goal but I couldn't decide how to phrase it. "I can't, I'm seeing Philippe." "Oh sure, right, foreigners first," I huffed and accidentally kicked a small hole in the grass. George was scanning the clouds. "*You* explain it," he shrugged, knowing I couldn't.

I couldn't even imagine us fucking without a lump in my throat. So every night when I lowered my eyelids I pictured George and his lover instead. It looked a bit like a scene from *The Blob*, an old sci-fi film I had mixed feelings about. George tripped and, as he fell, a flabby body just swallowed him up. I'd arch my back and come, dazed by the strange combination of lust and petty loss I felt.

Now George was sitting right next to me, staring up at a cloud bank. I couldn't guess how to get him in bed much less save him from "it." At least in fantasies I'd had some kind of effect on him, though he would never know how, when, where, what. "I should go home. I'm just boring you." "No, you're not," I whispered. "Well, I'm boring myself."

"I'll see you later," he yelled as he trudged up his front walk. I threw my car into drive and gunned it, searching for him in my rearview mirror. He'd stopped dead in his tracks and was watching me barrel off, arms wrapped around his chest, sure he had pissed me off. "Shit," I said, gripping the wheel, "no matter what I do . . ."

I climbed the stairs to my room. My mom had cleaned the house. The air smelled poisonous. I set an old Brian Wisdom LP on the turntable. There was a song on its second side called "Note to No One," in which the deeply depressed singer/songwriter moaned out some personal problems to a dead friend. It was a joke, in particular one couplet.

When it approached I sat forward. ". . . I'm as made-up as the TV star my lover's ogling / I feel like an empty exercise in acting . . ." That was so ludicrous. Why did it make me want to cry? Maybe because he was so out of touch with his thoughts he had to use unbelievably strained images to suggest the extent.

I could relate to that kind of approach. Still, every now and then, it helped to brush up.

The phone rang. "It's George. You're down on me, aren't you?" I said I wasn't. He sounded like he'd been crying. He claimed he hadn't although he admitted he'd tried. "I want to help you, George." "Well," he said and took a breath that sounded more like a hiccup, "you may." I let him sob for a while. The only words he could manage were, "Maybe it's . . . all this . . . Philippe . . . stuff."

I tried to find the right tone. Why not just say it? I thought. But before I could blurt that cliché I'd longed to get in the open for months, I saw his tears as a great opportunity. "I understand you, George. Give me less than a minute to think." I felt a weird grin spread over my face as I said this.

Once he'd calmed down I suggested a plan. I'd follow him to Philippe's. I'd hide outside and observe their sex. Afterward we'd go somewhere and I'd give him my honest opinion on what it meant. "Yeah, I guess so," he sighed, "but you'll be shocked." "No," I said. I grabbed a loose sheet of paper and scribbled down the directions. "Okay, got it."

I crawled through some bushes, careful to keep them from rustling. I found an unshuttered window and rose to my feet. The room was plush, overfurnished in shades of white. Philippe sat on a black sofa. He was ashen-faced, a little gray at the temples and saggy. To his left George was stumbling out of his Jockey shorts. Above their heads hung a charcoal drawing of somewhere that didn't exist.

I scooped some dirt off the sill and got my balance. Cars driving by couldn't see me. The lawn was deep, the foliage thick. The room was subtly lit like a case full of perishable objects. I wished I'd brought my old Konica. I could have gotten some great shots of George in the nude. As I'd hoped he was so pale and smooth he looked air-brushed.

He shut his eyes and felt his way through the furniture, stubbing a toe now and then. He ended up by a small air-conditioner, turned in slow circles for thirty seconds or so, then lay face down on the rug's smoky pattern. Philippe rose from his chair and knelt over the body. I thought, Religious, but what happened next made me think of a porn film I'd fidgeted through.

The starlet lay on her stomach. A fat man pried her ass open, stuck out his tongue and spread her privates with spit from the blond pubic bush to the small of her back, going over and over the same spots until they reflected the light, appeared monstrous one second, and toylike the next.

Philippe's tongue had a similar sweep. It climbed the rubble of George's balls, swabbed the crack and returned to base, again and again. At first that looked too mechanical, then I was struck by their grace. In comparison my fantasies were a scrawl. I nearly blushed at the thought of how close I'd come to subjecting this boy to them.

George got a fierce spanking. Philippe's arm seemed to move in slow motion, but I heard the slaps, even through plate glass. After a dozen he eased off, smiled down at his handprints and mouthed a few words. The asshole swelled, trembled, then very slowly produced a turd. It rose an inch in the air, toppled onto his waiting palm.

I thought I could make it but halfway down the street I splayed my hands on the nearest tree and threw up. A dog walked over and sniffed my splattered Adidas. "Go fuck yourself," I moaned. It backed off a few feet and watched me retch for a while with its confusing eyes. Thinking how it might have felt helped get my mind off my misery.

I thought of the first and last time I'd gone horseback riding. Those palominos resembled big dogs to me, with even kinder smiles. Dad helped me onto one's back whereupon it tore off down the trail. I gripped the reins in a terrified silence the more it snorted and tried to buck me off. Suddenly I lurched face-first toward the earth. The bored dog barked a few times and trotted under a bush.

Somehow I got to my car. Its chilly metal felt perfect. I lay on the hood taking deep, even breaths. After a while I stood up but was still much too shaky to form an opinion of what I'd seen. On the one hand I longed to find some sort of clinic and have my memory flushed. On the other hand I wanted to ring Philippe's bell, shake his hand and say, "Yeah, right."

I drove into a Shell station and phoned my friend Alex. He was the most callous, sarcastic person I knew, but we'd been friends since tenth grade. He knew me inside out. "We have to talk." I gave a quick sketch of what I'd seen. "Rush over here," he gasped. Ten minutes later I eased past two sleepy-eyed parents and into his bedroom. "So, tell all, Clifford." I pulled a chair up.

I loved seeing Alex. His face was covered with freckles, ten deep in some places. They camouflaged his quite commonplace features with startling images. I could connect up the dots and see galloping horses, a black man lifting a crate, a map of Oregon . . . It was the ideal appearance for someone so witty and complex.

Tonight I was too self-absorbed to see anything. I talked. He nodded occasionally. "Whew!" he said once I'd completed my tale, "Little George Miles? I can't fucking believe it." He crossed his arms and seemed deep in thought. I must have drifted off because the next thing I saw was a mouth smeared with toothpaste. "Rise and shine, pervert," it said.

While Alex showered I reached behind his cassette deck. I found the baggie where he hid his grass, rolled a joint, struck a match on my belt buckle. I tried the radio. Out popped Sparks' "Amateur Hour," a taut, experimental hit single that sounded best loud. I settled back on the bed, closed my eyes and pressed my thumbs on the lids until I could see pretty patterns wherever I looked.

Alex appeared in the doorway, a towel tied at his waist. Like his face, his chest was cluttered with freckles. Dripping wet it looked like polished stone, some sort of granite to be exact. I thought of a sculpture I'd seen at the County Museum. *Untitled Two* was gigantic and so brightly lit all I'd seen was the glare on its surface. Alex was like that.

"Sparks?!" He punched off the radio then plucked his joint from my lips. Without great music to structure my thoughts everything in the room became very abstract, not just ideas but objects. The world of George was one miniscule speck in that constellation. It was light brown and set next to a prominent cheekbone. A sarcastic voice boomed from deep inside it. "Cliff, you still with us?"

"Sort of." I shook my head when Alex held out the joint. I felt—I searched for an adequate word—weird. I had to wake up. "Hey man," I said, "is there any hot water left?" He grabbed my wrist, yanked me up to my feet and literally pushed me out into the hall. "Come back a new man!" I couldn't tell if he meant it or not.

I stood in the shower. I saw myself as a waterfall. Hot jet streams pounded my head, splashed my shoulders and upper chest, streaked down my ribs, made my pubic hair droop, spilled off the tip of my cock, exploded around my feet. I watched this chain of events for a half hour, struck by how worn out my thinking was.

I wrapped myself in a towel. When I got back to his room, Alex eyed me suspiciously. "I *said* come back a *nude* man." I was supposed to quip, "You wish"—my usual epithet—but I decided against it. I don't know why, and this left a small hole in our afternoon. He realized I had caught him at something. I understood what that was, but I wasn't sure whether he knew that I knew or not.

He plopped himself on the end of the bed, reached out, fiddled with the TV. I knew he was hot for my body. I'd been avoiding the issue for months. Why had I tiptoed around what he couldn't say? We were so much alike mentally. Surely our bodies would match. I closed my eyes and imagined us making out, then stole a glance at my towel. Guess not, I decided.

As a test I imagined a similar scene with George. I locked us in an embrace. But before I could fasten the lips our bodies started to move by themselves. It had the look of ballet, at least the one I'd been dragged to. I was so wowed by my own choreography I might have whipped out my cock if a lump in my throat hadn't woken me up.

I opened my eyes. I saw a pretty actress in a fake-looking

bathroom. Her mouth was open inhumanly wide. Her glazed eyes stared at a mirror. It reflected her screaming face and, further back, the burly chest of a beast with a leather hood over its head. It yanked a bloody ax out of her back and was wiping it off on the front of its T-shirt.

They were replaced by a bottle of Windex. Alex glanced over his shoulder. His face was mildly amused again. "This thing is great," he said. It was his kind of film—that is, it tried to make light of the worst thing in life, inadvertently making death witty and, therefore "great." Thanks to his lecturing I'd come around as well. "Yeah," I agreed, "the day's looking up."

He changed positions. His eyes came so close to mine I was sure I could see an emotion in them if one was back there. They were pea green with yellow flecks that looked like tiny dead leaves floating slowly around in two bowls of soup. Neat as a pin, I thought. Or as Alex liked to explain how he saw the world, "Tears are beside the point."

"Yes, may I help you?" "Oh," I gulped, shifting my gaze to the wall. "I was just spacing out." Being overly stoned was the perfect excuse. He gave me one of his skeptical glares, but I wouldn't be tripped up. I even asked for a hit off the joint. "Okay, I guess I believe you," he snapped and snatched the *TV Guide* off his alarm clock.

"*Young Blood Runs Wild*," he read aloud. "Three adventurous teenaged couples face horror and death at the hands of a half-human monster." As he spoke, a handsome boy on the TV was pointing his flashlight beam into a cobwebbed room. It found dusty books, a gruesome painting of lap dogs, chairs, overturned table . . . The jazzy soundtrack swelled-up as the murdered girl's face reappeared. His mouth opened inhumanly wide. The hooded beast bounded out of a closet.

He struck it over the head with his flashlight. It hit the floor. He staggered into the hall yelling, "I've killed it. Bobby? Jill?" They huddled down in a corner. "Come on, I'll show you," their hero said. "No way," Jill gasped, clutching Bobby's hand. But the brave boy ran ahead, gesturing into the death chamber. "See?" he grinned.

A very hairy arm dragged him away. I heard a scream, several yelps, then a gurgling noise. "That must be the air wheezing out of his chopped-open lungs," Alex mumbled. "Let's hope," I joked. The stunned couple eased through the hall and peered into the dark. Their handsome pal was face down with an ax sticking out of his haircut. "That's it?" Alex groaned. "What a rip-off!"

I knew what was coming next. "You know," he said, "I always say this but it's very true. If someone's cute and they have to die"—his eyes were almost emotional—"it's simple logic that someone who's beautiful is more important than some ugly guy. I mean, that actor"—he pointed at the TV—"he's cute. That's *all* he is. That's why he's in the film. Nobody cares if *he's* dead. All they know is his looks. If *I* were directing that scene I'd have totaled him."

I think he thought he could freak me out, but I was daydreaming. I saw the glare on a windowpane and, framed inside, a slightly sexier version of the shot we'd just been glued to. A pretty boy was face down in a living room. A man with leathery skin was pretending to finish him off. I was transfixed until one of the actors did something so realistic I jerked my head to the left.

My favorite porn stars were slim, pale teenagers with shoulder-length hair, preferably black. Take the boy sandwiched in between two musclemen in the magazine Alex had shoved at me. He had drab skin, shapely legs, a dated haircut and oversized eyes. Best of all he had one of those asses that opens unusually wide.

"Check out this page," Alex said. The star had shoved his ass right in the camera lens. What I'd thought pert at a distance was spooky close-up. "No matter how many times I see one of these," Alex leered, "it's still a shock. I mean, as hard as I try I can't look at this thing and recall the boy's face, even though I just told you how hot he is."

True enough, I also couldn't remember its owner. It seemed to have a hypnotic effect. I thought of aliens in sci-fi films who, catching humans' eyes, could wipe our memories clear. This boy's backside wasn't too far removed in appearance from one of those cheaply made monster masks. "Weird, Alex. You're right, as always."

"Let's jerk off," he whispered. We did that sometimes, each holding one end of a magazine, handling our cocks with the other. I didn't like it as much as my friend, but I did feel a certain thrill knowing how badly he wanted to turn on his side and have sex with me. "Let's share a joint first," I stalled. While he fixed us a fat one I scanned the small world in front of me.

Page eight: The two musclemen kiss; the porn star kneeling in front of them, both cocks between his teeth. Page twenty-two: Come dribbling down the star's chin. Page three: The men sixty-nine. Page eighteen: Two cocks inside the star's ass; his face grimacing. I was admiring the narrative when Alex entered my line of sight.

"Does he remind you of George?" he said. "I ask because I can see the resemblance, but I think this kid's really hot whereas I'm not attracted to George at all. Here." I took the joint. I was surprised, not that he'd claimed to be wild for George. I just assumed my friend's beauty was one of the earth's universals. "Yeah?"

"Sure. I mean, I'll admit George is cute although cutesy's more like it. He reminds me of a cartoon character. You know, the 'real boy' Pinocchio's forced to become in the old Disney film? Ugh. That's why I still can't imagine the scene you described last night. George's, uh, shit is supposed to be heavy I guess but to me the concept is incredibly lightweight."

Maybe it was the grass but I didn't know what he was talking about. I knew George wasn't the star's spitting image. This face was hot, whereas George's was so cute it seemed the work of a great plastic surgeon. Maybe it gave away too much too soon, but my friend's saving grace was his strange combination of idealized looks and whatever they bottled up.

I explained this to Alex. "Look," he sighed wearily, "you can't be objective. You're backstage. I'm talking about presentation because, Cliff, our world is a stage. If you buy that old metaphor, George is a character actor at best, not a sex symbol. Knowing you're hot for him is semi-interesting but, you'll admit this, they'll never base *Gone With the Wind Part II* on it."

"Well, even so, it's a monument to old-world values in other ways," I said, sounding as vague as I could. I was embarrassed to use the word *lust* around Alex, even ironically. He'd just guffaw. "Oh, believe me, I know," he smirked, stubbing the joint out. "Just make sure to keep Winnie the Pooh on *your* side of the bed." I slugged his arm and we settled down, magazine propped on our chests.

We agreed on a page where the star's upper half was in soft focus. Ass filled up most of the frame. The co-stars each held a big, creamy cheek. They grinned happily from either side of the page, as if they'd just won a loving cup. I liked the mixture of thoughts in their matching eyes: lust, greed, pride, boredom and maybe two or three others that didn't matter as much.

Alex unzipped his jeans which made the usual sputtering noise. I heard a crack as his head turned. Two short snorts rustled my sideburn. I smiled and met his eyes. I just assumed he had noticed how much we resembled the men in the picture. Instead his face looked extremely confused, about to burst into tears or bawl me out.

It made me think of the story an old girlfriend told me. When Joyce was young her family lived in a run-down apartment. Their landlord bragged that his collie could talk. One day it trotted in at the man's heels and when its master barked, "Greet the Benairs, Maxwell," it tried to mimic his voice. But its mouth wasn't built for speech so it took the dog an agonizingly long time to say in a strangled voice, "I . . . love . . . you."

Alex was like that. I couldn't imagine him mouthing the obvious: "I want to fuck with you, Cliff," or however he might have rephrased that. I realized it was up to me and, looking down at my hard-on I thought, Why not see what it means to be hot for a night? I closed my eyes and unfastened the front of my towel. The porn star's ass clattered onto the floor and flipped shut.

The result was too clumsy for my taste. We recreated a few poses we'd seen in magazines and spent far more time giggling than moaning each other's names. I thought of it as a sort of misplacement, kept George in mind and went right through the motions. I even gave my friend's ass a few superficially passionate strokes to make him think I hadn't tried to forget him.

We came and sat a few feet apart. "Well, Cliff," he said between breaths, "don't you think we've confirmed our big theory that sex is a blueprint for porn? I mean, we look at a photograph and get aroused yet we still have our wits. But just now I became so distracted by what you were doing I lost my perspective. You turned into someone I'd much rather see from a distance."

Driving home I debated for three seconds and made a sharp turn. George's house was lit up like a storefront so I rang the bell. His dad, a more wasted George on a much grander scale, pointed down a short corridor. "I think you'll find what you're seeking behind that locked door." We shared a nervous smile, then he went back to his coffee cup.

The hall was lined with family portraits that chronicled the enlargement of George. The storyline was okay but the pictures were blurry. The older their dates the cuter George grew. In '72 he'd looked girlish. In one snapped when he couldn't walk I'd have sworn his dad was kissing a doll's cheek.

"Oh, it's just you," George said. "Quick, come in." He double-bolted the door. The room was crammed to the ceiling with memorabilia, mostly from Disneyland. Everywhere I looked I saw a goofy sketch grinning at me. George dashed from wall to wall pointing out characters he liked the best. "Then over here's where I keep the attractions," he said, indicating a handmade altar which must have once been a desk.

He'd stapled photos of each of the famous amusement park's rides on its sides and filled the shelves with scale models of his particular favorites. ". . . The Haunted Mansion, Enchanted Tiki Room, Peter Pan, Space Mountain . . ." Finally he came to the centerpiece, a battered Mickey Mouse cap. He raised the lid ceremoniously. "Here," he said, "is where I keep my LSD. Want some?"

I shook my head. "Well, then . . ." He grabbed what I guessed was his diary and a small silver key about the size of a teardrop. ". . . Mind if I finish this?" I found a sittable spot on the floor and watched him write away. His eyes were wider than I'd ever seen them. His room was so dazzling it made the rest of the world seem as dull as a vacant lot.

I thought of my own bedroom. It was extremely plain: table, chairs, twin bed, and sometimes a poster of someone cute. The closest I'd come to creating a world for myself was a dusty storeroom in our basement. Dad kept it locked but one day years ago, I'd broken in. Every few months I'd crept down, stretched myself on the cold cement floor and jerked off.

Maybe that explained why, though surrounded by innocent icons, my mind was filled with pornographic ideas. I imagined George floating face down in the billows of his double bed. I felt my throat clogging up. I never would have believed I'd think of Alex at an emotional moment but, as tears threatened, I calmed myself by upgrading our time in the sack. At least I'd touched human flesh, even if my aim was off.

"I'm all yours," George said, clicking shut the tiny lock on his red leather booklet. He saw me eyeing it curiously. "Oh, this is where I hide my feelings. In here they don't get in anyone's way." While he buried it under his mattress I wondered how many times my name appeared in the scribbles. "Being articulate wears me out," he yawned, slapping himself in the face.

No kidding. Shortly thereafter his sentences shortened, then I was left asking dumb questions to which he'd shrug, nod or shake his head. During one particularly silent stretch I suggested a walk. "Huh? Oh, right," he shrugged. I followed him out a window. We walked a few blocks very slowly. When we reached a house with a huge front lawn, he stopped and stared at it. "Let's sit."

We perched side by side gazing out at the street. Once a big truck roared by, carrying some sort of carnival ride on its bed. I'd just decided to ask his opinion when . . . "So," he said softly, "the other night." I coughed, then blathered nonstop about how overcome I'd been. First he nodded along but his eyes grew so glazed that I stopped mid-apology, raising my eyebrows to mean, What's wrong?

Look at him, I thought. He's so fucked up, so far away from

the way I've felt. I'm sick of treating his moods with kid gloves. I want to figure his body out and get him over with if it comes down to that. He won't know the difference and whatever happens at least I'll stop feeling this weird.

"Let's go back." There was a flicker of warmth in his eyes. I helped him up to his feet. In the dark between streetlights my thoughts raced. When a yellowy glow made him visible, I reaffirmed what I already knew. The walk was lined with magnolia trees. Their strong, ambiguous odor had always repulsed me. Tonight they smelled like my come and I shared that perception with George. "How would I know," he whispered.

"Just stretch out here," I said, gesturing down at his unmade bed. I didn't have to say, "Face down." He naturally landed that way. As I undressed I glanced around at the walls completely covered with mice, ducks, dogs, crickets, etcetera. When I squinted they looked like the crowd at a strip joint. If life were a sketch I was sure I'd be deafened by high-pitched yells of encouragement.

I carefully recreated what I had seen through Philippe's window, up to the point when I'd felt nauseous. I was a little too tentative, but George's lack of response made it seem we'd rehearsed our parts hundreds of times. I left my come somewhere deep in his back. I was surprised by how coldly he watched me get dressed, but I figured I'd wait until we were a few miles apart.

The further I drove the more our sex mattered. George was a slight worry but, as I started to think how amused friends would be by the more bizarre aspects, he took a back seat. By the time I'd reached my house and dialed the only phone number I knew by heart, he was less of an issue. I thought the ringing would never stop. Then I heard a familiar voice. "Alex," I said, "get this."

SEPTEMBER

• KEVIN KILLIAN •

SEPTEMBER, AND HARRY had decided not to go to school any-more. What was the point, tell me? The thing was whether you knew how to read or write, or not, and he didn't, so he was stuck. Kids laughed at him, and who needs that shit? Harry stood in the doorway of Gunther's apartment and watched pas-sersby strolling along on their way to the beach, dressed in robes and towels and looking drugged, happy, in the Long Island summer heat. Every one of them probably knew how to read or write. Harry knew his letters and was good at remembering license plates. Listlessly he withdrew deeper into the house, away from the happy strangers, away from nature, and began to sharpen a pencil with his teeth.

He made up a list of all the license numbers he could remem-ber back to earliest childhood.

Who needed jokers like those kids in school, sneering? Tell me. Harry raised his suddenly heavy head and was confronted with Gunther's tall shelves of books. He had to laugh. Books, books, books. What the hell good were they anyhow, to Gunther or to anyone else? Harry grabbed one and flipped it open to find out what kind of book it was. He knew the format of all kinds of books. Cookbooks, for example, have pictures of delicious food and square box shapes with ingredients listed down them. But this was no cookbook. Okay then, spell it out. *The*.

One time a guy who lived in the same building in Boston brought him up to his place in the daytime, popped open some brandy, and lifted out some books from a plastic satchel, the kind you throw away trash in. "Like to read, kid?"

Old. The Old. All books are old, big deal.

"Yeah, I like to read but I like reading better when someone reads to me." A pampered perfumed cat went wiggling from room to room flipping her tail in a bossy way like she owned the place. The guy said, "Ever have a cat as a pet? She's my baby."

The Old. Wives. Gunther had a lot of books about husbands and wives.

"Read to me a little. What do you call this shit? Brandy you say? I'm drunk." "Want to lie down?" They smiled at each other filled with knowledge, the kind books don't teach you. Harry agreed; his head, he said, was spinning with planets and stars. "Read me some of those books you got there in that sack. Do some educating, mister." The pillow was dusty with perfumed cat hairs. The man pulled a hard wooden chair to one side of the bed and dragged the garbage bag over, and the bottle of brandy. "You must be new in this building, kid. Haven't seen you around." "I got here about two weeks ago," Harry said. "Everyone in Boston talks funny. Except for you: you talk fine. My head is spinning, clouds around the universe."

The Old Wives' Tale.

"How's your tail?" the guy said. Harry frowned. "It's okay. Hey man, you said you were gonna read, so read already." "Sure. I'll be right back, Kitty's calling for Daddy. Don't go away." So there he was already in some big mother bed acting drunk and the guy's falling for it. How's your tail? What a giveaway.

Harry tore up his list of license plate numbers and put the pieces inside Gunther's book, replaced it on the shelf. He'd like to burn all Gunther's books. The shit would hit the fan then, wouldn't it? He lit a match in his hand and peered at the books through the flame. The gold and silver on their bindings bobbed up and down like dancing lights in an acid hallucination. Yeah, burn all those fucking novels. He blew out the match. He'd been seduced many times by a combination of books and liquor or so, at any rate, had all those jerks believed. There must be something to books and booze that he, Harry, couldn't see. Gunther seemed to live his life through them, blinded by them, hypnotized by them. Harry's head was clear. He never fell for books or liquor, only let other people think so, in this way keeping an advantage over everyone, Gunther included. *The Old Wives' Tale.* What a name!

"I'll read you a nice fairy tale," the guy said. "Fairy?" "How old are you, kid?" "Old enough. I don't need no fairy tales." "Thirteen or fourteen?" "I am so drunk. How's Kitty? You get rid of Kitty?" "Did I tell you my name?" said the guy. "I forget." "Oh, so you don't even know my name." "What does Kitty call you? Oh yeah—Daddy." "Call me Sam. You like that name?" Sam's bedroom, curtained and musty, had too much perfume, too much talc. Big mother bed though. A cat's hair stuck in Harry's mouth. He took another sip of brandy and dribbled it down his cheek to make himself look prettier. Sam's chair squeaked as he drew it closer to the bed. "This fairy tale's called *Cadet Capers*, okay?" said Sam, drawing out a small book from the garbage bag. The heavy black plastic rustled as his hand withdrew, then collapsed in a heap on the carpet. "Takes place in a military school." "Go ahead," said Harry, struggling to sit up. But Sam wasn't having any of that. He hushed and sedated him. "Relax, kid. Settle that tail of yours into bed. Calm yourself. Relax." Booze and books.

Books and booze. Harry wondered which they'd invented first. "They" were the people who couldn't admit to themselves what they wanted. "Thirteen or fourteen's pretty close," he admitted. "How wise of you," Sam remarked. "Chapter One, A Day in the Barracks."

"That your favorite book?" he said to Sam.

"It is."

"I like it, Sam, but it's making me awfully horny."

Sam was alert. "What's that you say?" He'd drunk hardly any brandy. "You said horny?"

"I forget," said Harry, yawning, turning over.

Kevin's favorite book was something he called *Murder in Three Acts* by Agatha Christie. He was the neighbor upstairs with a bigger hard-on than Gunther's. And a writer. Jesus! You live with a *reader*, plus you got a writer tap-tap-typing all day and all night over your head like a—guardian angel, or a spy . . .

Gunther said he had no "favorite book," that the books he read were tools to open his mind. Harry's mind, said Gunther, was impossible to widen. Long ago all its circuits, its possibilities, had been fused. Harry would always be a dumb piece of shit. "But with a little time, asshole, I'll widen your asshole." "It's wide open already," said Harry, throwing up a fart at him. "And so is my mind if only you knew, bookworm." That was Gunther, a bookworm, a rundown worm who sometimes couldn't even get it up; and what was he, twenty-eight, twenty-nine, thirty-two? Tell me. Harry would lie there on the floor and watch Gunther shake his misshapen cock up and down, to and fro, watch him curse it, and he'd laugh. "Your cock is a worm, bookworm. Why don't you let it read a book, worm? Slip it in the pages like a bookmarker, bookworm. Yeah, Gunther, shake it! Go ahead and shake it good. Does a whole lot in motion. A whole hell lot of good." Gunther would get furious with him, go apeshit. At least he, Harry Van, had a cock that worked, that hardened on demand, that wasn't a limp pathetic spaghetti pink red and white thing like a dopey valentine. Gunther Fielder, who had so many books, that he called "tools," yet the tool he'd been born with couldn't cut mustard. Harry laughed. Even with a gag in his mouth laughter farted its way out of his body. Why not? Laughter's natural when you see something ludicrous. "Tools!" A thousand "tools" on these shelves, and Gunther was impotent.

No wonder then, as summer melted into September, Harry had come to feel closer to Gunther than to any other person in his life. The two of them were bound together not just by the sex they had, or the rooms they shared, but by all the lessons taught back and forth that don't come out of books but from the knowledge of what the body can and can't do. Sometimes Harry felt as though he had two bodies, his own and Gunther's, and when he was in Gunther's he felt sad, unable to exist happily inside him. Yet sometimes when Gunther began to punish him, for some petty shit thing, Harry was able to escape and inhabit instead the body Gunther lashed from, to feel from inside everything happening to them both. So Harry could think, and say, "This hurts him more than it hurts just me," and not feel he was lying one bit. That was okay, though. I mean what's the big deal.

Still he wandered through the furnishings of Gunther's apartment, this afternoon, feeling tired and weary. He needed some vitamin pills. His straps were beginning to chafe the red scratched spaces round his ankles. He needed Desenex too. "I feel sad more," he said. "There's not very much to do around here." He sat down and started to jerk off, then put his dick back in his shorts. Too much trouble. It was too gray an afternoon to waste. He stared at the whitish, graying, yellowing fly of his shorts, and imagined the sun rising and setting inside it. Everytime he came, a sun burst. But if he wasted it too soon, on this dingy summer day, that would leave twenty minutes or so of afternoon spread out before him like an uninviting, colorless rainbow. So instead Harry patted his crotch and whispered to it. Talking into the final thing that kept him alive like a Hot Line volunteer on a switchboard.

Then leaning back, he raised his legs above his head, and the long vinyl straps fell all around him like streamers, and gave him pleasure. He bicycled in the air, and the straps made a hissing noise round his head like the blades of a helicopter propeller. "Go, man, go," he whispered, in a melody of his own invention. "Go, man, go, Speed Angel. Go, man, go Sky King."

Sometimes he wished Gunther would get a tattoo on each shoulder. That would look cool. One arm could have Speed Angel on it, and the other arm—turn around Gunther—Sky King. "And it would be me!"

Gunther said he didn't want tattoos, but Harry talked about them so much that they decided to tattoo Harry. It didn't hurt as much as tickle, it was no worse than getting vaccinated. So far they'd only gotten up to the "e" in "Gunther." Gunther was performing the job very slowly, with a sewing needle, a candle, and a bottle of Waterman's blue ink. "Put clouds around it," Harry would urge, leaning back and straining to watch the name grow longer across his ass. "Or roses, or planets. Don't just make it just the name." "Quiet please," Gunther joked, "surgeon at work." To make sure the ink would never run, he had Harry sit in a handbasin filled with water for twenty-four hours. "Or do you think maybe thirty-six hours? What d'you think, Harry?" Gunther seemed so worried Harry had to share his concern. "I guess, wow, I don't know, we'll just see after twenty-four, see if the ink's still there." "Okay, we'll do it your way." "I like this," said Harry, sitting in the water, hands on his knees, as Gunther prowled around the bedroom dressing. "What about you, Gunther? This is kind of fun, ain't it?"

"I can't find my other tennis shoe," Gunther said, tearing the room apart. "Why can't you keep this place in some kind of order? You're home all day."

"I mean, like you do think it's fun?" Harry asked uncertainly. "I mean I do. Wow, wait till we get the whole word 'Gunther.' How many more letters you got after 'e' in your name? Just a couple? I forget."

Finally Gunther found the shoe next to the toilet. He must have kicked it off while relaxing, taking a shit.

"How many more letters past 'e,' huh, Gunther?"

"One," Gunther said, jiggling his car keys. He pointed to different spots around the apartment. "Try to get something done around here, okay? Today?"

"Oh, sure, Gunther, yeah, except I'll be sitting here in this tub all day like and I can't get up. Wow, I'm sorry. I know, Kevin will come over. He'll do it. I'll ask him. I'll ask Kevin to do it."

Gunther rushed to him. "I don't want him here," he said, his breath hot on Harry's chest. "Got me?"

Harry nodded.

"Nosy kind of guy," Gunther said after a beat, relenting, standing up again. "He'd like to break up our little arrangement here. He's that kind of guy, nosy. I hear he's been down here your ass is grass, got me?"

Harry yawned, waving him away. "You sound like *Cadet Capers*," he said. "Have a nice day."

Harry thought once more of that book, *The Old Wives' Tale*. What a crock of shit. Why did Gunther want to read a book about old ladies anyhow? Tell me. He let his legs fall and rested a minute. The straps settled along the rug like black curly snakes. His ankles itched but scratching makes things worse. Their color was bad. The red patches looked as red as blood now. Above the kitchen sink Gunther kept a grocery list, but Harry couldn't tell if Desenex was on the list because he forgot right now what letter "Desenex" begins with.

In the middle of the night Gunther would wake up, startled, sweating, and from his crib on the floor Harry could see his eyes wide and white as baseballs. "What's the matter?" "Ssshhh!"

Then Harry would focus and hear what Gunther was hearing: the tap tap tap of Kevin's typewriter upstairs. Gunther whispered, "Writing down our lives, and then what will happen!"

"Aw don't carry on about Kevin," Harry said muzzily. "He's harmless."

"He's a fly on the wall!" Gunther insisted, his face so white and his breath so labored that Harry would have rushed to comfort him were he not strapped down by the balls to his Pliofilm-covered pad. This would go on at intervals all night sometimes and could drive a person Looney Tunes and completely haywire.

It was true that Kevin was writing some kind of book, but he was secretive about it when asked. Was he really, as Gunther believed, listening in on their private talks and conversations? Was his book the story of their lives? "Well," Harry said, "I'll never read it so who cares?" And actually if a person is gonna get pushed around and get fucked all the time what's wrong with an audience? It makes your life dramatic anyhow. Gives you a sense of interest.

"One letter, moron. After 'e' just one letter. G U N T H E R, Gunther! One letter more." The ink was good ink, stayed in the

skin. Harry felt under the shorts for the raised fruity letters on
his backside, found them. Left cheek. Maybe they'd save the
right for Gunther's last name. That would look cool all right.
His ass was already the hottest square foot of flesh that ever was.
But there is always room for improvement. He forgot right now
what Gunther's last name says anyhow. Something stupid.
Many letters. Not "Van." "Van" is a good last name with not
many letters in it. Three. Easy to write. He spit on his fingers
and rubbed his left cheek up and down, loosening some of its
soreness. From there it was a natural thing to do, to grab hold
his hard-on and to pull on it. His fingers flew up and down, wet
with spit, warm, sweaty. Then he dropped his hands to his sides
and watched the underwear subside, still shaking, like ⌐ collapsed tent falling on some stupid Boy Scouts with merit badges
who go to school but have no common sense. Jerks.

Since his last escape from the Shelter, Harry had boarded
for six weeks with one woman and counted that a long spell.
Then with Paula and her mom I don't know how long: two,
three weeks, about average. Then ten days in New York City
with two well-to-do vampires, where he'd had a good time kind
of but still. Then living under the boardwalk down at the beach
like a homeless hobo. And since then—his lips opened and shut,
as he traced with a faltering finger the dates on the kitchen
calendar—and since then, ever since then, he'd been here. "This
is the longest time I've been in one place. This. This time. In
my life." No wonder then he felt settled at last. All this was his:
this accumulation of boxes of dates and days. With a red pen he
ran through the long seven-day weeks, all of which he'd spent
here, under Gunther's roof and thumb, and whooped, as happy
as he could possibly be or ever had been in memory.

Gunther had been in Kevin's apartment upstairs one time,
and he'd spotted a glass lying on the floor, and then he came
downstairs and went crazy. "He keeps that glass there to listen
through." "Ah, Gunther, come off it." "Whisper!" Gunther
said, his mouth tiny, his voice hissing like a dragonfly. "When
he's not typing his ear's to the floor, and do you hear him typing,

do you, asshole?" "Gunther, I don't even think he's home." "But how would we know!"

"God, a fucking glass on the floor and you're acting like this is what do you call it, Watergate?" "I said *whisper*." "Is it Watergate I mean?" "Yeah Einstein," said Gunther, resigned suddenly, his muscles relaxing as he came into Harry's mouth, "yeah, yeah, yeah it's Watergate you mean."

Gunther drove up and came in quietly. Harry didn't speak. What was there to talk about? The house? Gunther thought so. He came out of his room, spluttering like Elmer Fudd about dust.

"You can write your name on top of the dresser," he said in disgust. "Melanie always kept my room in order."

"Who's Melanie?"

"Never mind her," Gunther objected. "She's someone I should have stayed married to."

"Maybe so if you don't like dust," Harry said as he went to find the duster. "You need a good lady's maid if no dust is what you want. I've got too much to do already so fuck this dusting your dresser. I got allergies, you know." He didn't really, but he had to invent something, the way he thought that Gunther had invented a wife, to taunt him with, as if to say *I used to fuck women*. Jerk! He didn't remember right now what allergies are anyway but big shit.

Gunther returned to his car and shut the door, but remained seated there just watching him, an expression Harry couldn't read written across his face. The motor revved. Gunther picked his two front teeth with a fingernail.

"What are you waiting for, go, man, go!" Harry finally cried. He wondered about Gunther. When they'd first met, Gunther had been a mystery to him—now he thought he could see right through him, like glass. He used to fuck women. So did I, Harry thought dolefully. In the kitchen the floor and furniture looked dull and dark. As he began to clean them his heart just wasn't in it, but who cared.

For a long time Gunther sat without moving, his chin on his hand, looking out over the great billowing summer landscape which rolled away down the hill as if driven on an invisible flood toward the sea. When he turned to Harry his eyes were full of a puzzled sadness. "Clean up the house, okay pal?" In the old days, in their frenetic inconclusive talks, Gunther had often confessed his grief at being friendless. And now Harry heard in Gunther's voice the lonely man's indignation at the unworthiness of those given what he'd been denied. "Pal?" Gunther repeated.

"Yes," Harry said, turning away from the screen door. It was on the tip of his tongue to say, "Look, Gunther, I don't have any more friends than you do." Instead he shut the door and leaned against it, trailing his straps like a host of pups on leashes. In the old days, before he'd made Gunther take him in, the two of them had sat up all hours underneath the pier where they'd met, where he'd been crashing, talking about women, cars, the weather. Often, leaning back, real fucked up and giddy, Harry had imagined that there were no studded boards above their heads, that the delicate band of heaven itself is all we need or want of shelter. In those days he had had the advantage of Gunther's muted, suspicious friendship without having promised to make him happy. Now he'd lost that advantage, and brought happiness to neither of their lives, only a kind of sensual ecstasy that was, he began to see, his meat, not Gunther's especially. No wonder then he felt he had brought Gunther to the brink of misery by conjoining their bodies. And now it was September.

All through the house he crept, with a bucket of dirty water and a brush the size of a brick. Kitchen first, then Gunther's room, then the front room, and lastly he approached the spare room. He'd never been in this room before, he'd been warned, like Bluebeard's wife, to keep his ass out of it. "So it can't be very clean," he said, "and so it deserves a good scrubbing." Viciously he threw open the door and saw nothing. Dust, dust, more dust; a closet door, closed. Big mother room with nothing in it but dust and a door.

He took up the rug and dust flew into his sensitive sharp nose. "God bless me," he said aloud after a sneeze. At this he had to crack a smile, against his will. His upper lip curved like a mustache. "And God bless Uncle Joey and Aunt Rube and Uncle Flem and Uncle Pete." Forgotten people from forgotten territory. "Matthew, Mark, Luke and John, bless the bed that I lay down on." The tinny metal scrub bucket clattered to one side. Water and suds spilled across the wooden floor, under the closet door, so he opened it wide, noting how the water had soaked a throw rug inside, big shit. Nevertheless he took it up, swearing, and that's when he noticed the hole in the closet floor, something bright beneath it, glittering in oils. His soapy red hands trembled.

A secret!

After a minute he threw both brush and rug to one side and stared into the hole, then sat back, his face and throat hot among the cuffs and sleeves of Gunther's expensive winter clothes which hung above him, grinning and sneering like kids who go to school . . .

Then he forced himself to look down again. Gleaming from the open space was a small oil painting. A beautiful woman, a goddess, was leaping over a brook. Her legs were long and her white dress flew behind her, happy, and over her head in a blue sky Harry saw a string of flowers and ribbons with words written on them. He choked. Heavy tweed, brass buttons, tickled his upturned face.

"It's very quiet in here," Harry said. "It's just me and the oil painting." He looked downwards once more. "I can hear my own tears. Why, Gunther, why?"

For it must be that Gunther had hidden from him this beautiful oil painting. "Why? Why?" He must have thought Harry would steal it. Harry did not touch it. Already the oil painting seemed to have lost some of its beauty. He'd lost something too: that beautiful faith he had in the goodness of people. "Gunther," he said to himself. "Gunther suspicious. Gunther believing the worst of me, in this house, where I loved and trusted him. Gunther prying up the floorboards, sealing up valuables, pretending to be careless, letting me think I had the run of the house—but hiding his feelings from me, from Harry, Sky King, Speed Angel . . ."

The rug, the missing floorboards, the winter wardrobe and Gunther's insistence, like Bluebeard, that he keep out of this closet—all tied together now to make the situation bleak as road tar. They spoke to Harry of a past, or a future ("I can't decide which"), that belonged to Gunther Fielder and would never be his. But why hadn't Gunther given him his trust? He'd given Gunther everything he had, and ever would have. Then Harry remembered the burns that ran up his legs and spotted his scrotum like so many scraps of shiny cellophane. Maybe Gunther had been burned too. Burning makes a person paranoid and mistrustful. But he'd been so fond of Gunther that he'd asked him no questions, once he'd determined what kind of pleasure he could take from him, a bee at the lip of flower.

These burns that marked their love weren't his. They hardly hurt; but insofar as they once had stung they belonged, like everything else in and under this house, to Gunther Fielder. Nothing was Harry's. Gunther's name was written on every surface. Harry stood and felt the uncompleted name on his ass, rubbed it ruefully. "You could write your name on the top of my dresser," Gunther had complained. What an invitation! Like giving a blind man the run of your library. With a deep sigh, Harry replaced the boards carefully in the floor and spread out the rug. It was not until he reached the door that he thought of leaving Gunther.

One day, instead of going to work, Gunther cut out, taking Harry down the hill and to the beach. Harry seemed surprised. "I come here with Kevin sometimes. I try to get a tan."

He took off his pants and his T-shirt, and Gunther didn't recognize him at first. He looked like a little boy. Gunther hadn't remembered in a long time how young Harry was. They played cards a while, in the sand, then they went way out and let the swells rock them. Gunther liked to swim out as far as he could. Harry didn't swim well. He floated instead, and Gunther swam in lazy rings around him, trying to fluster him by splashing waves in his face. Harry looked at the sky. It was all he could see. Like God, he thought dismissively. Aloud he said:

"Gunther?"

"I'm right here."

"Gunther?"

"Yeah, I'm here, pal."

"You think salt water washes ink out more than regular tap water?"

"I don't know."

"Gunther?"

"Yes."

"I had to do what I did. I had to come into your life even though all I did was wreck it."

God is only a concept. The sky is only a thought in God's mind, and changes as often as breathing. Harry's throat stretched and fell, his cheeks puffed and pulled, but Gunther couldn't hear him breathing. Harry's eyes darted from side to side as though trying to judge the breadth of a universe that, Gunther knew, was narrow enough that he and Harry had found each other in it, and floated together, hand in hand, at this its watery deep base. Gunther wanted to sink like a stone, to immerse and die here, so that then he would be clean. Eventually, he supposed, the blue ink in Harry's tattoo would fade away. In a way it seemed a shame they had never gotten to put in the "r."

"You didn't wreck it," said Gunther wearily.

"Oh yeah, I sure did. But I didn't mean to. I'm not a bad guy really."

"I'm not blaming you," Gunther said. "My life is fine. I just wish I had a woman in it."

"That's because you hate women."

"I don't," Gunther said. But he did, really. They drifted back to the shore. Harry's bathing suit came from the Salvation Army. Gunther didn't know who had bought it for him. It sagged and bagged with running water. Probably Kevin had bought it. "My life is fine but someday, I know, I'm gonna hear from some authorities. We got that Kevin Killian up the stairs breathing in every word we say. I know he fucked you. I know you tell him every little thing I do. I know it's all gonna come back down on our heads."

"I made you," said Harry, looking into the sun. One hand fell across his eyes, and he glanced at Gunther guiltily. "It wasn't your decision. I wiggled my ass in your face."

"It's all wrong."

"I made the first move with you," Harry said. Gunther saw with shocking clarity the marks of their connection all over Harry's skinny childish legs. "That was wrong of me. But hey, don't worry about Kevin. I got him wrapped around my finger. And my lips are sealed."

"You like it here?" Gunther said, indicating with the sweep of a hand the sands, the Sound, the glistening white tide.

"Yes, Gunther."

"I do too. Where I come from we don't have the beaches."

"I put my hand on you, picked you out," Harry said. His wet head dropped beyond the towel, lay in sand. His hair was two colors, vanilla and chocolate, and swirled from the scalp in a dozen confusing directions. His upper lip curled under when he laughed like the crest of a wave. Under his arms sketchy tufts of hair dripped water, drooped and stunted. His narrow shoulders seemed freckled in the strong sunlight, and all his native intelligence beat behind his brown eyes in vain, trying to make sense of his circumstances. He was a kid fucked up as the scars on his lean body, but someday would grow up and think worse of Gunther than he did now. Gunther was all he had, and formed the boundaries of his world in the same way the lovely fresh horizons of the day and night formed Gunther's. He was, Gunther thought, too dumb to live, but life has loopholes through which swim or are borne like matchsticks all the dumbest kids in the world, carried by luck, good and bad, to go on suffering, with no ASPCAs to put them to sleep painlessly by gas. They're forced to live in beauty and splendor they can't understand except by translation.

Harry told Gunther he'd made up a song: "Want to hear it?"

"Sure."

He didn't have to sing very loud, because Gunther lay only a foot away, and because Kevin, no matter how far off, would hear him wherever he went, whatever he did. But he had to shut his eyes because he was kind of embarrassed. "Ready?" Like even though it was a real good song. "Ready?"

"Sure, pal," Gunther said.

"The girls all call me Speed Angel
Cause when I move I'm quick.
I got a girl in Manhattan
She loves me til she's sick.

Go, Speed Angel, go.
Go, Speed Angel, go.
Go, Speed Angel, go.
Go, man, go, Speed Angel."

AN ORACLE

• EDMUND WHITE •

For Herb Spiers

AFTER GEORGE DIED, Ray went through a long period of uncertainty. George's disease had lasted fifteen months and during that time Ray had stopped seeing most of his old friends. He'd even quarrelled with Betty, his best friend. Although she'd sent him little cards from time to time, including the ones made by a fifty-year-old California hippie whom she represented, he hadn't responded. He'd even felt all the more offended that she'd forgotten or ignored how sickening he'd told her he thought the pastel leaves and sappy sentiments were.

George had been a terrrible baby throughout his illness, but then again Ray had always babied him the whole twelve years they'd been together, so the last months had only dramatized what had been inherent from the beginning. Nor had George's crankiness spoiled their good times together. Of course they'd lived through their daily horrors (their dentist, an old friend, had refused to pull George's rotten tooth; George's mother had decided to "blame herself" for George's cowardice in the face of pain), but they still had fun. Ray leased a little Mercedes and they drove to the country whenever George was up to it. A friend had given them a three-hundred-dollar Siamese kitten he'd found at a pet show and they'd named her Anna, partly because of Anna and the King of Siam and partly in deference to an ancient nickname for Ray. They both showered her with affection.

Which she reciprocated. Indeed, the more they chased away their friends, the more they relished her obvious liking for them. When they'd lie in bed watching television at night, they'd take turns stroking Anna. If she purred, they'd say, "At least *she* likes us." After George became very feeble and emaciated, he would ignore his mother and father and refuse to stay even a single night at the hospital and would play with Anna if he had the strength and berate Ray for something or other.

George would become very angry at Ray for not calling to find out the results of his own blood test. "You're just being irresponsible," George would say. "To yourself." But Ray knew that the test would tell him nothing—or tell him that yes, he'd been exposed to the virus, but nothing more. And besides there was no preventive treatment. Anyway, he owed all his devotion to George; he didn't want to think for a second about his own potential illness.

Every moment of George's last four months had been absorbing. They quarreled a lot, specially about little dumb things, as though they needed the nagging and gibbering of everyday pettiness to drown out the roar of eternity. George, who'd never cared about anything except the day after tomorrow, suddenly became retrospective in a sour way.

They quarreled about whether Ray had ever needed George, which was absurd since until George had become ill Ray had been so deeply reliant on George's energy and contacts that Betty had repeatedly warned Ray against living forever in George's shadow. What she hadn't known was how much he, Ray, had always babied George at home—nursed him through hangovers, depressions, business worries, even attacks of self-hatred after he'd been rejected by a trick.

George, of course, was the famous one. Starting in the early Seventies he'd been called in by one major corporation after another to give each an image, and George had designed everything from the letterhead to the company jet. He'd think up a color scheme, a logo, a typeface, an overall look; he'd redo the layouts of the annual report. He'd even work with an advertising creative director on the product presentation and the campaign slogans. He'd demand control over even the tiniest details, down to the lettering on the business cards of the sales force. Since he was six-foot-three, rangy and athletic, had a deep voice, and had fathered a son during an early marriage, the executives he dealt with never suspected him of being gay, nor was George a crusader of any sort. He liked winning and he didn't want to start any game with an unfair handicap. George also had a temper, a drive to push his ideas through, and he wasn't handsome—three more things that counted as straight among straights.

He'd also had the heterosexual audacity to charge enormous fees. His job as corporate image-maker was something he'd more or less invented. He'd realized that most American corporations were paralyzed by pettiness, rivalry, and fear, and only an outsider could make things happen. George was able to bring about more changes in a month than some cringing and vicious vice-president could effect in a year if ever. George made sure he reported directly to the president or chairman, although as soon as he came "onstream" he solicited everyone else's "input."

On summer weekends George and Ray had flown in a seaplane to Fire Island, where they'd rented a big house on the ocean side complete with swimming pool. Around that pool they'd spent twelve summers with just a phone, a little acid, and thirty hunky men. They had, or Ray had, pounds of Polaroids to prove it. Here was the White Party and the house flying a thousand white balloons and Skipper in the foreground with his famous smile, the smile that earned him a hundred and fifty dollars an hour. Dead now of his own—not hand, but leap: he'd leapt from his penthouse on angel dust. And here was the Star Wars party with George as Darth Vader and his arm around little Tommy as R2D2, the cute kid who wanted to be a deejay but never made it though he did amazing disco tapes he sold to friends in editions of fifty.

And here's George as Darleen. Older guys hated George's dabbling in drag, since they associated it with the sissy 1950s. And the younger kids simply didn't get it; they'd heard of it, but it didn't seem funny to them. But for George and Ray's generation, the Stonewall generation, drag was something they'd come to late, after they'd worked their way through every other disguise. For George, such a sexy big man with a low voice and brash ways, the character he'd invented, Darleen, had provided a release—not a complete contrast, but a slight transposition. For one thing, she was a slut, but an intimidating one who when horny yanked much smaller men to her hairy chest without a second's hesitation. For another, she had a vulgar but on-target way of talking over George's current corporation and reducing it to its simplest profile; it was Darleen in her drugged way who'd mumbled forth the slogans now selling seven of the biggest American products.

And Darleen had introduced a certain variety into Ray's and George's sex life, for she liked to be passive in bed, whereas George was tirelessly active. No one would have believed it, not even their closest friends, but Ray had fucked Darleen whereas he could never have fucked George. After sex they'd weep from laughter, the two of them, Ray sweaty and gold with his white tan line and George, foundered, skinny legs in black net stockings and the lashes coming unglued on his, yes, his left eye.

When George died, Ray thought of burying him in his drag, but the two people he happened to mention it to (although fairly far-out numbers themselves) drew back in horror. "You've got to be kidding," one of them had said as though Ray were now committable for sure. Ray had wanted to say, "Shouldn't we die as we lived? Why put George in a dark suit that he never wore in life?"

But he didn't say anything, and George was buried as his parents wished. His father had been a cop, now retired, his mother a practical nurse, and in the last twenty years they'd made a lot of money in real estate. They liked fixing up old houses, as did George. Ray had a superstition that George had succumbed only because he'd worked so hard on his own loft. George was a perfectionist and he trusted no one else to do a job correctly. He'd spent hours crouched in the basement rewiring the whole building. Everything, and most especially the lacquering of the loft walls, was something he'd done by himself, again and again to get everything right.

Now he was dead and Ray had to go on with his own life, but he scarcely knew how or why to pick up the threads. The threads were bare, worn thin, so that he could see right through what should have been the thick stuff of everyday comings and goings, could see pale blue vistas it was death to look at. "You must look out for yourself," George had always said. But what self?

Ray still went to the gym three times a week as he'd done for almost twenty years. He never questioned anything there and resented even the smallest changes, such as the installation of a fruit juice bar or a computerized billing system always on the blink.

And then Ray had Anna to feed and play with. Since she'd been George's only other real companion toward the end, she felt comfortable and familiar. They'd lie in bed together and purr and that was nice, but it wasn't a sign pointing forward to a new life, only a burnt offering to his past, itself burnt and still smoking.

He thought he was too young to have had to renounce so much. He'd always known that he'd have to end in renunciation, but he didn't like being rushed. He thought of George's long femur bones slowly emerging in the expensive coffin.

And of course he had his job. He did public relations for a major chemical company with headquarters on Sixth Avenue. It was a gig George had found him; George had done a total face-lifting for Amalgamated Anodynes. Nearly everything about the company was reprehensible. It had a subsidiary in the Union of South Africa. Its biggest plant was in South Carolina, precisely because there the "right-to-work" laws, as they were called in the best Orwellian manner, had banned most of the unions. A.A. had produced a fabric for children's wear that had turned out to be flammable; Ray had even had to draft for the president's signature some very high-level waffling as a statement to the press. And Amalgamated Anodynes had a lousy record with women and minorities, although a creepy Uncle Tom headed up the company's equal hiring practices commission.

Worst of all was Ray's boss, Helen, the token female vice-president. Helen was by turns solicitous and treacherous, servile to superiors and tyrannical to her staff, an old-fashioned schemer who knew more about office politics than her job.

Following a run-in with Helen a few days after the funeral (which, of course, he hadn't been able to mention), he'd locked himself in the toilet and cried and cried, surprised there was so much mucous in his head. Where was it stored normally, in which secret cavity? He was also surprised by how lonely he felt. Lonely, or maybe spaced. George had always been barking at him, scolding or praising him; now the silence was oddly vacant, as though someone were to push past a last gate and enter into the limitless acreage of space and night.

To cry he had had to say to himself, "I'm giving in to total self-pity," because otherwise he was so stoic these post-mortem days that he'd never let himself be ambushed by despair. Why did he keep this job? Was it to please George, who always wanted him to go legit, who'd never approved of his "beatnik jobs." George had used "beatnik," "hippie," and "punk" interchangeably to dramatize the very carelessness of his contempt.

Ray had grown up on a farm in northern Ohio near Findlay and still had in his possession a second prize for his cow from the State Fair; he'd sewn it and his Future Farmers of America badge to his letter-jacket. What big-city sentimentalists never understood about the rural existence they so admired was that it was dull and lonely, unnaturally lonely, but it left lots of time for reading.

He'd read and read and won a first prize in the Belle Fontaine spelling bee and another as the captain of the Carrie debating team against Sandusky on the hot subject of "Free Trade." His grades were so good he received a scholarship to Oberlin, where, in his second year, he'd switched his major from agronomy to philosophy.

From there he'd gone on to the University of Chicago, where he'd joined the Committee on Social Thought and eventually written a thesis on Durkheim's concept of *anomie*. His father, who wore bib overalls and had huge, fleshy ears and read nothing but the Bible but that daily, would shake his head slowly and stare at the ground whenever the subject of his son's education came up. His mother, however, encouraged him. She was the school librarian, a thin woman with moist blue eyes and hands red from poor circulation, who drank coffee all day and read everything, everything. She'd been proud of him.

But she too had had her doubts when, after he received his doctorate, he'd drifted to Toronto and joined an urban gay commune, grown his blond hair to his shoulders, and done little else besides holding down part-time jobs and writing articles analyzing and lamenting the lesbian-gay male split. In the doctrinaire fashion of those days, he'd angrily denounced all gay men and assumed a female name for himself, "Anna." The name wasn't intended as a drag name (although later George had insisted he use it as one), but only as a statement of his position against gender distinctions. Only his friends in the commune could call him "Anna" with a straight face.

Unlike most of the other early gay liberationists, Ray had actually had sex with other men. His affairs were shy, poetic, and decidedly unfancy in bed. Despite his political beliefs, he insisted on being on top, which he admitted was a "phallocratic" hang-up, although nothing felt to him more natural than lavishing love on a subdued man, similarly smooth-skinned, slender, and pig-tailed.

Then one summer he'd met Jeff, a New Yorker and a contributor to the *Body Politic* who was every bit as ideological as Ray but much more muscular and amusing. When Jeff's Toronto vacation came to an end, Ray moved to New York to be with him. He justified the move to the other communards by pointing out that New York was a literary center. "So is Toronto!" they'd objected, for they were also Canadian patriots.

Ray had inchoate literary aspirations. For years he'd dutifully kept a journal. When he re-read it after living in New York a while, he found the voluminous self-analysis neither true nor false; the recorded ideas a good deal sharper than those he was currently entertaining; and the descriptions of nature accurate, and mildly, solidly of value.

When he looked for a job as a writer in New York, all he could find, given his lack of credentials (his Ph.D. in philosophy counted as a drawback) was a position on *Conquistador!*, a sleazy tits-and-ass magazine for which he invented the picture captions in the centerfold ("Lovely Linda is a stewardess and flies, natch, for Aer Lingus"). The indignities (plus low pay) of that job he tried to compensate for by reading manuscripts in the evening for Grove Press and evaluating them artistically and commercially. Since he'd read little except the classics in school, his standards were impossibly high, and since his acquaintanceship till now had included only Ohio farmers, Chicago intellectuals, and Toronto gay liberationists, his grasp of the potential market for any particular book was skewed.

He drifted from job to job, ghosted several chapters of a U.S. history college textbook for a tottering publishing house, worked as a bartender in a black-glass, red-velvet singles bar, taught one semester at a snooty Episcopalian boys school in Brooklyn Heights, spent one winter as a stock boy at a chic lucite boutique some friends owned, fled another winter to Key West, where he wore short shorts and served rum and coconut "Conch-outs" around the pool of a gay guest house (he saw the shells as shrunken skulls). He was hired because he'd long since joined a gym, acquired a beefy but defined body, traded in his pigtail and severe manner for a ready laugh and a crewcut ("Wear a Jantzen and a smile" as the old swimsuit slogan had put it). Naturally he no longer insisted on being called Anna. He'd also moved bumpily from one affairlet to another and had been embarrassed that most of them had ended in squabbles over money or fidelity.

Into this confusion, so rife with opportunities he was unable to see how little hope it held out, George had entered. They were both guests at someone's house in New York and when they helped out washing up their hands met under the suds. When he later tried to pinpoint what had made this relationship take and stick he thought it could be seen as a barter—George's forcefulness for Ray's beauty, say. George was homely if sexy, yet he didn't sense his own appeal and he dwelled on all his imperfections. Ray on the other hand was "pretty" in the special sense that word acquired in the mid-Seventies to mean massive shoulders, shaggy moustache, permanent tan, swelling chest. He was also pretty in the more usual sense, for his full lips seemed to be traced in light where a slightly raised welt outlined them, his deepest blue eyes contained an implosion of gold particles falling into the black holes of his pupils, his jaw had comic-book strength, and his teeth were so long and white a dentist had had to file them down once when he was twelve. And now that he was in his late twenties one could discern brown-gold hair on his chest spreading wings over his lungs like that goddess who spreads her arms to protect the pharaoh from all harm.

Ray didn't take his own beauty too seriously, though he maintained it as one might conserve a small inheritance for the sake of security. His spell in the gay commune had made him suspicious of all "objectifications of the body" and "commodification of sex," but his years in New York had taught him the importance of precisely these two operations. He was a bit of a star on the deck during tea dance on Fire Island, for his years of training had in point of absolute fact turned him into a physical commodity—but one he was too ironic, too human to sell to the highest bidder. That George was not at all an obvious candidate, that he was too skinny, too pockmarked, a diligent but unsuccessful dresser, made him all the more appealing to Ray.

George had a ravenous appetite to win, even in the most trivial contests, and that made him both infuriating and appealing. Ray had always been accommodating—too accommodating, he now saw in view of how little he'd accomplished. He deplored the way George cussed out every incompetent and sent back the wine and at every moment demanded satisfaction.

And yet George's life was royally satisfying. He drove his Chrysler station wagon full of friends to Vermont for ski weekends, he was doing the work he most enjoyed and making a minor fortune, and now, to put the final *u* on parvenu, he had . . . Ray. Until now, Ray had never thought of himself as primarily decorative, but George saw him obviously as a sort of superior home entertainment center—stylish, electric. Ray didn't like to stare into this reflection, he who'd won the Belle Fontaine spelling bee and written one hundred and twenty closely reasoned pages on *anomie*. He saw that without noticing it he'd drifted into the joking, irresponsible, anguished half-world of the gay actor-singer-dancer-writer-waiter-model who always knows what Sondheim has up his sleeve, who might delay his first spring visit to the island until he's worked on those forearms two more weeks, who feels confident Europe is as extinct as a dead star and all the heat and life for the planet must radiate from New York, who has heard most of his favorite songs from his chronological adolescence resurface fifteen years later in their disco versions, at once a reassurance about human continuity and a dismaying gauge of time's flight.

Lovers are attracted by opposites and then struggle to turn them into twins. Ray worked to mollify George's drive to win and George wanted Ray to turn into a winner. Work hard and play hard was George's motto, whereas Ray, without admitting it, wanted lots less work than play and wished both to be not hard but easy. Nevertheless, George, true to form, won. He nudged Ray into a series of well-paying jobs that ended him up at Amalgamated Anodynes. "You must look out for yourself," George was always saying. He said it over and over: "Look out for yourself." Ray would sit on his lap and say, "Why should I deprive you of a job you do so well?"

The one thing they'd agreed on from the first was not to be monogamous. Ray's ideological horror of marriage as a model and George's unreflecting appetite for pleasure neatly converged. What wasn't decided so easily were the terms under which they were to be unfaithful. George, who had a funny face, skinny body, and enormous penis, was always a hit at the baths; Ray, whose penis was of average dimensions ("a gay eight" meaning six inches), was more likely to attract another man for a lifetime than a night. Ray already had love, George's, but in order to get sex he had to seem to be offering love. When George would see some other beauty, as dark as Ray was fair, melting amorously around Ray, George would break glass, bellow, come crashing through doors, wounded bull in the china shop of Ray's delicate romantic lust. Of course Ray envied George his simpler, franker asset and wished he could score more efficiently, with fewer complications.

And now, a year after George's death, here he was learning all the ways in which he had accommodated George and was still doing so, even though George had broken camp. Ray saw how in their tiny group he'd been billed as the looker with the brain, exactly like the starlet whom the studio hypes wearing a mortarboard and specs above her adorable snub nose and bikini —yet he wasn't in Hollywood but New York City and he realized that he'd fallen way behind, hadn't read a book in ages or had a new, strenuous thought.

He still had the big showboat body that George had doted on and that Ray was vigorously maintaining two hours a day at the gym, even though personally (as in "If I may speak *personally* about my own life") he found the results caricatural and the waste of time ludicrous. And yet he was afraid to let go, stop pumping iron and deflate, sag, shrink, because if he was no longer the greatest brain he was at least a body; Some Body in the most concrete, painful sense. He looked around and realized he was still impersonating George's lover. He was even still using the same deodorant George had liked; George had had such an insinuating way of sticking his big, cratered nose into the most intimate aspects of Ray's habits. He'd made Ray switch from Jockey to boxer shorts, from cotton to cashmere stockings, from Pepsi to Coke, from ballpoint to fountain pen; like all people who make their living from publicity, George had believed that products and brand names determine destiny. Ray was still walking around like a doll George had dressed and wound up before taking off.

In the corner bookstore he picked up a remaindered large-format paperback called *The Death Rituals of Rural Greece*, by Loring M. Danforth. He liked the way the widows resented their husbands' deaths and said, "He wasn't very kind to me when he left me." That was closer to the truth than this twilit grief one was supposed to assume. He liked the funeral laments, specially the one in which a mother asks her dead daughter how Death, called Haros, received her. The daughter replies: "I hold him on my knees. He rests against my chest. If he is hungry, he eats from my body, and if he is thirsty, he drinks from my two eyes."

When he had a Midtown lunch with Betty she told him he was in an identity crisis precipitated by George's death. "But your real problem," she said, warming unbecomingly to her subject, "is that you're still seeking an authority, the answer. If you don't watch out, you'll find yourself saddled with another dominating lover; it's your passive Aquarian nature."

Ray could scarcely believe in how many ways his fur was being rubbed wrong, although he felt certain the prize had to go to Betty's insinuation that he was well rid of George. That night he found in an old linen jacket he took out of storage a joint of Acapulco gold George had rolled him—how long ago? Two years?—and he smoked it and cried and ordered in Chinese food and sat in bed and watched TV and played with Anna, who kept wandering over to the lit candle on the floor to sniff the flame. When she felt the heat her eyes would slit shut and she'd thrust her chin up, like a dowager who's smelled something rude.

Even though George had been a baby, he'd fought death with a winner's determination but he'd lost anyway. Ray thought that he wouldn't resist it for long. If and when the disease surfaced (for it seemed to him like a kid who's holding his nose underwater for an eerily long time but is bound to come crashing, gasping up for air), when the disease surfaced he wouldn't much mind. In a way dying would be easier than figuring out a new way of living.

Betty must have taken it on herself to contact Ralph Brooks and suggest he ask Ray to Greece. Otherwise Ray couldn't imagine why Ralph should have written him a belated condolence letter that ended with a very warm and specific invitation.

Ray was flattered. After all, Brooks was the celebrated painter. Betty would say that Ray accepted *because* Brooks was the celebrated painter. Not that she ever accused Ray of social-climbing. No, she just thought his "passivity" made him seek out authorities, no matter who or of what. Oddly enough, Betty's nagging, grating Brooklyn accent reassured him, because it was a voice made to complain, that stylized suffering, domesticated it. "Oy," Ray thought when he was with Betty. She wasn't even Jewish, but she was from Brooklyn, and if he used her accent he could actually say it to himself or to Anna, "Oy."

Ray welcomed the trip to Greece precisely because it didn't fit in. George had never been to Greece; Ralph had never met

George; Ray himself scarcely knew Ralph. They'd become friendly at the gym and worked out a dozen times together and Ralph had always asked him his bright, general questions that didn't seem to anticipate anything so concrete as an answer. Ralph, who'd worked out for years, had a big bearish body that was going to flab—exactly what envious, lazy people always say happens to weightlifters in middle age. His shoulders, chest, and biceps were still powerful, but his belly was as big as a bus driver's. Ralph said he hated the ruin of his looks, but he seemed so relaxed and sure of himself that this self-loathing struck Ray as an attitude he might once have held but had since outgrown without renouncing.

Then again Ray would so gladly have traded in his own prettiness for Ralph's success that perhaps he couldn't quite believe in Ralph's complaints. As for the three weeks in Crete (he found the town, Xania, on the map), it would be all new—new place, new language, no ghosts. He even liked going to the country where people expressed their grief over dying so honestly, so passionately. In that book he liked the way a mother, when she exhumed her daughter's body after three years of burial, said, "Look what I put in and look what I took out! I put in a partridge, and I took out bones."

Betty agreed to take care of Anna. "You must look out for yourself," George had said, and now he was trying.

Ralph had rented a floor of a Venetian palace on a hill overlooking the harbor; at least Ralph called it a "palace" in that hyperbolic way of of his. The town had been badly bombed during the war and empty lots and grass-growing ruins pocked even the most crowded blocks like shocking lapses in an otherwise good memory.

Nothing in town was taller than three stories except two minarets left over from the centuries of Turkish rule and allowed to stand more through indifference than ecumenism. At first Ray looked for the blazing whitewash and strong geometrical shapes he'd seen in trendy postcards from the Greek islands, but in Xania everything was crumbling brick, faded paint, mud or pebble alleyways, cement and rusting cement armatures sticking up out of unfinished upper stories, shabby exteriors and immaculate interiors, dusty carved-wood second stories overhanging the street in the Turkish fashion. Along the harbor a chrome-and-plastic disco, booming music and revolving lights as though it had just landed, made chic racket beside shadowy, abandoned arsenals where the Venetians had housed their warships. One of them had a stone balcony high above the harbor and two doors shaped like Gothic flames opening up onto a roofless void and a framed picture of the night sky—the half-waned moon.

Ralph and Ray ate fried squid and a feta cheese salad at a rickety table outside along the brackish-smelling harbor. The table could never quite find its footing. They were waited on by a Buddha-faced boy who smiled with mild amusement every time his few words in English were understood. The boy couldn't have been more than nine, but he already had a whole kit of skilled frowns, tongue-clicks, and body gestures and his grandfather's way of wiping his forehead with a single swipe of a folded fresh handkerchief as though he were ironing something. Ray found it hard to imagine having accumulated so many mannerisms before the dawn of sex, of the sexual need to please, of the staginess sex encourages or the tightly capped wells of poisoned sexual desire the disappointed must stand guard over.

Ralph, who was shoe-leather brown and so calm he let big gaps of comfortable silence open up in the conversation, was much fatter himself—all the olive oil and *rosé* and sticky desserts, no doubt. A cool wind was blowing up off the Aegean and Ray was glad he'd worn a long-sleeved shirt. Ralph had helped him unpack and had clucked over each article of clothing, all of which he found too stylish and *outré* for Xania. In fact Ralph seemed starved for company and gossip and far less vague than in New York. There he seemed always to be escaping sensory overload through benign nullity, the Andy Warhol strategy of saying "Oh great," to everything. Here he took a minute, gossipy interest in the details of everyday life. Ray thought we each need just the right weight of pettiness to serve as ballast; George's death had tossed all the sandbags overboard and Ray had been floating higher and higher toward extinction.

Ralph was specially interested in the "locals," as he called the young men. "Now this is the Black Adonis," he said of one tall, fair-skinned twenty-year-old strolling past with two younger boys. "He's in a different shirt every night. And would you look at that razor cut! Pure Frankie Avalon. . . . Oh my dear, what fun to have another golden oldie from the States with me, no need to explain my references for once."

Ralph had a nickname for every second young man who walked past in the slow, defiant, sharp-eyed parade beside the harbor. "This is the tail-end of the *volta*, as we call the evening *passeggiata*," Ralph said, typically substituting one incomprehensible word for another. "There's absolutely nothing to do in this town except cruise. In the hot weather they all stop working at two in the afternoon. Now here comes the Little Tiger—notice the feline tattoo?—a very bad character. He stole my Walkman when I invited him in for a night cap; Little Tiger, go to the rear of the class. He's bad because he's from the next town and he thinks he can get away with it. Stick with the locals; nothing like the high moral power of spying and gossip."

Ray had always heard of dirty old American men who'd gone to Greece for the summer "phallic cure," but he'd assumed gay liberation had somehow ended the practice, unshackled both predator and prey. Nevertheless, before they'd left the restaurant two more Americans, both in their sixties, had stopped by their table to recount their most recent adventures. Ray, used to fending off older men, was a bit put out that no one, not even Ralph, was flirting with him. In fact, the assumption, which he resented, was that he too was a golden oldie here "for the boys" and would be willing to pay for it.

"Aren't there any Greeks who do it for free?" Ray asked, not getting the smiles he'd anticipated.

"A few frightful pooves do, I suppose," Ralph drawled, looking offended by the notion. "But why settle for free frights when for ten bucks you can have anyone in town, absolutely anyone including the mayor and his wife, not to mention the odd god on the hoof?"

For a few days Ray held out. Betty, morbidly enough, had made a tape of all the crazy messages George had left on her answering machine during his last year. She'd given Ray the tape just before he'd left and now he sat in his bedroom, wearing gaudy drawstring shorts, and looked at the harbor lights and listened to George's voice.

Ray remembered a remark someone had once made: "Many people believe in God without loving him, but I love him without believing in him." Ray didn't know why the remark popped into his head just now. Did he love George without believing he existed? Ray described himself as a "mystical atheist." Maybe that was a complicated way of saying he believed George still loved him, or would if God would let him speak.

In his New York gay world, which was as carefully screened from men under twenty-five as from those over sixty, Ray counted as "young." That is, some old flame whom Ray had known fifteen years ago—a guy with a moustache gone gray and fanning squint lines but a still massive chest and thunder thighs under all that good tailoring—would spot Ray at a black-tie gay rights dinner or AIDS benefit and come up to him murmuring, "Lookin' good, kid," and would pinch his bottom. It was all continuing and Ray knew that despite the way his body had acquired a certain thickness, as though the original Greek statue had been copied by a Roman, he still looked youthful to his contemporaries.

In the first two weeks after George's death Ray had picked up three different men on the street and dragged them home. Ray had clung to their warm bodies, their air-breathing chests and blood-beating hearts, clung like a vampire to warm himself through transfusions of desire. He and Anna would sniff at these bewildered young men as though nothing could be less likely than a scabbed knee, furred buttocks, an uncollared collarbone, or the glamorous confusion of a cast-aside white shirt and silk rep tie. What they, the pick-ups, wanted, heart-to-heart post-coital chat, appealed to him not at all; all he wanted was to lie face down beside tonight's face-up partner and slide on top of him just enough to be literally heart-to-heart. Their carnality had seemed very fragile.

After this brief, irresponsible flaring up of lust, which had followed the sexless years of George's dying, Ray had gone back to celibacy. He thought it very likely that he was carrying death inside him, that it was ticking inside him like a time bomb but one he couldn't find because it had been secreted by an unknown terrorist. Even if it was located it couldn't be defused. Nor did he know when it might explode. He didn't want to expose anyone to contagion.

He wrote his will as he knew everyone should. That was the adult thing to do. But the paltry list of his possessions reminded him of how little he'd accumulated or accomplished; it was like the shame of moving day, of seeing one's cigarette-burned upholstery and scarred bureau on the curb under a hot, contemptuous sun. His relatively youthful looks had led him to go on believing in his youthful expectations; his life, he would have said as a philosophy student, was all becoming and no being. All in the future until this death sentence (never pronounced, daily remanded) had been handed down.

Occasionally he jerked off with poppers and dirty magazines. Although he found slaves and masters ludicrous and pathetic, his fantasies had not kept pace with the fashions and were mired somewhere in 1972, best simulated by the stories and photos in *Drummer*. He would read a hot tale about a violent encounter between two real pigs, sniff his amyl, even mutter a few words ("Give your boy that daddy-dick"), and then find himself, head aching, stomach sticky, heart sinking, erection melting, alone, posthumous. Anna wrinkled her nose and squinted at the fumes. He hoped his executor, who was his lawyer, would be able to bury him next to George as instructed, since he only slept really well when George was beside him. Once in a Philadelphia museum he'd seen the skeletons of a prehistoric man and woman, buried together (he couldn't remember how they'd come to die at the same time). He was lying on his back, she on her side, her hand placed delicately on his chest.

The days in Crete were big, cloudless hot days, heroic days, noisy with the saw rasp of insects. They were heroic days as though the sun were a lion-hearted hero. . . . Oh, but hadn't he just read in his beach book, *The Odyssey*, the words of the dead, lion-hearted Achilles: "Do not speak to me soothingly about death, glorious Odysseus; I should prefer as a slave to serve another man, even if he had no property and little to live on, than to rule over all these dead who have done with life." He'd cried on the white sand beach beside the lapis lazuli water and looked through his tears, amazed, at a herd of sheep trotting toward him. He stood and waded and waved, smiling, at the old shepherd in black pants and a carved stick in his hand, which itself looked carved; Ray, expensively muscular in his Valentino swim trunks, thought he was probably not much younger than this ancient peasant and suddenly his grief struck him as a costly gewgaw, beyond the means of the grievously hungry and hard-working world. Or maybe it was precisely his grief that joined him to this peasant. Every night he was dreaming about George, and in that book about the Greek death rituals he'd read the words of an old woman, "At death the soul emerges in its entirety, like a man. It has the shape of a man, only it's invisible. It has a mouth and hands and eats real food just like we do. When you see someone in your dreams, it's the soul you see. People in your dreams eat, don't they? The souls of the dead eat too." Ray couldn't remember if George ate in his dreams.

Ralph and Ray rented motor scooters and drove up a narrow road through chasms, past abandoned medieval churches and new cement-block houses, high into the mountains. They chugged slowly up to and away from a goat stretching to reach the lower branches of a tree. They saw a young Orthodox priest in a black soutane out strolling, preceded by a full black beard he seemed to be carrying in front of him as one might carry a salver. He remembered that Orthodox priests can marry and he vaguely thought of that as the reason this one looked so virile; he looked as though he'd just stepped out from behind the plow into this dress.

The summer drought had dwindled the stream to a brook within its still green bed. At a certain turn in the road the air turned cool, as though the frozen core of the mountain had gotten tired of holding its breath. In the shepherd's village where they stopped for lunch a smiling boy was found to speak English with them. He said he'd lived in New Zealand for a year with his aunt and uncle; that was why he knew English. Laughing, he offered them steaks and salads, but it turned out the only food available in the village was a runny sour cheese and bread and olives.

Every day, despite the climate's invitation to languor, Ray did his complete work-out, causing the heavy old wardrobe in his room to creak and throw open its door when he did pushups. Some days, specially around three, a wind would suddenly blow up and he and Ralph would run around battening down the twenty-three windows. At dusk on Sundays a naval band marched all the way around the harbor to the fortress opposite the lighthouse and played the national anthem ("Which was written by a German," Ralph couldn't resist throwing in) while the blue-and-white flag was lowered.

Although the days were cheerful—scooter rides to a deserted beach, vegetable and fish marketing, desultory house-hunting out beyond the town walls on which the Venetian lion had been emblazoned—the nights were menacing. He and Ralph would dress carefully for the *volta*, Ralph in a dark blue shirt and ironed slacks, Ray in a floating gown of a Japanese designer shirt and enormous one-size-drowns-all lime-green shorts, neon-orange cotton socks, black Adidas, and white sunglasses slatted like Venetian blinds angled down ("Perfect for the Saudi matron on the go," he said).

At least that's how he got himself up the first few nights until he sensed Ralph's embarrassment, the crowd's smiling contempt, and his own . . . what?

Desire?

Every night it was the same. The sun set, neon lights outlined the eaves and arches of the cafes, and an army of strollers, mostly young and male, sauntered slowly along the horseshoe-shaped stone walk beside the harbor. Sometimes it stank of pizza or what was called "Kantaki Fried Chicken" or of the sea urchins old fishermen had cleaned on the wharf earlier in the day. The route could be stretched out to twenty minutes if one lingered in conversation with friends, stopped to buy nuts from one vendor and to look at the jewelry sold by Dutch hippies. A drink at an outdoor cafe—ouzo and hors d'oeuvres (*"mezes"*)—could while away another forty minutes.

The full hour was always devoted to boy-watching. Ray looked, too, at the wonderful black hair, muscular bodies, red cheeks under deep tans, flamboyant moustaches, big noses, transparent arrogance, equally transparent self-doubt, black eyebrows yearning to meet above the nose and often succeeding. "Of course they need reassurance," Ralph said. "What actor doesn't?" These guys had loud voices, carnivorous teeth, strutting walks, big asses, broad shoulders. Ray thought they were more like American teenage boys than other European youths; they were equally big and loud and physical and sloppy and unveiled in their curiosity and hostility.

One of the sixty-year-old Americans, a classics professor in the States, was an amateur photographer of considerable refinement. He'd persuaded, it seemed, dozens of locals to pose nude for him. He paid them something. He was discreet. He flattered them as best he could in the modern language he'd pieced together out of his complete knowledge of ancient Greek. "Sometimes," he said, "they say a whole long improbable sentence in English—picked up from an American song or movie, no doubt."

Among the locals his ministrations to vanity made him popular, his scholarship made him impressive and his hobby risible, but since he always seemed to be laughing at himself in his ancient, elegant prep-school way, his laughter softened theirs. His photographic sessions he dismissed airily but pursued gravely.

Homer (for that was his name, absurdly, "Stranger than epic," as he said) took a polite but real interest in Ray—but strictly in Ray's mind. Ray—who expected, invited, and resented other men's sexual attraction to him—found Homer's sex-free attentiveness unsettling. And appealing. Maybe because Homer was a professor and had a professor's way of listening—which meant he winced slightly when he disagreed and cleaned his glasses when he deeply disagreed—Ray felt returned, if only for an instant, to his schooldays. To the days before he'd ever known George. To the days when he'd been not a New York know-it-all, but a Midwestern intellectual, someone who took nothing on authority and didn't even suspect there were such things as fashions in ideas.

This repatriation cheered him. Ralph had made a spaghetti dinner at home ("Enough with the swordfish and feta, already") and invited Homer. Ray's and Homer's conversation about the categorical imperative, the wager, the cave, the excluded middle astonished Ralph. "You girls are real bluestockings," he told them, "which is okay for a hen-party, but remember men don't make passes at girls who wear glasses." Ralph even seemed disconcerted by their intelligence, if that's what all this highbrow name-dropping had revealed.

After the wine and the laughter Ray thought it only natural to go on to the bar with his friends, the gay bar where they met with "true love" every night, as Ralph said. On the way along the harbor, Ray told Homer all about his sexual qualms. "I just don't think I should expose anyone else to this disease in case I've got it or in case I'm contagious. And I'm not disciplined enough to stick to safe sex."

Homer nodded and made the same noncommittal but polite murmur as when earlier they'd discussed the *Nicomachean Ethics.* Then, as though shaking himself awake, he asked, "What *is* safe sex, exactly?"

"Strictly safe is masturbation, no exchange of body fluids. Or if you fuck you can use a rubber. But I'm not worried about myself. The only one in danger where fucking and sucking is involved is the guy who gets the come."

Silence full of blinking in the dark, blinking with lashes growing longer, darker with mascara by the second. "But darling," Homer finally confided, hilariously woman-to-woman, "then the Greeks are *always* safe. They're the men; we're the girls."

"Call me square," Ray said, "but that's old-fashioned role-playing—and I've never, never paid—"

Homer interrupted him with a soft old hand on his arm. "Give it a try. After all, it's your only option."

The alley leading to the bar was too narrow for cars but wide enough to accommodate four noisy adolescents walking shoulder-to-shoulder; one of them stepped drunkenly down into the grass-sprouting ruins and pissed against a jagged wall. Ray thought of those jagged walls in . . . was it Giotto's murals in Santa Croce in Florence? The kid had a foolish grin and he seemed to have forgotten how to aim, shake, button up. The others started barking and mewing. Ray found the situation and the hoarse voices exciting. Had these guys come from the bar? Were they gay?

The bar was a low room, a basement grotto, one would have said, except it was on the ground floor. There were several dimly lit alcoves just off the room in which shadowy couples were smoking and drinking. The waiters or "hostessess" were two transvestites, Dmitri, who was chubby and brunette and kept a slightly deformed hand always just out of sight, flickering it behind his back or under a tray or into a pocket, and Adriana, who was slender, with straight, shoulder-length blond hair, and who responded to open jeers with a zonked-out grin that never varied, as though she were drugged on her own powerful fantasy of herself, which made her immune. Both were in jeans and T-shirts; Adriana had two small, hormone-induced breasts, but his arms were still muscular and his hips boyishly narrow. Dmitri, the brunette, had less beauty and still more vitality, a clown's vitality; he was the stand-up or run-past comic. He did pratfalls with his tray, twinkled past on point, sat on laps or wriggled deliciously against sailors, always keeping his hand in motion, out-of-focus. The bar was called "Fire Island."

At first this gay bar seemed to Ray an unexpected trove of sexy young guys until Homer explained that, technically, they (Ralph, Ray, and Homer) were the only gays, along with the two hostesses, of course. Everyone else was, well, a gigolo, although that was too coarse a word for it. "Greek men really do prefer male company. All their bars are like this one," Homer said with that ornithological pride all old-timer expatriates exhibit to the newcomer. "The women don't go out much. And the men all think it's normal to get money for sex—just remember the dowries they receive. And then they're terribly poor, the sailors, five bucks a week, that's all they get. So, you take all these horny nineteen-year-olds away from their villages for the first time in their lives. Here they are, bored, lonely, with too much time on their hands, no unmarried Greek girls in sight . . ."

"Where are the girls?" Ray asked, embarrassed he hadn't noticed their absence till now.

"Their mothers quite sensibly keep them under lock and key. I myself feel an infinite reverence for the intact maidenhead. Of course you know these scandalous mothers teach their daughters to take it up the ass if they must put out; anything to stay intact. Although why am I complaining? That's my philosophy exactly."

"So the sailors are alone and horny. . . ."

"And naturally they want to party. That's how they think of it. You buy them drinks and you're a real sport. You ask them home. It's a party. The only problem is how to wean them away from their *parea*."

"Come again?"

"*Parea*. That's their group, their friends, Oh, a very useful word. If you want to pick someone up, point to him, then yourself. Say, 'You, me, *parea?*' "

"And what do they call us, the faggots?"

Homer smiled and lowered his voice: "*Poosti*."

"So we're *poosti* on *parea*. . . . Don't rain on my *parea*."

"Yes," Homer said somewhat primly, "but not so loud. You'll scandalize the seafood," nodding toward a *parea* of five sailors, smiling at them with lofty politeness.

After two hours of drinking gin and tonic, Ray realized most of the boys weren't drinking at all and were just sitting over empty bottles of beer, bumming cigarettes from one another and hungrily staring at the door as each newcomer entered. Only a few were talking to each other. Sometimes they seemed to be inventing a conversation (involving lots of numbers, as even Ray could decode) and an emotion (usually indignation), but purely as a set piece to show them off to advantage to potential clients. The same tape of "Susanna" kept playing over and over, last year's disco tune, which didn't mean much to him since it had been popular when George was already sick and they had stopped going out dancing.

He excused himself, pecked Homer on the cheek, and squeezed past a suddenly amorous Dmitri, the hefty hostess, who smelled of sweat and Chanel.

Outside the night was airless, fragrant, the sky an enormous black colander held up to the light. Since it hadn't rained in months, dust filled the streets, dulled the store windows examined by veering headlights, rose in lazy devils behind passing shoes. In a bridal store the mannequin of the bride herself was snub-nosed and blonde, her hair bristling up under her veil at crazy shocked angles as though she'd stuck her finger in an electric socket. She was flanked by curious white cloth bouquets trailing white silk ribbons. Were they held by her bridesmaids? Ray had seen a woman bringing such a bouquet here on the plane from Athens. In that book he'd read the exhumations of a dead person's bones three years after death were compared to a wedding. The same songs were sung; the words varied only slightly. Both songs had begun with the words: "Now I have set out. Now I am about to depart. . . ." Something like that.

On the corner a man was selling round green melons out of a cart. Everywhere people seemed awake and watching—from a trellissed balcony, from a waiting cab, from a rooftop cafe. In such a hot country people stayed up to enjoy the cool of the night. Kids, calling out to one another, sped by on bicycles. In the square in front of the cathedral a whole line of taxis waited, five drivers standing in a circle and disputing—what? Soccer? Politics?

Ray turned onto a deserted street lined with notions shops displaying lace trimmings and bolts of fabric and spools of thread. At the corner an old man with yellowing hair, worn-down shoes, and no socks had fallen asleep with his feet up on his desk in an open-air stand that sold ex-votos in tin—a bent arm, an ear, an open eye, a soldier in World War I uniform and helmet—and also tin icons, the metal snipped away to frame crude tinted reproductions of the Virgin's face. He also had long and short candles and something (incense?) wrapped in red paper cylinders, stacked high like rolled coins from the bank.

Cars with bad mufflers blatted and farted through town or

throbbed beside a lit cigarette kiosk in front of the dim covered market. The cars were always full of teenage boys, and when they'd get out to buy cigarettes or to go into a bar and buy a paper, he'd see they were fat or thin, usually big handsome men with black moustaches or the first faint charcoal sketches of moustaches.

It struck Ray that it had been years since he'd seen guys this young. Expensive, childless Manhattan had banned them. Ray imagined that he was back in Findlay, Ohio, on a Saturday night, the dark silent streets suddenly glaring and noisy with a gang in two hotrods. He forgot for a moment that he was forty; he felt he was sixteen, afraid of the hoods who'd driven in from Sandusky or even from as far away as Toledo. He was afraid and curious and contemptuous and excited as he darted along under the old trees, hoping he was invisible.

He crossed the street to avoid two strolling straight couples, and now he did feel forty. And queer. And foreign. He wouldn't even know if they were gossiping about him. Worse, he knew he didn't exist for them, he was invisible.

As he headed up the gently winding street toward the town zoo, he passed a lone young guy coming down toward him, who stared at him hard, harder and longer even than the other Cretan men normally stared. The boy spit through his teeth as they passed. He struck his heels with spark-making violence against the pavement. And then stopped. Ray heard him stop behind him. If I turn around will he punch me?

When Ray finally turned around, the young man was standing there staring at him. "Ya," he said, that short form of *Yassou*, the all-purpose greeting. Ray could see he was handsome with regular features, an upper lip pulled back to show white teeth made whiter by his moustache and a black beard that he was letting grow in. He had on jeans and a denim jacket, and the jacket sleeves were tight enough to reveal well-muscled upper arms, not the netted cantaloupes Ray had for biceps, but longer, grooved haunches, the tightly muscled arms that the ancient Cretan youths had in those wall-paintings at absurdly over-restored Knossos: murderously slim-waisted matadors.

He was either very tan or very swarthy. His hair was long

and pushed back behind his ears. His slightly unshaved face (the look of the New York model who wears a two-days' growth of beard as an accessory to his smoking jacket or white silk pajamas), his obviously American jeans jacket, and his long hair were the three things that made him look fractionally different from all the other young men in this city of young men.

He kept staring, but then when Ray looked away for an instant, he slipped into a sidestreet. Ray wondered if he'd be jumped when he followed him. As he turned the corner, the boy was standing there and asked aggressively, "What you want?" and his faint smile suggested he already knew and that Ray's desire was disgusting and entirely practicable.

Ray said, "You," with the sort of airiness that ruined Oscar Wilde, but that word apparently was not one of the boy's dozen English words. He frowned angrily.

"Sex," Ray said, and this time the boy nodded.

"But money!" he threatened, rubbing his thumb and forefinger together. Ray nodded with a face-saving smirk he regretted but couldn't wipe away. "I fuck you!" the boy added. This time as Ray nodded his smile vanished, a little bit in awe at the mention of this intimacy, once so common, now so rare, so gravely admonished, so fearfully practiced in his plagued city.

"*Profilatikos*. You buy. Here." He pointed to the lit cigarette kiosk on the corner."

"No! *You* buy," Ray said, the facetious smile back in place but genuine alarm in his heart.

"You," the boy insisted, stepping into the shadows of a building.

Now all of his teenage qualms did come rushing back. He felt his fear of and fascination with the prophylactics dispenser in a Kentucky filling station toilet he'd glimpsed once during a family trip through the Smokies. Or he remembered the time when he'd helped his mother turn back the covers for a married couple who were visiting them, and he'd seen under the pillow the raised circle of the rolled rubber in its foil wrapper. The very width of that circumference had excited him.

He said the word to the impassive middle-aged woman in the kiosk. She lowered her head on an angle, dropped her eyes, said, "Ne," which means *yes* but sounds to English-speakers like *no*. A second later she'd fished up a box that read, in English, "Love Party" above a photo of a woman in provocative panties, one nyloned knee resting on the edge of a double bed.

Why rubbers? Ray wondered. Had he heard of our deadly new disease way out here at the end of the world, in a country where there are only two recorded cases, both of whom were visitors to New York? No, he must have in mind the old, curable maladies. Or maybe he just wants to dramatize our roles. I don't mind. Rubbers are terribly 1958 Saturday night at the drive-in. Maybe he needs a membrane intact to suggest his own virtual virginity.

A moment later, Ray was pursuing the boy through deserted night streets under big trees, big laurels so dry their gray-green leaves had started curling laterally. Distant motorbikes were test-drilling the night. The turn-of-the-century mansions lining these blocks were dilapidated, shuttered, and unlit behind rusting wrought-iron balconies, although trimmed hedges proved at least some of them were inhabited. The smells of garbage on a hot night alternated with the smell of jasmine, at first sniff slightly sweet, then ruttishly sweet. The boy wouldn't walk beside Ray, although Ray thought it must look much odder, this strange parade. They turned right off the boulevard and walked up, up a hill through residential streets. The boy's Keds shone almost phosphorescently white in the dark. Ray was calculating how much money he had in his wallet, while in his heart, his suddenly adolescent heart, he was exulting: "George, I've escaped you, I've gotten away from you."

In one sense he knew he was a slightly sissified middle-aged New York muscle queen somewhat out of her depth. In another sense he felt he was the teenage debating team captain in love again with Juan, son of a migrant Mexican worker who'd been brought to northern Ohio to pick fruit. The first confused conversation with Juan, the visit to the workers' compound, the smell of cooking chili, the sight of candles burning even by day before the tin shrine of the Virgin . . . The one thing certain was that whatever was going on in Crete came before or after George and precluded George.

As they walked along, the boy clicked a keychain, vestigial worry beads. Cats were everywhere, gliding in and out of shadows, daintily pawing black plastic garbage bags, slithering through gaps in fences, sitting on top of parked cars. Twice the boy stopped and scented the path—and now he looked like an Indian brave. Or so Ray thought, smiling at his own way of leafing through his boyhood anthology of erotic fantasies.

They reached what looked like a schoolyard, dark and empty because it was summer and night, but otherwise like any schoolyard in Ohio—broken concrete playing area, an orange metal basketball hoop dripping rust stains onto the wood backboard, peeling benches, a toilet with separate entrances for boys and girls, a high fence surrounding the whole. The boy scrambled over the fence in two quick steps up and a graceful pivot at the top. Ray followed fearfully, awkwardly ("Here, teach, lemme give you a hand"). The boy gave Ray his hand and produced his first real smile, as dazzling as a camel boy's (a new page in the anthology flipped open). His skin was surprisingly warm and plush and there were no calluses on his palm. Homer had told Ray that if parents could afford the luxury they preferred to shield their kids as long as possible from work. The boys, their adolescence extended well into their twenties, sat idly around the harbor at night, trying to pick up foreign girls (the sport was called *kemaki*, "harpooning").

When they ducked into the toilet, in the second that Ray's eyes took to adjust to the deeper dark, he walked by mistake right into the boy. They both gasped, the boy laughed, maybe a bit insultingly, his teeth lit up the room, Ray started to draw away but his hand had brushed against what could only be a big erection, "big" because of normal size; the boy's youth, the night, the danger, the fact he would be getting some money later on, all these things made it "big." Ray noticed the boy had already unzipped his fly. Out of eagerness?

Ray wanted him to be eager.

And then Ray, a famous beauty in his own right, a perennial hot number, hard to please, easily spooked by a maladroit cruiser, pursued throughout his twenty years of gay celebrity by hundreds of equally beautiful men, that elite corps of flight attendants, junior executives, and models—this Ray (he was trembling as he knelt) knelt before what could only be white Jockey shorts, yep, that's what they were, luminous under undone fly buttons, tugged the jeans down a notch, pulled down the elastic waist of the underpants, and tasted with gratitude the hot, slightly sour penis. He whose conscience years of political struggle had raised now sank into the delicious guilt of Anglo fag servicing Mexican worker, of cowboy face-fucked by Indian brave, of lost tourist waylaid by wily camel boy. He inhaled the smell of sweat and urine with heady, calm pleasure. He felt like E.T. being recharged by spaceship transfusion.

His mouth had been dry with fear. Now the penis striking his palate drew forth a flow of water in the desert. His knees already ached where he knelt on the wet cement floor. He took the boy's limp, hanging hand and laced his fingers into his. He looked up to catch the glance, but his eyes were shut and his face blank, which made him look much younger and almost absurdly unintimidating. At a certain point Ray pressed the unopened rubber into the boy's hand. Like a child peeping through a keyhole, Ray continued to kneel and to watch the boy breaking open the packet and methodically unrolling the rubber down the length of his penis. He got it going the wrong way, lubricated side in, and had to start over. Then the boy gripped him from behind and Ray felt the invasion, so complex psychologically, so familiar but still painful or pleasurable to accommodate, he couldn't tell which, he'd never known which. The boy breathed on his shoulder; he smelled of Kantaki Fried Chicken.

When Ray paid the boy, who aristocratically palmed the money without bothering to see how much it was, Ray used one of the few Greek words he'd picked up (this one at the laundry), *avrio*, the word for "tomorrow." The boy nodded, or rather did what Greeks do instead of nodding, he clicked a "Tsk" between his teeth and jerked his head down, lowering his eyelids. He pointed to this spot, to the ground in front of them. Then he flashed ten and two fingers. "You like?" he asked, pointing to his own chest.

"Yes, of course," Ray whispered, thinking: These men. . . .

He told the whole story at breakfast the next morning to Ralph, who was courteous enough to appear envious. After their yogurt and honey and the French roast coffee Ralph was at such pains to secure, they moved into Ralph's studio with its one small window looking down to the sea and the lighthouse. The studio had little in it besides a rocking chair, an old battered desk, a small kitchen table freighted with tubes of acrylics, a big, heavy wood easel and a rack for finished paintings. On the wall was a watercolor, poppies brilliant in a silky field of green and tan grasses. "Well, it's the only solution. For you," Ralph said.

Oh, he's turned his envy into pity, Ray thought, pity for me, the ticking timebomb, the young widow, but my "only solution" doesn't seem all that much of a hardship.

As Ray walked around and napped in the hot, airless late afternoon he could feel a small painful spot inside him where the boy had battered into him and he smiled to feel that pain again. "Oy," he said to himself in Betty's accent.

That night the boy was there exactly on time. His hair was cleaner and shinier and he'd shaved (not the moustache, of course). But he was wearing the same jeans jacket, although the T-shirt looked clean. They went through exactly the same routine, for Ray didn't want to scare him off. He wanted to build up a fixed routine, the same place, the same acts, the same price. Tonight the only innovation was that Ray pulled the kid's jeans and underpants all the way down below his knees and discovered that his testicles hadn't descended and that his ass was hairy with nice friendly fuzz. Nor did he have a tan line; his skin was naturally just this dark.

After sex the kid hopped over the fence and disappeared into the night and Ray walked home, downhill all the way through the silent, cat-quick, jasmine-scented streets. He felt sad and lyric and philosophical and happy as he'd felt as a teenager; since these encounters with the boy—strictly sexual—seemed a strangely insufficient pretext for so much emotion, he also felt something of a charlatan. "Objective correlative." That was the term. T. S. Eliot would have said that his emotion lacked an objective correlative.

The next night he asked him his name, which he discovered was Marco. "You must remember," Homer said during the *volta* the following evening, "the Italians ruled Crete for hundreds of years. Maybe he has some Italian blood." And again Ray had to describe his "find," for that's how the connoisseurs judged Marco. "Not the usual harbor trash," Homer said, and he announced that he was going to start harpooning in the zoological gardens again, which he'd assumed had long since been fished out. Ray refused to divulge where he met Marco every night. He wanted one secret at least, his dowry, the smallest secret he could keep and give to Marco, and again he thought of that book and the way they'd compared marriage to death, or rather marriage to the exhumation of bones.

Once he asked Marco where he lived, but Marco only waved vaguely in the direction of the shanty town inland and to the west of the harbor. *"Spiti mou, to limani,"* Ray announced, which he thought meant "My house is on the harbor," but Marco only lifted an indifferent eyebrow, the counterpart to the Frenchman's weary *"Eh alors?"* when smothered by Americans' doggy effusiveness. That night, Ray broadened his area of conquest and explored Marco's taut brown stomach up to his chest. By now there were several white rubbers on the wet cement floor like jellyfish washed up on the bleak shingle.

By day, Ray would go swimming or motorbiking to old churches or ruined monasteries or hidden beaches, but all day long and during the endless evenings, he'd daydream about Marco. He bought a phrasebook and pieced together Greek words for that night's rendezvous.

Once Marco asked Ray if he should bring along a friend, and Ray agreed because he thought Marco wanted him to. But the friend was a portly sailor ("Greeks go off early," Ralph had said, as though they were a temperamental triple cream cheese, a Brillat-Savarin, say). Ray sucked them both at the same time, doing one then the other, back and forth, but his only pleasure was in imagining reporting it to the other Americans tomorrow. The boys seemed embarrassed and talked loudly to each other and joked a lot and Marco kept losing

his erection and he sounded nasty and used the word
"*putana*," which surely meant "whore" in Greek as well as
Italian.

Ray paid them both and was tempted to mutter "putana"
while doing so, but that would be snapping the lime twig, so he
swallowed his resentment (yes, swallowed that, too) and drew
Marco aside and said "*Metavrio*," which meant "the day after
tomorrow" (*meta* as in "metaphysics, beyond physics"). The
delay was meant as some sort of punishment. He also indicated
he wanted to see Marco alone from now on. Marco registered
the compliment but not the punishment and smiled and asked
"You like?" pointing to himself, asked it loud and clear so the
other guy could hear.

"Yes," Ray said, "I like."

As he walked home, Ray took a stroll through the zoological
gardens, where there was also an outdoor movie theater. Inside
people sat on folding chairs and watched the huge screen on
which a street lamp had disobligingly cast the shadow of a leafy
branch. Tonight he sat outside but could hear the end of *Quer-
elle*, of all things, dubbed into Greek and offered to the extended
Cretan family, who chuckled over the perversities of northern
Europe. In the closing sequence, Jeanne Moreau laughed and
laughed a shattering laugh and the caged egrets dozing beside
Ray awakened and started to chatter and call. Then the house-
lights came up, the families streamed out, for a moment the park
was bright and vivid with crunched gravel and laughs and
shouts, then car doors slammed and motorbikes snarled, the
lights were dimmed and finally, conclusively, everything was
quiet. Ray sat in the dark, listening to the awakened birds pad-
dling the water, a leaf-spray of shadows across his face like an
old-fashioned figured veil. The jasmine gave off a shocking body
odor, as though one were to discover a pure girl was really a
slut.

Ray regretted his spiteful decision to skip a day with Marco.
The depth to which he felt Marco's absence, and his anxiety lest
Marco not show up at their next appointment, made Ray aware
of how much he liked Marco and needed him. Liked him?

There was nothing to like, nothing but a mindless, greedy

Cretan teen who was, moreover, heterosexual. Or worse, a complete mystery, a stranger, a minor tradesman with whom he was only on fucking terms.

Then Ray told himself he liked his own sense of gratitude to Marco, the silence imposed on them by the lack of a common language, liked the metered doses of sex fixed by fee and divergent appetites. He liked the high seriousness of the work they did together every night. He also liked stealing bits of affection from his co-worker, whose moustache was coming in as black and shiny as his eyebrows and whose chest (as Ray's hand had just discovered) was sprouting its first hair, this young man who would never love anyone, not even his wife, as much as Ray loved him.

One weekend Ralph went off on a yacht with a Greek collector of his paintings; they were sailing over to Thera and wouldn't be back till Monday. "Feel free to bring your child husband to the palace while I'm away," Ralph said as he pecked Ray on both cheeks in the French manner. And indeed that night Ray did say to Marco, *"Spiti mou,"* showed him the house keys, and led him through town, walking a few paces ahead just as on that first night Marco had preceded Ray. On the street of notions shops someone hailed Marco (*"Yassou"*) and talked to him and Ray, smiling at his own quick grasp of things, didn't look back but turned the corner and waited there, in the dark. After all, it was a little town. And only last week a shepherd had discovered his son was getting fucked and had killed him, which Homer said most of the locals had considered fair enough.

Marco in his white Keds and Levi jacket came treading stealthily around the corner, noble and balanced as a lion; he winked his approval and Ray felt his own pleasure spread over his whole body like the heat of the sun.

Marco was obviously impressed by the palace—impressed by its grandeur and, Ray imagined, proud that foreigners had furnished it with old Cretan furniture and folk embroideries.

Impressed? Nonsense, Ray thought, catching himself. Purest sentimental rubbish on my part. No doubt he'd prefer lavender Formica with embedded gold glitter.

Ray, who liked Marco and wanted to show that he did, felt

a new intimacy between them as he led him into his bedroom. He gently pushed him back on the bed and knelt to untie the Keds and take them off, then the smelly socks. Then he made Marco wriggle out of his jeans; he started to pull the T-shirt over his head but Marco stopped him, though he, too, was gentle. Every one of Marco's concessions meant so much more to Ray than all the sexual extravagances of New York in the old pre-plague days—the slings and drugs and filthy raps.

Ray undressed himself. He wondered what Marco thought of him, of this naked adult male body which he'd never seen before. How old does he think I am? Does he admire my muscles? Or does my role as *poosti* on *parea* keep him from seeing me?

Ray worried that the whole routine—nakedness, a bed, privacy—might be getting a little too queer for Marco, so he was quick to kneel and start sucking him, back to the tried and true. But Ray, carried away in spite of himself, couldn't resist adding a refinement. He licked the inside of Marco's thighs and Marco jumped, as he did a moment later when Ray's tongue explored his navel. Strange that his cock seems to be the least sensitive part of his body, Ray thought.

When the time for the rubber arrived, Ray thought that surely tonight might make some difference, and indeed for the first time Marco gasped at the moment of his climax. Ray said, "You like?" and Marco nodded vigorously and smiled, and a young male intimacy really had come alive between them, glued as they were together, their naked bodies sweaty.

Almost instantly Marco stood and dashed into the bathroom, pulled off the rubber, and washed while standing at the sink. Ray leaned against the door and watched him.

In this bright light the boy looked startlingly young and Ray realized, yes, he was young enough to be his son. But his other feeling was less easy to account for. It was of the oddness that a body so simple, with so few features, should have provoked so much emotion in him, Ray. Clothes with their colors and cuts seemed more adequate to what he was feeling.

Once again Ray noticed that he was feeling more, far more, than the occasion warranted. No objective correlative. Ray took

Marco up to the roof to see the panorama of the sea, the harbor, the far-flung villages, a car burrowing up the mountain with its headlights like a luminous insect. But now that the transaction was over, the tension between them had been cut.

The next night Marco came directly to the palace and Ray persuaded him to take off his T-shirt, too, so that now there was no membrane except the rubber between them. Before they got to the fucking part, Ray paused in his exertions and crept up beside Marco and rested his head on Marco's thumping chest. Marco's hand awkwardly grazed Ray's hair. Ray could smell the rank, ingenuous odor of Marco's underarm sweat—not old sweat or nervous sweat but the frank smell of a young summer body that had just walked halfway across town.

On the third and last night they'd have alone in the palace, Marco came up the steps not looking up, not giving his hearty greeting. *"Ti kanes? Kala?"* He simply walked right into the bedroom, threw his clothes off, fell back on the bed, and with a sneering smile parodied the moans and squirmings of sex.

"What's wrong?" Ray asked. Marco turned moodily on his side and Ray was grateful for this glimpse into the boy's discontent. When he sat down beside Marco he could smell beer on his breath and cigarette smoke in his hair, though Marco didn't smoke. At last, after a few words and much miming, Marco was able to indicate that he had a friend who was leaving the next morning for Athens to begin his compulsory military service and the guy was waiting for him in a bar down below along the harbor.

Ray pulled Marco to his feet, gave him double the ususal thousand drachmas, helped him dress, set tomorrow's date back in the schoolyard, and urged him to hurry off to his friend. He had a half-thought that Marco understood more English than he was letting on. For the first time Marco seemed to be looking at Ray not as a member of another race, sex, class, age, but as a friend.

Friend? Ray laughed at his own naivete. The boy's a hooker, he told himself. Don't get all moony over your beautiful budding friendship with the hooker.

After Marco had run down the steps, the thuds rattling the

whole house, Ray was alone. Definitely alone. He walked to the balcony and looked down at the harbor, most of its lights extinguished, the last waiters hosing down the boardwalk. He put on his headphones and listened to George's telephone messages to Betty. "Hi, doll, this is Darleen, now a stylishly anorectic 135 pounds. The Duchess of Windsor was wrong. You can be too thin." Oh yes, four months before the end. "Hi, doll, I know you're there with the machine on watching *The Guiding Light*. Can you believe that bitch Vanessa? Hi!" and a sudden happy duet of overlapping voices, since just then Betty picked up and confessed she had indeed been pigging out on the soaps and a pound of Godivas.

Ray snapped it off. "You must look out for yourself," George had said, and just now the best way seemed to be to forget George, at least for a while, to forget the atmosphere of dread, the midnight visits to the hospital, the horrifying outbreak of disease after disease—fungus in the throat, a bug in the brain, bleeding in the gut, herpes ringing the ass, every inch of the dwindling body explored by fiber optics, brain scanner, X-rays, the final agonies buried under blankets of morphine.

Ray received a call from Helen, his boss, and her tinny, crackling tirade sounded as remote as the final, angry emission from a dead star. He had no desire to leave Xania. With Homer as his translator he looked at a house for sale in the Turkish quarter and had a nearly plausible daydream of converting it into a guest house that he and Marco would run.

He started writing a story about Marco—his first story in fifteen years. He wondered if he could support himself by his pen. He talked to an Irish guy who made a meager living by teaching English at the prison nearby in their rehabilitation program. If he sold George's loft he could afford to live in Greece several years without working. He could even finance that guest house.

When he'd first arrived in Crete he'd had the vague feeling that this holiday was merely a detour and that when he rejoined his path George would be waiting for him. George or thoughts of George or the life George had custom-built for him, he wasn't quite sure which he meant. And yet now there was a real possibility that he might escape, start something new or transpose his old boyhood goals and values into a new key, the Dorian mode, say. Everything here seemed to be conspiring to reorient him, repatriate him, even the way he'd become in Greece the pursuer rather than the pursued.

One hot, sticky afternoon as he sat in a cafe with a milky ouzo and a dozing cat for company, a blond foreigner—a man, about twenty-five, in shorts and shirtless, barefoot—came walking along beside the harbor playing a soprano recorder. A chubby girl in a muumuu and with almost microscopic freckles dusted over her well-padded cheeks was following this ringleted Pan and staring at him devotedly.

Ray hated the guy's evident self-love and the way his head dropped to one side and he hated the complicity of the woman, hated even more that a grown-up man should still be pushing such an over-ripe version of the eternal boy. He really did look over-ripe. Even his lips, puckered for the recorder, looked too pulpy. Ray realized that he himself had played the boy for years and years. To be sure not when he'd chronologically been a boy, for then he'd been too studious for such posturing. But later, in his twenties and thirties. He saw that all those years of self-absorption had confused him. He had always been looking around to discover if older men were noticing him and he'd been distressed if they were or weren't. He hadn't read or written anything because he hadn't had the calm to submit to other people's thoughts or to summon his own. George had urged him to buy more and more clothes, always in the latest youthful style, and he'd fussed over Ray's workout, dentistry, haircut, even the state of his fingernails. When they'd doze in the sun on Fire Island, hour after hour George would stroke Ray's oiled back or legs. Ray had been the sultan's favorite.

Now he'd changed. Now he was like a straight man. He was the one who admired someone else. He wooed, he paid. At the same time he was the kneeling handmaiden to the Cretan youth, the slim-waisted matador. This funny complication suited him.

A journalist came down from Athens to Xania to interview Ralph for an Athens art magazine or maybe it was the paper.

Since he was gay, spoke English, and was congenial, Ralph invited him to stay on for the weekend. The day before Ray was due to fly back to New York, he asked the journalist to translate a letter for him into Greek, something he could give Marco along with the gold necklace he'd bought him, the sort of sleazy bauble all the kids here were wearing. Delighted to be part of the adventure and impressed by the ardor of the letter, the journalist readily accepted the commission. Ralph arranged to be away for a couple of hours on Ray's last night and insisted he bring Marco up to the palace for a farewell between sheets. Covering his friendliness with queenliness, Ralph said, "How else can you hold on to your nickname, La Grande Horizontale?"

In the palace bedroom that night, just as Marco was about to untie his laces and get down to work, Ray handed him the package and the letter. Before opening the package, Marco read the letter. It said: "I've asked a visitor from Athens to translate this for me because I have to tell you several things. Tomorrow I'm going back to New York, but I hope to sell my belongings there quickly. I'll be back in Xania within a month. I've already found a house I'd like to buy on Theotocopoulos Street. Perhaps you and I could live there someday or fix it up and run it as a guest house.

"I don't know what you feel for me if anything. For my part, I feel something very deep for you. Nor is it just sexual; the only reason we have so much sex is because we can't speak to each other. But don't worry. When I come back I'll study Greek and, if you like, I'll teach you English.

"Here's a present. If you don't like it you can exchange it."

After Marco finished reading the letter (he was sitting on the edge of the bed and Ray had snapped on the overhead light), he hung his head for a full minute. Ray had no idea what he'd say, but the very silence, the full stop, awed him. Then Marco looked at Ray and said in English, in a very quiet voice, "I know you love me and I love you. But Xania is no good for you. Too small. Do not rest here. You must go."

Although Ray felt so dizzy he sank into a chair, he summoned up the wit to ask, "And you? Will you leave Xania one day?" for he was already imagining their life together in New York.

"Yes, one day." Marco handed the unopened package back to Ray. "I won't see you again. You must look out for yourself."

And then he stood, left the room, thudded down the front steps, causing the whole house to rattle, and let himself out the front door. Ray felt blown back in a wind-tunnel of grief and joy. He felt his hair streaming, his face pressed back, the fabric of his pants fluttering. In pop-song phrases he thought this guy had walked out on him, done him wrong, broken his heart—a heart he was happy to feel thumping again with sharp, wounded life. He was blown back onto the bed and he smiled and cried as he'd never yet allowed himself to cry over George, who'd just spoken to him once again through the least likely oracle.

ABOUT THE AUTHORS

GEORGE STAMBOLIAN is professor of French and Interdisciplinary Studies at Wellesley College. His most recent books are *Homosexualities and French Literature* (co-edited with Elaine Marks) and *Male Fantasies / Gay Realities: Interviews with Ten Men*. His essays, interviews, and stories have been published in *Christopher Street* and *The Advocate*, and his column, "First Person," has appeared in *The New York Native*. Born in Bridgeport, Connecticut, he lives in New York City, Boston, and Amagansett, Long Island.

BRUCE BOONE has published a collection of stories, *My Walk with Bob*, a novel, *Century of Clouds*, and a collection of altered translations, *La Fontaine* (with Robert Glück). He was born in Portland, Oregon, did graduate work at the University of California (Berkeley), and lives in San Francisco where he is completing a translation of Georges Bataille's *Le Coupable*. His novel, *Carmen*, from which "David's Charm" is drawn, will be published in 1987.

C. F. BORGMAN was born in Cincinnati and lives in upstate New York. He attended Long Island University and is currently writing a novel, *River Road*. "A Queer Red Spirit" is his first published work.

DENNIS COOPER is the author of a novel, *Safe*, three volumes of poems and prose pieces, *The Tenderness of Wolves*, *The Missing Men*, *He Cried*, and two collections of poetry, *Tiger Beat* and *Idols*. His prose and poetry have appeared in *Semiotext(e)*, *Bomb*, *Mandate*, *Blueboy*, *Fag Rag*, and *Gay Sunshine*. He was born in Pasadena, California, and founded *Little Caesar* magazine and the Little Caesar Press. He now lives in Amsterdam where he is completing his second novel, *Closer*, which contains the narrative, "The Outsiders."

SAM D'ALLESANDRO has published a book of poems, *Slippery Sins*, and his stories have appeared in *No Apologies*, *Mirage*, and *Appearances*. He was born in New Orleans, attended the University of California (Santa Cruz). He died in 1987.

ROBERT FERRO divides his time between homes in New York City and Sea Girt, New Jersey. He is the author of three novels, *The Others*, *The Family of Max Desir*, *The Blue Star*, and a work of nonfiction, *Atlantis: The Autobiography of a Search* (with Michael Grumley). His stories and articles have appeared in *Christopher Street*, *The Advocate*, and the anthology, *A True Likeness*. Born in Cranford, New Jersey, he attended Rutgers University and the University of Iowa's Writers' Workshop. He has received an Ingram-Merrill Award, and his new novel, *Second Son*, which contains his narrative of the same title, was published in 1987. He died in 1988.

JOHN FOX was born in the Bronx and lives in Manhattan. He is the author of a novel, *The Boys on the Rock*, and his stories have appeared in *Christopher Street* and *Central Park*. He holds an MFA in writing from Columbia University and is the recipient of a Yaddo Fellowship. He is currently writing a second novel and several short stories.

ROBERT GLÜCK is the author of a narrative poem, *Andy*, three volumes of poems and prose pieces, *Family Poems*, *Metaphysics*, *Reader*, a collection of altered translations, *La Fontaine* (with

Bruce Boone), a collection of stories, *Elements of a Coffee Service*, and a novel, *Jack the Modernist*. His poems, stories, and articles have appeared in *Ironwood*, *Poetics Journal*, *Social Text*, *Christopher Street*, and *The Advocate*. Born in Cleveland, he holds an MFA in writing from San Francisco State University. He has received an Academy of American Poets Award and a Browning Award and lives in San Francisco where he is writing a novel.

BRAD GOOCH holds a Ph.D. in English Literature from Columbia University and is the recipient of a CAPS Fiction Grant. He is the author of a book of poetry, *The Daily News*, and a collection of stories, *Jailbait and Other Stories*, which received a Writer's Choice Award. His poems, stories, and articles have appeared in *The Paris Review*, *The Partisan Review*, *Christopher Street*, *Bomb*, *The Nation*, *Vanity Fair*, and *The New York Native*. Born in Kingston, Pennsylvania, he lives in New York City and has published a novel, *Scary Kisses*.

MICHAEL GRUMLEY has published four works of nonfiction, *Atlantis: The Autobiography of a Search* (with Robert Ferro), *There Are Giants in the Earth*, *Hard Corps*, and *After Midnight*. His articles and essays have appeared in *New York*, *New West*, *The Chicago Tribune*, *Grit*, *The New York Native*, and *Christopher Street*, and his fiction in the anthology, *A True Likeness*. He was born in Iowa and attended the University of Iowa's Writers' Workshop and the School of Visual Arts. He died in 1988.

RICHARD HALL is the author of a novel, *The Butterscotch Prince*, a volume of plays, *Three Plays for a Gay Theater*, and two collections of stories, *Couplings* and *Letter from a Great-Uncle*. A graduate of Harvard and New York University, his articles have appeared in *The New Republic*, *The New York Times*, *The Village Voice*, *The Saturday Review*, and *The Advocate*. Born in New York City, he lives in Oakland where he is writing a new collection of tales, *Story-Time*.

PATRICK HOCTEL was born in New Orleans, studied writing at the University of Arizona, and lives in San Francisco. His stories have been published in *The New Laurel Review*, *Pierian Spring*, *Sun Dog*, *The Tulane Literary Magazine*, and *Mirage*. He received a Breadloaf Writers' Conference scholarship and is currently writing a novella and a script for a rock video.

ANDREW HOLLERAN is the author of two novels, *Dancer From the Dance* and *Nights in Aruba*. His "New York Notebook" column in *Christopher Street* received a Gay Press Association Award, and his stories and articles have appeared in *New York*, *The New York Native*, and *Christopher Street*. Born in Aruba, N.A., he attended Harvard and the University of Iowa's Writers' Workshop. He divides his time between New York City and Florida where he is writing a novel.

KEVIN KILLIAN is the editor of the new literary journal, *Mirage*. He has published a book of prose fiction, *Desiree*, and his essays have appeared in *Soup*, *Poetry Flash*, and *Five Fingers Review*. He was born on Long Island, attended Fordham University and the State University of New York (Stony Brook), and lives in San Francisco where he is writing a series of memoirs, *Bedrooms Have Windows*.

ETHAN MORDDEN was born in Heavensville, Pennsylvania, and lives in New York City. He is the author of thirteen works of nonfiction, two collections of stories, *I've a Feeling We're Not in Kansas Anymore* and *Buddies*, and a novel, *One Last Waltz*. His column, "Is There a Book in This?," has appeared in *Christopher Street*, and his articles have been published in *Opera News*, *The New York Times*, *Harper's Bazaar*, and *The Baum Bugle*.

WALLACE PARR has lived in New York City and now resides in San Francisco where he attends Robert Glück's Writers' Workshop. His first published story recently appeared in *Mirage*.

FELICE PICANO is publisher of the SeaHorse Press and co-publisher of the Gay Presses of New York. He lives in New York

City and Fire Island Pines. His first novel, *Smart As the Devil*, was nominated for an Ernest Hemingway Award. He is the author of six other novels, *Eyes, The Mesmerist, The Lure, An Asian Minor, Late in the Season,* and *House of Cards,* two books of poetry, *The Deformity Lover* and *Window Elegies,* a collection of stories, *Slashed to Ribbons in Defense of Love,* a volume of memoirs, *Ambidextrous,* and a play, "Immortal!" He edited an anthology of gay fiction, *A True Likeness,* and his poems, reviews, and stories have been published in *Christopher Street, The Advocate, Ms, OMNI,* and *The Connecticut Poetry Review.* He is currently writing a screenplay based on *Eyes,* a novel, *E.D.G.E. Seven,* and the second volume of his memoirs, *Men Who Loved Me,* which includes his narrative, "The Most Golden Bulgari."

RICHARD UMANS grew up in suburban Boston and lived in New York City. His fiction appeared in *Christopher Street, The James White Review,* and in the anthology, *A True Likeness,* and his articles were published in *The New York Native* and *The Advocate.* He died of an AIDS-related illness on February 11, 1985. The Richard S. Umans Foundation has been established in his honor to support writers of gay fiction.

EDMUND WHITE is the author of four novels, *Forgetting Elena, Nocturnes for the King of Naples, A Boy's Own Story, Caracole,* and two works of nonfiction, *The Joy of Gay Sex* (with Dr. Charles Silverstein) and *States of Desire.* His stories, reviews, and essays have appeared in *The New York Times Book Review, The Washington Post, The Village Voice, Art in America, Rolling Stone, The Nation,* and *Christopher Street.* He is the recipient of a Guggenheim Fellowship, an Ingram-Merrill Award, and an Award for Literature from the American Academy of Arts and Letters. Born in Cincinnati, he studied at the University of Michigan, and now lives in Paris where he is a contributing editor to *Vogue* magazine and is writing a novel, *The Beautiful Room Is Empty.*

COMING OF AGE

☐ **THE SALT POINT by Paul Russell.** This compelling novel captures the restless heart of an ephemeral generation that has abandoned the future and all of its diminished promises. "Powerful, moving, stunning!"—*The Advocate* (265924—$8.95)

☐ **PEOPLE IN TROUBLE by Sarah Schulman.** Molly and her married lover Kate are playing out their passions in a city-scape of human suffering. "Funny, street sharp, gentle, graphic, sad and angry . . . probably the first novel to focus on aids activists."—*Newsday* (265681—$8.95)

☐ **THE BOYS ON THE ROCK, by John Fox.** Sixteen-year-old Billy Connors feels lost—he's handsome, popular, and a star member of the swim team, but his secret fantasies about men have him confused and worried—until he meets Al, a twenty-year-old aspiring politician who initiates him into a new world of love and passion. Combining uncanny precision and wild humor, this is a rare and powerful first novel. (262798—$8.95)

Prices slightly higher in Canada.

Buy them at your local bookstore or use this convenient coupon for ordering.

NEW AMERICAN LIBRARY
P.O. Box 999, Bergenfield, New Jersey 07621

Please send me the books I have checked above.
I am enclosing $_____ (please add $2.00 to cover postage and handling).
Send check or money order (no cash or C.O.D.'s) or charge by Mastercard or VISA (with a $15.00 minimum). Prices and numbers are subject to change without notice.

Card # _____ Exp. Date _____

Signature _____

Name _____

Address _____

City _____ State _____ Zip Code _____

For faster service when ordering by credit card call 1-800-253-6476

Allow a minimum of 4-6 weeks for delivery. This offer is subject to change without notice